W9-CUH-486

He knew the grand sweep of history, but he also knew the small tales; the intrigues and petty jealousies, heroism and cowardice, honor and betrayals.

This, I think, is why his stories have such a ring of truth . . . He was a story teller; a man who could keep you up all night with his books and tales . . . He was a cavalier.

—Jerry Pournelle,
Preface

FEDERATION

H. BEAM PIPER

SF
ace books
A Division of Charter Communications Inc.
A GROSSET & DUNLAP COMPANY
51 Madison Avenue
New York, New York 10010

An ACE Book

First Ace Printing: February 1981
Published Simultaneously in Canada
2 4 6 8 0 9 7 5 3 1
Manufactured in the United States of America

81 06084

TABLE OF CONTENTS

Preface: PIPER'S FOUNDATION
Jerry Pournelle

I have a unique privilege: I have the legal right, acknowl-
edged by the copyright owners, to do stories in H. Beam
Piper's worlds.

This didn't come lightly. It was given to me by Beam
Piper himself many years ago, long before I had any suspicion that I might write science fiction. Beam apparently
knew my future better than I did.

It happens sometimes: an instant bond between two
men on very short acquaintance. It was that way with
Beam. He was twice my age. I had admired his writing. He
had never heard of me, but was fascinated by my tales of
the space program. We met, I think, in Poul Anderson's
room, and we began talking; when we realized the time, it
was dawn. The next night also ended at dawn; and for
both of us the convention ended too quickly.

Afterwards we corresponded. I was then a graduate student in political science, studying the history of government, the pain and hopes and dreams of political
philosophers and statesmen, the brutal realities of politicians . . .

Our letters read like treatises. Beam, though not for-
mally educated, had read more books than most professors; and he was a keen observer of human nature. I for
my part asked questions, or called attention to works he
had not seen, adding little to the vast tapestry of the future
Beam had conceived; and he expressed his thanks by of-

fering me an equal right to the finished product. It was more than I had coming, but Beam never believed in doing anything by halves.

Then my degree was finished at last, and with my wife and young son I moved to California, where I was general editor of a top secret Air Force forecast of missile technology; a job that required me to understand everything, from warheads to guidance to rocket motor casings. I threw myself into the work. Beam continued to write, and I replied with post cards, or not at all; and one day I heard that he was dead by his own hand.

I didn't believe it. I called the police in Williamsport, convinced that he had been murdered by someone clever; but no, the note was authentically Beam Piper.

There remain questions. His extensive notes have never been found; yet I know that he kept a well-organized set of looseleaf notebooks, with entries color-coded; a star map of Federation and Empire; a history of the Systems States War; and other materials including some of my own letters which answered historical questions he had posed. Somewhere out there is a gold mine.

It isn't all lost. I have his letters; and some of his notes can be deduced from his writing. Beam firmly believed that history repeated itself; or at least that one can use real history to construct a future history. The casual reader will not easily deduce the historical models Beam employed. He was familiar with forgotten details: as an example, one of the battle scenes in *Lord Kalvan* is drawn directly from the obscure Battle of Barnet in the Wars of the Roses. He knew the grand sweep of history, but he also knew the small tales; the intrigues and petty jealousies, heroism and cowardice, honor and betrayals.

This, I think, is why his stories have such a ring of truth. They seem real because many were real. Such things as happen in Piper's statecraft have happened time and again to real politicians.

And to real heroes and heroines: for all his knowledge, Beam was no dry intellectual. He was a story teller; a man who could keep you up all night with his books and tales. He had respect for the intellect and for intellectuals, but he was never one of the breed.

He was a cavalier.

INTRODUCTION
John Carr

Acknowledgements

I would like to thank Jerry Pournelle for allowing me to use some of his personal reminiscences of H. Beam Piper and for allowing me to study the Piper notes and letters in his possession. I would also like to thank Charlie Brown for allowing me the use of his letters, Fred Pohl for his reminiscences, and Piper researchers William J. Denholm III, Richard A. Moore, and Paul Dellinger, for their encouragement and support.

SCENE: The Beckman Auditorium, Pasadena, California; the California Institute of Technology—a cement circus tent the size of a zepplin hanger. In the first two rows of the balcony; A. E. Van Vogt, Theodore Sturgeon, Jack Williamson, Larry Niven, Greg Bear and Astrid Anderson, Dr. Donald Kingsbury, Harlan Ellison, Gregory Benford, and others of the SF clan, including your intrepid reporter. All guests of NASA and Jerry Pournelle, our gracious host for the weekend. On stage: Ray Bradbury, sf poet laureate and Martian Chronicalist; Carl Sagan, Mr. Cosmos: Walter Sullivan, Science Editor of the *New York Times* since 1966; Dr. Philip Morrison, Institute Professor of Physics at M.I.T.—first scientist to call upon the professional community to begin a serious search for extraterrestial signals; and lastly, Dr. Bruce Murray, Director of J.P.L. and creator of Purple Physics.

TOPIC: SATURN AND THE MIND OF MAN: Fourth in a series of symposiums on man and the planets.

Dr. Murray, his short cropped silver hair gleaming in the spots, looking like a California-tanned version of one of the original astronauts ten years later, hunches forward: "Saturn, our first look at this most magnificent planet, and we are there! This first glimpse at the *terra incognita* of Saturn will remain one of the finer moments throughout the time of man."

Great stuff, but what does it have to do with Beam Piper?

He wasn't there; and he should have been.

In my study of the life of H. Beam Piper, I ran head-on into a number of perplexing questions: Why, despite numerous reprintings, have Piper's books been ignored by academic critics and scholars? How is it that the man who created one of science fictions most detailed future histories received the following note in Peter Nicholls' *The Science Fiction Encyclopedia:* "Many of his (Piper's) novels and stories . . . are set in a common future history, but are insufficiently connected to be regarded as a coherent series."? (This last comment is mere sloppy scholarship, as I shall show in the essay on the Federation.) And why is Piper, who published most of his best fiction in *Astounding/Analog,* seldom mentioned as one of the great Campbell writers although he always places in the top ten in the readers polls?

The answers to these questions are bound within the Gordian knot of Piper's character, the low stature of science fiction and sf writers in general during the fifties and early sixties, Piper's premature death, and the subsequent unavailability of most of his work.

Horace Beam Piper was born in 1904, the son of a Protestant minister. He had no formal education and at age eighteen went to work as a laborer for the Pennsylvania Railroad's Altoona yards. Throughout his life he was a reticent and guarded man and as a result we know little about his early years. He was largely self-educated; he obtained a deep knowledge of science and history: "without subjecting myself to the ridiculous misery of four years in the uncomfortable confines of a raccoon coat."

While still working for the Pennsy Railroad, he sold his first story to John W. Campbell at *Astounding Science Fiction*. "Time and Time Again" appeared in the April 1947 issue and was the first of many time travel tales. Like the themes of nuclear war and the lost Martian races, time travel was a theme that would appear in many guises. In a moment of guarded confidence, Piper once admitted to Jerry Pournelle that "He Walked Around the Horses"— another time travel tale—was a true story. "I know," said Piper, "I was born on another time line." Even now Jerry can only say, "Beam looked me right in the eye when he said it. And if there was a twinkle in his eye, I couldn't find it." Jerry's still not sure whether he believes it, but he's almost certain Beam did. This would certainly go a long way toward explaining Piper's fascination with time travel, his Paratime stories, and his interest in the time theories of John Dunne, which dealt with parallel worlds coexisting in time and space. Although on the other hand it raises some questions that are far beyond the scope of this short study.

In a self-revealing quote from *Murder in the Gun Room* (Piper's only published mystery novel) a character describes his own writing:

Science fiction. I do a lot of stories for the pulps. . . *Space-Trails,* and *Other Worlds,* and *Wonder*

Stories; mags like that. Most of it's standardized formula stuff; what's known in the trade as space-operas. My best stuff goes to *Astonishing*. Parenthetically, you mustn't judge any of these magazines by their names. It seems to be a convention to use hyperbolic names for science-fiction magazines; a heritage from what might be called an earlier and ruder day. What I do for *Astonishing* is really hard work, and I enjoy it. I'm working now on one of them, based on J. W. Dunne's time-theories, if you know what they are.

What was H. Beam Piper like? He was a lean man of medium height, with dark hair and a thin moustache. He was almost never seen without his pipe. A thin patrician nose bridged two flint-hard eyes which would occasionally twinkle as though listening to the punch line of some inner joke on the human condition. Jerry Pournelle describes him as a courtly gentleman of the old school; and even Jerry admits that Piper did not suffer fools gladly. He was soft-spoken and spent most of his time at sf conventions by himself, not even fraternizing much with the other writers.

I recently received a letter from Paul Dellinger, an old time fan, who had the following rememberance of H. Beam Piper. "My most vivid recollection of him (Piper) was his recalling attendance at a movie which sounded, from his description, like THEM. Anyway, he said about the time the giant insects appeared he stalked out in disgust. Another man who exited at the same time struck up a conversation with him, including the question of whether Piper had ever read any science-fiction. "Hell," Piper said, "I WRITE the stuff!" This is a rememberance from Mr. Dellinger's first sf con in Washington D.C. in 1963, not long after the publication of *Little Fuzzy*.

That Piper was a hard working and conscientious man,

there can be little doubt. From 1946 to 1956 he was a part-time writer and was published in *Astounding, Future Science Fiction, Space Stories,* and *Amazing Science Fiction.* All during this time he supported his elderly mother and continued to work for the Pennsy Railroad; it wasn't until 1956—after the death of his mother—that he was able to retire. Several years later he married a French woman whom he viewed with some ambivalence. He once confided to Jerry Pournelle that "she only married me to get an expensive Paris vacation." A letter to Charlie Brown, dated July 2, 1963:

> I am now in the process of being divorced, if my future-ex-wife can ever get her French lawyers to get all the red-tape untangled. I suspect that she just doesn't know who to bribe. We are writing to each other again, in a very cordial and friendly manner. She reports that our red dachshund, Verkan Vall, of whom she retained custody when we split up, was in a movie, along with Bridgitte Bardot and Jean Gabin, a couple of years ago.

Piper was also very fond of guns and had quite a respectable gun collection, one that would be valued in six or seven figures today.

John H. Costello described it for the fanzine *Renaissance:*

> His collection of more than 100 antique and modern weapons, ranging from a 450-year old French sword and a 400-year old Spanish poiniard with a gold inlaid blade, to a small brass cannon once mounted on a pioneer's blockhouse during the Indian fighting and a nine-millimeter pistol of the type used by German SS troops in World War II formed the background of his non-science fiction mystery, *Murder in the Gunroom,* published by Knopf in 1953.

While it's hard to judge the emotional effects of Piper's failed marriage, it is certain that the French honeymoon and subsequent divorce left him financially destitute. It was during this period that he wrote the *Fuzzy* novels, *Cosmic Computer*, *Space Viking*, and the "Lord Kalvan of Otherwhen" stories. It is a sad irony that while at the height of his writing prowess, he saw himself as a failure. When Ken White, his long-time agent, died, Piper was reduced to shooting pigeons from his hotel window to supplement his meager diet. White, who had kept all his clients' records inside his head, left Piper's business concerns in such a state of disarray that Piper was unaware of several sales to John W. Campbell. And when the third Fuzzy novel, *Fuzzies and Other People*, was rejected by Avon as being too dependent upon the other books in the series, he felt his career had come to an end. (The third Fuzzy novel has since become lost and is the property of the Piper estate now owned by Ace Books. Anyone aiding in its recovery will be amply rewarded.)

A solitary man to the end, Piper did not tell his friends of his financial predicament. Instead he took a way out that could only be reasonable to a man who abhorred state handouts and was determined not to burden his friends and family. On Monday, November 9th, 1964, H. Beam Piper shut off all the utilities to his apartment in Williamsport, Pennsylvania, put painter's drop-cloths over the walls and floor, and took his own life with a handgun from his collection.

In his suicide note, he gave an explanation that is pure Piper: "I don't like to leave messes when I go away, but if I could have cleaned up any of this mess, I wouldn't be going away. H. Beam Piper."

After ten years of neglect—from 1965 to 1976—due in large part to the problems of ownership and control of his estate, Piper's books have begun to fill the racks again in various Ace editions. The first to see print were the classic Fuzzy novels (often selling for $10 to $20 in their original Avon printings): *Little Fuzzy* and *Fuzzy Sapiens,* originally known as *The Other Human Race.* They have remained almost constantly in print ever since. These were followed by new editions of *Cosmic Computer* (Piper's title; the old Ace edition titled it *Junkyard Planet*), *Lord Kalvan of Otherwhen, Space Viking, Four-Day Planet/Planet for Texans.* With several more short story collections to come, the next few years should see the publication of almost the entire Piper cannon.

With the availability of Piper's short stories, many of which have been out of print since the forties and fifties, we should see a reevaluation of Piper's work and stature within the sf field. Had Piper lived to enjoy the sf boom of the late sixties and mid-seventies there is little doubt that he would be a major figure, standing among writers of *Astounding's* silver years such as Harry Harrison, Jerry Pournelle, Gordon Dickson, and Poul Anderson. In a recent poll of *Analog* readers' favorite writers, Piper placed well within the top ten—without having appeared there in 14 years.

While it is our loss that we will never know Beam Piper as a man, or read what he might have written had his life not come to such an abrupt end, it is our consolation that we can come to know and treasure him through his novels and stories.

I can still remember reading *Lord Kalvan of Otherwhen* and *Space Viking,* both good action-adventure novels, in the late sixties. But my real appreciation of H. Beam Piper didn't start until I went to work for Jerry Pournelle as his editorial assistant and researcher in 1977. Jerry had signed a contract several years before to do a sequel to *Space Viking* called *Return of Space Viking,* based on a rough outline and some notes Jerry had taken during talks with Beam. There had been some talk of a collaboration, and they continued to work on the project through their correspondence and late-night convention talks.

The project, of course, was shelved after Piper's tragic death. Jerry thought very little about it until the mid-seventies, when Roger Elwood, who had just become series editor of Laser Books, began to badger him about writing for the Laser line. Jerry eventually responded with several proposals, two of which eventually became the Laser Books titled *Birth of Fire* and *West of Honor.* The third of these proposed books, *Exiles to Glory,* was never released because of the internal problems which eventually brought an end to Laser Books. Of the four books Jerry proposed, only *Return of Space Viking* was never written, for several good reasons. While on casual inspection *Space Viking* may look like just another space opera, in reality it is one of the most complex and historically developed books in the science fiction field. As Jerry told me then, "It just seemed easier to write a new book from scratch than to spend several years doing the research necessary to do justice to Beam's *Viking* book."

So naturally my first research assignment was to take extensive notes on all the planets, history, characters, artifacts, and personal and political relationships contained in *Space Viking.* I thought it would be a piece of cake; after all, hadn't I done post-graduate work in history? My surprise! There aren't more than one or two pages in *Space Viking* that don't have some kind of historical or planetary reference, some which run for pages. On the first reading

I picked up only the obvious; it took two more readings and several hundred note cards before I was finished.

But, of course, I wasn't done; now that I had discovered the fascinating and intricate tapestry of Beam's History of the Future I had to know it all. This meant reading everything he ever wrote as well as making elaborate charts and chronologies, and spending hours talking with Jerry about the historical events and models Piper used. Then, using Beam's correspondence and Jerry's notes, I tried with Jerry to plot the uncharted areas of the TerroHuman Future History.

Slowly and steadily we began to fill in large chunks of the missing territory. We began to gather steam as more and more of his conversations with Piper began to return to Jerry. Piper's original plan had been to write at least one novel per century of his future history; accordingly he had file folders for each century containing all the pertinent historical data and characters. Even had he lived his full life span it is doubtful that he would have ever finished this monumental task, for there is evidence that the Terro-Human Future History (to simplify matters, we will call it TFH) was to continue for over six thousand years. It is hard to believe that even Beam could have written another fifty to sixty books in the twenty years he might have been expected to live—although it would have been nice to see him try. But he had already admitted the futility of this plan to Jerry during one of their discussions on the popularity of the Fuzzy novels—a popularity which forced him to write two sequels, only one of which was published, in the Seventh Century Atomic Era.

While my research on *Space Viking* was completed some time back, my interest in Piper, his works, and personality has continued to grow. I have managed to obtain copies of every story he ever published, many of which have been out of print for over thirty years. One result of this mild obsession with Piper—in addition to this essay—was a rather long article for "The Bulletin of the Science Fiction Writers of America" on the "TerroHuman Future History of H. Beam Piper".

As for *Return of Space Viking,* Jerry Pournelle is still working on that book. Jerry thrives on having four or five simultaneous projects competing for his attention: witness, three columns, several ongoing anthologies, at least two collaborations with Larry Niven always in the works, plus several independent sf novels and his new mystery series, and the new non-fiction book he just decided to do last week. During the sixties when he was working with NASA Jerry grew to like, make that love, the constructive chaos of the space program. However, *Return of Space Viking* is now somewhere near the top of that list and should be completed within the next year or two.

H. Beam Piper had a lifelong love affair with history. Off and on during the last few years of his life he was working on a major work he called in one letter *Only the Arquebus,* a historical novel about Gonzalo de Córdoba and the Italian Wars of the early sixteenth century. Unfortunately it is not known whether Piper ever finished *Only the Arquebus,* and as far as I know no trace of it has been found among his effects. Jerry Pournelle still remembers many an evening spent with Piper discussing historical figures and events and how they might apply to the future. Piper had many a keen insight into the past and often expressed a longing that he had been alive in the simpler days of the Christian Era, when Clausewitzian politics and nuclear war were a faraway nightmare.

In a number of his works Piper created major characters

who are historians or study history as a hobby. In "The Edge of the Knife," a story about a college history professor who can sometimes see into the future, the professor says, "History follows certain patterns. I'm not a Toynbean, but any historian can see that certain forces geneally tend to produce similar effects." Piper set forth a great number of his views concerning history in his works. In *Space Viking* we learn from Otto Harkaman, a Space Viking captain whose hobby is the study of history, "I study history. You know, it's odd; practically everything that's happened on any of the inhabited planets had happened on Terra before the first spaceship." Vilfredo Pareto, a famous mid-twentieth century Italian sociologist, once made a very similar statement; almost every known form of government or political-science possibility existed at one time or another among the Italian city-states of the Renaissance.

Piper also used past events as plot models and for inspiration for future history. In *Uller Uprising,* the first published work in Piper's TFH, he used the Sepoy Mutiny, a revolt started in British-held India when Bengalese soldiers were issued cartridges coated with what they believed to be the fat of cows (sacred to Hindus) and pigs (sacred to Moslems), as the basis for his plot. This is confirmed by Piper in "The Edge of the Knife," an interesting story that fits sideways into his future history, where the history professor who sees into the future compares a planetary rebellion in the Fourth Century A.E. (the Uller Uprising) to the Sepoy Mutiny. He also compares the early expansion of the Federation to the Spanish conquest of the New World.

Another historical analog used by Piper was the war in the Pacific during World War II. In *Cosmic Computer* the planet Poictesme, the former headquarters of the Third

Terran Force during the System States War, has become
in the post-war period a deserted backwater. Most of those
remaining on Poictesme earn their living by salvaging old
army vehicles and stores—a way of life that still continues
on one or two Pacific atolls. The survivors have created a
belief-system around Merlin, the legendary computer that
was reputed to have won the war for the Federation, rem-
iniscent of the Cargo Cults much in vogue among Pacific
Islanders after the parachute drops of W.W.II.

Piper also paid great attention to historical detail, more
so than any other major sf writer since Olaf Stapledon. In
Space Viking he gives the names of over fifty-five planets
and goes into some historical, sociological, and political
detail on about twenty of them. This detail ranges from a
short clause to pages of exposition concerning Federation
history, past wars, and historical figures, and comments on
their political and sociological foibles.

Piper himself had a cyclical view of human history, one
based on his study of history and certainly influenced by
Arnold Toynbee, the English historian whose *A Study of
History* had a great impact on the historical consciousness
of the mid-twentieth century. Piper's TerroHuman Future
History, which covers the fall of the Federation, the
Sword-Worlds, and at least four Galactic Empires, has
much of the depth of Toynbee's major study of human
civilizations. Furthermore, it can easily be shown that
Piper's civilizations pass through many of the same
phases, the *universal state,* the *time of troubles,* and the
interregnum, that Toynbee used to describe past civilizations.

Where Piper and Toynbee diverge is on Toynbee's be-
lief that psychic forces determine the course of history. In
The Study of History Toynbee says, "The Human protag-
onist in the divine drama not only serves God by enabling

him to renew His creation but also serves his fellow man
by pointing the way for others to follow" Piper, although—
or maybe because—he was the son of a minister, was a
confirmed agnostic. Although fascinated by psychic research, and a believer in reincarnation, he was outwardly
antagonistic towards organized religion, be it Buddhism or
Christianity. There is no analogy in Piper's work to the
early Christian Church, which Toynbee saw as the womb
of western culture after the Fall of Rome. Throughout
Piper's history, religion is played down or is the butt of
satire, as in *Space Viking,* where he gives the following
description of the pious Gilgameshers: "Their society
seemed to be a loose theo-socialism, and their religion an
absurd potpourri of most of the major monotheisms of the
Federation period, plus doctrinal and ritualistic innova-
tions of their own."

It is clear from his conception of history and his
TerroHuman Future History that Piper believed no human civilization would ever be more than a short stanza
before the next verse of human history. Lucas Trask, near
the end of *Space Viking,* says, "It may just be that there is
something fundamentally unworkable about government
itself. As long as *Homo sapiens terra* is a wild animal, which
he always has been and always will be until he evolves into
something different in a million years or so, maybe a work-
able system of government is a political science impossibility . . ." This is a political reality which Piper accepts as
neither good nor bad—just a law like the Second Law of
Thermodynamics.

We find Piper's use of historical models, fine historical
detail, and political philosophy throughout his Terro-
Human Future History—a history which spans thousands
of years across the First and Second Federation, the System States Alliance, the Interstellar Wars, the Neo-Barbar-

ian Age, the Sword-World Conquests, the formation of the League of Civilized Worlds, the Mardukan Empire, the First, Second, Third, and Fourth Galactic Empires; just the first of which is described as containing 3,365 worlds, 1.5 trillion people, and 15 intelligent races. But, of the whole TerroHuman Future History, it is the early Federation that receives most of Piper's attention, contains the most novels and stores, is the focus of this collection, and is what we shall turn our attention to next.

The Terran Federation included an area of over two hundred billion cubic light years and held over five million planets that could sustain life in a natural or artificial environment. Although internal evidence leaves us to suspect that only one thousand or more of these worlds were inhabited by man during the Federation, there were new worlds being colonized up until the time of the System States War in the late ninth century A.E., when the Federation began to turn back into itself. The language of the Federation was the universal Lingua Terra, an English-Spanish-Afrikaani-Portugese mixture of old Terran tongues. Time is kept according to Glactic Standard, based on earth time in seconds, minutes, and hours.

By the First Century, A.E. *homo sapiens* has become racially homogeneous; in *Four-Day Planet,* Piper states, "The amount of intermarriage that's gone on since the First Century, [had made] any resemblance between people's names and their appearances purely coincidental." Lingua Terra was also universal; by the seventeenth century, A.E. it was "spoken, in one form or another, by every descendant of the race that had gone out from the Sol System in the Third Century." Once could assume that by the time of *Space Viking* all racial differences had been lost, although there is some mention of new species differentiation. On Agni, a hot-star planet mentioned in *Space*

Viking, the inhabitants were said to be tough for Neo-Barbarians, and to have very dark skin.

Where are the American-Sino-Soviet superpowers in Piper's history of the future? And what has happened to the cultural domination of North America and Europe?

To understand the answer to this question we have to go back to Piper's early short stories and novelettes, many of which are not in his TFH. Throughout his body of work, Piper shows a fondness for certain themes: nuclear war, lost Martian races, the cyclical nature of civilization, the threat of barbarism from within and without, the citizen patriot, parallel time lines, etc.. In the stories published in the early fifties (and in some of his letters, too) it is the threat of a global nuclear holocaust that is clearly on his mind—as it was on the mind of any sane person in that era of nuclear brinkmansship.

One of the most important of these stories is "Flight From Tomorrow," *Future Science Fiction,* Sept.–Oct. 1950, the first story using Atomic Era dating and one in which he explores the concept of rising and ebbing civilizations on earth. There are some glaring inconsistances with later stories, which makes "Flight From Tomorrow" impossible to place in the TFH, and the central idea—that man could adapt to radiation—is false, although that wasn't quite so obvious at the time the story was written. It is certainly one of the more curious tales in the Piper canon, and is a springboard for many of the ideas which we find in later future history stories.

The next story of interest is "Time and Time Again," Piper's first published story. In this one we find mention of a Third World War, one that takes place in 1975 (only one year before the date given to that war in the TFH). The next tale, "Day of the Morn", could almost be called a part of the TFH; Piper is clearly working out some of the back-

ground he used in later TFH stories. However, there is no
internal evidence that could allow us to legitimately place
it in the history.

It isn't until we get to *Uller Uprising* that we have the first
true story of the TerroHuman Future History. *Uller Uprising* has an interesting history of its own; it first appeared as
a Twayne Triplet (a series of three novels along a similar
theme published in one large book by Twayne) in 1952—
a very rare item—and was later published in 1953 in
Space Science Fiction; it is somewhat unusual for a book
to be serialized after its initial book publication! The
Twayne version, about 20,000 words longer, is by far the
more interesting of the two. (Ace Books may publish *Uller
Uprising* in its original form in the future.) Since all the
stories in the Twayne book were based on a science essay
by Dr. John D. Clark, we find that many so-called Piper-
isms, *Niflheim,* for example, come right out of Dr. Clark's
essay! Piper, in a letter to Charlie Brown dated June 6,
1964, had the following to say about *Uller Uprising:* "I'm
glad to hear that the paperback *Junkyard Planet (The
Cosmic Computer,* for Christ's sake!)—parenthesis
Piper's—is selling well. I will probably be reaping the harvest in six months or so; they got the rights on it from Putnam's, and Putnam's will pay me. A paperback *Uller
Uprising* I have been thinking about for some time; some
day something will get done on it."

But while *Uller Uprising* is a treasure trove of information on the Fourth Century A.E., it tells very little about the
early Federation. Instead we have to go to "The Edge of
the Knife," the story published in *Amazing Stories* that I
mentioned earlier—about the history prof who sees into
the future (Beam's TerroHuman Future History, that is).
The professor's foresight is phenomenal, from the Third
World War to the Third Imperium, and he stores his data

in file folders much as Beam did. However, this story is
most valuable for data on the early Federation.

In "Edge of the Knife":

> He sighed and sat down at Marjorie's typewriter and
> began transcribing his notes. Assassination of Khalid ib'n
> Hussein, the pro-Western leader of the newly formed Is-
> lamic Caliphate; period of anarchy in the Middle East; in-
> terfactional power-struggles; Turkish intervention. He
> wondered how long that would last; Khalid's son, Tallal
> ib'n Khalid, was at school in England when his father
> was—would be—killed. He would return, and eventually
> take his father's place, in time to bring the Caliphate into
> the Terran Federation when the general war came. There
> were some notes on that already; the war would result
> from an attempt by the Indian Communists to seize East
> Pakistan. The trouble was that he so seldom "remem-
> bered" an exact date.

Later in "Edge of the Knife":

> There would be an Eastern (Axis) inspired uprising in
> Azerbaijan by the middle of the next year; before autumn,
> the Indian Communists would make their fatal attempt to
> seize East Pakistan. The Thirty Days' War would be the
> immediate result. By that time, the Lunar Base would be
> completed and ready; the enemy missiles would be aimed
> primarily at the rocketports from which it was supplied.
> Delivered without warning, it should have succeeded—
> except that every rocketport had its secret duplicate and
> triplicate. That was Operation Triple Cross; no wonder
> Major Cutler had been so startled at the words, last eve-
> ning. The enemy would be utterly overwhelmed under the
> rain of missiles from across space, but until the moon rock-
> ets began to fall, the United States would suffer grievously.

The end result, according to Piper, is World War III—
the nightmare we all dread come true. The new order is

the Pan-Federation, otherwise known as the First Federation, formed after the Thirty Days War. According to a security officer who talks to our time-seeing historian: "It's
all pretty hush-hush, but this term Terran Federation [is]
for a proposed organization to take the place of the U.N. if
that organization breaks up . . ."

In "The Mercenaries" mention is made of the same Is-
lamic Caliphate and a Fourth Komintern, which clearly
puts this story, which first appeared in *Analog* in 1962, into
the TFH cannon. Caliphate is spelled with a "K" in "The
Mercenaries" but this could easily be a stylistic difference
in copy-editing between the two houses. Certainly by
1962 everything Piper was writing was either part of the
future history or a Lord Kalvan story (In the introduction
to "When in the Course" we show that the Lord Kalvan
stories are really offshoots of the TFH; so it could well be
said that nothing Piper wrote after the fifties was not part
of his future history.)

But what is this about a First and Second Federation? In
Space Viking I found this note: "[Terra even] had anti-
technological movements after Venus seceded from the
First Federation, before the Second Federation was organized." Some scholars have tried to argue that this sentence proves that Pipers TFH is nothing but a copy of
Asimov's *Foundation* trilogy, but I believe that's bunk.
There is sufficient evidence to show that Piper was not re-
writing Asimov and that instead of appearing after the System States War (as his critics claim); the Second Federation appeared during the Second Century A.E. before the
real push toward interstellar colonization came in The
Third Century A.E. In "Omnilingual" there is mention
made of the Thirty Days War—which clearly makes that
story part of the TFH cannon—and of a Pan-Federation
Telecast System. (Pan-Federation is a term used only in
early TFH stories mentioning the Federation, and I believe

it is translatable as First Federation.) Then, in *Uller Uprising,* there is talk of a "revolt of the colonies on Mars and
Venus"—certainly the same revolt mentioned in *Space
Viking*—which means the revolt had to take place sometime earlier than the Fourth Century A.E., the time of *Uller
Uprising.* And in "The Edge of the Knife" Piper states,
"the world of 2050—2070 . . . [was a] completely unified
world, abolition of all national states under a single world
soverignity, colonies on Mars and Venus." This, I think we
can safely say, is Piper's Second Federation, since the First
began in 31 A.E.

There is little mention of what happened on earth after
the Third Global War, although by reading "The Return"
(by H. Beam Piper and John J. McGuire) we see a very
convincing portrait of a far-future earth devestated by a
long-ago nuclear war. Nature in "The Return" has run riot
and the human survivors are slowly beginning to rebuild
civilization again. There are some interesting parallels here
with the far-far-future earth described in "The Keeper,"
which does belong in the TFH—but I will save those for
my introduction to *Empire,* the next Piper collection due
from Ace.

So how did Terran civilization rebuild itself after the
Third World War? Certainly by 54 A.E. (1996 A.D.) civilization had reasserted itself sufficiently enough to mount a
major archeological expedition to Mars, as described in
"Omnilingual." Piper's own definition of Lingua Terra—if
you remember, a combination of English (probably Aus-
tralian) and Spanish (South American) and Afrikaans
(South African) and Portugese (Brazilian)—provides us
with the major loci of early Federation civilization, especially since all are in the Southern Hemisphere. In *Four-
Day Planet* two major papers are named, the *La Presna*

from Buenos Aires and the *Melbourne Times,* "formerly
London Times, when there was still a London." From this
and other evidence, it is apparent that South America and
Australia were the cradles of First Federation culture and
technology.

As we mentioned earlier, the government of the First
Federation was based on the Corporate State—quite dis-
tinct from the Second Federation. For by the time of the
Second Federation, the Federation government most
closely approaches that of Georgian England—a representative government with colonies and member states—
rather than a monarchy. We also have chartered companies (remember the British East India Company) like the
Chartered Zarathustran Company, which tried to enslave
the Fuzzies. Also many of the planets had appointed colonial governors, who could only be overthrown by direct
military intervention, and who governed through and with
the consent of a legislature.

What about the expansion of the Federation (as Piper
did, we will now drop the needless appellation "Second")
into intergalactic space?

Again in "The Edge of the Knife" we find the answer:
"And when Mars and Venus are colonized, there will be
the same historic situations, at least in general shape, as
arose when the European powers were colonizing the
New Worlds or, for that matter, when the Greek city-states
were throwing out colonies across the Aegean." Later in
that story he compares the early Federation with the Spanish Conquest. And, as we discussed earlier, we have
events like the Uller Uprising and the Loki Enslavement
which sound like events from our own past.

Since most of these stories, with the exception of
"Graveyard of Dreams," are concerned with man's con-

quest of new worlds, I will leave it up to you to draw further conclusions about the Federation's subjugation of space as you enjoy the following yarns.

John Carr

Introduction to "Omnilingual"

In The <u>Science Fiction Encyclopedia</u> John Clute, British sf scholar noted for his reviews in the English journal Foundation, states that "Omnilingual" is probably H. Beam Piper's best short story. It may be one of Piper's best known and most anthologized, but I'm not certain it is his best as there are several other very good stories just in this collection alone. I'm sure you will have your own favorite. "Omnilingual" is however a powerful story about unlocking the key to an ancient and unknown civilization and, even if the Viking landers have made Beam's Mars somewhat suspect, no one can fault his anthropology and cryptography.

"Omnilingual" takes place in 54 A.E. and is the first story in Piper's TerroHuman Future History to take place after the founding of the First Federation. In this story Piper shows another of his unrecognized strengths: the creation of a strong central woman character, long before it became politically expedient.

OMNILINGUAL

Martha Dane paused, looking up at the purple-tinged copper sky. The wind had shifted since noon, while she had been inside, and the dust storm that was sweeping the high deserts to the east was now blowing out over Syrtis. The sun, magnified by the haze, was a gorgeous magenta ball, as large as the sun of Terra, at which she could look directly. Tonight, some of that dust would come sifting down from the upper atmosphere to add another film to what had been burying the city for the last fifty thousand years.

The red loess lay over everything, covering the streets and the open spaces of park and plaza, hiding the small houses that had been crushed and pressed flat under it and the rubble that had come down from the tall buildings when roofs had caved in and walls had toppled outward. Here where she stood, the ancient streets were a hundred to a hundred and fifty feet below the surface; the breach they had made in the wall of the building behind her had opened into the sixth story. She could look down on the cluster of prefabricated huts and sheds, on the brush-grown flat that had been the waterfront when this place had been a seaport on the ocean that was now Syrtis Depression; already, the bright metal was thinly coated with red dust. She thought, again, of what clearing this city would mean, in terms of time and labor, of people and supplies and equipment brought across fifty million miles of space. They'd have to use machinery; there was no other way it could be done. Bulldozers and power shovels and draglines; they were fast, but they were rough and indiscriminate. She remembered the digs around Harappa and Mohenjo-Daro, in the Indus Valley, and the careful, patient native laborers—the painstaking foremen, the pickmen and spademen, the long files of basketmen carrying away the earth. Slow and primitive as the civilization whose ruins they were uncovering, yes, but she could count on the fingers of one hand the times one of her pickmen had damaged a valuable object in the ground. If it hadn't been for the underpaid and uncomplaining native laborer, archaeology would still be back where Wincklemann had found it. But on Mars there was no native labor; the last Martian had died five hundred centuries ago.

Something started banging like a machine gun four or five hundred yards to her left. A solenoid jackhammer; Tony Lattimer must have decided which building he wanted to break into next. She became conscious, then, of the awkward weight of her equipment, and began redistributing it, shifting the straps of her oxy-tank pack, slinging the camera from one shoulder and the board and drafting tools from the other, gathering the notebooks and sketchbooks under her left arm. She started walking down the road, over hillocks of buried rubble, around snags of wall jutting up out of the loess, past buildings still standing, some of them already breached and explored, and across the brushgrown flat to the huts.

There were ten people in the main office room of Hut One when she entered. As soon as she had disposed of her oxygen equipment, she lit a cigarette, her first since noon, then looked from one to another of them. Old Selim von Ohlmhorst, the Turco-German, one of her two fellow archaeologists, sitting at the end of the long table against the farther wall, smoking his big curved pipe and going through a looseleaf notebook. The girl ordnance officer, Sachiko Koremitsu, between two droplights at the other end of the table, her head bent over her work. Colonel Hubert Penrose, the Space Force CO, and Captain Field, the intelligence officer, listening to the report of one of the airdyne pilots, returned from his afternoon survey flight. A couple of girl lieutenants from Signals, going over the script of the evening telecast, to be transmitted to the *Cyrano,* on orbit five thousand miles off planet and relayed from thence to Terra via Lunar. Sid Chamberlain, the Trans-Space News Service man, was with them. Like Selim and herself, he was a civilian; he was advertising the fact with a white shirt and a sleeveless blue sweater. And Major Lindemann, the engineer officer, and one of his assistants, arguing over some plans on a drafting board. She hoped, drawing a pint of hot water to wash her hands and sponge off her face, that they were doing something about the pipeline.

She started to carry the notebooks and sketchbooks over to where Selim von Ohlmhorst was sitting, and then, as she always did, she turned aside and stopped to watch Sachiko. The Japanese girl was restoring what had been a book, fifty thousand years ago; her eyes were masked by a binocular loup, the black headband invisible against her glossy black hair, and she was picking delicately at the crumbled page with a hair-fine wire set in a handle of copper tubing. Finally, loosening a particle as tiny as a snowflake, she grasped it with tweezers, placed it on the sheet of transparent plastic on which she was reconstructing the page, and set it with a mist of fixitive from a little spraygun. It was a sheer joy to watch her; every movement was as graceful and precise as though done to music after being rehearsed a hundred times.

"Hello, Martha. It isn't cocktail-time yet, is it?" The girl at the table spoke without raising her head, almost without moving her lips, as though she were afraid that the slightest breath would disturb the flaky stuff in front of her.

"No, it's only fifteen-thirty. I finished my work, over there. I didn't find any more books, if that's good news for you."

Sachiko took off the loup and leaned back in her chair, her palms cupped over her eyes.

"No, I like doing this. I call it micro-jigsaw puzzles. This book, here, really is a mess. Selim found it lying open, with some heavy stuff on top of it; the pages were simply crushed. She hesitated briefly. "If only it would mean something, after I did it."

There could be a faintly critical overtone to that. As she replied, Martha realized that she was being defensive.

"It will, some day. Look how long it took to read Egyptian hieroglyphics, even after they had the Rosetta Stone."

Sachiko smiled. "Yes, I know. But they did have the Rosetta Stone."

"And we don't. There is no Rosetta Stone, not anywhere on Mars. A whole race, a whole species, died while the first Crô-Magnon caveartist was daubing pictures of reindeer and bison, and across fifty thousand years and fifty million miles there was no bridge of understanding.

"We'll find one. There must be something, somewhere, that will give us the meaning of a few words, and we'll use them to pry meaning out of more words, and so on. We may not live to learn this language, but we'll make a start, and some day somebody will."

Sachiko took her hands from her eyes, being careful not to look toward the unshaded lights, and smiled again. This time Martha was sure that it was not the Japanese smile of politeness, but the universally human smile of friendship.

"I hope so, Martha; really I do. It would be wonderful for you to be the first to do it, and it would be wonderful for all of us to be able to read what these people wrote. It would really bring this dead city to life again." The smile faded slowly. "But it seems so hopeless."

"You haven't found any more pictures?"

Sachiko shook her head. Not that it would have meant much if she had. They had found hundreds of pictures with captions; they had never been able to establish a positive relationship between any pictured object and any printed word. Neither of them said anything more, and after a moment Sachiko replaced the loup and bent her head forward over the book.

Selim von Ohlmhorst looked up from his notebook, taking his pipe out of his mouth.

"Everything finished, over there?" he asked, releasing a puff of smoke.

"Such as it was." She laid the notebooks and sketches on the table. "Captain Gicquel's started airsealing the buidling from the fifth floor down, with an entrance on the sixth; he'll start putting in oxygen generators as soon as that's done. I have everything cleared up where he'll be working."

Colonel Penrose looked up quickly, as though making a mental note to attend to something later. Then he returned his attention to the pilot, who was pointing something out on a map.

Von Ohlmhorst nodded. "There wasn't much to it, at that," he agreed. "Do you know which building Tony has decided to enter next?"

"The tall one with the conical thing like a candle extinguisher on top, I think. I heard him drilling for the blasting shots over that way."

"Well, I hope it turns out to be one that was occupied

up to the end."

The last one hadn't. It had been stripped of its contents and fittings, a piece of this and a bit of that, haphazardly, apparently over a long period of time, until it had been almost gutted. For centuries, as it had died, this city had been consuming itself by a process of autocannibalism. She said something to that effect.

"Yes. We always find that—except, of course, at places like Pompeii. Have you seen any of the other Roman cities in Italy?" he asked. "Minturnae, for instance? First the inhabitants tore down this to repair that, and then, after they had vacated the city, other people came along and tore down what was left, and burned the stones for lime, or crushed them to mend roads, till there was nothing left but the foundation traces. That's where we are fortunate; this is one of the places where the Martian race perished, and there were no barbarians to come later and destroy what they had left." He puffed slowly at this pipe. "Some of these days, Martha, we are going to break into one of these buildings and find that it was one in which the last of these people died. Then we will learn the story of the end of this civilization."

And if we learn to read their language, we'll learn the whole story, not just the obituary. She hesitated, not putting the thought into words. "We'll find that, sometime, Selim," she said, then looked at her watch. "I'm going to get some more work done on my lists, before dinner."

For an instant, the old man's face stiffened in disapproval; he started to say something, thought better of it, and put his pipe back into his mouth. The brief wrinkling around his mouth and the twitch of his white mustache had been enough, however; she knew what he was thinking. She was wasting time and effort, he believed; time and effort belonging not to herself but to the expedition. He could be right, too, she realized. But he had to be wrong; there had to be a way to do it. She turned from him silently and went to her own packing-case seat, at the middle of the table.

Photographs, and photostats of restored pages of books, and transcripts of inscriptions, were piled in front of her, and the notebooks in which she was compiling her lists. She sat down, lighting a fresh cigarette, and reached over to a stack of unexamined material, taking off the top sheet. It was a photostat of what looked like the title page and contents of some sort of a periodical. She remembered it; she had found it herself, two days before, in a closet in the basement of the building she had just finished examining.

She sat for a moment, looking at it. It was readable, in the sense that she had set up a purely arbitrary but consistently pronounceable system of phonetic values for the letters. The long vertical symbols were vowels. There were only ten of them; not too many, allowing separate characters for long and short sounds. There were twenty of the short horizontal letters, which meant that sounds like -ng or -ch or -sh were single letters. The odds were millions to one against her system being anything like the original sound of the language, but she had listed several thousand Martian words, and she could pronounce all of them.

And that was as far as it went. She could pronounce between three and four thousand Martian words, and she couldn't assign a meaning to one of them. Selim von Ohlmhorst believed that she never would. So did Tony Lattimer, and he was a great deal less reticent about saying so. So, she was sure, did Sachiko Koremitsu. There were times, now and then, when she began to be afraid that they were right.

The letters on the page in front of her began squirming

and dancing, slender vowels with fat little consonants.
They did that, now, every night in her dreams. And there
were other dreams, in which she read them as easily as
English; waking, she would try desperately and vainly to
remember. She blinked, and looked away from the pho-
tostated page; when she looked back, the letters were be-
having themselves again. There were three words at the
top of the page, over-and-underlined, which seemed to be
the Martian method of capitalization. *Mastharnorvod Tadavas Sornhulva.* She pronounced them mentally, leafing
through her notebooks to see if she had encountered them
before, and in what contexts. All three were listed. In addition, *mastbar* was a fairly common word, and so was
norvod, and so was *nor,* but *-vod* was a suffix and nothing
but a suffix. *Davas,* was a word, too, and *ta-* was a common prefix; *sorn* and *hulva* were both common words.
This language, she had long ago decided, must be something like German; when the Martians had needed a new
word, they had just pasted a couple of existing words together. It would probably turn out to be a grammatical
horror. Well, they had published magazines, and one of
them had been called *Mastharnorvod Tadavas Sornhulva.*
She wondered if it had been something like the *Quarterly
Archaeological Review,* or something more on the order
of *Sexy Stories.*

A smaller line, under the title, was plainly the issue number and date; enough things had been found numbered in
series to enable her to identify the numerals and determine
that a decimal system of numeration had been used. This
was the one thousand and seven hundred and fifty-fourth
issue, for Doma, 14837; then Doma must be the name of
one of the Martian months. The word had turned up several times before. She found herself puffing furiously on
her cigarette as she leafed through notebooks and piles of

already examined material.

Sachiko was speaking to somebody, and a chair scraped at the end of the table. She raised her head, to see a big man with red hair and a red face, in Space Force green, with the single star of a major on his shoulder, sitting down. Ivan Fitzgerald, the medic. He was lifting weights from a book similar to the one the girl ordnance officer was restoring.

"Haven't had time, lately," he was saying, in reply to Sachiko's question. "The Finchley girl's still down with whatever it is she has, and its something I haven't been able to diagnose yet. And I've been checking on bacteria cultures, and in what spare time I have, I've been dissecting specimens for Bill Chandler. Bill's finally found a mammal. Looks like a lizard, and it's only four inches long, but it's a real warm-blooded, gamogenetic, placental, viviparous mammal. Burrows, and seems to live on what pass for insects here."

"Is there enough oxygen for anything like that?" Sachiko was asking.

"Seems to be, close to the ground." Fitzgerald got the headband of his loup adjusted, and pulled it down over his eyes. "He found this thing in a ravine down on the sea bottom— Ha, this page seems to be intact; now, if I can get it out all in one piece—"

He went on talking inaudibly to himself, lifting the page a little at a time and sliding one of the transparent plastic sheets under it, working with minute delicacy. Not the delicacy of the Japanese girl's small hands, moving like the paws of a cat washing her face, but like a steam-hammer cracking a peanut. Field archaeology requires a certain delicacy of touch, too, but Martha watched the pair of them with envious admiration. Then she turned back to her own work, finishing the table of contents.

The next page was the beginning of the first article listed; many of the words were unfamiliar. She had the impression that this must be some kind of scientific or technical journal; that could be because such publications made up the bulk of her own periodical reading. She doubted if it were fiction; the paragraphs had a solid, factual look.

At length, Ivan Fitzgerald gave a short, explosive grunt. "Ha! Got it!"

She looked up. He had detached the page and was cementing another plastic sheet onto it.

"Any pictures?" she asked.

"None on this side. Wait a moment." He turned the sheet. "None on this side, either." He sprayed another sheet of plastic to sandwich the page, then picked up his pipe and relighted it.

"I get fun out of this, and it's good practice for my hands, so don't think I'm complaining," he said, "but, Martha, do you honestly think anybody's ever going to get anything out of this?"

Sachiko held up a scrap of the silicone plastic the Martians had used for paper with her tweezers. It was almost an inch square.

"Look; three whole words on this piece," she crowed. "Ivan, you took the easy book."

Fitzgerald wasn't being sidetracked. "This stuff's absolutely meaningless," he continued. "It had a meaning fifty thousand years ago, when it was written, but it has none at all now."

She shook her head. "Meaning isn't something that evaporates with time," she argued. "It has just as much meaning now as it ever had. We just haven't learned how to decipher it."

"That seems like a pretty pointless distinction," Selim von Ohlmhorst joined the conversation. "There no longer exists a means of deciphering it.''

"We'll find one." She was speaking, she realized, more in self-encouragement than in controversy.

"How? From pictures and captions? We've found captioned pictures, and what have they given us? A caption is intended to explain the picture, not the picture to explain the caption. Suppose some alien to our culture found a picture of a man with a white beard and mustache sawing a billet from a log. He would think the caption meant, 'Man Sawing Wood.' How would he know that it was really 'Wilhelm II in Exile at Doorn?' ''

Sachiko had taken off her loup and was lighting a cigarette.

"I can think of pictures intended to explain their captions," she said. "These picture language-books, the sort we use in the Service—little line drawings, with a word or phrase under them."

"Well, of course, if we found something like that," von Ohlmhorst began.

"Michael Ventris found someting like that, back in the Fifties," Hubert Penrose's voice broke in from directly behind her.

She turned her head. The colonel was standing by the archaeologists' table; Captain Field and the airdyne pilot had gone out.

"He found a lot of Greek inventories of military stores," Penrose continued. "They were in Cretan Linear B script, and at the head of each list was a little picture, a sword or a helmet or a cooking tripod or a chariot wheel. That's what gave him the key to the script."

"Colonel's getting to be quite an archaeologist," Fitzgerald commented. "We're all learning each others' specialties, on this expedition."

"I heard about that long before this expedition was even

contemplated." Penrose was tapping a cigarette on his gold case. "I heard about that back before the Thirty Days' War, at Intelligence School, when I was a lieutenant. As a feat of cryptanalysis, not an archaeological discovery."

"Yes, cryptanalysis," von Ohlmhorst pounced. "The reading of a known language in an unknown form of writing. Ventris' lists were in the known language, Greek. Neither he nor anybody else ever read a word of the Cretan language until the finding of the Greek-Cretan bilingual in 1963, because only with a bilingual text, one language already known, can an unknown ancient language be learned. And what hope, I ask you, have we of finding anything like that here? Martha, you've been working on these Martian texts ever since we landed here—for the last six months. Tell me, have you found a single word to which you can positively assign a meaning?"

"Yes, I think I have one." She was trying hard not to sound too exultant. "*Doma.* It's the name of one of the months of the Martian calendar."

"Where did you find that?" von Ohlmhorst asked. "And how did you establish—?"

"Here." She picked up the photostat and handed it along the table to him. "I'd call this the title page of a magazine."

He was silent for a moment, looking at it. "Yes. I would say so, too. Have you any of the rest of it?"

"I'm working on the first page of the first article, listed there. Wait till I see; yes, here's all I found, together, here." She told him where she had gotten it. "I just gathered it up, at the time, and gave it to Geoffrey and Rosita to photostat; this is the first I've really examined it."

The old man got to his feet, brushing tobacco ashes from the front of his jacket, and came to where she was sitting, laying the title page on the table and leafing quickly through the stack of photostats.

"Yes, and here is the second article, on page eight, and here's the next one." He finished the pile of photostats. "A couple of pages missing at the end of the last article. This is remarkable; surprising that a thing like a magazine would have survived so long."

"Well, this silicone stuff the Martians used for paper is pretty durable," Hubert Penrose said. "There doesn't seem to have been any water or any other fluid in it originally, so it wouldn't dry out with time."

"Oh, it's not remarkable that the material would have survived. We've found a good many books and papers in excellent condition. But only a really vital culture, an organized culture, will publish magazines, and this civilization had been dying for hundreds of years before the end. It might have been a thousand years before the time they died out completely that such activities as publishing ended."

"Well, look where I found it; in a closet in a cellar. Tossed in there and forgotten, and then ignored when they were stripping the building. Things like that happen."

Penrose had picked up the title page and was looking at it.

"I don't think there's any doubt about this being a magazine, at all." He looked again at the title, his lips moving silently. *"Mastharnorvod Tadavas Sornhulva.* Wonder what it means. But you're right about the date—*Doma* seems to be the name of a month. Yes, you have a word, Dr. Dane."

Sid Chamberlain, seeing that something unusual was going on, had come over from the table at which he was working. After examining the title page and some of the inside pages, he began whispering into the stenophone he had taken from his belt.

"Don't try to blow this up to anything big, Sid," she cautioned. "All we have is the name of a month, and Lord only knows how long it'll be till we even find out which month it was."

"Well, it's a start, isn't it?" Penrose argued. "Grotefend only had the word for 'king' when he started reading Persian cuneiform."

"But I don't have the word for month; just the name of a month. Everybody knew the names of the Persian kings, long before Grotefend."

"That's not the story," Chamberlain said. "What the public back on Terra will be interested in is finding out that the Martians published magazines, just like we do. Something familiar; make the Martians seem more real. More human."

Three men had come in, and were removing their masks and helmets and oxy-tanks, and peeling out of their quilted coveralls. Two were Space Force lieutenants; the third was a youngish civilian with close-cropped blond hair, in a checked woolen shirt. Tony Lattimer and his helpers.

"Don't tell me Martha finally got something out of that stuff?" he asked, approaching the table. He might have been commenting on the antics of the village half-wit, from his tone.

"Yes; the name of one of the Martian months." Hubert Penrose went on to explain, showing the photostat.

Tony Lattimer took it, glanced at it, and dropped it on the table.

"Sounds plausible, of course, but just an assumption. That word may not be the name of a month, at all—could mean 'published' or 'authorized' or 'copyrighted' or anything like that. Fact is, I don't think it's more than a wild guess that that thing's anything like a periodical." He dis-

missed the subject and turned to Penrose. "I picked out
the next building to enter; that tall one with the conical
thing on top. It ought to be in pretty good shape inside; the
conical top wouldn't allow dust to accumulate, and from
the outside nothing seems to be caved in or crushed.
Ground level's higher than the other one, about the seventh floor. I found a good place and drilled for the shots;
tomorrow I'll blast a hole in it, and if you can spare some
people to help, we can start exploring it right away."

"Yes, of course, Dr. Lattimer. I can spare about a dozen,
and I suppose you can find a few civilian volunteers," Penrose told him. "What will you need in the way of equipment?"

"Oh, about six demolition-packets; they can all be shot
together. And the usual thing in the way of lights, and
breaking and digging tools, and climbing equipment in
case we run into broken or doubtful stairways. We'll divide
into two parties. Nothing ought to be entered for the first
time without a qualified archaeologist along. Three parties,
if Martha can tear herself away from this catalogue of sys-
tematized incomprehensibilities she's making long enough
to do some real work."

She felt her chest tighten and her face become stiff. She
was pressing her lips together to lock in a furious retort
when Hubert Penrose answered for her.

"Dr. Dane's been doing as much work, and as important work, as you have," he said brusquely. "More important work, I'd be inclined to say."

Von Ohlmhorst was visibly distressed; he glanced once
toward Sid Chamberlain, then looked hastily away from
him. Afraid of a story of dissension among archaeologists
getting out.

"Working out a system of pronunciation by which the
Martian language could be transliterated was a most im-

portant contribution," he said. "And Martha did that al-most unassisted."

"Unassisted by Dr. Lattimer, anyway," Penrose added. "Captain Field and Lieutenant Koremitsu did some work, and I helped out a little, but nine-tenths of it she did her-self."

"Purely arbitrary," Lattimer disdained. "Why, we don't even know that the Martians could make the same kind of vocal sounds we do."

"Oh, yes, we do," Ivan Fitzgerald contradicted, safe on his own ground. "I haven't seen any actual Martian skulls—these people seem to have been very tidy about disposing of their dead—but from statues and busts and pictures I've seen, I'd say that their vocal organs were identical with our own."

"Well, grant that. And grant that it's going to be impres-sive to rattle off the names of Martian notables whose stat-ues we find, and that if we're ever able to attribute any placenames, they'll sound a lot better than this horse-doc-tors' Latin the old astronomers splashed all over the map of Mars," Lattimer said. "What I object to is her wasting time on this stuff, of which nobody will ever be able to read a word if she fiddles around with those lists till there's an-other hundred feet of loess on this city, when there's so much real work to be done and we're as shorthanded as we are."

That was the first time that had come out in just so many words. She was glad Lattimer had said it and not Selim von Ohlmhorst.

"What you mean," she retorted, "is that it doesn't have the publicity value that digging up statues has."

For an instant, she could see that the shot had scored. Then Lattimer, with a side glance at Chamberlain, an-swered:

"What I mean is that you're trying to find something that any archaeologist, yourself included, should know doesn't exist. I don't object to your gambling your professional reputation and making a laughing stock of yourself; what I object to is that the blunders of one archaeologist discredit the whole subject in the eyes of the public."

That seemed to be what worried Lattimer most. She was framing a reply when the communication-outlet whistled shrilly, and then squawked: "Cocktail time! One hour to dinner; cocktails in the library, Hut Four!"

The library, which was also lounge, recreation room, and general gathering-place, was already crowded; most of the crowd was at the long table topped with sheets of glasslike plastic that had been wall panels out of one of the ruined buildings. She poured herself what passed, here, for a martini, and carried it over to where Selim von Ohlmhorst was sitting alone.

For a while, they talked about the building they had just finished exploring, then drifted into reminiscences of their work on Terra—von Ohlmhorst's in Asia Minor, with the Hittite Empire, and hers in Pakistan, excavating the cities of the Harappa Civilization. They finished their drinks— the ingredients were plentiful; alcohol and flavoring extracts synthesized from Martian vegetation—and von Ohlmhorst took the two glasses to the table for refills.

"You know, Martha," he said, when he returned, "Tony was right about one thing. You are gambling your professional standing and reputation. It's against all archaeological experience that a language so completely dead as this one could be deciphered. There was a continuity between all the other ancient languages—by knowing Greek, Champollion learned to read Egyptian; by knowing Egyptian, Hittite was learned. That's why you and your colleagues have never been able to translate the

Harappa hieroglyphics; no such continuity exists there. If you insist that this utterly dead language can be read, your reputation will suffer for it."

"I heard Colonel Penrose say, once, that an officer who's afraid to risk his military reputation seldom makes much of a reputation. It's the same with us. If we really want to find things out, we have to risk making mistakes. And I'm a lot more interested in finding things out than I am in my reputation."

She glanced across the room, to where Tony Lattimer was sitting with Gloria Standish, talking earnestly, while Gloria sipped one of the counterfeit martinis and listened. Gloria was the leading contender for the title of Miss Mars, 1996, if you liked big bosomy blondes, but Tony would have been just as attentive to her if she'd looked like the Wicked Witch in "The Wizard of Oz," because Gloria was the Pan-Federation Telecast System commentator with the expedition.

"I know you are," the old Turco-German was saying. "That's why, when they asked me to name another archaeologist for this expedition, I named you."

He hadn't named Tony Lattimer; Lattimer had been pushed onto the expedition by his university. There'd been a lot of high-level string-pulling to that; she wished she knew the whole story. She'd managed to keep clear of universities and university politics; all her digs had been sponsored by non-academic foundations or art museums.

"You have an excellent standing; much better than my own, at your age. That's why it disturbs me to see you jeapordizing it by this insistence that the Martian language can be translated. I can't, really, see how you can hope to succeed."

She shrugged and drank some more of her cocktail, then lit another cigarette. It was getting tiresome to try to verbalize something she only felt.

"Neither do I, now, but I will. Maybe I'll find something like the picture-books Sachiko was talking about. A child's primer, maybe; surely they had things like that. And if I don't, I'll find something else. We've only been here six months. I can wait the rest of my life, if I have to, but I'll do it sometime."

"I can't wait so long," von Ohlmhorst said. "The rest of my life will only be a few years, and when the *Schiaparelli* orbits in, I'll be going back to Terra on the *Cyrano*."

"I wish you wouldn't. This is a whole new world of archaeology. Literally."

"Yes." He finished the cocktail and looked at his pipe as though wondering whether to re-light it so soon before dinner, then put it in his pocket. "A whole new world—but I've grown old, and it isn't for me. I've spent my life studying the Hittites. I can speak the Hittite language, though maybe King Muwatallis wouldn't be able to understand my modern Turkish accent. But the things I'd have to learn, here—chemistry, physics, engineering, how to run analytic tests on steel girders and beryllo-silver alloys and plastics and silicones. I'm more at home with a civilization that rode in chariots and fought with swords and was just learning how to work iron. Mars is for young people. This expedition is a cadre of leadership—not only the Space Force people, who'll be the commanders of the main expedition, but us scientists, too. And I'm just an old cavalry general who can't learn to command tanks and aircraft. You'll have time to learn about Mars. I won't."

His reputation as the dean of Hittitologists was solid and secure, too, she added mentally. Then she felt ashamed of the thought. He wasn't to be classed with Tony Lattimer.

"All I came for was to get the work started," he was continuing. "The Federation Government felt that an old hand should do that. Well, it's started, now; you and Tony and whoever come out on the *Schiaparelli* must carry it on. You said it, yourself; you have a whole new world. This is only one city, of the last Martian civilization. Behind this, you have the Late Upland Culture, and the Canal Builders, and all civilizations and races and empires before them, clear back to the Martian Stone Age." He hesitated for a moment. "You have no idea what all you have to learn, Martha. This isn't the time to start specializing too narrowly."

They all got out of the truck and stretched their legs and looked up the road to the tall building with the queer conical cap askew on its top. The four little figures that had been busy against its wall climbed into the jeep and started back slowly, the smallest of them, Sachiko Koremitsu, paying out an electric cable behind. When it pulled up beside the truck, they climbed out; Sachiko attached the free end of the cable to a nuclear-electric battery. At once, dirty gray smoke and orange dust puffed out from the wall of the building, and, a second later, the multiple explosion banged.

She and Tony Lattimer and Major Lindemann climbed onto the truck, leaving the jeep stand by the road. When they reached the building, a satisfyingly wide breach had been blown in the wall. Lattimer had placed his shots between two of the windows; they were both blown out along with the wall between, and lay unbroken on the ground. Martha remembered the first building they had entered. A Space Force officer had picked up a stone and thrown it at one of the windows, thinking that would be all they'd need to do. It had bounced back. He had drawn his pistol—they'd all carried guns, then, on the principle that what they didn't know about Mars might easily hurt

them—and fired four shots. The bullets had ricochetted,
screaming thinly; there were four coppery smears of
jacket-metal on the window, and a little surface spalling.
Somebody tried a rifle; the 4000-f.s. bullet had cracked
the glasslike pane without penetrating. An oxyacetylene
torch had taken an hour to cut the window out; the lab
crew, aboard the ship, were still trying to find out just what
the stuff was.

Tony Lattimer had gone forward and was sweeping his
flashlight back and forth, swearing petulantly, his voice
harshened and amplified by his helmet-speaker.

"I thought I was blasting into a hallway; this lets us into
a room. Careful; there's about a two-foot drop to the floor,
and a lot of rubble from the blast just inside."

He stepped down through the breach; the others began
dragging equipment out of the trucks—shovels and picks
and crowbars and sledges, portable floodlights, cameras,
sketching materials, an extension ladder, even Alpinists'
ropes and crampons and pickaxes. Hubert Penrose was
shouldering something that looked like a surrealist machine gun but which was really a nuclear-electric jackhammer. Martha selected one of the spike-shod
mountaineer's ice axes, with which she could dig or chop
or poke or pry or help herself over rough footing.

The windows, grimed and crusted with fifty millennia of
dust, filtered in a dim twilight; even the breach in the wall,
in the morning shade, lighted only a small patch of floor.
Somebody snapped on a floodlight, aiming it at the ceiling.
The big room was empty and bare; dust lay thick on the
floor and reddened the once-white walls. It could have
been a large office, but there was nothing left in it to indicate its use.

"This one's been stripped up to the seventh floor!" Lattimer exclaimed. "Street level'll be cleaned out, com-

pletely."

"Do for living quarters and shops, then," Lindemann said. "Added to the others, this'll take care of everybody on the *Schiaparelli.*"

"Seem to have been a lot of electric or electronic apparatus over along this wall," one of the Space Force officers commented. "Ten or twelve electric outlets." He brushed the dusty wall with his glove, then scraped on the floor with his foot. "I can see where things were pried loose."

The door, one of the double sliding things the Martians had used, was closed. Selim von Ohlmhorst tried it, but it was stuck fast. The metal latch-parts had frozen together, molecule bonding itself to molecule, since the door had last been closed. Hubert Penrose came over with the jackhammer, fitting a spear-point chisel into place. He set the chisel in the joint between the doors, braced the hammer against his hip, and squeezed the trigger-switch. The hammer banged briefly like the weapon it resembled, and the doors popped a few inches apart, then stuck. Enough dust had worked into the recesses into which it was supposed to slide to block it on both sides.

That was old stuff; they ran into that every time they had to force a door, and they were prepared for it. Somebody went outside and brought in a power-jack and finally one of the doors inched back to the door jamb. That was enough to get the lights and equipment through; they all passed from the room to the hallway beyond. About half the other doors were open; each had a number and a single word, *Darfhulva,* over it.

One of the civilian volunteers, a woman professor of natural ecology from Penn State University, was looking up and down the hall.

"You know," she said, "I feel at home here. I think this

was a college of some sort, and these were classrooms. That word, up there; that was the subject taught, or the department. And those electronic devices, all where the class could face them; audio-visual teaching aids."

"A twenty-five-story university?" Lattimer scoffed. "Why, a building like this would handle thirty thousand students."

"Maybe there were that many. This was a big city, in its prime," Martha said, moved chiefly by a desire to oppose Lattimer.

"Yes, but think of the snafu in the halls, every time they changed classes. It'd take half an hour to get everybody back and forth from one floor to another." He turned to von Ohlmhorst. "I'm going up above this floor. This place has been looted clean up to here, but there's a chance there may be something above," he said.

"I'll stay on this floor, at present," the Turco-German replied. "There will be much coming and going, and dragging things in and out. We should get this completely examined and recorded first. Then Major Lindemann's people can do their worst, here."

"Well, if nobody else wants it, I'll take the downstairs," Martha said.

"I'll go along with you," Hubert Penrose told her. "If the lower floors have no archaeological value, we'll turn them into living quarters. I like this building; it'll give everybody room to keep out from under everybody else's feet." He looked down the hall. "We ought to find escalators at the middle."

The hallway, too, was thick underfoot with dust. Most of the open rooms were empty, but a few contained furniture, including small seat-desks. The original proponent of the university theory pointed these out as just what might be found in classrooms. There were escalators, up and down, on either side of the hall, and more on the intersecting passage to the right.

"That's how they handled the students, between classes," Martha commented. "And I'll bet there are more ahead, there."

They came to a stop where the hallway ended at a great square central hall. There were elevators, there, on two of the sides, and four escalators, still usable as stairways. But it was the walls, and the paintings on them, that brought them up short and staring.

They were clouded with dirt—she was trying to imagine what they must have looked like originally, and at the same time estimating the labor that would be involved in cleaning them—but they were still distinguishable, as was the word, *Darfhulva*, in golden letters above each of the four sides. It was a moment before she realized, from the murals, that she had at last found a meaningful Martian word. They were a vast historical panorama, clockwise around the room. A group of skin-clad savages squatting around a fire. Hunters with bows and spears, carrying the carcass of an animal slightly like a pig. Nomads riding long-legged, graceful mounts like hornless deer. Peasants sowing and reaping; mud-walled hut villages, and cities; processions of priests and warriors; battles with swords and bows, and with cannon and muskets; galleys, and ships with sails, and ships without visible means of propulsion, and aircraft. Changing costumes and weapons and machines and styles of architecture. A richly fertile landscape, gradually merging into barren deserts and bushlands—the time of the great planet-wide drought. The Canal Builders—men with machines recognizable as steam-shovels and derricks, digging and quarrying and driving across the empty plains with aquaducts. More cities—seaports on the shrinking oceans; dwindling, half-deserted cities; an abandoned city, with four tiny humanoid figures and a thing like a combat-car in the middle of a brush-grown plaza, they and their vehicle dwarfed by the huge lifeless buildings around them. She had not the least doubt; *Darfhulva* was History.

"Wonderful!" von Ohlmhorst was saying. "The entire history of this race. Why, if the painter depicted appropriate costumes and weapons and machines for each period, and got the architecture right, we can break the history of this planet into eras and periods and civilizations."

"You can assume they're authentic. The faculty of this university would insist on authenticity in the *Darfhulva* — History — Department," she said.

"Yes! *Darfhulva*—History! And your magazine was a journal of *Somhulva!*" Penrose exclaimed. "You have a word, Martha!" It took her an instant to realize that he had called her by her first name, and not Dr. Dane. She wasn't sure if that weren't a bigger triumph than learning a word of the Martian language. Or a more auspicious start. "Alone, I suppose that *hulva* means something like science or knowledge, or study; combined, it would be equivalent to our 'ology. And *darf* would mean something like past, or old times, or human events, or chronicles."

"That gives you three words, Martha!" Sachiko jubilated. "You did it."

"Let's don't go too fast," Lattimer said, for once not derisively. "I'll admit that *darfhulva* is the Martian word for history as a subject of study; I'll admit that *hulva* is the general word and *darf* modifies it and tells us which subject is meant. But as for assigning specific meanings, we can't do that because we don't know just how the Martians thought, scientifically or otherwise."

He stopped short, startled by the blue-white light that

blazed as Sid Chamberlain's Kliegettes went on. When the whirring of the camera stopped, it was Chamberlain who was speaking:

"This is the biggest thing yet; the whole history of Mars, stone age to the end, all on four walls. I'm taking this with the fast shutter, but we'll telecast it in slow motion, from the beginning to the end. Tony, I want you to do the voice for it—running commentary, interpretation of each scene as it's shown. Would you do that?"

Would he do that! Martha thought. If he had a tail, he'd be wagging it at the very thought.

"Well, there ought to be more murals on the other floors," she said. "Who wants to come downstairs with us?"

Sachiko did; immediately, Ivan Fitzgerald volunteered. Sid decided to go upstairs with Tony Lattimer, and Gloria Standish decided to go upstairs, too. Most of the party would remain on the seventh floor, to help Selim von Ohlmhorst get it finished. After poking tentatively at the escalator with the spike of her ice axe, Martha led the way downward.

The sixth floor was *Darfhulva*, too; military and technological history, from the character of the murals. They looked around the central hall, and went down to the fifth; it was like the floors above except that the big quadrangle was stacked with dusty furniture and boxes. Ivan Fitzgerald, who was carrying the floodlight, swung it slowly around. Here the murals were of heroic-sized Martians, so human in appearance as to seem members of her own race, each holding some object—a book, or a testtube, or some bit of scientific apparatus, and behind them were scenes of laboratories and factories, flame and smoke, lightning-flashes. The word at the top of each of the four walls was one with which she was already familiar—*Som-*

hulva.

"Hey, Martha; there's that word." Ivan Fitzgerald exclaimed. "The one in the title of your magazine." He looked at the paintings. "Chemistry, or physics."

"Both," Hubert Penrose considered. "I don't think the Martians made any sharp distinction between them. See, the old fellow with the scraggly whiskers must be the inventor of the spectroscope; he has one in his hands, and he has a rainbow behind him. And the woman in the blue smock, beside him, worked in organic chemistry; see the diagrams of long-chain molecules behind her. What word would convey the idea of chemistry and physics taken as one subject?"

"Somhulva," Sachiko suggested. "If *hulva's* something like science, *som* must mean matter, or substance, or physical object. You were right, all along, Martha. A civilization like this would certainly leave something like this, that would be self-explanatory."

"This'll wipe a little more of that superior grin off Tony Lattimer's face," Fitzgerald was saying, as they went down the motionless escalator to the floor below. "Tony wants to be a big shot. When you want to be a big shot, you can't bear the possibility of anybody else being a bigger big shot, and whoever makes a start on reading this language will be the biggest big shot archaeology ever saw."

That was true. She hadn't thought of it, in that way, before, and now she tried not to think about it. She didn't want to be a big shot. She wanted to be able to read the Martian language, and find things out about the Martians.

Two escalators down, they came out on a mezzanine around a wide central hall on the street level, the floor forty feet below them and the ceiling thirty feet above. Their lights picked out object after object below—a huge group of sculptured figures in the middle; some kind of a motor vehicle jacked up on trestles for repairs; things that looked like machine-guns and auto-cannon; long tables, tops littered with a dust-covered miscellany; machinery; boxes and crates and containers.

They made their way down and walked among the clutter, missing a hundred things for every one they saw, until they found an escalator to the basement. There were three basements, one under another, until at last they stood at the bottom of the last escalator, on a bare concrete floor, swinging the portable floodlight over stacks of boxes and barrels and drums, and heaps of powdery dust. The boxes were plastic—nobody had ever found anything made of wood in the city—and the barrels and drums were of metal or glass or some glasslike substance. They were outwardly intact. The powdery heaps might have been anything organic, or anything containing fluid. Down here, where wind and dust could not reach, evaporation had been the only force of destruction after the minute life that caused putrefaction had vanished.

They found refrigeration rooms, too, and using Martha's ice axe and the pistollike vibratool Sachiko carried on her belt, they pounded and pried one open, to find dessicated piles of what had been vegetables, and leathery chunks of meat. Samples of that stuff, rocketed up to the ship, would give a reliable estimate, by radio-carbon dating, of how long ago this building had been occupied. The refrigeration unit, radically different from anything their own culture had produced, had been electrically powered. Sachiko and Penrose, poking into it, found the switches still on; the machine had only ceased to function when the power-source, whatever that had been, had failed.

The middle basement had also been used, at least toward the end, for storage; it was cut in half by a partition pierced by but one door. They took half an hour to force this, and were on the point of sending above for heavy equipment when it yielded enough for them to squeeze through. Fitzgerald, in the lead with the light, stopped short, looked around, and gave a groan that came through his helmet-speaker like a foghorn.

"Oh, no! *No!*"

"What's the matter, Ivan?" Sachiko, entering behind him, asked anxiously.

He stepped aside. "Look at it Sachi! Are we going to have to do all that?"

Martha crowded through behind her friend and looked around, then stood motionless, dizzy with excitement. Books. Case on case of books, half an acre of cases, fifteen feet to the ceiling. Fitzgerald, and Penrose, who had pushed in behind her, were talking in rapid excitement; she only heard the sound of their voices, not their words. This must be the main stacks of the university library—the entire literature of the vanished race of Mars. In the center, down an aisle between the cases, she could see the hollow square of the librarians' desk, and stairs and a dumbwaiter to the floor above.

She realized that she was walking forward, with the others, toward this. Sachiko was saying: "I'm the lightest; let me go first." She must be be talking about the spidery metal stairs.

"I'd say they were safe," Penrose answered. "The trouble we've had with doors around here shows that the metal hasn't deteriorated."

In the end, the Japanese girl led the way, more catlike than ever in her caution. The stairs were quite sound, in spite of their fragile appearance, and they all followed her. The floor above was a duplicate of the room they had entered, and seemed to contain about as many books. Rather than waste time forcing the door here, they re-

turned to the middle basement and came up by the escalator down which they had originally decended.

The upper basement contained kitchens—electric
stoves, some with pots and pans still on them—and a big
room that must have been, originally, the students' dining
room, though when last used it had been a workshop. As
they expected, the library reading room was on the street-
level floor, directly above the stacks. It seemed to have
been converted into a sort of common living room for the
building's last occupants. An adjoining auditorium had
been made into a chemical works; there were vats and
distillation apparatus, and a metal fractionating tower that
extended through a hole knocked in the ceiling seventy
feet above. A good deal of plastic furniture of the sort they
had been finding everywhere in the city was stacked
about, some of it broken up, apparently for reprocessing.
The other rooms on the street floor seemed also to have
been devoted to manufacturing and repair work; a considerable industry, along a number of lines, must have been
carried on here for a long time after the university had
ceased to function as such.

On the second floor, they found a museum; many of the
exhibits remained, tantalizingly half-visible in grimed glass
cases. There had been administrative offices there, too.
The doors of most of them were closed, and they did not
waste time trying to force them, but those that were open
had been turned into living quarters. They made notes,a
and rough floor-plans, to guide them in future more thor-
ough examination; it was almost noon before they had
worked their way back to the seventh floor.

Selim von Ohlmhorst was in a room on the north side
of the building, sketching the position of things before examining them and collecting them for removal. He had the
floor checkerboarded with a grid of chalked lines, each

numbered.

"We have everything on this floor photographed," he
said. "I have three gangs—all the floodlights I have—
sketching and making measurements. At the rate we're
going, with time out for lunch, we'll be finished by the middle of the afternoon."

"You've been working fast. Evidently you aren't being
high-church about a 'qualified archaeologist' entering
rooms first," Penrose commented.

"Ach, childishness!" the old man exclaimed impatiently. "These officers of yours aren't fools. All of them
have been to Intelligence School and Criminal Investiga-
tion School. Some of the most careful amateur archaeologists I ever knew were retired soldiers or policemen. But
there isn't much work to be done. Most of the rooms are
either empty or like this one—a few bits of furniture and
broken trash and scraps of paper. Did you find anything
down on the lower floors?"

"Well, yes," Penrose said, a hint of mirth in his voice.
"What would you say, Martha?"

She started to tell Selim. The others, unable to restrain
their excitement, broke in with interruptions. Von Ohlmhorst was staring in incredulous amazement.

"But this floor was looted almost clean, and the buildings we've entered before were all looted from the street
level up," he said, at length.

"The people who looted this one lived here," Penrose
replied. "They had electric power to the last; we found
refrigerators full of food, and stoves with the dinner still on
them. They must have used the elevators to haul things
down from the upper floor. The whole first floor was converted into workshops and laboratories. I think that this
place must have been something like a monastery in the
Dark Ages in Europe, or what such a monastery would

have been like if the Dark Ages had followed the fall of a highly developed scientific civilization. For one thing, we found a lot of machine guns and light auto-cannon on the street level, and all the doors were barricaded. The people here were trying to keep a civilization running after the rest of the planet had gone back to barbarism; I suppose they'd have to fight off raids by the barbarians now and then."

"You're not going to insist on making this building into expedition quarters, I hope, colonel?" von Ohlmhorst asked anxiously.

"Oh, no! This place is an archaeological treasure-house. More than that; from what I saw, our technicians can learn a lot, here. But you'd better get this floor cleaned up as soon as you can, though. I'll have the subsurface part, from the sixth floor down, airsealed. Then we'll put in oxygen generators and power units, and get a couple of elevators into service. For the floors above, we can use temporary airsealing floor by floor, and portable equipment; when we have things atmosphered and lighted and heated, you and Martha and Tony Lattimer can go to work systematically and in comfort, and I'll give you all the help I can spare from the other work. This is one of the biggest things we've found yet."

Tony Lattimer and his companions came down to the seventh floor a little later.

"I don't get this, at all," he began, as soon as he joined them. "This building wasn't stripped the way the others were. Always, the procedure seems to have been to strip from the bottom up, but they seem to have stripped the top floors first, here. All but the very top. I found out what that conical thing is, by the way. It's a wind-rotor, and under it there's an electric generator. This building generated its own power."

"What sort of condition are the generators in?" Penrose

asked.

"Well, everything's full of dust that blew in under the rotor, of course, but it looks to be in pretty good shape. Hey, I'll bet that's it! They had power, so they used the elevators to haul stuff down. That's just what they did. Some of the floors above here don't seem to have been touched, though." He paused momentarily; back of his oxy-mask, he seemed to be grinning. "I don't know that I ought to mention this in front of Martha, but two floors above we hit a room—it must have been the reference library for one of the departments—that had close to five hundred books in it."

The noise that interrupted him, like the squawking of a Brobdingnagian parrot, was only Ivan Fitzgerald laughing through his helmet-speaker.

Lunch at the huts was a hasty meal, with a gabble of full-mouthed and excited talking. Hubert Penrose and his chief subordinates snatched their food in a huddled consultation at one end of the table; in the afternoon, work was suspended on everything else and the fifty-odd men and women of the expedition concentrated their efforts on the University. By the middle of the afternoon, the seventh floor had been completely examined, photographed and sketched, and the murals in the square central hall covered with protective tarpaulins, and Laurent Gicquel and his airsealing crew had moved in and were at work. It had been decided to seal the central hall at the entrances. It took the French-Canadian engineer most of the afternoon to find all the ventilation-ducts and plug them. An elevator-shaft on the north side was found reaching clear to the twenty-fifth floor; this would give access to the top of the building; another shaft, from the center, would take care of the floors below. Nobody seemed willing to trust the

ancient elevators, themselves; it was the next evening before a couple of cars and the necessary machinery could
be fabricated in the machine shops aboard the ship and
sent down by landing-rocket. By that time, the airsealing
was finished, the nuclear-electric energy-converters were
in place, and the oxygen generators set up.

Martha was in the lower basement, an hour or so before
lunch the day after, when a couple of Space Force officers
came out of the elevator, bringing extra lights with them.
She was still using oxygen-equipment; it was a moment
before she realized that the newcomers had no masks, and
that one of them was smoking. She took off her own helmet-speaker, throat-mike and mask and unslung her tank-
pack, breathing cautiously. The air was chilly, and musty-
acrid with the odor of antiquity—the first Martian odor she
had smelled—but when she lit a cigarette, the lighter
flamed clear and steady and the tobacco caught and
burned evenly.

The archaeologists, many of the other civilian scientists,
a few of the Space Force officers and the two news-corre-
spondents, Sid Chamberlain and Gloria Standish, moved
in that evening, setting up cots in vacant rooms. They installed electric stoves and a refrigerator in the old Library
Reading Room, and put in a bar and lunch counter. For a
few days, the place was full of noise and activity, then,
gradually, the Space Force people and all but a few of the
civilians returned to their own work. There was still the
business of airsealing the more habitable of the buildings
already explored, and fitting them up in readiness for the
arrival, in a year and a half, of the five hundred members
of the main expedition. There was work to be done enlarg-
ing the landing field for the ship's rocket craft, and building
new chemical-fuel tanks.

There was the work of getting the city's ancient reser-

voirs cleared of silt before the next spring thaw brought
more water down the underground aquaducts everybody
called canals in mistranslation of Schiaparelli's Italian
word, though this was proving considerably easier than
anticipated. The ancient Canal-Builders must have anticipated a time when their decendents would no longer be
capable of maintenance work, and had prepared against
it. By the day after the University had been made completely habitable, the actual work there was being done by
Selim, Tony Lattimer and herself, with half a dozen Space
Force officers, mostly girls, and four or five civilians, helping.

They worked up from the bottom, dividing the floor-
surfaces into numbered squares, measuring and listing
and sketching and photographing. They packaged samples of organic matter and sent them up to the ship for
Carbon-14 dating and analysis; they opened cans and jars
and bottles, and found that everything fluid in them had
evaporated, through the porosity of glass and metal and
plastic if there were no other way. Wherever they looked,
they found evidence of activity suddenly suspended and
never resumed. A vise with a bar of metal in it, half cut
through and the hacksaw beside it. Pots and pans with
hardened remains of food in them; a leathery cut of meat
on a table, with the knife ready at hand. Toilet articles on
washstands; unmade beds, the bedding ready to crumble
at a touch but still retaining the impress of the sleeper's
body; papers and writing materials on desks, as though
the writer had gotten up, meaning to return and finish a
fifty-thousand-year-ago moment.

It worried her. Irrationally, she began to feel that the
Martians had never left this place; that they were still
around her, watching disapprovingly every time she
picked up something they had laid down. They haunted

her dreams, now, instead of their enigmatic writing. At first, everybody who had moved into the University had taken a separate room, happy to escape the crowding and lack of privacy of the huts. After a few nights, she was glad when Gloria Standish moved in with her, and accepted the newswoman's excuse that she felt lonely without somebody to talk to before falling asleep. Sachiko Koremitsu joined them the next evening, and before going to bed, the girl officer cleaned and oiled her pistol, remarking that she was afraid some rust may have gotten into it.

The others felt it, too. Selim von Ohlmhorst developed the habit of turning quickly and looking behind him, as though trying to surprise somebody or something that was stalking him. Tony Lattimer, having a drink at the bar that had been improvised from the librarian's desk in the Reading Room, set down his glass and swore.

"You know what this place is? It's an archaeological *Marie Celeste!*" he declared. "It was occupied right up to the end—we've all seen the shifts these people used to keep a civilization going here—but what was the end? What happened to them? Where did they go?"

"You didn't expect them to be waiting out front, with a red carpet and a big banner, *Welcome Terrans,* did you, Tony?" Gloria Standish asked.

"No, of course not; they've all been dead for fifty thousand years. But if they were the last of the Martians, why haven't we found their bones, at least? Who buried them, after they were dead?" He looked at the glass, a bubble-thin goblet, found, with hundreds of others like it, in a closet above, as though debating with himself whether to have another drink. Then he voted in the affirmative and reached for the cocktail pitcher. "And every door on the old ground level is either barred or barricaded from the inside. How did they get out? And why did they leave?"

The next day, at lunch, Sachiko Koremitsu had the answer to the second question. Four or five electrical engineers had come down by rocket from the ship, and she had been spending the morning with them, in oxy-masks, at the top of the building.

"Tony, I thought you said those generators were in good shape," she began, catching sight of Lattimer. "They aren't. They're in the most unholy mess I ever saw. What happened, up there, was that the supports of the wind-rotor gave way, and weight snapped the main shaft, and smashed everything under it."

"Well, after fifty thousand years, you can expect something like that," Lattimer retorted. "When an archaeologist says something's in good shape, he doesn't necessarily mean it'll start as soon as you shove a switch in."

"You didn't notice that it happened when the power was on, did you," one of the engineers asked; nettled at Lattimer's tone. "Well, it was. Everything's burned out or shorted or fused together; I saw one busbar eight inches across melted clean in two. It's a pity we didn't find things in good shape, even archaeologically speaking. I saw a lot of interesting things, things in advance of what we're using now. But it'll take a couple of years to get everything sorted out and figure what it looked like originally."

"Did it look as though anybody'd made any attempt to fix it?" Martha asked.

Sachiko shook her head. "They must have taken one look at it and given up. I don't believe there would have been any possible way to repair anything."

"Well, that explains why they left. They needed electricity for lighting, and heating, and all their industrial equipment was electrical. They had a good life, here, with power; without it, this place wouldn't have been habitable."

"Then why did they barricade everything from the inside, and how did they get out?" Lattimer wanted to know.

"To keep other people from breaking in and looting. Last man out probably barred the last door and slid down a rope from upstairs," von Ohlmhorst suggested. "This Houdini-trick doesn't worry me too much. We'll find out eventually."

"Yes, about the time Martha starts reading Martian," Lattimer scoffed.

"That may be just when we'll find out," von Ohlmhorst replied seriously. "It wouldn't surprise me if they left something in writing when they evacuated this place."

"Are you really beginning to treat this pipe dream of hers as a serious possibility, Selim?" Lattimer demanded. "I know, it would be a wonderful thing, but wonderful things don't happen just because they're wonderful. Only because they're possible, and this isn't. Let me quote that distinguished Hittitologist, Johannes Friedrich: 'Nothing can be translated out of nothing.' Or that later but not less distinguished Hittitologist, Selim von Ohlmhorst: 'Where are you going to get your bilingual?' "

"Friedrich lived to see the Hittite language deciphered and read," von Ohlmhorst reminded him.

"Yes, when they found Hittite-Assyrian bilinguals." Lattimer measured a spoonful of coffee-powder into his cup and added hot water. "Martha, you ought to know, better than anybody, how little chance you have. You've been working for years in the Indus Valley; how many words of Harappa have you or anybody else ever been able to read?"

"We never found a university, with a half-million-volume library, at Harappa or Mohenjo-Daro."

"And, the first day we entered this building, we established meanings for several words," Selim von Ohlmhorst added.

"And you've never found another meaningful word since," Lattimer added. And you're only sure of general meaning, not specific meaning of word-elements, and you have a dozen different interpretations for each word."

"We made a start," von Ohlmhorst maintained. "We have Grotefend's word for 'king.' But I'm going to be able to read some of those books, over there, if it takes me the rest of my life here. It probably will, anyhow."

"You mean you've changed your mind about going home on the *Cyrano?*" Martha asked. "You'll stay on here?"

The old man nodded. "I can't leave this. There's too much to discover. The old dog will have to learn a lot of new tricks, but this is where my work will be, from now on."

Lattimer was shocked. "You're nuts!" he cried. "You mean you're going to throw away everything you've accomplished in Hittitology and start all over again here on Mars? Martha, if you've talked him into this crazy decision, you're a criminal!"

"Nobody talked me into anything," von Ohlmhorst said roughly. "And as for throwing away what I've accomplished in Hittitology, I don't know what the devil you're talking about. Everything I know about the Hittite Empire is published and available to anybody. Hittitology's like Egyptology; it's stopped being research and archaeology and become scholarship and history. And I'm not a scholar or a historian; I'm a pick-and-shovel field archaeologist— a highly skilled and specialized grave-robber and junk-picker—and there's more pick-and-shovel work on this planet than I could do in a hundred lifetimes. This is something new; I was a fool to think I could turn my back on it and go back to scribbling footnotes about Hittite kings."

"You could have anything you wanted, in Hittitology. There are a dozen universities that'd sooner have you than a winning football team. But no! You have to be the top man in Martiology, too. You can't leave that for anybody else—" Lattimer shoved his chair back and got to his feet, leaving the table with an oath that was almost a sob of exasperation.

Maybe his feelings were too much for him. Maybe he realized, as Martha did, what he had betrayed. She sat, avoiding the eyes of the others, looking at the ceiling, as embarrassed as though Lattimer had flung something dirty on the table in front of them. Tony Lattimer had, desperately, wanted Selim to go home on the *Cyrano*. Martiology was a new field; if Selim entered it, he would bring with him the reputation he had already built in Hittitology, automatically stepping into the leading role that Lattimer had coveted for himself. Ivan Fitzgerald's words echoed back to her—when you want to be a big shot, you can't bear the possibility of anybody else being a bigger big shot. His derision of her own efforts became comprehensible, too. It wasn't that he was convinced that she would never learn to read the Martian language. He had been afraid that she would.

Ivan Fitzgerald finally isolated the germ that had caused the Finchly girl's undiagnosed illness. Shortly afterward, the malady turned into a mild fever, from which she recovered. Nobody else seemed to have caught it. Fitzgerald was still trying to find out how the germ had been transmitted.

The found a globe of Mars, made when the city had been a seaport. They located the city, and learned that its name had been Kukan—or something with a similar vowel-consonant ratio. Immediately, Sid Chamberlain and Gloria Standish began giving their telecasts a Kukan dateline, and Hubert Penrose used the name in his official reports. They also found Martian calendar; the year had been divided into ten more or less equal months, and one of them had been Doma. Another month was Nor, and that was a part of the name of the scientific journal Martha had found.

Bill chandler, the zoologist, had been going deeper and deeper into the old sea bottom of Syrtis. Four hundred miles from Kukan, and at fifteen thousand feet lower altitude, he shot a bird. At least, it was a something with wings and what were almost but not quite feathers, though it was more reptilian than avian in general characteristics. He and Ivan Fitzgerald skinned and mounted it, and then dissected the carcass almost tissue by tissue. About seven-eights of its body capacity was lungs; it certainly breathed air containing at least half enough oxygen to support human life, or five times as much as the air around Kukan.

That took the center of interest away from archaeology, and started a new burst of activity. All the expedition's aircraft—four jetticopters and three wingless airdyne reconnaissance fighters—were thrown into intensified exploration of the lower sea bottoms, and the bio-science boys and girls were wild with excitement and making new discoveries on each flight.

The University was left to Selim and Martha and Tony Lattimer, the latter keeping to himself while she and the old Turco-German worked together. The civilian specialists in other fields, and the Space Force people who had been holding tape lines and making sketches and snapping cameras, were all flying to lower Syrtis to find out how much oxygen there was and what kind of life it supported.

Sometimes Sachiko dropped in; most of the time she was busy helping Ivan Fitzgerald dissect specimens. They

had four or five species of what might loosely be called
birds, and something that could easily be classed as a rep-
tile, and a carnivorous mammal the size of a cat with bird-
like claws, and a herbivore almost identical with the piglike
thing in the big *Darfhulva* mural, and another like a gazelle
with a single horn in the middle of its forehead.

The high point came when one party, at thirty thousand
feet below the level of Kukan, found breathable air. One
of them had a mild attack of *sorroche* and had to be flown
back for treatment in a hurry, but the others showed no ill
effects.

The daily newscasts from Terra showed a correspond-
ing shift in interest at home. The discovery of the University had focused attention on the dead past of Mars; now
the public was interested in Mars as a possible home for
humanity. It was Tony Lattimer who brought archaeology
back into the activities of the expedition and the news at
home.

Martha and Selim were working in the museum on the
second floor, scrubbing the grime from the glass cases,
noting contents, and grease-penciling numbers; Lattimer
and a couple of Space Force officers were going through
what had been the administrative offices on the other side.
It was one of these, a young second lieutenant, who came
hurrying in from the mezzanine, almost bursting with excitement.

"Hey, Martha! Dr. von Ohlmhorst!" he was shouting.
"Where are you? Tony's found the Martians!"

Selim dropped his rag back in the bucket; she laid her
clipboard on top of the case beside her.

"Where?" they asked together.

"Over on the north side." The lieutenant took hold of
himself and spoke more deliberately. "Little room, back
of one of the old faculty offices—conference room. It was

locked from the inside, and we had to burn it down with a torch. That's where they are. Eighteen of them, around a long table—"

Gloria Standish, who had dropped in for lunch, was on the mezzanine, fairly screaming into a radiophone extension:

". . . Dozen and a half of them! Well, of course they're dead. What a question! They look like skeletons covered with leather. No, I do not know what they died of. Well, forget it; I don't care if Bill 'Chandler's found a three-headed hippopotamus. Sid, don't you get it? We've found the *Martians!*"

She slammed the phone back on its hook, rushing away ahead of them.

Martha remembered the closed door; on the first survey, they hadn't attempted opening it. Now it was burned away at both sides and lay still hot along the edges, on the floor of the big office room in front. A floodlight was on in the room inside, and Lattimer was going around looking at things while a Space Force officer stood by the door. The center of the room was filled by a long table; in armchairs around it sat the eighteen men and women who had occupied the room for the last fifty millennia. There were bottles and glasses on the table in front of them, and, had she seen them in a dimmer light, she would have thought that they were merely dozing over their drinks. One had a knee hooked over his chair-arm and was curled in foetus-like sleep. Another had fallen forward onto the table, arms extended, the emerald set of a ring twinkling dully on one finger. Skeletons covered with leather, Gloria Standish had called them, and so they were—faces like skulls, arms and legs like sticks, the flesh shrunken onto the bones under it.

"Isn't this something!" Lattimer was exulting. "Mass suicide, that's what it was. Notice what's in the corners?"

Braziers, made of perforated two-gallon-odd metal cans, the white walls smudged with smoke above them. Von Ohlmhorst had noticed them at once, and was poking into one of them with his flashlight.

"Yes; charcoal. I noticed a quantity of it around a couple of hand-forges in the shop on the first floor. That's why you had so much trouble breaking in; they'd sealed the room on the inside." He straightened and went around the room, until he found a ventilator, and peered into it. "Stuffed with rags. They must have been all that were left, here. Their power was gone, and they were old and tired, and all around them their world was dying. So they just came in here and lit the charcoal, and sat drinking together till they all fell asleep. Well, we know what became of them, now, anyhow."

Sid and Gloria made the most of it. The Terran public wanted to hear about Martians, and if live Martians couldn't be found, a room full of dead ones was the next best thing. Maybe an even better thing; it had been only sixty-odd years since the Orson Welles invasion-scare. Tony Lattimer, the discoverer, was beginning to cash in on his attentions to Gloria and his ingratiation with Sid; he was always either making voice-and-image talks for telecast or listening to the news from the home planet. Without question, he had become, overnight, the most widely known archaeologist in history.

"Not that I'm interested in all this, for myself," he disclaimed, after listening to the telecast from Terra two days after his discovery. "But this is going to be a big thing for Martian archaeology. Bring it to the public attention; dramatize it. Selim, can you remember when Lord Carnarvon and Howard Carter found the tomb of Tutankhamen?"

"In 1923? I was two years old, then," von Ohlmhorst
chuckled. "I really don't know how much that publicity
ever did for Egyptiology. Oh, the museums did devote
more space to Egyptian exhibits, and after a museum department head gets a few extra showcases, you know how
hard it is to make him give them up. And, for a while, it
was easier to get financial support for new excavations.
But I don't know how much good all this public excitement
really does, in the long run."

"Well, I think one of us should go back on the *Cyrano,*
when the *Schiaparelli* orbits in," Lattimer said. "I'd hoped
it would be you; your voice would carry the most weight.
But I think it's important that one of us go back, to present
the story of our work, and what we have accomplished
and what we hope to accomplish, to the public and to the
universities and the learned societies, and to the Federation Government. There will be a great deal of work that
will have to be done. We must not allow the other scientific
fields and the so-called practical interests to monopolize
public and academic support. So, I believe I shall go back
at least for a while, and see what I can do—"

Lectures. The organization of a Society of Martian Archaeology, with Anthony Lattimer, Ph.D., the logical can-
didate for the chair. Degrees, honors; the deference of the
learned, and the adulation of the lay public. Positions, with
impressive titles and salaries. Sweet are the uses of publicity.

She crushed out her cigarette and got to her feet. "Well,
I still have the final lists of what we found in *Halvhulva*—
Biology—department to check over. I'm starting on Sornhulva tomorrow, and I want that stuff in shape for expert
evaluation."

That was the sort of thing Tony Lattimer wanted to get

away from, the detail-work and the drudgery. Let the infantry do the slogging through the mud; the brass-hats got
the medals.

She was halfway through the fifth floor, a week later, and
was having midday lunch in the reading room on the first
floor when Hubert Penrose came over and sat down beside her, asking her what she was doing. She told him.

"I wonder if you could find me a couple of men, for an
hour or so," she added. "I'm stopped by a couple of
jammed doors at the central hall. Lecture room and library, if the layout of that floor's anything like the ones
below it."

"Yes. I'm a pretty fair door-buster, myself." He looked
around the room. "There's Jeff Miles; he isn't doing much
of anything. And we'll put Sid Chamberlain to work, for a
change, too. The four of us ought to get your doors open."
He called to Chamberlain, who was carrying his tray over
to the dish washer. "Oh, Sid; you doing anything for the
next hour or so?"

"I was going up to the fourth floor, to see what Tony's
doing."

"Forget it. Tony's bagged his season limit of Martians.
I'm going to help Martha bust in a couple of doors; we'll
probably find a whole cemetery full of Martians."

Chamberlain shrugged. "Why not. A jammed door can
have anything back of it, and I know what Tony's doing—
just routine stuff."

Jeff Miles, the Space Force captain, came over, accompanied by one of the lab-crew from the ship who had come
down on the rocket the day before.

"This ought to be up your alley, Mort," he was saying
to his companion. "Chemistry and physics department.
Want to come along?"

The lab man, Mort Tranter, was willing. See the sights was what he'd come down from the ship for. She finished her coffee and cigarette, and they went out into the hall together, gathered equipment and rode the elevator to the fifth floor.

The lecture hall door was the nearest; they attacked it first. With proper equipment and help, it was no problem and in ten minutes they had it open wide enough to squeeze through with the floodlights. The room inside was quite empty, and like most of the rooms behind closed doors, comparatively free from dust. The students, it appeared, had sat with their backs to the door, facing a low platform, but their seats and the lecturer's table and equipment had been removed. The two side walls bore inscriptions: on the right, a pattern of concentric circles which she recognized as a diagram of atomic structure, and on the left a complicated table of numbers and words, in two columns. Tranter was pointing at the diagram on the right.

"They got as far as the Bohr atom, anyhow," he said. "Well, not quite. They knew about electron shells, but they have the nucleus pictured as a solid mass. No indication of proton-and-neutron structure. I'll bet, when you come to translate their scientific books, you'll find that they taught that the atom was the ultimate and indivisible particle. That explains why you people never found any evidence that the Martians used nuclear energy."

"That's a uranium atom," Captain Miles mentioned.

"It is?" Sid Chamberlain asked, excitedly. "Then they did know about atomic energy. Just because we haven't found any pictures of A-bomb mushrooms doesn't mean—"

She turned to look at the other wall. Sid's signal reactions were getting away from him again; uranium meant nuclear power to him, and the two words were inter-

changeable. As she studied the arrangement of the numbers and words, she could hear Tranter saying:

"Nuts, Sid. We knew about uranium a long time before
anybody found out what could be done with it. Uranium
was discovered on Terra in 1789, by Klaproth."

There was something familiar about the table on the left
wall. She tried to remember what she had been taught in
school about physics, and what she had picked up by accident afterward. The second column was a continuation
of the first: there were forty-six items in each, each item
numbered consecutively—

"Probably used uranium because it's the largest of the
natural atoms," Penrose was saying. "The fact that there's
nothing beyond it there shows that they hadn't created
any of the transuranics. A student could go to that thing
and point out the outer electron of any of the ninety-two
elements."

Ninety-two! That was it; there were ninety-two items in
the table on the left wall! Hydrogen was Number One, she
knew; One, *Sarfaldsorn*. Helium was Two; that was *Tir-
faldsorn*. She couldn't remember which element came
next, but in Martian it was *Sarfalddavas*. *Sorn* must mean
matter, or substance, then. And *davas;* she was trying to
think of what it could be. She turned quickly to the others,
catching hold of Hubert Penrose's arm with one hand and
waving her clipboard with the other.

"Look at this thing, over here," she was clamoring excitedly. "Tell me what you think it is. Could it be a table of
the elements?"

They all turned to look. Mort Tranter stared at it for a
moment.

"Could be. If I only knew what those squiggles
meant—"

That was right; he'd spent his time aboard the ship.

"If you could read the numbers, would that help?" she asked, beginning to set down the Arabic digits and their Martian equivalents. "It's decimal system, the same as we use."

"Sure. If that's a table of elements, all I'd need would be the numbers. Thanks," he added as she tore off the sheet and gave it to him.

Penrose knew the numbers, and was ahead of him. "Ninety-two items, numbered consecutively. The first number would be the atomic number. Then a single word, the name of the element. Then the atomic weight—"

She began reading off the names of the elements. "I know hydrogen and helium; what's *tirfalddavas,* the third one?"

"Lithium," Tranter said. "The atomic weights aren't run out past the decimal point. Hydrogen's one plus, if that double-hook dingus is a plus sign; Helium's four-plus, that's right. And lithium's given as seven, that isn't right. It's six-point nine-four-oh. Or is that thing a Martian minus sign?"

"Of course! Look! A plus sign is a hook, to hang things together; a minus sign is a knife, to cut something off from something—see, the little loop is the blade. Stylized, of course, but that's what it is. And the fourth element, *kira-davas;* what's that?"

"Beryllium. Atomic weight given as nine-and-a-hook; actually it's nine-point-oh-two."

Sid Chamberlain had been disgruntled because he couldn't get a story about the Martians having developed atomic energy. It took him a few minutes to understand the newest development, but finally it dawned on him.

"Hey! You're reading that!" he cried. "You're reading Martian!"

"That's right," Penrose told him. "Just reading it right

off. I don't get the two items after the atomic weight, though. They look like months of the Martian calendar. What ought they to be, Mort?"

Tranter hesitated. "Well, the next information after the atomic weight ought to be the period and group numbers. But those are words."

"What would the numbers be for the first one, hydrogen?"

"Period One, Group One. One electron shell, one electron in the outer shell," Tranter told her. "Helium's period one, too, but it has the outer—only—electron shell full, so it's in the group of inert elements."

"*Trav, Trav. Trav's* the first month of the year. And helium's *Trav, Yenth; Yenth* is the eighth month."

"The inert elements could be called Group Eight, yes. And the third element, lithium, is Period Two, Group One. That check?"

"It certainly does. *Sanv, Trav; Sanv's* the second month. What's the first element in Period Three?"

"Sodium, Number Eleven."

"That's right; its *Krav, Trav.* Why, the names of the months are simply numbers, one to ten, spelled out."

"*Doma's* the fifth month. That was your first Martian word, Martha," Penrose told her. "The word for five. And if *davas* is the word for metal, and *sornhulva* is chemistry and/or physics, I'll bet *Tadavas Sornhulva* is literally translated as: 'Of-Metal Matter-Knowledge.' Metallurgy, in other words. I wonder what *Mastharnorvod* means." It surprised her that, after so long and with so much happening in the meantime, he could remember that. "Something like 'Journal,' or 'Review,' or maybe 'Quarterly.' "

"We'll work that out, too," she said confidently. After this, nothing seemed impossible. "Maybe we can find—" Then she stopped short. "You said 'Quarterly.' I think it was 'Monthly,' instead. It was dated for a specific month, the fifth one. And if *nor* is ten, *Mastharnorvod* could be 'Year-Tenth'. And I'll bet we'll find that *masthar* is the word for year." She looked at the table on the wall again. "Well, let's get all these words down, with translations for as many as we can."

"Let's take a break for a minute," Penrose suggested, getting out his cigarettes. "And then, let's do this in comfort. Jeff, suppose you and Sid go across the hall and see what you find in the other room in the way of a desk or something like that, and a few chairs. There'll be a lot of work to do on this."

Sid Chamberlain had been squirming as though he were afflicted with ants, trying to contain himself. Now he let go with an excited jabber.

"This is really it! *The* it, not just it-of-the-week, like finding the reservoirs or those statues or this building, or even the animals and the dead Martians! Wait till Selim and Tony see this! Wait till Tony sees it; I want to see his face! And when I get this on telecast, all Terra's going to go nuts about it!" He turned to Captain Miles. "Jeff, suppose you take a look at that other door, while I find somebody to send to tell Selim and Tony. And Gloria; wait till she sees this—"

"Take it easy, Sid," Martha cautioned. "You'd better let me have a look at your script, before you go too far overboard on the telecast. This is just a beginning; it'll take years and years before we're able to read any of those books downstairs."

"It'll go faster than you think, Martha," Hubert Penrose told her. "We'll all work on it, and we'll teleprint material to Terra, and people there will work on it. We'll send them everything we can . . . everything we work out, and copies of books, and copies of your wordlists—"

And there would be other tables—astronomical tables, tables in physics and mechanics, for instance—in which words and numbers were equivalent. The library stacks, below, would be full of them. Transliterate them into Roman alphabet spellings and Arabic numerals, and somewhere, sombody would spot each numerical significance, as Hubert Penrose and Mort Tranter and she had done with the table of elements. And pick out all the chemistry textbooks in the Library; new words would take on meaning from contexts in which the names of elements appeared. She'd have to start studying chemistry and physics, herself—

Sachiko Koremitsu peeped in through the door, then stepped inside.

"Is there anything I can do—?" she began. "What's happened? Something important?"

"Important?" Sid Chamberlain exploded. "Look at that, Sachi! We're reading it! Martha's found out how to read Martian!" He grabbed Captain Miles by the arm. "Come on, Jeff; let's go. I want to call the others—" He was still babbling as he hurried from the room.

Sachi looked at the inscription. "Is it true?" she asked, and then, before Martha could more than begin to explain, flung her arms around her. "Oh, it really is! You are reading it! I'm so happy!"

She had to start explaining again when Selim von Ohlmhorst entered. This time, she was able to finish.

"But, Martha, can you be really sure? You know, by now, that learning to read this language is as important to me as it is to you, but how can you be so sure that those words really mean things like hydrogen and helium and boron and oxygen? How do you know that their table of elements was anything like ours?"

Tranter and Penrose and Sachiko all looked at him in amazement.

"That isn't just the Martian table of elements; that's *the* table of elements. It's the only one there is," Mort Tranter almost exploded. "Look, hydrogen has one proton and one electron. If it had more of either, it wouldn't be hydrogen, it'd be something else. And the same with all the rest of the elements. And hydrogen on Mars is the same as hydrogen on Terra, or on Alpha Centauri, or in the next galaxy—"

"You just set up those numbers, in that order, and any first-year chemistry student could tell you what elements they represented," Penrose said. "Could if he expected to make a passing grade, that is."

The old man shook his head slowly, smiling. "I'm afraid I wouldn't make a passing grade. I didn't know, or at least didn't realize, that. One of the things I'm going to place an order for, to be brought on the *Schiaparelli,* will be a set of primers in chemistry and physics, of the sort intended for a bright child of ten or twelve. It seems that a Martiologist has to learn a lot of things the Hittites and the Assyrians never heard about."

Tony Lattimer, coming in, caught the last part of the explanation. He looked quickly at the walls and, having found out just what had happened, advanced and caught Martha by the hand.

"You really did it, Martha! You found your bilingual! I never believed that it would be possible; let me congratulate you!"

He probably expected that to erase all the jibes and sneers of the past. If he did, he could have it that way. His friendship would mean as little to her as his derision—except that his friends had to watch their backs and his knife. But he was going home on the *Cyrano,* to be a bigshot. Or had this changed his mind for him again?

"This is something we can show the world, to justify any expenditure of time and money on Martian archaeological work. When I get back to Terra, I'll see that you're given full credit for this achievement—"

On Terra, her back and his knife would be out of her watchfulness.

"We won't need to wait that long," Hubert Penrose told him dryly. "I'm sending off an official report, tomorrow; you can be sure Dr. Dane will be given full credit, not only for this but for her previous work, which made it possible to exploit this discovery."

"And you might add, work done in spite of the doubts and discouragements of her colleagues," Selim von Ohlmhorst said. "To which I am ashamed to have to confess my own share."

"You said we had to find a bilingual," she said. "You were right, too."

"This is better than a bilingual, Martha," Hubert Penrose said. "Physical science expresses universal facts; necessarily it is a universal language. Heretofore archeologists have dealt only with pre-scientific cultures."

Introduction to "Naudsonce"

"Naudsonce" takes place almost six centuries after "Omni-lingual," sometime in the Seventh Century A.E. The Federation is still expanding, although Terra's bureaucracy is more and more making its weight felt. "But if he failed, he was through . . . When he got back to Terra, he would be promoted to some home office position at slightly higher base pay but without the three hundred per cent extraterrestrial bonus, and he would vegetate there till he retired." No longer is exploration enough incentive to get people out of their safe sinecures; although there will always be those few who decry the safe harbor. . . .

This is another anthropological detective story and while the solution is just as snappy, the ethical outcome is no longer quite so clear.

56

NAUDSONCE

The sun warmed Mark Howell's back pleasantly. Under-foot, the mosslike stuff was soft and yielding, and there was a fragrance in the air unlike anything he had ever smelled. He was going to like this planet; he knew it. The question was, how would it, and its people, like him? He watched the little figures advancing across the fields from the mound, with the village out of sight on the other end of it and the combat-car circling lazily on contragravity above.

Major Luis Gofredo, the Marine officer, spoke without lowering his binoculars:

"They have a tubular thing about twelve feet long; six of them are carrying it on poles, three to a side, and a couple more are walking behind it. Mark, do you think it could be a cannon?"

So far, he didn't know enough to have an opinion, and said so, adding:

"What I saw of the village in the screen from the car, it looked pretty primitive. Of course, gunpowder's one of those things a primitive people could discover by accident, if the ingredients were available."

"We won't take any chances, then."

"You think they're hostile? I was hoping they were com-ing out to parley with us."

That was Paul Meillard. He had a right to be anxious; his whole future in the Colonial Office would be made or ruined by what was going to happen here.

The joint Space Navy-Colonial Office expedition was looking for new planets suitable for colonization; they had been out, now, for four years, which was close to maximum for an exploring expedition. They had entered eleven systems, and made landings on eight planets. Three had been reasonably close to Terra-type. There had been Fafnir; conditions there would correspond to Terra during the Cretaceous Period, but any Cretaceous dinosaur would have been cute and cuddly to the things on Fafnir. Then there had been Imhotep; in twenty or thirty thousand years, it would be a fine planet, but at present it was undergoing an extensive glaciation. And Irminsul, covered with forests of gigantic trees; it would have been fine except for the fauna, which was nasty, especially a race of subsapient near-humanoids who had just gotten as far as clubs and *coup-de-poing* axes. Contact with them had entailed heavy ammunition expenditure, with two men and a woman killed and a dozen injured. He'd had a limp, himself, for a while as a result.

As for the other five, one had been an all-out hell-planet, and the rest had been the sort that get colonized by irreconcilable minority-groups who want to get away from everybody else. The Colonial Office wouldn't even consider any of them.

Then they had found this one, third of a GO-star, eighty million miles from primary, less axial inclination than Terra, which would mean a more uniform year-round temperature, and about half land surface. On the evidence of a couple of sneak landings for specimens, the biochemistry was identical with Terra's and the organic matter was edible. It was the sort of planet every explorer dreams of finding, except for one thing.

It was inhabited by a sapient humanoid race, and some of them were civilized enough to put it in Class V, and

Colonial Office doctrine on Class V planets was rigid. Friendly relations with the natives had to be established, and permission to settle had to be guaranteed in a treaty of some sort with somebody more or less authorized to make one.

If Paul Meillard could accomplish that, he had it made. He would stay on with forty or fifty of the ship's company to make preparations. In a year a couple of ships would come out from Terra, with a thousand colonists, and a battalion or so of Federation troops, to protect them from the natives and vice versa. Meillard would automatically be appointed governor-general.

But if he failed, he was through. Not out—just through. When he got back to Terra, he would be promoted to some home office position at slightly higher base pay but without the three hundred per cent extraterrestrial bonus, and he would vegetate there till he retired. Every time his name came up, somebody would say, "Oh, yes; he flubbed the contact on Whatzit."

It wouldn't do the rest of them any good, either. There would always be the suspicion that they had contributed to the failure.

Bwaaa-waaa-waaanh!

The wavering sound hung for an instant in the air. A few seconds later, it was repeated, then repeated again.

"Our cannon's a horn," Gofredo said. "I can't see how they're blowing it, though."

There was a stir to right and left, among the Marines deployed in a crescent line on either side of the contact team; a metallic clatter as weapons were checked. A shadow fell in front of them as a combat-car moved into position above.

"What do you suppose it means?" Meillard wondered.

"Terrans, go home." He drew a frown from Meillard with the suggestion. "Maybe it's supposed to intimidate us."

"They're probably doing it to encourage themselves," Anna de Jong, the psychologist, said. "I'll bet they're really scared stiff."

"I see how they're blowing it," Gofredo said. "The man who's walking behind it has a hand-bellows." He raised his voice. "Fix bayonets! These people don't know anything about rifles, but they know what spears are. They have some of their own."

So they had. The six who walked in the lead were un-armed, unless the thing one of them carried was a spear. So, it seemed, were the hornbearers. Behind them, how-ever, in an open-order skirmish-line, came fifty-odd with weapons. Most of them had spears, the points glinting redly. Bronze, with a high copper content. A few had bows. They came slowly; details became more plainly vis-ible.

The leader wore a long yellow robe; the thing in his hand was a bronze-headed staff. Three of his companions also wore robes; the other two were bare-legged in short tunics. The horn-bearers wore either robes or tunics; the spearmen and bowmen behind either wore tunics or were naked except for breechclouts. All wore sandals. They were red-brown in color, completely hairless; they had long necks, almost chinless lower jaws, and fleshy, beak-like noses that gave them an avian appearance which was heightened by red crests, like roosters' combs, on the tops of their heads.

"Well, aren't they something to see?" Lillian Ransby, the linguist asked.

"I wonder how we look to them," Paul Meillard said.

That was something to wonder about, too. The differences between one and another of the Terrans must puzzle them. Paul Meillard, as close to being a pure Negro as anybody in the Seventh Century of the Atomic Era was to being pure anything. Lillian Ransby, almost ash-blond. Major Gofredo, barely over the minimum Service height requirement; his name was Old Terran Spanish, but his ancestry must have been Polynesian, Amerind and Mongolian. Karl Dorver, the sociographer, six feet six, with red hair. Bennet Fayon, the biologist and physiologist, plump, pink-faced and balding. Willi Schallenmacher, with a bushy black beard . . .

They didn't have any ears, he noticed, and then he was taking stock of the things they wore and carried. Belts, with pouches, and knives with flat bronze blades and riveted handles. Three of the delegation had small flutes hung by cords around their necks, and a fourth had a reed Panpipe. No shields, and no swords; that was good. Swords and shields mean organized warfare, possibly a warrior-caste. This crowd weren't warriors. The spearmen and bowmen weren't arrayed for battle, but for a drive-hunt, with the bows behind the spears to stop anything that broke through the line.

"All right; let's go meet them." The querulous, uncertain note was gone from Meillard's voice; he knew what to do and how to do it.

Gofredo called to the Marines to stand fast. Then they were advancing to meet the natives, and when they were twenty feet apart, both groups halted. The horn stopped blowing. The one in the yellow robe lifted his staff and said something that sounded like, *"Tweedle-eedle-oodly-eenk."*

The horn, he saw, was made of strips of leather, wound spirally and coated with some kind of varnish. Everything

these people had was carefully and finely made. An old
culture, but a static one. Probably tradition-bound as all
get-out.

Meillard was raising his hands; solemnly he addressed
the natives:

"Twas brillig and the slithy toves were whooping it up in
the Malemute Saloon, and the kid that handled the music
box did gyre and gimble in the wabe, and back of the bar
in a solo game all mimsy were the borogoves, and the
mome raths outgabe the lady that's known as Lou."

That was supposed to show them that we, too, have a
spoken language, to prove that their language and ours
were mutually incomprehensible, and to demonstrate the
need for devising a means of communication. At least that
was what the book said. It demonstrated nothing of the
sort to this crowd. It scared them. The dignitary with the
staff twittered excitedly. One of his companions agreed
with him at length. Another started to reach for his knife,
then remembered his manners. The bellowsman pumped
a few blasts on the horn.

"What do you think of the language?" he asked Lillian.

"They all sound that bad, when you first hear them.
Give them a few seconds, and then we'll have Phase
Two."

When the gibbering and skreeking began to fall off, she
stepped forward. Lillian was, herself, a good test of how
human aliens were; this gang weren't human enough to
whistle at her. She touched herself on the breast. "Me,"
she said.

The natives seemed shocked. She repeated the gesture
and the word, then turned and addressed Paul Meillard.
"You."

"Me," Meillard said, pointing to himself. Then he said,
"You," to Luis Gofredo. It went around the contact team;

when it came to him, he returned it to point of origin.

"I don't think they get it at all," he added in a whisper.

. "They ought to," Lillian said. "Every language has a word for self and a word for person-addressed."

"Well, look at them," Karl Dorver invited. "Six different opinions about what we mean, and now the band's starting an argument of their own."

"Phase Two-A," Lillian said firmly, stepping forward. She pointed to herself. "Me—Lillian Ransby. Lillian Ransby—me *name*. You—*name?*"

"Bwoooo!" the spokesman screamed in horror, clutching his staff as though to shield it from profanation. The others howled like a hound-pack at a full moon, except one of the short-tunic boys, who was slapping himself on the head with both hands and yodeling. The horncrew hastily swung their piece around at the Terrans, pumping frantically.

"What do you suppose I said?" Lillian asked.

"Oh, something like, 'Curse your gods, death to your king, and spit in your mother's face,' I suppose."

"Let me try it," Gofredo said.

The little Marine major went through the same routine. At his first word, the uproar stopped; before he was through, the natives' faces were sagging and crumbling into expressions of utter and heart-broken grief.

"It's not as bad as all that, is it?" he said. "You try it, Mark."

"Me . . . Mark . . . Howell . . ." They looked bewildered.

"Let's try objects, and play-acting," Lillian suggested. "They're farmers; they ought to have a word for water."

They spent almost an hour at it. They poured out two gallons of water, pretended to be thirsty, gave each other drinks. The natives simply couldn't agree on the word, in

their own language, for water. That or else they missed the
point of the whole act. They tried fire, next. The efficiency
of a steel hatchet was impressive, and so was the sudden
flame of a pocket-lighter, but no word for fire emerged,
either.

"Ah, to Nifflheim with it!" Luis Gofredo cried in exasperation. "We're getting nowhere at five times light speed.
Give them their presents and send them home, Paul."

"Sheath-knives; they'll have to be shown how sharp
they are," he suggested. "Red bandannas. And costume
jewelry."

"How about something to eat, Bennet?" Meillard asked
Fayon.

"Extee Three, and C-H trade candy," Fayon said. Field
Ration, Extraterrestrial Service, Type Three, could be eat-
en by anything with a carbon-hydrogen metabolism, and
so could the trade candy. "Nothing else, though, till we
have some idea what goes on inside them."

Dorver thought the six members of the delegation
would be persons of special consequence, and should
have something extra. That was probably so. Dorver was
as quick to pick up clues to an alien social order as he was,
himself, to deduce a culture pattern from a few artifacts.
He and Lillian went back to the landing craft to collect the
presents.

Everybody, horn-detail, armed guard and all, got one
ten-inch bowie knife and sheath, a red bandanna neck-
cloth, and a piece of flashy junk jewelry. The (town council? prominent citizens? or what?) also received a colored
table-spread apiece; these were draped over their shoulders and fastened with two-inch plastic pins advertising the
candidacy of somebody for President of the Federation
Member Republic of Venus a couple of elections ago.
They all looked woebegone about it; that would be their

expression of joy. Different type nerves and different facial musculature, Fayon thought. As soon as they sampled the Extee Three and candy, they looked crushed under all the sorrows of the galaxy.

By pantomime and pointing to the sun, Meillard managed to inform them that the next day, when the sun was in the same position, the Terrans would visit their village, bringing more gifts. The natives were quite agreeable, but Meillard was disgruntled that he had to use signtalk. The natives started off toward the village on the mound, munching Extee Three and trying out their new knives. This time tomorrow, half of them would have bandaged thumbs.

The Marine riflemen and submachine-gunners were coming in, slinging their weapons and lighting cigarettes. A couple of Navy technicians were getting a snooper—a thing shaped like a short-tailed tadpole, six feet long by three at the widest, fitted with visible-light and infra-red screen pickups and crammed with detection instruments—ready to relieve the combat car over the village. The contact team crowded into the Number One landing craft, which had been fitted out as a temporary headquarters. Prefab-hut elements were already being unloaded from the other craft.

Everybody felt that a drink was in order, even if it was two hours short of cocktail time. They carried bottles and glasses and ice to the front of the landing craft and sat down in front of the battery of view and communication screens. The central screen was a two-way, tuned to one in the officers' lounge aboard the *Hubert Penrose,* two hundred miles above. In it, also provided with drinks, were Captain Guy Vindinho and two orther Navy officers, and a Marine captain in shipboard blues. Like Gofredo, Vindinho must have gotten into the Service on tiptoe; he had a bald dome and a red beard, and he always looked as though he were gloating because nobody knew that his name was really Rumplestiltskin. He had been watching the contact by screen. He lifted his glass toward Meillard.

"Over the hump, Paul?"

Meillard raised his drink to Vindinho. "Over the first one. There's a whole string of them ahead. At least, we sent them away happy. I hope."

"You're going to make permanent camp where you are now?" one of the other officers asked. Lieutenant-Commander Dave Questell; ground engineering and construction officer. "What do you need?"

There were two viewscreens from pickups aboard the 2500-foot battle cruiser. One, at ten-power magnification, gave a maplike view of the broad valley and the uplands and mountain foothills to the south. It was only by tracing the course of the main river and its tributaries that they could find the tiny spot of the native village, and they couldn't see the landing craft at all. The other, at a hundred power, showed the oblong mound, with the village on its flat top, little dots around a circular central plaza. They could see the two turtle-shaped landing-craft, and the combat car, that had been circling over the mound, landing beside them, and, sometimes, a glint of sunlight from the snooper that had taken its place.

The snooper was also transmitting in, to another screen, from two hundred feet above the village. From the sound outlet came an incessant gibber of native voices. There were over a hundred houses, all small and square, with pyramidal roofs. On the end of the mound toward the Terran camp, animals of at least four different species were crowded, cattle that had been herded up from the meadows at the first alarm. The open circle in the middle of the village was crowded, and more natives lined the low palisade along the edge of the mound.

"Well, we're going to stay here till we learn the language," Meillard was saying. "This is the best place for it. It's completely isolated, forests on both sides, and seventy miles to the nearest other village. If we're careful, we can stay here as long as we want to and nobody'll find out about us. Then, after we can talk with these people, we'll go to the big town."

The big town was two hundred and fifty miles down the valley, at the forks of the main river, a veritable metropolis of almost three thousand people. That was where the treaty would have to be negotiated.

"You'll want more huts. You'll want a water tank, and a pipeline to that stream below you, and a pump," Questell said. "You think a month?"

Meillard looked at Lillian Ransby. "What do you think?"

"*Poodly-doodly-oodly-foodle,*" she said. "You saw how far we didn't get this afternoon. All we found out was that none of the standard procedures work at all." She made a tossing gesture over her shoulder. "There goes the book; we have to do it off the cuff from here."

"Suppose we make another landing, back in the mountains, say two or three hundred miles south of you," Vindinho said. "It's not right to keep the rest aboard two hundred miles off planet, and you won't be wanting liberty parties coming down where you are."

"The country over there looks uninhabited," Meillard said. "No villages, anyhow. That wouldn't hurt, at all."

"Well, it'll suit me," Charley Loughran, the xeno-naturalist, said. "I want a chance to study the lifeforms in a state of nature."

Vindinho nodded. "Luis, do you anticipate any trouble with this crowd here?" he asked.

"How about it, Mark? What do they look like to you? Warlike?"

"No." He stated the opinion he had formed. "I had a close look at their weapons when they came in for their presents. Hunting arms. Most of the spears have cross-guards, usually wooden, lashed on, to prevent a wounded animal from running up the spear-shaft at the hunter. They made boar-spears like that on Terra a thousand years ago. Maybe they have to fight raiding parties from the hills once in a while, but not often enough for them to develop special fighting weapons or techniques."

"Their village is fortified," Meillard mentioned.

"I question that," Gofredo differed. "There won't be more than a total of five hundred there; call that a fighting strength of two hundred, to defend a twenty-five-hundred-meter perimeter, with woodchoppers' axes and bows and spears. If you notice, there's no wall around the village itself. That palisade is just a fence."

"Why would they mound the village up?" Questell, in the screen wondered. "You don't think the river gets up that high, do you? Because if it does—"

Schallenmacher shook his head. "There just isn't enough watershed, and there's too much valley. I'll be very much surprised if that stream, there"—he nodded at the hundred-power screen—"ever gets more than six inches over the bank."

"I don't know what those houses are built of. This is all alluvial country; building stone would be almost unobtainable. I don't see anything like a brick kiln. I don't see any evidence of irrigation, either, so there must be plenty of rainfall. If they use adobe, or sun-dried brick, houses would start to crumble in a few years, and they would be pulled down and the rubble shoved aside to make room for a new house. The village has been rising on its own ruins, probably shifting back and forth from one end of that mound to the other."

"If that's it, they've been there a long time," Karl Dorver said. "And how far have they advanced?"

"Early bronze; I'll bet they still use a lot of stone implements. Pre-dynastic Egypt, or very early Tigris-Euphrates, in Terran terms. I can't see any evidence that they have the wheel. They have draft animals; when we were coming down, I saw a few of them pulling pole travoises. I'd say they've been farming for a long time. They have quite a diversity of crops, and I suspect that they have some idea of crop-rotation. I'm amazed at their musical instruments; they seem to have put more skill into making them than anything else. I'm going to take a jeep, while they're all in the village, and have a look around the fields, now."

Charley Loughran went along for specimens, and, for the ride, Lillian Ransby. Most of his guesses, he found had been correct. He found a number of pole travoises, from which the animals had been unhitched in the first panic when the landing craft had been coming down. Some of them had big baskets permanently attached. There were dragmarks everywhere in the soft ground, but not a single wheel track. He found one plow, cunningly put together with wooden pegs and rawhide lashings; the point was stone, and it would only score a narrow groove, not a proper furrow. It was, however, fitted with a big bronze ring to which a draft animal could be hitched. Most of the cultivation seemed to have been done with spades and hoes. He found a couple of each, bronze, cast flat in an open-top mold. They hadn't learned to make composite molds.

There was an even wider variety of crops than he had

expected: two cereals, a number of different rootplants, and a lot of different legumes, and things like tomatoes and pumpkins.

"Bet these people had a pretty good life, here—before the Terrans came," Charley observed.

"Don't say that in front of Paul," Lillian warned. "He has enough to worry about now, without starting him on whether we'll do these people more harm than good."

Two more landing craft had come down from the *Hubert Penrose;* they found Dave Questell superintending the unloading of more prefab-huts, and two were already up that had been brought down with the first landing.

A name for the planet had also arrived.

"Svantovit," Karl Dorver told him. "Principal god of the Baltic Slavs, about three thousand years ago. Guy Vindinho dug it out of the 'Encyclopedia of Mythology.' Svantovit was represented as holding a bow in one hand and a horn in the other."

"Well, that fits. What will we call the natives; Svantovitians, or Svantovese?"

"Well, Paul wanted to call them Svantovese, but Luis persuaded him to call them Svants. He said everybody'd call them that, anyhow, so we might as well make it official from the start."

"We can call the language Svantovese," Lillian decided. "After dinner, I am going to start playing back recordings and running off audiovisuals. I will be so happy to know that I have a name for what I'm studying. Probably be all I will know."

After dinner, he and Karl and Paul went into a huddle on what sort of gifts to give the natives, and the advisability of trading with them, and for what. Nothing too far in advance of their present culture level. Wheels; they could be made in the fabricating shop aboard the ship.

"You know, it's odd," Karl Dorver said. "These people here have never seen a wheel, and, except in documentary or historical-drama films, neither have a lot of Terrans."

That was true. As a means of transportation, the wheel had been completely obsolete since the development of contragravity, six centuries ago. Well, a lot of Terrans in the Year Zero had never seen a suit of armor, or an harquebus, or even a tinder box or a spinning wheel.

Wheelbarrows; now there was something they'd find useful. He screened Max Milzer, in charge of the fabricating and repair shops on the ship. Max had never even heard of a wheelbarrow.

"I can make them up, Mark; better send me some drawings, though. Did you just invent it?"

"As far as I know, a man named Leonardo da Vinci invented it, in the Sixth Century Pre-Atomic. How soon can you get me half a dozen of them?"

"Well, let's see. Welded sheet metal, and pipe for the frame and handles. I'll have some of them for you by noon tomorrow. Now, about hoes; how tall are these people, and how long are their arms, and how far can they stoop over?"

They were all up late, that night. So were the Svants; there was a fire burning in the middle of the village, and watchfires along the edge of the mound. Luis Gofredo was just as distrustful of them as they were of the Terrans; he kept the camp lighted, a strong guard on the alert, and the area of darkness beyond infra red lighted and covered by photoelectric sentries on the ground and snoopers in the air. Like Paul Meillard, Luis Gofredo was a worrier and a pessimist. Everything happened for the worst in this worst of all possible galaxies, and if anything could conceivably go wrong, it infallibly would. That was probably why he was still alive and had never had a command massacred.

The wheelbarrows, four of them, came down from the ship by mid-morning. With them came a grindstone, a couple of crosscut saws, and a lot of picks and shovels and axes, and cases of sheath knives and mess gear and miscellaneous trade goods, including a lot of the empty wine and whisky bottles that had been hoarded for the past four years.

At lunch, the talk was almost exclusively about the language problem. Lillian Ransby, who had not gotten to sleep before sunrise and had just gotten up, was discouraged.

'I don't know what we're going to do next,'' she admitted. ''Glenn Orent and Anna and I were on it all night, and we're nowhere. We have about a hundred wordlike sounds isolated, and twenty or so are used repeatedly, and we can't assign a meaning to any of them. And none of the Svants ever reacted the same way twice to anything we said to them. There's just no one-to-one relationship anywhere.''

''I'm beginning to doubt they have a language,'' the Navy intelligence officer said. ''Sure, they make a lot of vocal noise. So do chipmunks.''

''They have to have a language,'' Anna de Jong declared. ''No sapient thought is possible without verbalization.''

''Well, no society like that is possible without some means of communication,'' Karl Dorver supported her from the other flank. He seemed to have made that point before. ''You know,'' he added, ''I'm beginning to wonder if it mightn't be telepathy.''

He evidently hadn't suggested that before. The others looked at him in surprise. Anna started to say, ''Oh, I doubt if—" and then stopped.

"I know, the race of telepaths is an old gimmick that's been used in new-planet adventure stories for centuries, but maybe we've finally found one."

"I don't like it, Karl," Loughran said. "If they're telepaths, why don't they understand us? And if they're telepaths, why do they talk at all? And you can't convince me that this boodly-oodly-doodle of theirs isn't talking."

"Well, our neural structure and theirs won't be nearly alike," Fayon said. "I know, this analogy between telepathy and radio is full of holes, but it's good enough for this. Our wave length can't be picked up with their sets."

"The deuce it can't, Gofredo contradicted. "I've been bothered about that from the beginning. These people act as though they got meaning from us. Not the meaning we intend, but some meaning. When Paul made the gobbledygook speech, they all reacted in the same way—frightened, and then defensive. The you-me routine simply bewildered them, as we'd be at a set of semantically lucid but self-contradictory statements. When Lillian tried to introduce herself, they were shocked and horrified . . ."

"It looked to me like actual physical disgust," Anna interpolated.

"When I tried it, they acted like a lot of puppies being petted, and when Mark tried it, they were simply baffled. I watched Mark explaining that steel knives were dangerously sharp; they got the demonstration, but when he tried to tie words onto it, it threw them completely."

"All right. Pass that," Loughran conceded. "But if they have telepathy, why do they use spoken words?"

"Oh, I can answer that," Anna said. "Say they communicated by speech originally, and developed their telepathic faculty slowly and without realizing it. They'd go on using speech, and since the message would be received telepathically ahead of the spoken message, nobody would pay any attention to the words as such. Everybody would have a spoken language of his own; it would be sort of the instrumental accompaniment to the song."

"Some of them don't bother speaking," Karl nodded. "They just toot."

"I'll buy that, right away," Loughran agreed. "In mating, or in group-danger situations, telepathy would be a race-survival characteristic. It would be selected for genetically, and the non-gifted strains would tend to die out."

It wouldn't do. It wouldn't do at all. He said so.

"Look at their technology. We either have a young race, just emerged from savagery, or an old, stagnant race. All indications seem to favor the latter. A young race would not have time to develop telepathy as Anna suggests. An old race would have gone much farther than these people have. Progress is a matter of communication and pooling ideas and discoveries. Make a trend-graph of technological progress on Terra; every big jump comes after an improvement in communications. The printing press; railways and steamships; the telegraph; radio. Then think how telepathy would speed up progress."

The sun was barely past noon meridian before the Svants, who had ventured down into the fields at sunrise, were returning to the mound-village. In the snooper-screen, they could be seen coming up in tunics and breechclouts, entering houses, and emerging in long robes. There seemed to be no bows or spears in evidence, but the big horn sounded occasionally. Paul Meillard was pleased. Even if it had been by signtalk, which he rated with worm-fishing for trout or shooting sitting rabbits, he had gotten something across to them.

When they went to the village, at 1500, they had trouble

getting their lorry down. A couple of Marines in a jeep had to go in first to get the crowd out of the way. Several of the locals, including the one with the staff, joined with them; this quick co-operation delighted Meillard. When they had the lorry down and were all out of it, the dignitary with the staff, his scarlet tablecloth over his yellow robe, began an oration, apparently with every confidence that he was being understood. In spite of his objections at lunch, the telepathy theory was beginning to seem more persuasive.

"Give them the Shooting of Dan McJabberwock again," he told Meillard. "This is where we came in yesterday."

Something Meillard had noticed was exciting him. "Wait a moment. They're going to do something."

They were indeed. The one with the staff and three of his henchmen advanced. The staff bearer touched himself on the brow. *"Fwoonk,"* he said. Then he pointed to Meillard. *"Hoonkle,"* he said.

"They got it!" Lillian was hugging herself joyfully. "I knew they ought to!"

Meillard indicated himself and said, *"Fwoonk."*

That wasn't right. The village elder immediately corrected him. The word, it seemed, was, *"Fwoonk."*

His three companions agreed that that was the word for self, but that was as far as the agreement went. They rendered it, respectively, as *"Pwink,"* *"Tweelt"* and *"Kroosh."*

Gofredo gave a barking laugh. He was right; anything that could go wrong would go wrong. Lillian used a word; it was not a ladylike word at all. The Svants looked at them as though wondering what could possibly be the matter. Then they went into a huddle, arguing vehemently. The argument spread, like a ripple in a pool; soon everybody was twittering vocally or blowing on flutes and Panpipes.

Then the big horn started blaring. Immediately, Gofredo
snatched the handphone of his belt radio and began
speaking urgently into it.

"What are you doing, Luis?" Meillard asked anxiously.

"Calling the reserve in. I'm not taking chances on this."
He spoke again into the phone, then called over his shoulder: "Rienet; three one-second bursts, in the air!"

A Marine pointed a submachine gun skyward and
ripped off a string of shots, then another, and another.
There was silence after the first burst. Then a frightful
howling arose.

"Luis, you imbecile!" Meillard was shouting.

Gofredo jumped onto the top of an airjeep, where they
could all see him; drawing his pistol, he fired twice into the
air.

"Be quiet, all of you!" he shouted, as though that would
do any good.

It did. Silence fell, bounced noisily, and then settled over
the crowd. Gofredo went on talking to them: "Take it easy,
now; easy." He might have been speaking to a frightened
dog or a fractious horse. "Nobody's going to hurt you.
This is nothing but the great noise-magic of the
Terrans . . ."

"Get the presents unloaded," Meillard was saying.
"Making a big show of it. The table first."

The horn, which had started, stopped blowing. As they
were getting off the long table and piling it with trade
goods, another lorry came in, disgorging twenty Marine
riflemen. They had their bayonets fixed; the natives
looked apprehensively at the bare steel, but went on listening to Gofredo. Meillard pulled the (Lord Mayor? Arch-
bishop? Lord of the Manor?) aside, and began making
sign-talk to him.

When quiet was restored, Howell put a pick and shovel

into a wheelbarrow and pushed them out into the space that had been cleared in front of the table. He swung the pick for a while, then shoveled the barrow full of ground. After pushing it around for a while, he dumped it back in the hole and leveled it off. Two Marines brought out an eight-inch log and chopped a couple of billets off it with an ax, than cut off another with one of the saws, split them up, and filled the wheelbarrow with the firewood.

The knives, jewelry and other small items would be no problem; they had enough of them to go around. The other stuff would be harder to distribute, and Paul Meillard and Karl Dorver were arguing about how to handle it. If they weren't careful, a lot of new bowie knives would get bloodied.

"Have them form a queue," Anna suggested. "That will give them the idea of equal sharing, and we'll be able to learn something about their status levels and social hierarchy and agonistic relations."

The one with the staff took it as a matter of course that he would go first; his associates began falling in behind him, and the rest of the villagers behind them. Whether they'd gotten one the day before or not, everybody was given a knife and a bandanna and one piece of flashy junk-jewelry, also a stainless steel cup and mess plate, a bucket, and an empty bottle with a cork. The women didn't carry sheath knives, so they got Boy Scout knives on lanyards. They were all lavishly supplied with Extee Three and candy. Any of the children who looked big enough to be trusted with them got knives too, and plenty of candy.

Anna and Karl were standing where the queue was forming, watching how they fell into line; so was Lillian, with an audiovisual camera. Having seen that the Marine enlisted men were getting the presents handed out prop-

erly, Howell strolled over to them. Just as he came up, a
couple approached hesitantly, a man in a breechclout under a leather apron, and a woman, much smaller, in a ragged and soiled tunic. As soon as they fell into line, another
Svant, in a blue robe, pushed them aside and took their
place.

"Here, you can't do that!" Lillian cried. "Karl, make
him step back.".

Karl was saying something about social status and precedence. The couple tried to get into line behind the man
who had pushed them aside. Another villager tried to
shove them out of his way. Howell advanced, his right fist
closing. Then he remembered that he didn't know what
he'd be punching; he might break the fellow's neck, or his
own knuckles. He grabbed the blue-robed Svant by the
wrist with both hands, kicked a foot out from under him,
and jerked, sending him flying for six feet and then sliding
in the dust for another couple of yards. He pushed the
others back, and put the couple into place in the line.

"Mark, you shouldn't have done that," Dorver was ex-
postulating. "We don't know . . ."

The Svant sat up, shaking his head groggily. Then he
realized what had been done to him. With a snarl of rage,
he was on his feet, his knife in his hand. It was a Terran
bowie knife. Without conscious volition, Howell's pistol
was out and he was thumbing the safety off.

The Svant stopped short, then dropped the knife,
ducked his head, and threw his arms over it to shield his
comb. He backed away a few steps, then turned and
bolted into the nearest house. The others, including the
woman in the ragged tunic, were twittering in alarm. Only
the man in the leather apron was calm; he was saying,
tonelessly, *"Ghrooogh-ghrooogh."*

Luis Gofredo was coming up on the double, followed

by three of his riflemen.

"What happened, Mark? Trouble?"

"All over now." He told Gofredo what had happened. Dorver was still objecting:

". . . Social precedence; the Svant may have been right, according to local customs."

"Local customs be damned!" Gofredo became angry. "This is a Terra Federation handout; we make the rules, and one of them is, no pushing people out of line. Teach the buggers that now and we won't have to work so hard at it later." He called back over his shoulder, "Situation under control; get the show going again."

The natives were all grimacing heartbrokenly with pleasure. Maybe the one who got thrown on his ear—no, he didn't have any—was not one of the more popular characters in the village.

"You just pulled your gun, and he dropped the knife and ran?" Gofredo asked. "And the others were scared, too?"

"That's right. They all saw you fire yours; the noise scared them."

Golfredo nodded. "We'll avoid promiscuous shooting, then. No use letting them find out the noise won't hurt them any sooner than we have to."

Paul Meillard had worked out a way to distribute the picks and shovels and axes. Considering each house as representing a family unit, which might or might not be the case, there were picks and shovels enough to go around, and an ax for every third house. They took them around in an airjeep and left them at the doors. The houses, he found, weren't adobe at all. They were built of logs, plastered with adobe on the outside. That demolished his theory that the houses were torn down periodically, and left the mound itself unexplained.

The wheelbarrows and the grindstone and the two crosscut saws were another matter. Nobody was quite sure that the (nobility? capitalist-class? politicians? prominent citizens?) wouldn't simply appropriate them for themselves. Paul Meillard was worried about that; everybody else was willing to let matters take their course. Before they were off the ground in their vehicles, a violent dispute had begun, with a badlam of jabbering and shrieking. By the time they were landing at the camp, the big laminated leather horn had begun to bellow.

One of the huts had been fitted as contact-team headquarters, with all the view and communication screens installed, and one end partitioned off and soundproofed for Lillian to study recordings in. It was cocktail time when they returned; conversationally, it was a continuation from lunch. Karl Dorver was even more convinced than ever of his telepathic hypothesis, and he had completely converted Anna de Jong to it.

"Look at that." He pointed at the snooper screen, which gave a view of the plaza from directly above. "They're reaching an agreement already."

So they seemed to be, though upon what was less apparent. The horn had stopped, and the noise was diminishing. The odd thing was that peace was being restored, or was restoring itself, as the uproar had begun—outwardly from the center of the plaza to the periphery of the crowd. The same thing had happened when Gofredo had ordered the submachine gun fired, and, now that he recalled, when he had dealt with the line-crasher.

"Suppose a few of them, in the middle, are agreed," Anna said. "They are all thinking in unison, combining their telepathic powers. They dominate those nearest to them, who join and amplify their telepathic signal, and it spreads out through the whole group. A mental chain-re-action."

"That would explain the mechanism of community leadership, and I'd been wondering about that," Dorver said, becoming more excited. "It's a mental aristocracy; an especially gifted group of telepaths, in agreement and using their powers in concert, implanting their opinions in the minds of all the others. I'll bet the purpose of the horn is to distract the thoughts of the others, so that they can be more easily dominated. And the noise of the shots shocked them out of communication with each other; no wonder they were frightened."

Bennet Fayon was far from convinced. "So far, this telepathy theory is only an assumption. I find it a lot easier to assume some fundamental difference between the way they translate sound into sense-data and the way we do. We *think* those combs on top of their heads are their external hearing organs, but we have no idea what's back of them, or what kind of a neural hookup is connected to them. I wish I knew how these people dispose of their dead. I need a couple of fresh cadavers. Too bad they aren't warlike. Nothing like a good bloody battle to advance the science of anatomy, and what we don't know about Svant anatomy is practically the entire subject."

"I should imagine the animals hear in the same way," Meillard said. "When the wagon wheels and the hoes and the blacksmith tools come down from the ship, we'll trade for cattle."

"When they make the second landing in the mountains, I'm going to do a lot of hunting," Loughran added. "I'll get wild animals for you."

"Well, I'm going to assume that the vocal noises they make are meaningful speech," Lillian Ransby said. "So far, I've just been trying to analyze them for phonetic values. Now I'm going to analyze them for soundwave patterns. No matter what goes on inside their private nervous systems, the sounds exist as waves in the public atmosphere. I'm going to assume that the Lord Mayor and his stooges were all trying to say the same thing when they were pointing to themselves, and I'm going to see if all four of those sounds have any common characteristic.''

By the time dinner was over, they were all talking in circles, none of them hopefully. They all made recordings of the speech about the slithy toves in the Malemute Saloon; Lillian wanted to find out what was different about them. Luis Gofredo saw to it that the camp itself would be visible-lighted, and beyond the lights he set up more photoelectric robot sentries and put a couple of snoopers to circling on contragravity, with infra-red lights and receptors. He also insisted that all his own men and all Dave Questell's Navy construction engineers keep their weapons ready to hand. The natives in the village were equally distrustful. They didn't herd the cattle up from the meadows where they had been pastured, but they lighted watchfires along the edge of the mound as soon as it became dark.

It was three hours after nightfall when something on the indicator board for the robot sentries went off like a startled rattlesnake. Everybody, talking idly or concentrating on writing up the day's observations, stiffened. Luis Gofredo, dozing in a chair, was on his feet instantly and crossing the hut to the instruments. His second-in-command, who had been playing chess with Willi Schallenmacher, rose and snatched his belt from the back of his chair, putting it on.

"Take it easy," Gofredo said. "Probably just a cow or a horse—local equivalent—that's strayed over from the other side."

He sat down in front of one of the snooper screens and twisted knobs on the remote controls. The monochrome view, transformed from infra red, rotated as the snooper circled and changed course. The other screen showed the camp receding and the area around it widening as its snooper gained altitude.

"It's not a big party," Gofredo was saying. "I can't see— Oh, yes I can. Only two of them."

The humanoid figures, one larger than the other, were moving cautiously across the fields, crouching low. The snooper went down toward them, and then he recognized them. The man and woman whom the blue-robed villager had tried to shove out of the queue, that afternoon. Gofredo recognized them, too.

"Your friends, Mark. Harry," he told his subordinate, "go out and pass the word around. Only two, and we think they're friendly. Keep everybody out of sight; we don't want to scare them away."

The snooper followed closely behind them. The man was no longer wearing his apron; the woman's tunic was even more tattered and soiled. She was leading him by the hand. Now and then, she would stop and turn her head to the rear. The snooper over the mound showed nothing but half a dozen fire-watchers dozing by their fires. Then the pair were at the edge of the camp lights. As they advanced, they seemed to realize that they had passed a point-of-no-return. They straightened and came forward steadily, the woman seeming to be guiding her companion.

"What's happening, Mark?"

It was Lillian; she must have just come out of the sound-proof speechlab.

"You know them; the pair in the queue, this afternoon.

I think we've annexed a couple of friendly natives."

They all went outside. The two natives, having come into the camp, had stopped. For a moment, the man in the breechclout seemed undecided whether he was more afraid to turn and run than advance. The woman, holding his hand, led him forward. They were both bruised, and both had minor cuts, and neither of them had any of the things that had been given to them that afternoon.

"Rest of the gang beat them up and robbed them," Gofredo began angrily.

"See what you did?" Dorver began. "According to their own customs, they had no right to be ahead of those others, and now you've gotten them punished for it."

"I'd have done more to that fellow then Mark did, if I'd been there when it happened." The Marine officer turned to Meillard. "Look, this is your show, Paul; how you run it is your job. But in your place, I'd take that pair back to the village and have them point out who beat them up, and teach the whole gang of them a lesson. If you're going to colonize this planet, you're going to have to establish Federation law, and Federation law says you mustn't gang up on people and beat and rob them. We don't have to speak Svantese to make them understand what we'll put up with and what we won't."

"Later, Luis. After we've gotten a treaty with somebody." Meillard broke off. "Watch this!"

The woman was making sign-talk. She pointed to the village on the mound. Then, with her hands, she shaped a bucket like the ones that had been given to them, and made a snatching gesture away from herself. She indicated the neckcloths, and the sneath knife and the other things, and snatched them away too. She made beating motions, and touched her bruises and the man's. All the time she was talking excitedly, in a high shrill noice. The man made the same *ghroogh-ghroogh* noises that he had that afternoon.

"No; we can't take any punitive action. Not now," Meillard said. "But we'll have to do something for them."

Vengeance, it seemed, wasn't what they wanted. The woman made vehement gestures of rejection toward the village, then bowed, placing her hands on her brow. The man imitated her obeisance, then they both straightened. The woman pointed to herself and to the man, and around the circle of huts and landing craft. She began scuttling about, picking up imaginary litter and sweeping with an imaginary broom. The man started pounding with an imaginary hammer, then chopping with an imaginary ax.

Lillian was clapping her hand softly. "Good; got it the first time. 'You let us stay; we work for you.' How about it, Paul?"

Meillard nodded. "Punitive action's unadvisable, but we will show our attitude by taking them in. You tell them, Luis; these people seem to like your voice."

Gofredo put a hand on each of their shoulders. "You . . . stay . . . with us." He pointed around the camp. "You . . . stay . . . this . . . place."

Their faces broke into that funny just-before-tears expression that meant happiness with them. The man confined his vocal expressions to his odd *ghroogh-ghroogh*-ing; the woman twittered joyfully. Gofredo put a hand on the woman's shoulder, pointed to the man and from him back to her. "Unh?" he inquired.

The woman put a hand on the man's head, then brought it down to within a foot of the ground. She picked up the imaginary infant and rocked it in her arms, then set it down and grew it up until she had her hand on the top of the man's head again.

"That was good, Mom," Gofredo told her. "Now, you and Sonny come along; we'll issue you equipment and find you billets." He added, "What in blazes are we going to feed them; Extee Three?"

They gave them replacements for all the things that had been taken away from them. They gave the man a one-piece suit of Marine combat coveralls; Lillian gave the woman a lavender bathrobe, and Anna contributed a red scarf. They found them quarters in one end of a store shed, after making sure that there was nothing they could get at that would hurt them or that they could damage. They gave each of them a pair of blankets and a pneumatic mattress, which delighted them, although the cots puzzled them at first.

"What do you think about feeding them, Bennet?" Meillard asked, when the two Svants had gone to bed and they were back in the headquarters hut. "You said the food on this planet is safe for Terrans."

"So I did, and it is, but the rule's not reversible. Things we eat might kill them," Fayon said. "Meats will be especially dangerous. And no caffein, and no alcohol."

"Alcohol won't hurt them," Schallenmacher said. "I saw big jars full of fermenting fruit-mash back of some of those houses; in about a year, it ought to be fairly good wine. C^2H_5OH is the same on any planet."

"Well, we'll get native foodstuffs tomorrow," Meillard said. "We'll have to do that by signs, too," he regretted.

"Get Mom to help you; she's pretty sharp," Lillian advised. "But I think Sonny's the village half-wit."

Anna de Jong agreed. "Even if we don't understand. Svant psychology, that's evident; he's definitely subnormal. The way he clings to his mother for guidance is absolutely pathetic. He's a mature adult, but mentally he's still a little child."

"That may explain it!" Dorver cried. "A mental defective, in a community of telepaths, constantly invading the minds of others with irrational and disgusting thoughts; no wonder he is rejected and persecuted. And in a community on this culture level, the mother of an abnormal child is often regarded with superstitious detestation—"

"Yes, of course!" Anna de Jong instantly agreed, and began to go into the villagers' hostility to both mother and son; both of them were now taking the telepathy hypothesis for granted.

Well, maybe so. He turned to Lillian.

"What did you find out?"

"Well, there is a common characteristic in all four sounds. A little patch on the screen at seventeen-twenty cycles. The odd thing is that when I try to repeat the sound, it isn't there."

Odd indeed. If a Svant said something, he made sound waves; if she imitated the sound, she ought to imitate the wave pattern. He said so, and she agreed.

"But come back here and look at this," she invited.

She had been using a visibilizing analyzer; in it, a sound was broken by a set of filters into frequency-groups, translated into light from dull red too violet paling into pure white. It photographed the light-pattern on high-speed film, automatically developed it, and then made a print-copy and projected the film in slow motion on a screen. When she pressed a button, a recorded voice said, *"Fwoonk."* An instant later, a pattern of vertical lines in various colors and lengths was projected on the screen.

"Those green lines," she said." "That's it. Now, watch this."

She pressed another button, got the photoprint out of a slot, and propped it beside the screen. Then she picked up

a hand-phone and said, *"Fwoonk,"* into it. It sounded like
the first one, but the pattern that danced onto the screen
was quite different. Where the green had been there was
a patch of pale-blue line. She ran the other three Svant
voices, each saying, presumably "Me." Some were
mainly up in blue, others had a good deal of yellow and
orange, but they all had the little batch of green lines.

"Well, that seems to be the information," he said. "The
rest is just noise."

"Maybe one of them is saying, John Doe, *me*, son of
Joe Blow,' and another is saying, 'Tough guy, *me; kick
anybody in town.' "

"All in one syllable?" Then he shrugged. How did he
know what these people could pack into one syllable? He
picked up the handphone and said, "Fwoonk," into it.
The pattern, a little deeper in color and with longer lines,
was recognizably like stars, and unlike any of the Svants'.

The others came in, singly and in pairs and threes. They
watched the colors dance on the screen to picture the four
Svant words which might or might not all mean *me*. They
tried to duplicate them. Luis Gofredo and Lilli Schallenmacher came closest of anybody. Bennet Fayon was still
insisting that the Svants had a perfectly comprehensible
language—to other Svants. Anna de Jong had started to
steer a little away from the Dorver hypothesis. There was
a difference between event-level sound, which was a series of waves of alternately crowded and rarefied molecules of t, and object-level sound, which was an auditory
sensation inside the nervous system, she admitted. That,
they crowed, was what he'd been doing all along; their
auditory system was probably such that *fwoonk* and *pwink*
and *tweelt* and *kroosh* all sounded alike to them.

By this time, *fwoonk* and *pwink* and *tweelt* and *kroosh*
had become swear words among the joint Space Navy-

Colonial Office contact team.

"Well, if I hear the two sounds alike, why doesn't the analyzer hear them alike?" Karl Dorver demanded.

"It has better ears than you do, Karl. Look how many different frequencies there are in that word, all crowding up behind each other," Lillian said. "But it isn't sensitive or selective enough. I'm going to see what Ayesha Keithley can do about building me a better one."

Ayesha was signals and detection officer on the *Hubert Penrose*. Dave Questell mentioned that she'd had a hard day, and was probably making sack-time, and she wouldn't welcome being called at 0130. Nobody seemed to have realized that it had gotten that late.

"Well, I'll call the ship and have a recording made for her for when she gets up. But till we get something that'll sort this mess out and make sense of it, I'm stopped."

"You're stopped, period, Lillian," Dorver told her. "What these people gibber at us doesn't even make as much sense as the Shooting of Dan McJabberwock. The real information is conveyed by telepathy."

Lieutenant j.g. Ayesha Keithley was on the screen the next morning while they were eating breakfast. She was a blonde, like Lillian.

"I got your message; you seem to have problems, don't you?"

"Speaking conservatively, yes. You see what we're up against?"

"You don't know what their vocal organs are like, do you?" the girl in naval uniform in the screen asked.

Lillian shook her head. "Bennet Fayon's hoping for a war, or an epidemic, or something to break out, so that he can get a few cadavers to dissect."

"Well, he'll find that they're pretty complex," Ayesha

Keithley said. "I identified stick-and-slip sounds and percussion sounds, and plucked-string sounds, along with the
ordinary hiss-and-buzz speech-sounds. Making a vocoder
to reproduce that speech is going to be fun. Just what are
you using, in the way of equipment?"

Lillian was still talking about that when the two landing
craft from the ship were sighted, coming down. Charley
Loughran and Willi Schallenmacher, who were returning
to the *Hubert Penrose* to join the other landing party, began assembling their luggage. The others went outside,
Howell among them.

Mom and Sonny were watching the two craft grow
larger and closer above, keeping close to a group of space-
men; Sonny was looking around excitedly, while Mom
clung to his arm, like a hen with an oversized chick. The
reasoning was clear—these people knew all about big
things that came down out of the sky and weren't afraid of
them; stick close to them, and it would be perfectly safe.
Sonny saw the contact team emerging from their hut and
grabbed his mother's arm, pointing. They both beamed
happily; that empression didn't look sad, at all, now that
you knew what it meant. Sonny began ghroogh-ghroogh-
ing hideously; Mom hushed him with a hand over his
mouth, and they both made eating gestures, rubbed their
abdomens comfortably, and pointed toward the mess hut.
Bennet Fayon was frightened. He turned and started on
the double toward the cook who was standing in the doorway of the hut, calling out to him.

The cook spoke inaudibly. Fayon stopped short. "Unholy Saint Beelzebub, no!" he cried. The cook said something in reply, shrugging. Fayon on came back, talking to
himself.

"Terran carniculture pork," he said, when he returned.
"Zarathustra pool-ball fruit. Potato-flour hotcakes with

Baldur honey and Odin flameberry jam. And two big cups of coffee apiece. It's a miracle they aren't dead now. If they're alive for lunch, we won't need to worry about feeding them anything we eat, but I'm glad somebody else has the moral responsibility for this."

Lillian Ransby came out of the headquarters hut. "Ayesha's coming down this afternoon, with a lot of equipment," she said. "We're not exactly going to count air molecules in the sound waves, but we'll do everything short of that. We'll need more lab space, soundproofed."

"Tell Dave Questell what you want," Meillard said. "Do you really think you can get anything?"

She shrugged. "If there's anything there to get. How long it'll take is another question."

The two sixty-foot collapsium-armored turtles settled to the ground and went off contragravity. The ports opened, and things began being floated off on lifter-skids: framework for the water tower, and curved titanium sheets for the tank. Anna de Jong said something about hot showers, and not having to take any more sponge-baths. Howell was watching the stuff come off the other landing craft. A dozen pairs of four-foot wagon wheels, with axles. Hoes, in bundles. Scythe blades. A hand forge, with a crank-driven fan blower, and a hundred and fifty pound anvil, and sledges and cutters and swages and tongs.

Everybody was busy, and Mom and Sonny were fidgeting, gesturing toward the work with their own empty hands. *Hey, boss; whatta we gonna do?* He patted them on the shoulders.

"Take it easy." He hoped his tone would convey nonurgency. "We'll find something for you to do."

He wasn't particularly happy about most of what was coming off. Giving these Svants tools was fine, but it was

more important to give them technologies. The people on
the ship hadn't thought of that. These wheels, now; machined steel hubs, steel rims, tubular steel spokes, drop-
forged and machined axles. The Svants wouldn't be able
to copy them in a thousand years. Well, in a hundred, if
somebody showed them where and how to mine iron and
how to smelt and work it. And how to build a steam engine.

He went over and pulled a hoe out of one of the bundles. Blades stamped out with power press, welded to tubular steel handles. Well, wood for hoe handles was hard
to come by on a spaceship, even a battle cruiser almost
half a mile in diameter; he had to admit that. And they
were about two thousand percent more efficient than the
bronze scrapers the Svants used. That wasn't the idea,
though. Even supposing that the first wave of colonists
came out in a year and a half, it would be close to twenty
years before Terran-operated factories would be in mass
production for the native trade. The idea was to teach
these people to make better things for themselves; give
them a leg up, so that the next generation would be ready
for contragravity and nuclear and electric power.

Mom didn't know what to make of any of it. Sonny did,
though; he was excited, grabbing Howell's arm, pointing,
saying, *"Ghroogh! Ghroogh!"* He pointed at the wheels,
and made a stooping, lifting and pushing gesture. *Like
wheelbarrow?*

"That's right." He nodded, wondering if Sonny recognized that as an affirmative sign. "Like big wheelbarrow."

One thing puzzled Sonny, though. Wheelbarrow
wheels were small—his hands indicated the size—and single. These were big, and double.

"Let me show you this, Sonny."

He squatted, took a pad and pencil from his pocket, and

drew two pairs of wheels, and then put a wagon on them, and drew a quadruped hitched to it, and a Svant with a stick walking beside it. Sonny looked at the picture— Svants seemed to have pictoral sense, for which make us thankful!—and then caught his mother's sleeve and showed it to her. Mom didn't get it. Sonny took the pencil and drew another animal, with a pole travois. He made gestures. A travois dragged; it went slow. A wagon had wheels that went around; it went fast.

So Lillian and Anna thought he was the village half-wit. Village genius, more likely; the other peasants didn't understand him, and resented his superiority. They went over for a closer look at the wheels, and pushed them. Sonny was almost beside himself. Mom was puzzled, but she thought they were pretty wonderful.

Then they looked at blacksmith tools. Tongs; Sonny had never seen anything like them. Howell wondered what the Svants used to handle hot metal; probably big tweezers made by tying two green sticks together. There was an old Arabian legend that Allah had made the first tongs and given them to the first smith, because nobody could make tongs without having a pair already.

Sonny didn't understand the fan blower until it was taken apart. Then he made a great discovery. The wheels, and the fan, and the pivoted tongs, all embodied the same principle, one his people had evidently never discovered. A whole new world seemed to open before him from then on, he was constantly finding things pierced and rotating on pivots.

By this time, Mom was fidgeting again. She ought to be doing something to justify her presence in the camp. He was wondering what sort of work he could invent for her when Karl Dorver called to him from the door of the headquarters hut.

"Mark, can you spare Mom for a while?" he asked. "We want her to look at pictures and show us which of the animals are meat-cattle, and which of the crops are ripe."

"Think you can get anything out of her?"

"Sign-talk, yes. We may get a few words from her, too."

At first, Mom was unwilling to leave Sonny. She finally decided that it would be safe, and trotted over to Dorver, entering the hut.

Dave Questell's construction crew began at once on the water tank using a power shovel to dig the foundation. They had to haul water in a tank from the river a quarter-mile away to mix the concrete. Sonny watched that interestedly. So did a number of the villagers, who gathered safely out of bowshot. They noticed Sonny among the Terrans and pointed at him. Sonny noticed that. He unobtrusively picked up a double-bitted ax and kept it to hand.

He and Mom had lunch with the contact team. As they showed no ill effects from breakfast, Fayon decided that it was safe to let them have anything the Terrans ate or drank. They liked wine; they knew what it was, all right, but this seemed to have a delightfully different flavor. They each tried a cigarette, choked over the first few puffs, and decided that they didn't like smoking.

"Mom gave us a lot of information, as far as she could, on the crops and animals. The big things, the size of rhinoceroses, are draft animals and nothing else; they're not eaten," Dorver said. "I don't know whether the meat isn't good, or is taboo, or they are too valuable to eat. They eat all the other three species, and milk two of them. I have an idea they grind their grain in big stone mortars as needed."

That was right; he'd seen things like that.

"Willi, when you're over in the mountains, see if you

can find something we can make millstones out of. We can shape them with sono-cutters; after they get the idea, they can do it themselves by hand. One of those big animals could be used to turn the mill. Did you get any words from her?"

Paul Meillard shook his head gloomily. "Nothing we can be sure of. It was the same thing as in the village, yesterday. She'd say something, I'd repeat it, and she'd tell us it was wrong and say the same thing over again. Lillian took recordings; she got the same results as last night. Ask her about it later."

"She has the same effect on Mom as on the others?"

"Yes. Mom was very polite and tried not to show it, but—"

Lillian took him aside, out of earshot of the two Svants, after lunch. She was almost distracted.

"Mark, I don't know what I'm going to do. She's like the others. Every time I open my mouth in front of her, she's simply horrified. It's as though my voice does something loathsome to her. And I'm the one who's supposed to learn to talk to them."

"Well, those who can do, and those who can't teach," he told her. "You can study recordings, and tell us what the words are and teach us how to recognize and pronounce them. You're the only linguist we have."

That seemed to comfort her a little. He hoped it would work out that way. If they could communicate with these people and did leave a party here to prepare for the first colonization, he'd stay on, to teach the natives Terran technologies and study theirs. He'd been expecting that Lillian would stay, too. She was the linguist; she'd have to stay. But now, if it turned out that she would be no help but a liability, she'd go back with the *Hubert Penrose*. Paul wouldn't keep a linquist who offended the natives' every

sensibility with every word she spoke. He didn't want that
to happen. Lillian and he had come to mean a little too
much to each other to be parted now.

Paul Meillard and Karl Dorver had considerable diffi-
culty with Mom, that afternoon. They wanted her to go
with them and help trade for cattle. Mom didn't want to;
she was afraid. They had to do a lot of playacting, with half
a dozen Marines pretending to guard her with fixed bayonets from some of Dave Questell's Navy construction men
who had red bandannas on their heads to simulate combs
before she got the idea. Then she was afraid to get into the
contragravity lorry that was to carry the hoes and the wagon wheels. Sonny managed to reassure her, and insisted
on going along, and he insisted on taking his ax with him.
That meant doubling the guard, to make sure Sonny
didn't lose his self-control when he saw his former perse-
cutors within chopping distance.

It went off much better than either Paul Meillard or Luis
Gofredo expected. After the first shock of being air-borne
had worn off, Mom found that she liked contragravity-rid-
ing; Sonny was wildly delighted with it from the start. The
natives showed neither of them any hostility. Mom's lavender bathrobe and Sonny's green coveralls and big ax
seemed to be symbols of a new and exalted status; even
the Lord Mayor was extremely polite to them.

The Lord Mayor and half a dozen others got a contragravity ride, too, to the meadows to pick out cattle. A
dozen animals, including a pair of the two-ton draft beasts,
were driven to the Terran camp. A couple of lorry-loads of
assorted vegetables were brought in, too. Everybody
seemed very happy about the deal, especially Bennet Fayon. He wanted to slaughter one of the sheep-sized meat-
and-milk animals at once and get to work on it. Gofredo

advised him to put it off till the next morning. He wanted a large native audience to see the animal being shot with a rifle.

The water tower was finished, and the big spherical tank hoisted on top of it and made fast. A pump, and a filter-system were installed. There was no water for hot showers that evening, though. They would have to run a pipeline to the river, and that would entail a ditch that would cut through several cultivated fields, which, in turn, would provoke an uproar. Paul Meillard didn't want that happening until he'd concluded the cattle-trade.

Charley Loughran and Willi Schallenmacher had gone up to the ship on one of the landing craft; they accompanied the landing party that went down into the mountains. Ayesha Keithley arrived late in the afternoon on another landing craft, with five or six tons of instruments and parts and equipment, and a male Navy warrant-officer helper.

They looked around the lab Lillian had been using at one end of the headquarters hut.

"This won't do," the girl Navy officer said. "We can't get a quarter of the apparatus we're going to need in here. We'll have to build something."

Dave Questell was drawn into the discussion. Yes, he could put up something big enough for everything the girls would need to install, and soundproof it. Concrete, he decided; they'd have to wait till he got the water line down and the pump going, though.

There was a crowd of natives in the fields, gaping at the Terran camp, the next morning, and Gofredo decided to kill the animal—until they learned the native name, they were calling it Domesticated Type C. It was herded out where everyone could watch, and a Marine stepped forward unslung his rifle took a kneeling position, and aimed at it. It was a hundred and fifty yards away. Mom had come out to see what was going on; Sonny and Howell, who had been consulting by signs over the construction of a wagon, were standing side by side. The Marine squeezed his trigger. The rifle banged, and the Domesticated-C bounded into the air, dropped, and kicked a few times and was still. The natives, however, missed that part of it; they were howling piteously and rubbing their heads. All but Sonny. He was just mildly surprised at what had happened to the Dom.-C.

Sonny, it would appear, was stone deaf.

As anticipated, there was another uproar later in the morning when the ditching machine started north across the meadow. A mob of Svants, seeing its relentless progress toward a field of something like turnips, gathered in front of it, twittering and brandishing implements of agriculture, many of them Terran-made.

Paul Meillard was ready for this. Two lorries went out; one loaded with Marines, who jumped off with their rifles ready. By this time, all the Svants knew what rifles would do beside make a noise. Meillard, Dorver, Gofredo and a few others got out of the other vehicle, and unloaded presents. Gofredo did all the talking. The Svants couldn't understand him, but they liked it. They also liked the presents, which included a dozen empty half-gallon rum demijohns, tarpaulins, and a lot of assorted knickknacks. The pipeline went through.

He and Sonny got the forge set up. There was no fuel for it. A party of Marines had gone out to the woods to the east to cut wood; when they got back, they'd burn some charcoal in the pit that had been dug beside the camp. Until then, he and Sonny were drawing plans for a wooden wheel with a metal tire when Lillian came out of the headquarters hut with a clipboard under her arm. She motioned to him.

"Come on over," he told her. "You can talk in front of Sonny; he won't mind. He can't hear."

"Can't hear?" she echoed. "You mean—?"

"That's right. Sonny's stone deaf. He didn't even hear that rifle going off. The only one of this gang that has brains enough to pour sand out of a boot with directions on the bottom of the heel, and he's a total linguistic loss."

"So he isn't a half-wit, after all."

"He's got an IQ close to genius level. Look at this; he never saw a wheel before yesterday; new he's designing one."

Lillian's eyes widened. "So that's why Mom's so sharp about sign-talk. She's been doing it all his life." Then she remembered what she had come out to show him, and held out the clipboard. "You know how that analyzer of mine works? Well, here's what Ayesha's going to do. After breaking a sound into frequency bands instead of being photographed and projected, each band goes to an analyzer of its own, and is projected on its own screen. There'll be forty of them, each for a band of a hundred cycles, from zero to four thousand. That seems to be the Svant vocal range."

The diagram passed from hand to hand during cocktail time, before dinner. Bennet Fayon had been working all day dissecting the animal they were all calling a *domsee,* a name which would stick even if and when they learned the native name. He glanced disinterestedly at the drawing, then looked again, more closely. Then he set down the drink he was holding in his other hand and studied it intently.

"You know what you have here?" he asked. "This is a very close analogy to the hearing organs of that animal I was working on. The comb, as we've assumed, is the external organ. It's covered with small flaps and fissures. Back of each fissure is a long, narrow membrane; they're paired, one on each side of the comb, and from them nerves lead to clusters of small round membranes. Nerves lead from them to a complex nerve-cable at the bottom of the comb and into the brain at the base of the skull. I couldn't understand how the system functioned, but now I see it. Each of the larger membrances on the outside responds to a sound-frequency band, and the small ones on the inside break the bands down to individual frequencies."

"How many of the little ones are there?" Ayesha asked.

"Thousands of them; the inner comb is simply packed with them. Wait; I'll show you."

He rose and went away, returning with a sheaf of photo-enlargements and a number of blocks of lucite in which specimens were mounted. Everybody examined them. Anna de Jong, as a practicing psychologist, had an M.D. and to get that she'd had to know a modicum of anatomy; she was puzzled.

"I can't understand how they hear with those things. I'll grant that the membranes will respond to sound, but I can't see how they transmit it."

"But they do hear," Meillard said. "Their musical instruments, their reactions to our voices, the way they are affected by sounds like gunfire—"

"They hear, but they don't hear in the same way we do," Fayon replied. "If you can't be convinced by anything else, look at these things, and compare them with the structure of the human ear, or the ear of any member of any other sapient race we've ever contacted. That's what I've been saying from the beginning."

"They have sound-perception to an extent that makes

ours look almost like deafness," Ayesha Keithley said. "I wish I could design a sound-detector one-tenth as good as this must be."

Yes. The way the Lord Mayor said *fwoonk* and the way Paul Meillard said it sounded entirely different to them. Of course, *fwoonk* and *pwink* and *tweelt* and *kroosh* sounded alike to them, but let's don't be too picky about things.

There were no hot showers that evening; Dave Questell's gang had trouble with the pump and needed some new parts made up aboard the ship. They were still working on it the next morning. He had meant to start teaching Sonny blacksmithing, but during the evening Lillian and Anna had decided to try teaching Mom a nonphonetic, ideographic, alphabet, and in the morning they co-opted Sonny to help. Deprived of his disciple, he strolled over to watch the work on the pump. About twenty Svants had come in from the fields and were also watching, from the meadow.

After a while, the job was finished. The petty officer in charge of the work pushed in the switch, and the pump started, sucking dry with a harsh racket. The natives twittered in surprise. Then the water came, and the pump settled down to a steady *thugg-thugg, thugg-thugg.*

The Svants seemed to like the new sound; they grimaced in pleasure and moved closer; within forty or fifty feet, they all squatted on the ground and sat entranced. Others came in from the fields, drawn by the sound. They, too, came up and squatted, until there was a semicircle of them. The tank took a long time to fill; until it did, they all sat immobile and fascinated. Even after it stopped, many remained, hoping that it would start again. Paul Meillard began wondering, a trifle uneasily, if that would happen every time the pump went on.

"They get a positive pleasure from it. It affects them the same way Luis' voice does."

"Mean I have a voice like a pump?" Gofredo demanded.

"Well, I'm going to find out," Ayesha Keithley said. "The next time that starts, I'm going to make a recording, and compare it with your voice-recording. I'll give five to one there'll be a similarity."

Questell got the foundation for the sonics lab dug, and began pouring concrete. That took water, and the pump ran continuously that afternoon. Concrete-mixing took more water the next day, and by noon the whole village population, down to the smallest child, was massed at the pumphouse, enthralled. Mom was snared by the sound like any of the rest; only Sonny was unaffected. Lillian and Ayestha compared recordings of the voices of the team with the pump-sound; in Gofredo's they found an identical frequency-pattern.

"We'll need the new apparatus to be positive about it, but it's there, all right," Ayesha said. "That's why Luis' voice pleases them."

"That tags me: Old Pump-Mouth," Gofredo said. "It'll get all through the Corps, and they'll be calling me that when I'm a four-star general, if I live that long."

Meillard was really worried, now. So was Bennet Fayon. He said so that afternoon at cocktail time.

"It's an addiction," he declared. "Once they hear it, they have no will to resist; they just squat and listen. I don't know what it's doing to them, but I'm scared of it."

"I know one thing it's doing," Meillard said. "It's keeping them from their work in the fields. For all we know, it may cause them to lose a crop they need badly for subsistence."

The native they had come to call the Lord Mayor evidently thought so, too. He was with the others, the next morning, squatting with his staff across his knees, as bemused as any of them, but when the pump stopped he rose and approached a group of Terrans, launching into what could only be an impassioned tirade. He pointed with his staff to the pump house, and to the semicircle of still motionless villagers. He pointed to the fields, and back to the people, and to the pump house again, gesturing vehemently with his other hand.

You make the noise. My people will not work while they hear it. The fields lie untended. Stop the noise, and let my people work.

Couldn't possibly be any plainer.

Then the pump started again. The Lord Mayor's hands tightened on the staff; he was struggling tormentedly with himself, in vain. His face relaxed into the heartbroken expression of joy; he turned and shuffled over, dropping onto his haunches with the others.

"Shut down the pump, Dave!" Meillard called out. "Cut the power off."

The *thugg-thugg*-ing stopped. The Lord Mayor rose, made an odd salaamlike bow toward the Terrans, and then turned on the people, striking with his staff and shrieking at them. A few got to their feet and joined him, screaming, pushing, tugging. Others joined. In a little while, they were all on their feet, straggling away across the fields.

Dave Questell wanted to know what it meant; Meillard explained.

"Well, what are we going to do for water?" the Navy engineer asked.

"Soundproof the pump house. You can do that, can't

you?''

"Sure. Mound it over with earth. We'll have that done in a few hours."

That started Gofredo worrying. "This happens every time we colonize an inhabited planet. We give the natives something new. Then we find out it's bad for them, and we try to take it away from them. And then the knives come out, and the shooting starts."

Luis Gofredo was also a specialist, speaking on his subject.

While they were at lunch, Charley Loughran screened in from the other camp and wanted to talk to Bennet Fayon.

"A funny thing, Bennet. I took a shot at a bird . . . no, a flying mammal . . . and dropped it. It was dead when it hit the ground, but there isn't a mark on it. I want you to do an autopsy, and find out how I can kill things by missing them."

"How far away was it?"

"Call it forty feet; no more."

"What were you using, Charley?" Ayesha Keithley called from the table.

"Eight-point-five Mars-Consolidated pistol," Loughran said. "I'd laid my shotgun down and walked away from it—"

"Twelve hundred foot-seconds," Ayesha said. "Bow-wave as well as muzzle-blast."

"You think the report was what did it?" Fayon asked.

"You want to bet it didn't?" she countered.

Nobody did.

Mom was sulky. She didn't like what Dave Questell's men were doing to the nice-noise-place. Ayesha and Lillian consoled her by taking her into the soundproofed room and playing the recording of the pump-noise for her. Sonny couldn't care less, one way or another; he spent the afternoon teaching Mark Howell what the marks on paper meant. It took a lot of signs and play-acting. He had learned about thirty ideographs; by combining them and drawing little pictures, he could express a number of simple ideas. There was, of course, a limit to how many of those things anybody could learn and remember—look how long it took an Old Terran Chinese scribe to learn his profession—but it was the beginning of a method of communication.

Questell got the pump house mounded over. Ayesha came out and tried a sound-meter, and also Mom, on it while the pump was running. Neither reacted.

A good many Svants were watching the work. They began to demonstrate angrily. A couple tried to interfere and were knocked down with rifle butts. The Lord Mayor and his Board of Aldermen came out with the big horn and harangued them at length, and finally got them to go back to the fields. As nearly as anybody could tell, he was friendly to and co-operative with the Terrans. The snooper over the village reported excitement in the plaza.

Bennet Fayon had taken an air-jeep to the other camp immediately after lunch. He was back by 1500, accompanied by Loughran. They carried a cloth-wrapped package into Fayon's dissecting-room. At cocktail time, Paul Meillard had to go and get them.

"Sorry," Fayon said, joining the group. "Didn't notice how late it was getting. We're still doing a post on this svant-bat; that's what Charley's calling it, till we get the native name.

"The immediate cause of death was spasmodic contraction of every muscle in the thing's body; some of them

were partly relaxed before we could get to work on it, but
not completely. Every bone that isn't broken is dislocated;
a good many both. There is not the slightest trace of external injury. Everything was done by its own muscles." He
looked around. "I hope nobody covered Ayesha's bet,
after I left. If they did, she collects. The large outer membranes in the comb seem to be unaffected, but there is
considerable compression of the small round ones inside,
in just one area, and more on the left side than on the right.
Charley says it was flying across in front of him from left to
right."

"The receptor-area responding to the frequencies of the
report," Ayesha said.

Anna de Jong made a passing gesture toward Fayon.
"The baby's yours, Bennet," she said. "This isn't psychological. I won't accept a case of psychosomatic compound
fracture."

"Don't be too premature about it, Anna. I think that's
more or less what you have, here."

Everybody looked at him, surprised. His subject was
comparative technology. The bio- and psycho-sciences
were completely outside his field.

"A lot of things have been bothering me, ever since the
first contact. I'm beginning to think I'm on the edge of understanding them, now. Bennet, the higher life-forms
here—the people, and that domsee, and Charley's svant-
bat—are structurally identical with us. I don't mean gross
structure, -like ears and combs. I mean molecular and cel-
lular and tissue structure. Is that right?"

Fayon nodded. "Biology on this planet is exactly Terra
type. Yes. With adequate safeguards, I'd even say you
could make a viable tissue-graft from a Svant to a Terran,
or vice versa."

"Ayesha, would the sound waves from that pistol-shot

in any conceivable way have the sort of physical effect we're considering?"

"Absolutely not," she said, and Luis Gofredo said: "I've been shot at and missed with pistols at closer range than that."

"Then it was the effect on the animal's nervous system."

Anna shrugged. "It's still Bennet's baby. I'm a psychologist, not a neurologist."

"What I've been saying, all along," Fayon reiterated complacently. "Their hearing is different from ours. This proves it.

"It proves that they don't hear at all."

He had expected an explosion; he wasn't disappointed. They all contradicted him, many derisively. Signal reactions. Only Paul Meillard made the semantically appropriate response:

"What do you mean, Mark?"

"They don't *hear* sound; they *feel* it. You saw what they have inside their combs. Those things don't transmit sound like the ears of any sound-sensitive life-form we've ever seen. They transform sound waves into tactile sensations."

Fayon cursed, slowly and luridly. Anna de Jong looked at him wide-eyed. He finished his cocktail and poured another. In the snooper screen, what looked like an indignation meeting was making uproar in the village plaza. Gofredo cut the volume of the speaker even lower.

"That would explain a lot of things," Meillard said slowly. "How hard it was for them to realize that we didn't understand when they talked to us. A punch in the nose feels the same to anybody. They thought they were giving us bodily feelings. They didn't know we were insensible to them."

"But they do . . . they do have a language," Lillian faltered. "They talk."

"Not the way we understand it. If they want to say, 'Me,' it's *tickle-pinch-rub*, even if it sounds like *fwoonk* to us, when it doesn't sound like *pwink* or *tweelt* or *kroosh*. The tactile sensations, to a Svant, feel no more different than a massage by four different hands. Analogous to a word pronounced by four different voices, to us. They'll have a code for expressing meanings in tactile sensation, just as we have a code for expressing meanings in audible sound."

"Except that when a Svant tells another, 'I am happy,' or 'I have a stomach-ache,' he makes the other one feel that way too," Anna said. "That would carry an awful lot more conviction. I don't imagine symptom-swapping is popular among Svants. Karl! You were nearly right, at that. This isn't telepathy, but it's a lot like it."

"So it is," Dorver, who had been mourning his departed telepathy theory, said brightly. "And look how it explains their society. Peaceful, everybody in quick agreement—" He looked at the screen and gulped. The Lord Mayor and his party had formed one clump, and the opposition was grouped at the other side of the plaza; they were screaming in unison at each other. "They make their decisions by endurance; the party that can resist the feelings of the other longest converts their opponents."

"Pure democracy," Gofredo declared. "Rule by the party that can make the most noise."

"And I'll bet that when they're sick, they go around chanting, 'I am well; I feel just fine!'" Anna said. "Auto-suggestion would really work, here. Think of the feedback, too. One Svant has a feeling. He verbalizes it, and the sound of his own voice re-enforces it in him. It is induced in his hearers, and they verbalize it, re-enforcing it in themselves and in him. This could go on and on."

"Yes. It has. Look at their technology." He felt more comfortable, now he was on home ground again. "A friend of mine, speaking about a mutual acquaintance, once said, 'When they installed her circuits, they put in such big feeling circuits that there was no room left for any thinking circuits.' I think that's a perfect description of what I estimate Svant mentality to be. Take these bronze knives, and the musical instruments. Wonderful; the work of individuals trying to express feeling in metal or wood. But get an idea like the wheel, or even a pair of tongs? Poo! How would you state the First Law of Motion, or the Second Law of Thermodynamics, in tickle-pinch-rub terms? Sonny could grasp an idea like that. Sonny's handicap, if you call it that, cuts him off from feel-thinking; he can think logically instead of sensually."

He sipped his cocktail and continued: "I can understand why the village is mounded up, too. I realized that while I was watching Dave's gang bury the pump house. I'd been bothered by that, and by the absence of granaries for all the grain they raise, and by the number of people for so few and such small houses. I think the village is mostly underground, and the houses are just entrances, sound-proofed, to shelter them from uncomfortable natural noises—thunderstorms, for instance."

The horn was braying in the snooper-screen speaker; somebody wondered what it was for. Gofredo laughed.

"I thought, at first, that it was a war-horn. It isn't. It's a peace-horn," he said. "Public tranquilizer. The first day, they brought it out and blew it at us to make us peaceable."

"Now I see why Sonny is rejected and persecuted," Anna was saying. "He must make all sorts of horrible noises that he can't hear . . . that's not the word; we have none for it . . . and nobody but his mother can stand being near him."

"Like me," Lillian said. "Now I understand. Just think of the most revolting thing that could be done to you physically; that's what I do to them every time I speak. And I always thought I had a nice voice," she added, pathetically.

"You have, for Terrans," Ayesha said. "For Svants, you'll just have to change it."

"But how—?"

"Use an analyzer; train it. That was why I took up sonics, in the first place. I had a voice like a crow with a sore throat, but by practicing with an analyzer, an hour a day, I gave myself an entirely different voice in a couple of months. Just try to get some pump-sound frequencies into it, like Luis'."

"But why? I'm no use here. I'm a linguist, and these people haven't any language that I could ever learn, and they couldn't even learn ours. They couldn't learn to make sounds, as sounds."

"You've been doing very good work with Mom on those ideographs," Meillard said. "Keep it up till you've taught her the Lingua Terra Basic vocabulary, and with her help we can train a few more. They can be our interpreters; we can write what we want them to say to the others. It'll be clumsy, but it will work, and it's about the only thing I can think of that will."

"And it will improve in time," Ayesha added. "And we can make vocoders and visibilizers. Paul, you have authority to requisiton personnel from the ship's company. Draft me; I'll stay here and work on it."

The rumpus in the village plaza was getting worse. The Lord Mayor and his adherents were being outshouted by the opposition.

"Better do something about that in a hurry, Paul, if you don't want a lot of Svants shot," Gofredo said. "Give that another half hour and we'll have visitors, with bows and spears."

"Ayesha, you have a recording of the pump," Meillard said. "Load a record-player onto a jeep and fly over the village and play it for them. Do it right away. Anna, get Mom in here. We want to get her to tell that gang that from now on, at noon and for a couple of hours after sunset, when the work's done, there will be free public pump-concerts, over the village plaza."

Ayesha and her warrant-officer helper and a Marine lieutenant went out hastily. Everybody else faced the screen to watch. In fifteen minutes, an airjeep was coming in on the village. As it circled low, a new sound, the steady *thugg-thugg, thugg-thugg* of the pump, began.

The yelling and twittering and the blaring of the peace-horn died out almost at once. As the jeep circled down to housetop level, the two contending faction-clumps broke apart; their component individuals moved into the center of the plaza and squatted, staring up, letting the delicious waves of sound caress them.

"Do we have to send a detail in a jeep to do that twice a day?" Gofredo asked. "We keep a snooper over the village; fit it with a loud-speaker and a timer; it can give them their *thugg-thugg*, on schedule, automatically."

"We might give the Lord Mayor a recording and a player and let him decide when the people ought to listen—if that's the word—to it," Dorver said. "Then it would be something of their own."

"No!" He spoke so vehemently that the others started. "You know what would happen? Nobody would be able to turn it off; they'd all be hypnotized, or doped, or whatever it is. They'd just sit in a circle around it till they starved to death, and when the power-unit gave out, the record-player would be surrounded by a ring of skeletons. We'll just have to keep on playing it for them ourselves. Terrans' Burden."

"That'll give us a sanction over them," Gofredo observed. "Extra *thugg-thugg* if they're very good; shut it off on them if they act nasty. And find out what Lillian has in her voice that the rest of us don't have, and make a good loud recording of that, and stash it away along with the rest of the heavy-weapons ammunition. You know, you're not going to have any trouble at all, when we go down-country to talk to the king or whatever. This is better than fire-water ever was."

"We must never misuse our advantage, Luis," Meillard said seriously. "We must use it only for their good."

He really meant it. Only—You had to know some general history to study technological history, and it seemed to him that that pious assertion had been made a few times before. Some of the others who had made it had really meant it, too, but that had made little difference in the long run.

Fayon and Anna were talking enthusiastically about the work ahead of them.

"I don't know where your subject ends and mine begins," Anna was saying. "We'll just have to handle it between us. What are we going to call it? We certainly can't call it hearing."

"Nonauditory sonic sense is the only thing I can think of," Fayon said. "And that's such a clumsy term."

"Mark; you thought of it first," Anna said. "What do you think?"

"Nonauditory sonic sense. It isn't any worse than Domesticated Type C, and that got cut down to size. *Naudsonce.*"

Introduction to "Oomphel in the Sky"

"Oomphel in the Sky" takes place in the early Ninth Century A.E. on the planet Kwann where the Terrans are having trouble with the local natives, the Kwannons. In this story we find a classic Piper conflict: inefficient government vs. efficient private enterprise. Terra is a hotbed of Neo-Marxist liberalism and we get the idea that it is beginning to fall into decadence, and that in large part the colonial spirit of the outer worlds is all that is keeping the Federation alive and functioning.

In this story we see the first appearance of Captain Foxx Travis, a young army officer who will become the Napoleon of this far future earth during the System States War.

113

Oomphel In The Sky

Miles Gilbert watched the landscape slide away below him, its quilt of rounded treetops mottled red and orange in the double sunlight and, in shaded places, with the natural yellow of the vegetation of Kwannon. The aircar began a slow swing to the left, and Gettler Alpha came into view, a monstrous smear of red incandescence with an optical diameter of two feet at arm's length, slightly flattened on the bottom by the western horizon. In another couple of hours it would be completely set, but by that time Beta, the planet's G-class primary, would be at its midafternoon hottest. He glanced at his watch. It was 1005, but that was Galactic Standard Time, and had no relevance to anything that was happening in the local sky. It did mean, though, that it was five minutes short of two hours to 'cast-time.

He snapped on the communication screen in front of him, and Harry Walsh, the news editor, looked out of it at him from the office in Bluelake, halfway across the continent. He wanted to know how things were going.

"Just about finished. I'm going to look in at a couple more native villages, and then I'm going to Sanders' plantation to see Gonzales. I hope I'll have a personal statement from him, and the final situation-progress map, in time for the 'cast. I take it Maith's still agreeable to releasing the story at twelve-hundred?"

"Sure; he was always agreeable. The Army wants publicity; it was Government House that wanted to sit on it, and they've given that up now. The story's all over the place here, native city and all."

"What's the situation in town, now?"

"Oh, it's still going on. Some disorders, mostly just unrest. Lot of street meetings that could have turned into frenzies if the police hadn't broken them up in time. A couple of shootings, some sleep-gassing, and a lot of arrests. Nothing to worry about—at least, not immediately."

That was about what he thought. "Maybe it's not bad to have a little trouble in Bluelake," he considered. "What happens out here in the plantation country the Government House crowd can't see, and it doesn't worry them. Well, I'll call you from Sanders'."

He blanked the screen. In the seat in front, the native pilot said: "Some contragravity up ahead, boss." It sounded like two voices speaking in unison, which was just what it was. "I'll have a look."

The pilot's hand, long and thin, like a squirrel's, reached up and pulled down the fifty-power binoculars on their swinging arm. Miles looked at the screen-map and saw a native village just ahead of the dot of light that marked the position of the aircar. He spoke the native name of the village aloud, and added:

"Let down there, Heshto. I'll see what's going on."

The native, still looking through the glasses, said, "Right, boss." Then he turned.

His skin was blue-gray and looked like sponge rubber. He was humanoid, to the extent of being an upright biped, with two arms, a head on top of shoulders and a torso that housed, among other oddities, four lungs. His face wasn't even vaguely human. He had two eyes in front, close enough for stereoscopic vision, but that was a common characteristic of sapient life forms everywhere. His mouth was strictly for eating; he breathed through separate in-

takes and outlets, one of each on either side of his neck;
he talked through the outlets and had his scent and hearing organs in the intakes. The car was air-conditioned,
which was a mercy; an overheated Kwann exhaled
through his skin, and surrounded himself with stenches
like an organic chemistry lab. But then, Kwanns didn't
come any closer to him than they could help when he was
hot and sweated, which, lately, had been most of the time.

"A V and a half of air cavalry, circling around," Heshto
said. "Making sure nobody got away. And a combat car at
a couple of hundred feet and another one just at treetop
level."

He rose and went to the seat next to the pilot, pulling
down the binoculars that were focused for his own eyes.
With them, he could see the air cavalry—egg-shaped
things just big enough for a seated man, with jets and contragravity field generators below and a bristle of machine
gun muzzles in front. A couple of them jetted up for a look
at him and then went slanting down again, having recognized the Kwannon Planetwide News Service car.

The village was typical enough to have been an illustration
in a sociography textbook—fields in a belt for a couple of
hundred yards around it, dome-thatched mud-and-wattle
huts inside a pole stockade with log storehouses built
against it, their flat roofs high enough to provide platforms
for defending archers, the open oval gathering-place in the
middle. There was a big hut at one end of this, the khamdoo, the sanctum of the adult males, off limits for women
and children. A small crowd was gathered in front of it;
fifteen or twenty Terran air cavalrymen, a couple of enlisted men from the Second Kwannon Native Infantry, a
Terran second lieutenant, and half a dozen natives. The
rest of the village population, about two hundred, of both

sexes and all ages, were lined up on the shadier side of the gathering-place, most of them looking up apprehensively at the two combat cars which were covering them with their guns.

Miles got to his feet as the car lurched off contragravity and the springs of the landing-feet took up the weight. A blast of furnacelike air struck him when he opened the door; he got out quickly and closed it behind him. The second lieutenant had come over to meet him; he extended his hand.

"Good day, Mr. Gilbert. We all owe you our thanks for the warning. This would have been a real baddie if we hadn't caught it when we did."

He didn't even try to make any modest disclaimer; that was nothing more than the exact truth.

"Well, lieutenant, I see you have things in hand here." He glanced at the line-up along the side of the oval plaza, and then at the selected group in front of the khamdoo. The patriarchal village chieftain in a loose slashed shirt; the shoonoo, wearing a multiplicity of amulets and nothing else; four or five of the village elders. "I take it the word of the swarming didn't get this far?"

"No, this crowd still don't know what the flap's about, and I couldn't think of anything to tell them that wouldn't be worse than no explanation at all."

He had noticed hoes and spades flying in the fields, and the cylindrical plastic containers the natives bought from traders, dropped when the troops had surprised the women at work. And the shoonoo didn't have a fire-dance cloak or any other special regalia on. If he'd heard about the swarming, he'd have been dressed to make magic for it.

"What time did you get here, lieutenant?"

"Oh-nine-forty. I just called in and reported the village

occupied, and they told me I was the last one in, so the operation's finished."

That had been smart work. He got the lieutenant's name and unit and mentioned it into his memophone. That had been a little under five hours since he had convinced General Maith, in Bluelake, that the mass labor-desertion from the Sanders plantation had been the beginning of a swarming. Some division commanders wouldn't have been able to get a brigade off the ground in that time, let alone landed on objective. He said as much to the young officer.

"The way the Army responded, today, can make the people of the Colony feel a lot more comfortable for the future."

"Why, thank you, Mr. Gilbert." The Army, on Kwannon, was rather more used to obloquy than praise. "How did you spot what was going on so quickly?"

This was the hundredth time, at least, that he had been asked that today.

"Well, Paul Sanders' labor all comes from neighboring villages. If they'd just wanted to go home and spend the end of the world with their families, they'd have been dribbling away in small batches for the last couple of hundred hours. Instead, they all bugged out in a bunch, they took all the food they could carry and nothing else, and they didn't make any trouble before they left. Then, Sanders said they'd been building fires out in the fallow ground and moaning and chanting around them for a couple of days, and idling on the job. Saving their strength for the trek. And he said they had a shoonoo among them. He's probably the lad who started it. Had a dream from the Gone Ones, I suppose."

"You mean, like this fellow here?" the lieutenant asked. "What are they, Mr. Gilbert; priests?"

He looked quickly at the lieutenant's collar-badges. Yellow trefoil for Third Fleet-Army Force, Roman IV for Fourth Army, 907 for his regiment, with C under it for cavalry. That outfit had only been on Kwanon for the last two thousand hours, but somebody should have briefed him better than that.

He shook his head. "No, they're magicians. Everything these Kwanns do involves magic, and the shoonoon are the professionals. When a native runs into something serious, that his own do-it-yourself magic can't cope with, he goes to the shoonoo. And, of course, the shoonoo works all the magic for the community as a whole—rain-magic, protective magic for the village and the fields, that sort of thing."

The lieutenant mopped his face on a bedraggled handkerchief. "They'll have to struggle along somehow for a while; we have orders to round up all the shoonoon and send them in to Bluelake."

"Yes." That hadn't been General Maith's idea; the governor had insisted on that. "I hope it doesn't make more trouble than it prevents."

The lieutenant was still mopping his face and looking across the gathering-place toward Alpha, glaring above the huts.

"How much worse do you think this is going to get?" he asked.

"The heat, or the native troubles?"

"I was thinking about the heat, but both."

"Well, it'll get hotter. Not much hotter, but some. We can expect storms, too, within twelve to fifteen hundred hours. Nobody has any idea how bad they'll be. The last periastron was ninety years ago, and we've only been here for sixty-odd; all we have is verbal accounts from memory from the natives, probably garbled and exaggerated. We had pretty bad storms right after transit a year ago; they'll be much worse this time. Thermal convections; air starts to cool when it gets dark, and then heats up again in double-sun daylight."

It was beginning, even now; starting to blow a little after Alpha-rise.

"How about the natives?" the lieutenant asked. "If they can get any crazier than they are now—"

"They can, and they probably will. They think this is the end of the world. The Last Hot Time." He used the native expression, and then translated it into Lingua Terra. "The Sky Fire—that's Alpha—will burn up the whole world."

"But this happens every ninety years. Mean they always acted this way at periastron?"

He shook his head. "Race would have exterminated itself long ago if they had. No, this is something special. The coming of the Terrans was a sign. The Terrans came and brought oomphel to the world; this a sign that the Last Hot Time is at hand."

"What the devil *is* oomphel?" The lieutenant was mopping the back of his neck with one hand, now, and trying to pull his sticky tunic loose from his body with the other. "I hear that word all the time."

"Well, most Terrans, including the old Kwannon hands, use it to mean trade-goods. To the natives, it means any product of Terran technology, from paper-clips to spaceships. They think it's . . . well, not exactly supernatural; extranatural would be closer to expressing their idea. Terrans are natural; they're just a different kind of people. But oomphel isn't; it isn't subject to any of the laws of nature at all. They're all positive that we don't make it. Some of them even think it makes us."

When he got back in the car, the native pilot, Heshto, was lolling in his seat and staring at the crowd of natives along the side of the gathering-place with undisguised disdain. Heshto had been educated at one of the Native Welfare Commission schools, and post-graded with Kwannon Planetwide News. He could speak, read and write Lingua Terra. He was a mathematician as far as long division and decimal fractions. He knew that Kwannon was the second planet of the *Gettler* Beta system, 23,000 miles in circumference, rotating on its axis once in 22.8 Galactic Standard hours and making an orbital circuit around *Gettler* Beta once in 372.06 axial days, and that Alpha was an M-class pulsating variable with an average period of four hundred days, and that Beta orbited around it in a long elipse every ninety years. He didn't believe there was going to be a Last Hot Time. He was an intellectual, he was.

He started the contragravity-field generator as soon as Miles was in his seat. "Where now, boss?" he asked.

"Qualpha's Village. We won't let down; just circle low over it I want some views of the ruins. Then to Sanders' plantation."

"O.K., boss; hold tight."

He had the car up to ten thousand feet. Aiming it in the map direction of Qualpha's Village, he let go with everything he had—hot jets, rocketbooster and all. The forest landscape came hurtling out of the horizon toward them.

Qualpha's was where the trouble had first broken out, after the bug-out from Sanders; the troops hadn't been able to get there in time, and it had been burned. Another village, about the same distance south of the plantation, had also gone up in flames, and at a dozen more they had found the natives working themselves into frenzies and had had to sleep-gas them or strum them with concussion-bombs. Those had been the villages to which the deserters from Sanders' had themselves gone; from every one, runners had gone out to neighboring villages—"The Gone Ones are returning; all the People go to greet them at the

Deesha-Phoo. Burn your villages; send on the word. Has-
ten; the Gone Ones return!"

Saving some of those villages had been touch-and-go,
too; the runners, with hours lead-time, had gotten there
ahead of the troops, and there had been shooting at a
couple of them. Then the Army contragravity began landing at villages that couldn't have been reached in hours by
foot messengers. It had been stopped—at least for the
time, and in this area. When and where another would
break out was anybody's guess.

The car was slowing and losing altitude, and ahead he
could see thin smoke rising above the trees. He moved
forward beside the pilot and pulled down his glasses; with
them he could distinguish the ruins of the village. He called
Bluelake, and then put his face to the view-finder and began transmitting in the view.

It had been a village like the one he had just visited, mud-
and-wattle huts around an oval gathering-place, stockade,
and fields beyond. Heshto brought the car down to a few
hundred feet and came coasting in on momentum helped
by an occasional spurt of the cold-jets. A few sections of
the stockade still stood, and one side of the khamdoo
hadn't fallen, but the rest of the structures were flat. There
wasn't a soul, human or parahuman, in sight; the only living thing was a small black-and-gray quadruped investi-
gating some bundles that had been dropped in the fields,
in hope of finding something tasty. He got a view of that—
everybody liked animal pictures on a newscast—and then
he was swinging the pickup over the still-burning ruins. In
the ashes of every hut he could see the remains of something like a viewscreen or a nuclear-electric stove or a refrigerator or a sewing machine. He knew how dearly the
Kwanns cherished such possessions. That they had de-

stroyed them grieved him. But the Last Hot Time was at hand; the whole world would be destroyed by fire, and then the Gone Ones would return.

So there were uprisings on the plantations. Paul Sanders had been lucky; his Kwanns had just picked up and left. But he had always gotten along well with the natives, and his plantation house was literally a castle and he had plenty of armament. There had been other planters who had made the double mistake of incurring the enmity of their native labor and of living in unfortified houses. A lot of them weren't around, any more, and their plantations were gutted ruins.

And there were plantations on which the natives had destroyed the klooba plants and smashed the crystal which lived symbiotically upon them. They thought the Terrans were using the living crystals to make magic. Not too far off, at that; the properties of Kwannon biocrystals had opened a major breakthrough in subnucleonic physics and initiated half a dozen technologies. New kinds of oomphel. And down in the south, where the spongy and resinous trees were drying in the heat, they were starting forest fires and perishing in them in hecatombs. And to the north, they were swarming into the mountains; building great fires there, too, and attacking the Terran radar and radio beacons.

Fire was a factor common to all these frenzies. Nothing could happen without magical assistance; the way to bring on the Last Hot Time was People.

Maybe the ones who died in the frenzies and the swarmings were the lucky ones at that. They wouldn't live to be crushed by disappointment when the Sky Fire receded as Beta went into the long swing toward apastron. The surviving shoonoon wouldn't be the lucky ones, that was for sure. The magician-in-public-practice needs only to make

one really bad mistake before he is done to some unpleas-
antly ingenious death by his clientry, and this was going to
turn out to be the biggest magico-prophetic blooper in all
the long unrecorded history of Kwannon.

A few minutes after the car turned south from the ruined
village, he could see contragravity-vehicles in the air
ahead, and then the fields and buildings of the Sanders
plantation. A lot more contragravity was grounded in the
fallow fields, and there were rows of pneumatic balloon-
tents, and field-kitchens, and a whole park of engineering
equipment. Work was going on in the klooba-fields, too;
about three hundred natives were cutting open the six-foot
leafy balls and getting out the biocrystals. Three of the
plantation airjeeps, each with a pair of machine guns, were
guarding them, but they didn't seem to be having any
trouble. He saw Sanders in another jeep, and had Heshto
put the car alongside.

"How's it going, Paul?" he asked over his radio. "I see
you have some help, now."

"Everybody's from Qualpha's, and from Darshat's,"
Sanders replied. "The Army had no place to put them,
after they burned themselves out." He laughed happily.
"Miles, I'm going to save my whole crop! I thought I was
wiped out, this morning."

He would have been, if Gonzales hadn't brought those
Kwanns in. The klooba was beginning to wither; if left un-
harvested, the biocrystals would die along with their hosts
and crack into worthlessness. Like all the other planters,
Sanders had started no new crystals since the hot weather,
and would start none until the worst of the heat was over.
He'd need every crystal he could sell to tide him over.

"The Welfarers'll make a big forced-labor scandal out
of this," he predicted.

"Why, such an idea." Sanders was scandalized. "I'm

not forcing them to eat."

"The Welfarers don't think anybody ought to have to work to eat. They think everybody ought to be fed whether they do anything to earn it or not, and if you try to make people earn their food, you're guilty of economic coercion. And if you're in business for yourself and want them to work for you, you're an exploiter and you ought to be eliminated as a class. Haven't you been trying to run a plantation on this planet, under this Colonial Government, long enough to have found that out, Paul?"

Brigadier General Ramón Gonzales had taken over the first—counting down from the landing-stage—floor of the plantation house for his headquarters. His headquarters company had pulled out removable partitions and turned four rooms into one, and moved in enough screens and teleprinters and photoprint machines and computers to have outfitted the main newsroom of *Planetwide News*. The place had the feel of a newsroom—a newsroom after a big story has broken and the cast has gone on the air and everybody—in this case about twenty Terran officers and non-coms, half women—standing about watching screens and smoking and thinking about getting a follow-up ready.

Gonzales himself was relaxing in Sanders' business-room, with his belt off and his tunic open. He had black eyes and black hair and mustache, and a slightly equine face that went well with his Old Terran Spanish name. There was another officer with him, considerably younger—Captain Foxx Travis, Major General Maith's aide.

"Well, is there anything we can do for you, Miles?" Gonzales asked, after they had exchanged greetings and sat down.

"Why, could I have your final situation-progress map?

And would you be willing to make a statement on audio-visual." He looked at his watch. "We have about twenty minutes before the 'cast."

"You have a map," Gonzales said, as though he were walking tiptoe from one word to another. "It accurately represents the situation as of the moment, but I'm afraid some minor unavoidable inaccuracies may have crept in while marking the positions and times for the earlier phases of the operation. I teleprinted a copy to *Planetwide* along with the one I sent to Division Headquarters."

He understood about that and nodded. Gonzales was zipping up his tunic and putting on his belt and sidearm. That told him, before the brigadier general spoke again, that he was agreeable to the audio-visual appearance and statement. He called the recording studio at *Planetwide* while Gonzales was inspecting himself in the mirror and told them to get set for a recording. It only ran a few minutes; Gonzales, speaking without notes, gave a brief description of the operation.

"At present," he concluded, "we have every native village and every plantation and trading-post within two hundred miles of the Sanders plantation occupied. We feel that this swarming has been definitely stopped but we will continue the occupation for at least the next hundred to two hundred hours. In the meantime, the natives in the occupied villages are being put to work building shelters for themselves against the anticipated storms."

"I hadn't heard about that," Miles said, as the general returned to his chair and picked up his drink again.

"Yes. They'll need something better than these thatched huts when the storms start, and working on them will keep them out of mischief. Standard megaton-kilometer field shelters, earth and log construction. I think they'll be adequate for anything that happens at periastron."

Anything designed to resist the heat, blast and radiation effects of a megaton thermonuclear bomb at a kilometer ought to stand up under what was coming. At least, the periastron effects; there was another angle to it.

"The Native Welfare Commission isn't going to take kindly to that. That's supposed to be their job."

"Then why the devil haven't they done it?" Gonzales demanded angrily. "I've viewed every native village in this area by screen, and I haven't seen one that's equipped with anything better than those log storagebins against the stockades."

"There was a project to provide shelters for the periastron storms set up ten years ago. They spent one year arguing about how the natives survived storms prior to the Terrans' arrival here. According to the older natives, they got into those log storagehouses you were mentioning; only about one out of three in any village survived. I could have told them that. Did tell them, repeatedly, on the air. Then after they decided that shelters were needed, they spent another year hassling over who would be responsible for designing them. Your predecessor here, General Nokami, offered the services of his engineer officers. He was frostily informed that this was a humanitarian and not a military project."

Ramon Gonzales began swearing, then apologized for the interruption. "Then what?" he asked.

"Apology unnecessary. Then they did get a shelter designed, and started teaching some of the students at the native schools how to build them, and then the meteorologists told them it was no good. It was a dugout shelter; the weathermen said there'd be rainfall measured in meters instead of inches and anybody who got caught in one of those dugouts would be drowned like a rat."

"Ha, I thought of that one." Gonzales said. "My shelters are going to be mounded up eight feet above the ground."

"What did they do then?" Foxx Travis wanted to know.

"There the matter rested. As far as I know, nothing has been done on it since."

"And you think, with a disgraceful record of non-accomplishment like that, that they'll protest General Gonzales' action on purely jurisdictional grounds?" Travis demanded.

"Not jurisdictional grounds, Foxx. The general's going at this the wrong way. He actually knows what has to be done and how to do it, and he's going right ahead and doing it, without holding a dozen conferences and round-table discussions and giving everybody a fair and equal chance to foul things up for him. You know as well as I do that that's undemocratic. And what's worse, he's making the natives build them themselves, whether they want to or not, and that's forced labor. That reminds me; has anybody started raising the devil about those Kwanns from Qualpha's and Darshat's you brought here and Paul put to work?"

Gonzales looked at Travis and then said: "Not with me. Not yet, anyhow."

"They've been at General Maith," Travis said shortly. After a moment, he added: "General Maith supports General Gonzales completely; that's for publication. I'm authorized to say so. What else was there to do? They'd burned their villages and all their food stores. They had to be placed somewhere. And why in the name of reason should they sit around in the shade eating Government native-type rations while Paul Sanders has fifty to a hundred thousand sols' worth of crystals dying on him?"

"Yes; that's another thing they'll scream about. Paul's

making a profit out of it."

"Of course he's making a profit," Gonzales said. "Why else is he running a plantation? If planters didn't make profits, who'd grow biocrystals?"

"The Colonial Government. The same way they built those storm-shelters. But that would be in the public interest, and if the Kwanns weren't public-spirited enough to do the work, they'd be made to—at about half what planters like Sanders are paying them now. But don't you realize that profit is sordid and dishonest and selfish? Not at all like drawing a salary-cum-expense-account from the Government."

"You're right, it isn't," Gonzales agreed. "People like Paul Sanders have ability. If they don't, they don't stay in business. You have ability and people who don't never forgive you for it. Your very existence is a constant reproach to them."

"That's right. And they can't admit your ability without admitting their own inferiority, so it isn't ability at all. It's just dirty underhanded trickery and selfish ruthlessness." He thought for a moment. "How did Government House find out about these Kwanns here?"

"The Welfare Commission had people out while I was still setting up headquarters," Gonzales said. "That was about oh-seven-hundred."

"This isn't for publication?" Travis asked. "Well, they know, but they can't prove, that our given reason for moving in here in force is false. Of course, we can't change our story now; that's why the situation-progress map that was prepared for publication is incorrect as to the earlier phases. They do not know that it was you who gave us our first warning; they ascribe that to Sanders. And they are claiming that there never was any swarming; according to them, Sanders' natives are striking for better pay and conditions, and Sanders got General Maith to use troops to break the strike. I wish we could give you credit for putting us onto this, but it's too late now."

He nodded. The story was that a battalion of infantry had been sent in to rescue a small detail under attack by natives, and that more troops had been sent into re-enforce them, until the whole of Gonzales' brigade had been committed.

"That wasted an hour, at the start," Gonzales said. "We lost two native villages burned, and about two dozen casualties, because we couldn't get our full strength in soon enough."

"You'd have lost more than that if Maith had told the governor general the truth and requested orders to act. There'd be a hundred villages and a dozen plantations and trading posts burning now, and Lord knows how many dead, and the governor general would still be arguing about whether he was justified in ordering troop-action." He mentioned several other occasions when something like that had happened. "You can't tell that kind of people the truth. They won't believe it. It doesn't agree with their preconceptions."

Foxx Travis nodded. "I take it we are still talking for nonpublication?" When Miles nodded, he continued: "This whole situation is baffling, Miles. It seems that the government here knew all about the weather conditions they could expect at periastron, and had made plans for them. Some of them excellent plans, too, but all based on the presumption that the natives would co-operate or at least not obstruct. You see what the situation actually is. It should be obvious to everybody that the behavior of these natives is nullifying everything the civil government is trying to do to ensure the survival of the Terran colonists, the production of Terrantype food without which we would all starve, the biocrystal plantations without which the Colony would perish, and even the natives themselves. Yet the Civil Government will not act to stop these native frenzies and swarmings which endanger everything and everybody here, and when the Army attempts to act, we must use every sort of shabby subterfuge and deceit or the Civil Government will prevent us. What ails these people?''

"You have the whole history of the Colony against you, Foxx," he said. "You know, there never was any Chartered Kwannon Company set up to exploit the resources of the planet. At first, nobody realized that there were any resources worth exploiting. This plan was just a scientific curiosity; it was and is still the only planet of a binary system with a native population of sapient beings. The first people who came here were scientists, mostly sociographers and para-anthropologists. And most of them came from the University of Adelaide."

Travis nodded. Adelaide had a Federation-wide reputation for left-wing neo-Marxist "liberalism."

"Well, that established the political and social orientation of the Colonial Government, right at the start, when study of the natives was the only business of the Colony. You know how these ideological cliques form in a government—or any other organization. Subordinates are always chosen for their agreement with the views of their superiors, and the extremists always get to the top and shove the moderates under or out. Well, the Native Affairs Administration became the tail that wagged the Government dog, and the Native Welfare Commission is the big muscle in the tail."

His parents hadn't been of the left-wing Adelaide clique. His mother had been a biochemist; his father a roving news correspondent who had drifted into trading with the natives and made a fortune in keffa-gum before the chemists on Terra had found out how to synthesize hopkinsine.

"When the biocrystals were dicovered and the plantations started, the Government attitude was set. Biocrystal culture is just sordid money grubbing. The real business of the Colony is to promote the betterment of the natives, as defined in University of Adelaide terms. That's to say, convert them into ersatz Terrans. You know why General Maith ordered these shoonoon rounded up?"

Travis made a face. "Governor general Kovac insisted on it; General Maith thought that a few minor concessions would help him on his main objective, which was keeping a swarming from starting out here."

"Yes. The Commissioner of Native Welfare wanted that done, mainly at the urging of the Director of Economic, Educational and Technical Assistance. The EETA crowd don't like shoonoon. They have been trying, ever since their agency was set up, to undermine and destroy their influence with the natives. This looked like a good chance to get rid of some of them."

Travis nodded. "Yes. And as soon as the disturbances in Bluelake started, the Constabulary started rounding them up there, too, and at the evacuee contonments. They got about fifty of them, mostly from the cantonments east of the city—the natives brought in from the flooded tidewater area. They just dumped the lot of them onto us. We have them penned up in a lorry-hangar on the military reservation now." He turned to Gonzales. "How many do you think you'll gather up out here, general?" he asked.

"I'd say about a hundred and fifty, when we have them all."

Travis groaned. "We can't keep all of them in that hangar, and we don't have anywhere else—"

Sometimes a new idea sneaked up on Miles, rubbing

against him and purring like a cat. Sometimes one hit him like a sledgehammer. This one just seemed to grow inside him.

"Foxx, you know I have the top three floors of the Suzikami Building; about five hundred hours ago, I leased the fourth and fifth floors, directly below. I haven't done anything with them, yet; they're just as they were when Trans-Space Imports moved out. There are ample water, light, power, air-conditioning and toilet facilities, and they can be sealed off completely from the rest of the building. If General Maith's agreeable, I'll take his shoonoon off his hands."

"What in blazes will you do with them?"

"Try a little experiment in psychological warfare. At minimum, we may get a little better insight into why these natives think the Last Hot Time is coming. At best, we may be able to stop the whole thing and get them quieted down again."

"Even the minimum's worth trying for," Travis said. "What do you have in mind, Miles? I mean, what procedure?"

"Well, I'm not quite sure, yet." That was a lie; he was very sure. He didn't think it was quite time to be specific, though. "I'll have to size up my material a little, before I decide on what to do with it. Whatever happens, it wont hurt the shoonoon, and it won't make any more trouble than arresting them has made already. I'm sure we can learn something from them, at least."

Travis nodded. "General Maith is very much impressed with your grasp of native psychology," he said. "What happened out here this morning was exactly as you predicted. Whatever my recommendation's worth, you have it. Can you trust your native driver to take your car back to Bluelake alone?"

"Yes, of course."

"Then suppose you ride in with me in my car. We'll talk about it on the way in, and go see General Maith at once."

Bluelake was peaceful as they flew in over it, but it was an uneasy peace. They began running into military contra-gravity twenty miles beyond the open farmlands—they were the chlorophyll green of Terran vegetation—and the natives at work in the fields were being watched by more military and police vehicles. The carniculture plants, where Terran-type animal tissue was grown in nutrient-vats, were even more heavily guarded, and the native city was being patroled from above and the streets were empty, even of the hordes of native children who usually played in them.

The Terran city had no streets. Its dwellers moved about on contragravity, and tall buildings rose singly or in clumps, among the landing-staged residences and the green transplanted trees. There was a triple wire fence around it, the inner one masked by vines and the middle one electrified, with warning lights on. Even a government dedicated to the betterment of the natives and unwilling to order military action against them was, it appeared, un-willing to take too many chances.

Major General Denis Maith, the Federation Army com-mander on Kwannon, was considerably more than willing to find a temporary home for his witch doctors, now num-bering close to two hundred. He did insist that they be kept under military guard, and on assigning his aide, Captain Travis, to co-operate on the project. Beyond that, he gave Miles a free hand.

Miles and Travis got very little rest in the next ten hours. A half-company of engineer troops was also kept busy, as were a number of Kwannon Planetwide News technicians and some Terran and native mechanics borrowed from different private business concerns in the city. Even the most guarded hints of what he had in mind were enough to get this last co-operation; he had been running a news-service in Bluelake long enough to have the confidence of the business people.

He tried, as far as possible, to keep any intimation of what was going on from Government House. That, unfortunately, hadn't been far enough. He found that out when General Maith was on his screen, in the middle of the work on the fourth and fifth floors of the Suzikami Building.

"The governor general just screened me," Maith said. "He's in a tizzy about our shoonoon. Claims that keeping them in the Suzikami Building will endanger the whole Terran city."

"Is that the best he can do? Well, that's rubbish, and he knows it. There are less than two hundred of them, I have them on the fifth floor, twenty stories above the ground, and the floor's completely sealed off from the floor below. They can't get out, and I have tanks of sleep-gas all over the place which can be opened either individually or all together from a switch on the fourth floor, where your sepoys are quartered."

"I know, Mr. Gilbert; I screenviewed the whole installation. I've seen regular maximum-security prisons that would be easier to get out of."

"Governor general Kovac is not objecting personally. He has been pressured into it by this Native Welfare government-within-the-Government. They don't know what I'm doing with those shoonoon, but whatever it is, they're afraid of it."

"Well, for the present," Maith said, "I think I'm holding them off. The Civil Government doesn't want the responsibility of keeping them in custody, I refused to assume responsibility for them if they were kept anywhere else,

and Kovac simply won't consider releasing them, so that
leaves things as they are. I did have to make one compro-
mise, though." That didn't sound good. It sounded less so
when Maith continued: "They insisted on having one of
their people at the Suzikami Building as an observer. I had
to grant that."

"That's going to mean trouble."

"Oh, I shouldn't think so. This observer will observe,
and nothing else. She will take no part in anything Your're
doing, will voice no objections, and will not interrupt anything you are saying to the shoonoon. I was quite firm on
that, and the governor general agreed completely."

"She?"

"Yes. A Miss Edith Shaw; do you know anything about
her?"

"I've met her a few times; cocktail parties and so on."
She was young enough, and new enough to Kwannon,
not to have a completely indurated mind. On the other
hand, she was EETA which was bad, and had a master's
in sociography from Adelaide, which was worse. "When
can I look for her?"

"Well, the governor general's going to screen me and
find out when you'll have the shoonoon on hand."

Doesn't want to talk to me at all, Miles thought. Afraid
he might say something and get quoted.

"For your information, they'll be here inside an hour.
They will have to eat, and they're all tired and sleepy. I
should say bout oh-eight-hundred. Oh, and will you tell
the governor general to tell Miss Shaw to bring an overnight kit with her. She's going to need it."

He was up at 0400, just a little after Beta-rise. He might
be a civilian big wheel in an Army psychological warfare
project, but he still had four newscasts a day to produce.

He spent a couple of hours checking the 0600 cast and briefing Harry Walsh for the indeterminate period in which he would be acting chief editor and producer. At 0700, Foxx Travis put in an appearance. They went down to the fourth floor, to the little room they had fitted out as command-post, control room and office for Operation Shoonoo.

There was a rectangular black traveling-case, initialed E. S., beside the open office door. Travis nodded at it, and they grinned at one another; she'd come early, possibly hoping to catch them hiding something they didn't want her to see. Entering the office quietly, they found her seated facing the big viewscreen, smoking and watching a couple of enlisted men of the First Kwannon Native Infantry at work in another room where the pickup was. There were close to a dozen lipstick-tinted cigarette butts in the ashtray beside her. Her private face wasn't particularly happy. Maybe she was being earnest and concerned about the betterment of the underpriviledged, or the satanic maneuvers of the selfish planters.

Then she realized that somebody had entered; with a slight start, she turned, then rose. She was about the height of Foxx Travis, a few inches shorter than Miles, and slender. Light blond; green suit costume. She ditched her private face and got on her public one, a pleasant and deferential smile, with a trace of uncertainty behind it. Miles introduced Travis, and they sat down again facing the screen.

It gave a view, from one of the long sides and near the ceiling, of a big room. In the center, a number of seats— the drum-shaped cushions the natives had adopted in place of the seats carved from sections of tree trunk that they had been using when the Terrans had come to Kwannon—were arranged in a semicircle, one in the middle slightly in advance of the others. Facing them were three armchairs, a remote-control box beside one and another Kwann cushion behind and between the other two. There was a large globe of Kwannon, and on the wall behind the chairs an array of viewscreens.

"There'll be an interpreter, a native Army sergeant, between you and Captain Travis." he said. "I don't know how good you are with native languages, Miss Shaw; the captain is not very fluent."

"Cushions for them, I see, and chairs for the lordly Terrans," she commented. "Never miss a chance to rub our superiority in, do you?"

"I never deliberately force them to adopt our ways," he replied. "Our chairs are as uncomfortable for them as their low seats are for us. Difference, you know, doesn't mean inferiority or superiority. It just means difference."

"Well, what are you trying to do, here?"

"I'm trying to find out a little more about the psychology back of these frenzies and swarmings."

"It hasn't occurred to you to look for them in the economic wrongs these people are suffering at the hands of the planters and traders, I suppose."

"So they're committing suicide, and that's all you can call these swarmings, and the fire-frenzies in the south, from economic motives," Travis said. "How does one better oneself economically by dying?"

She ignored the question, which was easier than trying to answer it.

"And why are you bothering to talk to these witch doctors? They aren't representative of the native people. They're a lot of cynical charlatans, with a vested interest in ignorance and superstition—"

"Miss Shaw, for the past eight centuries, earnest souls have been bewailing the fact that progress in the social sciences has always lagged behind progress in the physical sciences. I would suggest that the explanation might be in difference of approach. The physical scientist works *with* physical forces, even when he is trying, as in the case of contragravity, to nullify them. The social scientist works *against* social forces."

"And the result's usually a miserable failure, even on the physical-accomplishment level," Foxx Travis added. "This storm shelter project that was set up ten years ago and got nowhere, for instance. Ramón Gonzales set up a shelter project of his own seventy-five hours ago, and he's half through with it now."

"Yes, by forced labor!"

"Field surgery's brutal, too, especially when the anaesthetics run out. It's better than letting your wounded die, though."

"Well, we were talking about these shoonoon. They are a force among the natives; that can't be denied. So, since we want to influence the natives, why not use them?"

"Mr. Gilbert, these shoonoon are blocking everything we are trying to do for the natives. If you use them for propaganda work in the villages, you will only increase their prestige and make it that much harder for us to better the natives' condition, both economically and culturally—"

"That's it, Miles," Travis said. "She isn't interested in facts about specific humanoid people on Kwannon. She has a lot of high-order abstractions she got in a classroom at Adelaide on Terra."

"No. Her idea of bettering the natives' condition is to rope in a lot of young Kwanns, put them in Government schools, overload them with information they aren't prepared to digest, teach them to despise their own people, and then send them out to the villages, where they behave with such insufferable arrogance that the wonder is that so few of them stop an arrow or a charge of buckshot, instead of so many. And when that happens, as it does occasionally, Welfare says they're murdered at the instigation of the shoonoon.''

"You know, Miss Shaw, this isn't just the roughneck's scorn for the egghead," Travis said. "Miles went to school on Terra, and majored in extraterrestrial sociography, and got a master's, just like you did. At Montevideo," he added. "And he spent two more years traveling on a Paula von Schlicten Fellowship."

Edith Shaw didn't say anything. She even tried desperately not to look impressed. It occurred to him that he'd never mentioned that fellowship to Travis. Army Intelligence must have a pretty good *dossier* on him. Before anybody could say anything further, a Terran captain and a native sergeant of the First K.N.I. came in. In the screen, the four sepoys who had been fussing around straightening things picked up auto-carbines and posted themselves two on either side of a door across from the pickup, taking positions that would permit them to fire into whatever came through without hitting each other.

What came through was one hundred and eighty-four shoonoon. Some wore robes of loose gauze strips, and some wore fire-dance cloaks of red and yellow and orange ribbons. Many were almost completely naked, but they were all amulet-ed to the teeth. There must have been a couple of miles of brass and bright-alloy wire among them, and half a ton of bright scrap-metal, and the skulls, bones, claws, teeth, tails and other components of most of the native fauna. They debouched into the big room, stopped, and stood looking around them. A native sergeant and a couple more sepoys followed. They got the shoonoon over to the semicircle of cushions, having to chase a couple of them away from the single seat at front and center, and

induced them to sit down.

The native sergeant in the little room said something under his breath; the captain laughed. Edith Shaw gaped for an instant and said, *"Muggawsh!"* Travis simply remarked that he'd be damned.

"They do look kind of unusual, don't they?" Miles said. "I wouldn't doubt that this is the biggest assemblage of shoonoon in history. They aren't exactly a gregarious lot."

"Maybe this is the beginning of a new era. First meeting of the Kwannon Thaumaturgical Society."

A couple more K.N.I. Privates came in with serving-tables on contragravity floats and began passing bowls of a frozen native-food delicacy of which all Kwanns had become passionately fond since its introduction by the Terrans. He let them finish, and then, after they had been relieved of the empty bowls, he nodded to the K.N.I. sergeant, who opened a door on the left. They all went through into the room they had been seeing in the screen. There was a stir when the shoonoon saw him, and he heard his name, in its usual native mispronunciation, repeated back and forth.

"You all know me," he said, after they were seated. "Have I ever been an enemy to you or to the People?"

"No," one of them said. "He speaks for us to the other Terrans. When we are wronged, he tries to get the wrongs righted. In times of famine he has spoken of our troubles, and gifts of food have come while the Government argued about what to do."

He wished he could see Edith Shaw's face.

"There was a sickness in our village, and my magic could not cure it," another said. "Mailsh Heelbare gave me oomphel to cure it, and told me how to use it. He did this privately, so that I would not be made to look small to the people of the village."

And that had infuriated EETA; it was a question whether
unofficial help to the natives or support of the prestige of a
shoonoo had angered them more.

"His father was a trader; he gave good oomphel, and
did not cheat. Mailsh Heelbare grew up among us; he took
the Manhood Test with the boys of the village," another
oldster said. "He listened with respect to the grandfather-
stories. No, Mailsh Heelbare is not our enemy. He is our
friend."

And so I will prove myself now," he told them. "The
Government is angry with the People, but I will try to take
their anger away, and in the meantime I am permitted to
come here and talk with you. Here is a chief of soldiers,
and one of the Government people, and your words will
be heard by the oomphel machine that remembers and
repeats, for the Governor and the Great Soldier Chief."

They all brightened. To make a voice recording was a
wonderful honor. Then one of them said:

"But what good will that do now? The Last Hot Time is
here. Let us be permitted to return to our villages, where
our people need us."

"It is of that that I wish to speak. But first of all, I must
hear your words, and know what is in your minds. Who is
the eldest among you? Let him come forth and sit in the
front, where I may speak with him."

Then he relaxed while they argued in respectfully subdued voices. Finally one decrepit oldster, wearing a cloak
of yellow ribbons and carrying a highly obscene and inef-
ably sacred wooden image, was brought forward and in-
talled on the front-and-center cushion. He'd come from
some village to the west that hadn't gotten the word of the
warming; Gonzales' men had snagged him while he was
making crop-fertility magic.

Miles showed him the respect due his advanced age and

obviously great magical powers, displaying, as he did, an understanding of the regalia.

"I have indeed lived long," the old shoonoo replied. "I saw the Hot Time before; I was a child of so high." He measured about two and a half feet off the floor; that would make him ninety-five or thereabouts. "I remember it."

"Speak to us, then. Tell us of the Gone Ones, and of the Sky Fire, and of the Last Hot Time. Speak as though you alone knew these things, and as though you were teaching me."

Delighted, the oldster whooshed a couple of times to clear his outlets and began:

"In the long-ago time, there was only the Great Spirit. The Great Spirit made the World, and he made the People. In that time, there were no more People in the World then would be in one village, now. The Gone Ones dwelt among them, and spoke to them as I speak to you. Then, as more People were born, and died and went to join the Gone Ones, the Gone Ones became many, and they went away and built a place for themselves, and built the Sky Fire around it, and in the Place of the Gone Ones, at the middle of the Sky Fire, it is cool. From their place in the Sky Fire, the Gone Ones send wisdom to the people in dreams.

"The Sky Fire passes across the sky, from east to west, as the Always-Same does, but it is farther away than the Always-Same, because sometimes the Always Same passes in front of it, but the Sky Fire never passes in front of the Always-Same. None of the grandfather-stories, not even the oldest, tell of a time when this happened.

"Sometimes the Sky Fire is big and bright; that is when the Gone Ones feast and dance. Sometimes it is smaller and dimmer; then the Gone Ones rest and sleep. Some times it is close, and there is a Hot Time; sometimes it goes far away, and then there is a Cool Time.

"Now, the Last Hot Time has come. The Sky Fire will come closer and closer, and it will pass the Always Same, and then it will burn up the World. Then will be a new World, and the Gone Ones will return, and the People will be given new bodies. When this happens, the sky Fire will go out, and the Gone Ones will live in the World again with the People; the Gone Ones will make great magic and teach wisdom as I teach to you, and will no longer have to send dreams. In that time the crops will grow without planting or tending or the work of women; in that time, the game will come into the villages to be killed in the gathering-places. There will be no more of hunger and no more hard work, and no more the People will die or be slain. And that time is now here," he finished. "All the People know this."

"Tell me, Grandfather; how is this known? There have been many Hot Times before. Why should this one be the Last Hot Time?"

"The Terrans have come, and brought oomphel into the World," the old shoonoo said. "It is a sign."

"It was not prophesied beforetime. None of the People had prophesies of the coming of the Terrans. I ask you, who were the father of children and the grandfather of children's children when the Terrans came; was there any such prophesy?"

The old shoonoo was silent, turning his pornographic ikon in his hands and looked at it.

"No," he admitted, at length. "Before the Terrans came, there were no prophesies among the People of their coming. Afterward, of course, there were many such prophesies, but there were none before."

"That is strange. When a happening is a sign of something to come, it is prophesied beforetime." He left that seed of doubt alone to grow, and continued: "Now, Grandfather, speak to us about what the People believe concerning the Terrans."

"The Terrans came to the World when my eldest daughter bore her first child," the old shoonoo said. "They came in great round ships, such as come often now, but which had never before been seen. They said that they came from another world like the World of People, but so far away that even the Sky Fire could not be seen from it. They still say this, and many of the People believe it, but it is not real.

"At first, it was thought that the Terrans were great shoonoon who made powerful magic, but this is not real either. The Terrans have no magic and no wisdom of their own. All they have is the oomphel, and the oomphel works magic for them and teaches them their wisdom. Even in the schools which the Terrans have made for the People, it is the oomphel which teaches." He went on to describe, not too incorrectly, the reading-screens and viewscreens and audio-visual equipment. "Nor do the Terrans make the oomphel, as they say. The oomphel makes more oomphel for them."

"Then where did the Terrans get the first oomphel?"

"They stole it from the Gone Ones,' the old shoonoo replied. "The Gone Ones make it in their place in the middle of the Sky Fire, for themselves and to give to the People when they return. The Terrans stole it from them. For this reason, there is much hatred of the Terrans among the People. The Terrans live in the Dark Place, under the World, where the Sky Fire and the Always-Same go when they are not in the sky. It is there that the Terrans get the oomphel from the Gone Ones, and now they have come to the World, and they are using oomphel to hold back the Sky-Fire and keep it beyond the Always-Same so that the Last Hot Time will not come and the Gone Ones will not return. For this reason, too, there is much hatred of the Terrans among the People."

"Grandfather, if this were real there would be good reason for such hatred, and I would be ashamed for what my people had done and were doing. But it is not real." He had to rise and hold up his hands to quell the indignant outcry. "Have any of you known me to tell not-real things and try to make the People act as though they were real? Then trust me in this. I will show you real things, which you will all see, and I will give you great secrets, which it is now time for you to have and use for the good of the People. Even the greatest secret," he added.

There was a pause of a few seconds. Then they burst out, in a hundred and eighty-four—no, three hundred and sixty eight—voices:

"The Oomphel Secret, Mailsh Heelbare?"

He nodded slowly. "Yes. The Oomphel Secret will be given."

He leaned back and relaxed again while they were getting over the excitement. Foxx Travis looked at him apprehensively.

"Rushing things, aren't you? What are you going to tell them?"

"Oh, a big pack of lies, I suppose," Edith Shaw said scornfully.

Behind her and Travis, the native noncom interpreter was muttering something in his own language that translated roughly as: "This better be good!"

The shoonoon had quieted, now, and were waiting breathlessly.

"But if the Oomphel Secret is given, what will become

of the shoonoon?" he asked. "You, yourselves, say that we Terrans have no need for magic, because the oomphel works magic for us. This is real. If the People get the Oomphel Secret, how much need will they have for you shoonoon?"

Evidently that hadn't occurred to them before. There was a brief flurry of whispered—whooshed, rather—conversation, and then they were silent again. The eldest shoonoo said:

"We trust you, Mailsh Heelbare. You will do what is best for the People, and you will not let us be thrown out like broken pots, either."

"No, I will not," he promised. "The Oomphel Secret will be given to you shoonoon." He thought for a moment of Foxx Travis' joking remark about the Kwannon Thaumaturgical Society. "You have been jealous of one another, each keeping his own secrets," he said. "This must be put away. You will all receive the Oomphel Secret equally, for the good of all the People. You must all swear brotherhood, one with another, and later if any other shoonoo comes to you for the secret, you must swear brotherhood with him and teach it to him. Do you agree to this?"

The eldest shoonoo rose to his feet, begged leave, and then led the others to the rear of the room, where they went into a huddle. They didn't stay huddled long; inside of ten minutes they came back and took their seats.

"We are agreed, Mailsh Heelbare," the spokesman said.

Edith Shaw was impressed, more than by anything else she had seen. "Well, that was a quick decision!" she whispered.

"You have done well, Grandfathers. You will not be

thrown out by the People like broken pots; you will be greater among them than ever. I will show you how this will be.

"But first, I must speak around the Oomphel Secret." He groped briefly for a comprehensible analogy, and thought of a native vegetable, layered like an onion, with a hard kernel in the middle. "The Oomphel Secret is like a fooshkoot. There are many lesser secrets around it, each of which must be peeled off like the skins of a fooshkoot and eaten. Then you will find the nut in the middle."

"But the nut of the fooshkoot is bitter," somebody said.

He nodded, slowly and solemnly. "The nut of the fooshkoot is bitter," he agreed.

They looked at one another, disquieted by his words. Before anybody could comment, he was continuing:

"Before this secret is given, there are things to be learned. You would not understand it if I gave it to you now. You believe many not-real things which must be chased out of your minds, otherwise they would spoil your understanding."

That was verbatim what they told adolescents before giving them the Manhood Secret. Some of them huffed a little; most of them laughed. Then one called out: "Speak on, Grandfather of Grandfathers," and they all laughed. That was fine, it had been about time for teacher to crack his little joke. Now he became serious again.

"The first of these not-real things you must chase from your mind is this which you believe about the home of the Terrans. It is not real that they come from the Dark Place under the World. There is no Dark Place under the World."

Bedlam for a few seconds; that was a pretty stiff jolt. No Dark Place; who ever heard of such a thing? The eldest shoonoo rose, cradling his graven image in his arms, and the noise quieted.

"Mailsh Heelbare, if there is no Dark Place where do the Sky Fire and the Always-Same go when they are not in the sky?"

"They never leave the sky; the World is round, and there is sky everywhere around it."

They knew that, or had at least heard it, since the Terrans had come. They just couldn't believe it. It was against common sense. The oldest shoonoo said as much, and more:

"These young ones who have gone to the Terran schools have come to the villages with such tales, but who listens to them? They show disrespect for the chiefs and the elders, and even for the shoonoon. They mock at the Grandfather-stories. They say men should do women's work and women do no work at all. They break taboos, and cause trouble. They are fools."

"Am I a fool, Grandfather? Do I mock at the old stories, or show disrespect to elders and shoonoon? Yet I, Mailsh Heelbare, tell you this. The World is indeed round, and I will show you."

The shoonoo looked contemptuously at the globe. "I have seen those things," he said. "That is not the World; that is only a make-like. He held up his phalic wood-carving. "I could say that this is a make-like of the World, but that would not make it so."

"I will show you for real. We will all go in a ship." He looked at his watch. "The Sky Fire is about to set. We will follow it all around the world to the west, and come back here from the east, and the Sky Fire will still be setting when we return. If I show you that, will you believe me?"

"If you show us for real, and it is no a trick, we will have to believe you."

When they emerged from the escalators, Alpha was just touching the western horizon, and Beta was a little past zenith. The ship was moored on contragravity beside the landing stage, her gangplank run out. The shoonoon, who had gone up ahead, had all stopped short and were starting at her; then they began gabbling among themselves, overcome by the wonder of being about to board such a monster and ride on her. She was the biggest ship any of them had ever seen. Maybe a few of them had been on small freighters; many of them had never been off the ground. They didn't look or act like cynical charlatans or implacable enemies of progress and enlightenment. They were more like a lot of schoolboys whose teacher is taking them on a surprise outing.

"Bet this'll be the biggest day in their lives," Travis said.

"Oh, sure. This'll be a grandfatherstory ten generations from now."

"I can't get over the way they made up their minds, down there," Edith Shaw was saying. "Why, they just went and talked for a few minutes and came back with a decision."

They hadn't any organization, or any place to maintain on an organizational pecking-order. Nobody was obliged to attack anybody else's proposition in order to keep up his own status. He thought of the Colonial Government taking ten years not to build those storm-shelters.

Foxx Travis was commenting on the ship, now:

"I never saw that ship before; didn't know there was anything like that on the planet. Why, you could lift a whole regiment, with supplies and equipment—"

"She's been laid up for the last five years, since the heat and the native troubles stopped the tourist business here. She's the old *Hesperus*. Excursion craft. This sun-chasing trip we're going to make used to be a must for tourists here."

"I thought she was something like that, with all the

glassed observation deck forward. Who's the owner?"

"Kwannon Air Transport, Ltd. I told them what I needed her for, and they made her available and furnished officers and crew and provisions for the trip. They were working to put her in commission while we were fitting up the fourth and fifth floors, downstairs."

"You just asked for that ship, and they just let you have it?" Edith Shaw was incredulous and shocked. They wouldn't have done that for the Government.

"They want to see these native troubles stopped, too. Bad for business. You know; selfish profit-move. That's another social force it's a good idea to work with instead of against."

The shoonoon were getting aboard, now, shepherded by the K.N.I. officer and a couple of his men and some of the ship's crew. A couple of sepoys were lugging the big globe that had been brought up from below after them. Everybody assembled on the forward top observation deck, and Miles called for attention and, finally, got it. He pointed out the three viewscreens mounted below the bridge, amidships. One on the left, was tuned to a pickup on the top of the Air Terminal tower, where the Terran city, the military reservation and the spaceport met. It showed the view to the west, with Alpha on the horizon. The one on the right, from the same point, gave a view in the opposite direction, to the east. The middle screen presented a magnified view of the navigational globe on the bridge.

Viewscreens were no novelty to the shoonoon. They were a very familiar type of oomphel. He didn't even need to do more than tell them that the little spot of light on the globe would show the position of the ship. When he was sure that they understood that they could see what was happening in Bluelake while they were away, he called the

bridge and ordered Up Ship, telling the officer on duty to
hold her at five thousand feet.

The ship rose slowly, turning toward the setting M-giant.
Somebody called attention that the views in the screens
weren't changing. Somebody else said:

"Of course not. What we see for real changes because
the ship is moving. What we see in the screens is what the
oomphel on the big building sees, and it does not move.
That is for real as the oomphel sees it."

"Nice going," Edith said. "Your class has just discovered relativity." Travis was looking at the eastward viewscreen. He stepped over beside Miles and lowered his
voice.

"Trouble over there to the east of town. Big swarm of
combat contragravity working on something on the
ground. And something's on fire, too."

"I see it."

"That's where those evacuees are camped. Why in
blazes they had to bring them here to Bluelake—"

That had been EETA, too. When the solar tides had
gotten high enough to flood the coastal area, the natives
who had been evacuated from the district had been
brought here because the Native Education people
wanted them exposed to urban influences. About half of
the shoonoon who had been rounded up locally had come
in from the tide-innundated area.

"Parked right in the middle of the Terran-type food production area," Travis was continuing.

That was worrying him. Maybe he wasn't used to
planets where the biochemistry wasn't Terra-type and a
Terran would be poisoned or, at best, starve to death, on
the local food; maybe, as a soldier he knew how fragile
even the best logistics system can be. It was something to
worry about. Travis excused himself and went off in the

direction of the bridge. Going to call HQ and find out what was happening.

Excitement among the shoonoon; they had spotted the ship on which they were riding in the westward screen. They watched it until it had vanished from "sight of the seeing-oomphel," and by then were over the upland forests from whence they had been brought to Bluelake. Now and then one of them would identify his own village, and that would start more excitement.

Three infantry troop-carriers and a squadron of air cavalry were rushing past the eastward pickup in the right hand screen; another fire had started in the trouble area.

The crowd that had gathered around the globe that had been brought aboard began calling for Mailsh Heelbare to show them how they would go around the world and what countries they would pass over. Edith accompanied him and listened while he talked to them. She was bubbling with happy excitement, now. It had just dawned on her that shoonoon were fun.

None of them had ever seen the mountains along the western side of the continent except from a great distance. Now they were passing over them; the ship had to gain altitude and even then make a detour around one snow-capped peak. The whole hundred and eighty-four rushed to the starboard side to watch it as they passed. The ocean, half an hour later, started a rush forward. The score or so of them from the Tidewater knew what an ocean was, but none of them had known that there was another one to the west. Miles' view of the education program of the EETA, never bright at best, became even dimmer. *The young men who have gone to the Terran schools . . . who listens to them? They are fools.*

There were a few islands off the coast; the shoonoon

identified them on the screen globe, and on the one on deck. Some of them wanted to know why there wasn't a spot of light on this globe, too. It didn't have the oomphel inside to do that; that was a satisfactory explanation. Edith started to explain about the orbital beacon-stations ox-planet and the radio beams, and then stopped.

"I'm sorry; I'm not supposed to say anything to them," she apologized.

"Oh, that's all right. I wouldn't go into all that, though. We don't want to overload them."

She asked permission, a little later, to explain why the triangle tip of the arctic continent, which had begun to edge into sight on the screen globe, couldn't be seen from the ship. When he told her to go ahead, she got a platinum half-sol piece from her purse, held it on the globe from the classroom and explained about the curvature and told them they could see nothing farther away than the circle the coin covered. It was beginning to look as though the psychological-warfare experiment might show another, unexpected, success.

There was nothing, after the islands passed, but a lot of empty water. The shoonoon were getting hungry, but they refused to go below to eat. They were afraid they might miss something. So their dinner was brought up on deck for them. Miles and Travis and Edith went to the officers' dining room back of the bridge. Edith, by now, was even more excited than the shoonoon.

"They're so anxious to learn"' She was having trouble adjusting to that; that was dead against EETA doctrine. "But why wouldn't they listen to the teachers we sent to the villages?"

"You heard old Shatresh—the fellow with the porno-graphic sculpture and the yellow robe. These young twerps act like fools, and sensible people don't pay any

attention to fools. What's more, they've been sent out in-
doctrinated with the idea that shoonoon are a lot of lying
old fakes, and the shoonoon resent that. You know,
they're not lying old fakes. Within their limitations, they
are honest and ethical professional people."

"Oh, come, now! I know, I think they're sort of wonderful, but let's don't give them too much credit."

"I'm not. You're doing that."

"*Huh?*" She looked at him in amazement. "Me?"

"Yes, you. You know better than to believe in magic, so
you expect them to know better, too. Well, they don't.
You know that under the macroscopic world-of-the senses
there exists a complex of biological, chemical and physical
phenomena down to the subnucleonic level. They realize
that there must be something beyond what they can see
and handle, but they think it's magic. Well, as a race, so
did we until only a few centuries pre-atomic. These people
are still lower Neolithic, a hunting people who have just
learned agriculture. Where we were twenty thousand
years ago.

"You think any glib-talking Kwann can hang a lot of
rags, bones and old iron onto himself, go through some
impromptu mummery, and set up as shoonoo? Well, he
can't. The shoonoon are a hereditary caste. A shoonoo
father will begin teaching his son as soon as he can walk
and talk, and he keeps on teaching him till he's the age-
equivalent of a graduate M.D. or a science Ph. D."

"Well, what all is there to learn—?"

"The theoretical basis and practical applications of sym-
pathetic magic. Action-at-a-distance by one object upon
another. Homeopathic magic: the principle that things
which resemble one another will interact. For instance,
there's an animal the natives call a shynph. It has an ex-
crescence of horn on its brow like an arrowhead, and it

arches its back like a bow when it jumps. Therefore, a shynph is equal to a bow and arrow, and for that reason the Kwanns made their bowstrings out of shynph-gut. Now they use tensilon because it won't break as easily or get wet and stretch. So they have to turn the tensilon into shynph-gut. They used to do that by drawing a picture of a shynph on the spool, and then the traders began labeling the spools with pictures of shynph. I think my father was one of the first to do that.

"Then, there's contagious magic. Anything that's been part of anything else or come in contact with it will interact permanently with it. I wish I had a sol for every time I've seen a Kwann pull the wad out of a shot-shell, pick up a pinch of dirt from the footprint of some animal he's tracking, put it in among the buckshot, and then crimp the wad in again.

"Everything a Kwann does has some sort of magical implications. It's the shoonoo's business to know all this; to be able to tell just what magical influences have to be produced, and what influences must be avoided. And there are circumstances in which magic simply will not work, even in theory. The reason is that there is some powerful counter-influence at work. He has to know when he can't use magic, and he has to be able to explain why. And when he's theoretically able to do something by magic, he has to have a plausible explanation why it won't produce results—just as any highly civilized and ethical Terran M.D. has to be able to explain his failures to the satisfaction of his late patient's relatives. Only a shoonoo doesn't get sued for malpractice; he gets a spear stuck in him. Under those circumstances, a caste of hereditary magicians is literally bred for quick thinking. These old gaffers we have aboard are the intellectual top crust among the natives. Any of them can think rings around your Government school products. As for preying on the ignorance and credulity of the other natives, they're only infinitesmally less ignorant and credulous themselves. But they want to learn—from anybody who can gain their respect by respecting them."

Edith Shaw didn't say anything in reply. She was thoughtful during the rest of the meal, and when they were back on the observation deck he noticed that she seemed to be looking at the shoonoon with new eyes.

In the screen-views of Bluelake, Beta had already set, and the sky was fading; stars had begun to twinkle. There were more fires—one, close to the city in the east, a regular conflagration—and fighting had broken out in the native city itself. He was wishing now, that he hadn't thought it necessary to use those screens. The shoonoon were noticing what was going on in them, and talking among themselves. Travis, after one look at the situation, hurried back to the bridge to make a screen-call. After a while, he returned, almost crackling with suppressed excitement.

"Well, it's finally happened! Maith's forced Kovac to declare martial rule!" he said in an exultant undertone.

"Forced him?" Edith was puzzled. "The Army can't force the Civil Government—"

"He threatened to do it himself. Intervene and suspend civil rule."

"But I thought only the Navy could do that."

"Any planetary commander of Armed Forces can, in a state of extreme emergency. I think you'll both agree that this emergency is about as extreme as they come. Kovac knew that Maith was unwilling to do it—he'd have to stand court-martial to justify his action—but he also knew that a governor general who has his Colony taken away from him by the Armed Forces never gets it back; he's finished. So it was just a case of the weaker man in the weaker position yielding."

"Where does this put us?"

"We are a civilian scientific project. You are under orders of General Maith. I am under your orders. I don't know about Edith."

"Can I draft her, or do I have to get you to get General Maith to do it?"

"Listen, don't do that," Edith protested. "I still have to work for Government House, and this martial rule won't last forever. They'll all be prejudiced against me—"

"You can shove your Government job on the air lock," Miles told her. "You'll have a better one with Planetwide News, at half again as much pay. And after the shakeup at Government House, about a year from now, you may be going back as director of EETA. When they find out on Terra just how badly this Government has been mismanaging things there'll be a lot of vacancies."

The shoonoon had been watching the fighting in the viewscreens. Then somebody noticed that the spot of light on the navigational globe was approaching a coastline, and they all rushed forward for a look.

Travis and Edith slept for a while; when they returned to relieve him, Alpha was rising to the east of Bluelake, and the fighting in the city was still going on. The shoonoon were still wakeful and interested; Kwanns could go without sleep for much longer periods than Terrans. The lack of any fixed cycle of daylight and darkness on their planet had left them unconditioned to any regular sleeping-and-walking rhythm.

"I just called in," Travis said. "Things aren't good, at all. Most of the natives in the evacuee cantonments have gotten into the native city, now, and they've gotten hold of a lot of firearms somehow. And they're getting nasty in the west, beyond where Gonzales is occupying, and in the northeast, and we only have about half enough troops to cope with everything. The general wants to know how your're making out with the shoonoon."

"I'll call him before I get in the sack."

He went up on the bridge and made the call. General Maith looked as sleepy as he felt; they both yawned as they greeted each other. There wasn't much he could tell the general, and it sounded like the glib reassurances one gets from a hospital about a friend's condition.

"We'll check in with you as soon as we get back and get our shoonoon put away. We understand what's motivating these frenzies, now, and in about twenty-five to thirty hours we'll be able to start doing something about it.

The general, in the screen, grimaced.

"That's a long time, Mr. Gilbert. Longer than we can afford to take, I'm afraid. You're not cruising at full speed now, are you?"

"Oh, no, general. We're just trying to keep Alpha level on the horizon." He thought for a moment. "We don't need to keep down to that. It may make an even bigger impression if we speed up."

He went back to the observation deck, picked up the PA-phone, and called for attention.

"You have seen, now, that we can travel around the world, so fast that we keep up with the Sky Fire and it is not seen to set. Now we will travel even faster, and I will show you a new wonder. I will show you a new wonder. I will show you the Sky Fire rising in the west; it and the Always-Same will seem to go backward in the sky. This will not be for real; it will only be seen so because we will be traveling faster. Watch, now, and see." He called the bridge for full speed, and then told them to look at the Sky-Fire and then see in the screens where it stood over Bluelake.

That was even better; now they were racing with the Sky-Fire and catching up to it. After half an hour he left them still excited and whooping gleefully over the steady gain. Five hours later, when he came back after a nap and a hasty breakfast, they were still whooping. Edith Shaw was excited, too; the shoonoon were trying to estimate how soon they would be back to Bluelake by comparing the position of the Sky Fire with its position in the screen.

General Maith received them in his private office at Army HQ; Foxx Travis mixed drinks for the four of then while the general checked the microphones to make sure they had privacy.

"I blame myself for not having forced martial rule on them hundreds of hours ago," he said. "I have three brigades; the one General Gonzales had here originally, and the two I brought with me when I took over here. We have to keep at least half a brigade in the south, to keep the tribes there from starting any more forest fires. I can't hold Bluelake with anything less than half a brigade. Gonzales has his hands full in his area. He had a nasty business while you were off on that world cruise—natives in one village caught the men stationed there off guard and wiped them out, and then started another frenzy. It spread to two other villages before he got it stopped. And we need the Third Brigade in the northeast; there are three quarters of a million natives up there, inhabiting close to a million square miles. And if anything really breaks loose here, and what's been going on in the last few days is nothing even approaching what a real outbreak could be like, we'll have to pull in troops from everywhere. We must save the Terran-type crops and the carniculture plants. If we don't, we all starve."

Miles nodded. There wasn't anything he could think of saying to that.

"How soon can you begin to show results with those shoonoon, Mr. Gilbert?" the general asked. "You said from twenty-five to thirty hours. Can you cut that any? In twenty-five hours, all hell could be loose all over the continent."

Miles shook his head. "So far, I haven't accomplished anything positive," he said. "All I did with this trip around the world was convince them that I was telling the truth when I told them there was no Dark Place under the World, where Alpha and Beta go at night." He hastened, as the general began swearing, to add: "I know, that doesn't sound like much. But it was necessary. I have to convince them that there will be no Last Hot Time, and then—"

The shoonoon, on their drumshaped cushions, stared at him in silence, aghast. All the happiness over the wonderful trip in the ship, when they had chased the Sky Fire around the World and caught it over Bluelake, and even their pleasure in the frozen delicacies they had just eaten, was gone.

"No—Last—Hot—Time?"

"Mailsh Heelbare, this is not real! It cannot be"

"The Gone Ones—"

"The Always-Cool Time, when there will be no more hunger or hard work or death; it cannot be real that this will never come!"

He rose, holding up his hands; his action stopped the clamor.

"Why should the Gone Ones want to return to this poor world that they have gladly left?" he asked. "Have they not a better place in the middle of the Sky Fire, where it is always cool? And why should you want them to come back to this world? Will not each one of you pass, sooner or later, to the middle of the Sky Fire; will you not there be given new bodies and join the Gone Ones? There is the Always-Cool; there the crops grow without planting and without the work of women; there the game come into the villages to be killed in the gathering-places, without hunting. There you will talk with the other Gone Ones, your fathers and your fathers' fathers, as I talk with you. Why do you think this must come to the World of People? Can you not wait to join the Gone Ones in the Sky Fire?"

Then he sat down and folded his arms. They were looking at him in amazement; evidently they all saw the logic, but none of them had ever thought of it before. Now they would have to turn it over in their minds and accustom themselves to the new viewpoint. They began whooshing among themselves. At length, old Shatresh, who had seen the Hot Time before, spoke:

"Mailsh Heelbare, we trust you," he said. "You have told us of wonders, and you have shown us that they were real. But do you know this for real?"

"Do you tell me that you do not?" he demanded in surprise. "You have had fathers, and fathers' fathers. They have gone to join the Gone Ones. Why should you not, also? And why should the Gone Ones come back and destroy the World of People? Then your chilren will have no more children, and your children's children will never be. It is in the World of People that the People are born; it is in the World that they grow and gain wisdom to fit themselves to live in the Place of the Gone Ones when they are through with the bodies they use in the World. You should be happy that there will be no Last Hot Time, and that the line of your begettings will go on and not be cut short."

There were murmurs of agreement with this. Most of

them were beginning to be relieved that there wouldn't be a Last Hot Time, after all. Then one of the class asked:

"Do the Terrans also go to the Place of the Gone Ones, or have they a place of their own?"

He was silent for a long time, looking down at the floor. Then he raised his head.

"I had hoped that I would not have to speak of this," he said. "But, since you have asked, it is right that I should tell you." He hesitated again, until the Kwannos in front of him had begun to fidget. Then he asked old Shatresh: "Speak of the beliefs of the People about how the World was made."

"The great Spirit made the world." He held up his carven obscenity. "He made the World out of himself. This is a makelike to show it."

"The Great Spirit made many worlds. The stars which you see in dark-time are all worlds, each with many smaller worlds around it. The Great Spirit made them all at one time, and made people on many of them. The Great Spirit made the World of People, and made the Always-Same and the Sky Fire, and inside the Sky Fire he made the Place of the Gone Ones. And when he made the Place of the Gone Ones, he put an Oomphel-Mother inside it, to bring forth oomphel."

This created a brief sensation. An Oomphel-Mother was something they had never thought of before, but now they were wondering why they hadn't. Of course there'd be an Oomphel-Mother; how else would there be oomphel?

"The World of the Terrans is far away from the World of People, as we have always told you. When the Great Spirit made it He gave it only an Always-Same, and no Sky Fire. Since there was no Sky Fire, there was no place to put a Place of the Gone Ones, so the Great Spirit made the Terrans so that they would not die, but live forever in

their own bodies. The Oomphel-Mother for the World of
the Terrans the Great Spirit hid in a cave under a great
mountain.

"The Terrans whom the Great Spirit made lived for a
long time, and then, one day, a man and a woman found
a crack in a rock, and went inside, and they found the cave
of the Oomphel-Mother, and the Oomphel-Mother in it.
So they called all the other Terrans, and they brought the
Oomphel-Mother out, and the Oomphel-Mother began to
bring forth Oomphel. The Oomphel-Mother brought forth
metal, and cloth, and glass, and plastic; knives, and axes
and guns and clothing—" He went on, cataloguing the
products of human technology, the shoonoon staring
more and more wide-eyed at him. "And oomphel to make
oomphel, and oomphel to teach wisdom," he finished.
"They became very wise and very rich.

"Then the Great Spirit saw what the Terrans had done,
and became angry, for it was not meant for the Terrans to
do this, and the Great Spirit cursed the Terrans with a
curse of death. It was not death as you know it. Because
the Terrans had sinned by laying hands on the Oomphel-
Mother, not only their bodies must die, but their spirits
also. A Terran has a short life in the body, after that no
life.

"This, then, is the Oomphel Secret. The last skin of the
fooshkoot has been peeled away; behold the bitter nut,
upon which we Terrans have chewed for more time than
anybody can count. Happy people! When you die or are
slain, you go to the Place of the Gone Ones, to join your
fathers and your fathers' fathers and to await your childen
and children's children. When we die or are slain, that is
the end of us."

"But you have brought your oomphel into this world;
have you not brought the curse with it?" somebody asked,

frightened.

"No. The People did not sin against the Great Spirit; they have not laid hands on an Oomphel-Mother as we did. The oomphel we bring you will do no harm; do you think we would be so wicked as to bring the curse upon you? It will be good for you to learn about oomphel here; in your Place of the Gones One there is much oomphel."

"Why did your people come to this world, Mailsh Heelbare?" old Shatresh asked. "Was it to try to hide from the curse?"

"There is no hiding from the curse of the Great Spirit, but we Terrans are not a people who submit without strife to any fate. From the time of the Curse of Death on, we have been trying to make spirits for ourselves."

"But how can you do that?"

"We do not know. The oomphel will not teach us that, though it teaches everything else. We have only learned many ways in which it cannot be done. It cannot be done with oomphel, or with anything that is in our own world. But the Oomphel-Mother made us ships to go to otherworlds, and we have gone to many of them, this one among them, seeking things from which we try to make spirits. We are trying to make spirits for ourselves from the crystals that grow in the Klooba plants; we may fail with them, too. But I say this; I may die, and all the other Terrans now living may die, and be as though they had never been, but someday we will not fail. Someday our children, or our children's children, will make spirits for themselves and live forever, as you do."

"Why were we not told this before, Mailsh Heelbare?"

"We were ashamed to have you know it. We are ashamed to be people without spirits."

"Can we help you and your people? Maybe our magic might help."

"It well might. It would be worth trying. But first, you must help yourselves. You and your people are sinning against the Great Spirit as grievously as did the Terrans of old. Bewarned in time, lest you answer it as grievously."

"What do you mean, Mailsh Heelbare?" Old Shatresh was frightened.

"You are making magic to bring the Sky Fire to the World. Do you know what will happen? The World of People will pass whole into the place of the Gone Ones, and both will be destroyed. The World of People is a world of death; everything that lives on it must die. The Place of the Gone Ones is a world of life; everything in it lives forever. The two will strive against each other, and will destroy one another, and there will be nothing in the Sky Fire or the World but fire. This is wisdom which our oomphel teaches us. We know this secret, and with it we make weapons of great destruction." He looked over the seated shoonoon, picking out those who wore the flamecolored cloaks of the fire-dance. "You—and you—and you," he said. "You have been making this dreadful magic, and leading your people in it. And which among the rest of you have not been guilty?"

"We did not know," one of them said. "Mailsh Heelbare, have we yet time to keep this from happening?"

"Yes. There is only a little time, but there is time. You have until the Always-Same passes across the face of the Sky-Fire." That would be seven hundred and fifty hours. "If this happens, all is safe. If the Sky Fire blots out the Always Same, we are all lost together. You must go among your people and tell them what madness they are doing, and command them to stop. You must command them to lay down their arms and cease fighting. And you must tell them of the awful curse that was put upon the Terrans in the long-ago time, for a lesser sin than they are now committing."

"If we say that Mailsh Heelbare told us this, the people may not believe us. He is not known to all, and some would take no Terran's word, not even his."

"Would anybody tell a secret of this sort, about his own people, if it were not real?"

"We had better say nothing about Mailsh Heelbare. We will say that the Gone Ones told us in dreams."

"Let us say that the Great Spirit sent a dream of warning to each of us," another shoonoo said. "There has been too much talk about dreams from the Gone Ones already."

"But the Great Spirit has never sent a dream—"

""Nothing like this has ever happened before, either."

He rose, and they were silent. "Go to your living-place, now," he told them. "Talk of how best you may warn your people." He pointed to the clock. "You have an oomphel like that in your living-place; when the shorter spear has moved three places, I will speak with you again, and then you will be sent in air cars to your people to speak to them."

They went up the escalator and down the hall to Miles' office on the third floor without talking. Foxx Travis was singing softly, almost inaudibly:

"You will eeeat . . . in the sweeet . . . bye-and-bye,

You'll get oooom . . . phel in the sky . . . when you die!"

Inside, Edith Shaw slumped dispiritedly in a chair. Foxx Travis went to the coffee-maker and started it. Miles snapped on the communication screen and punched the combination of General Maith's headquarters. As soon as the uniformed girl who appeared in it saw him, her hands moved quickly; the screen flickered, and the general appeared in it.

"We have it made, general. They're sold; we're ready to start them out in three hours."

Maith's thin, weary face suddenly lighted. "You mean they are going to co-operate?"

He shook his head. "They think they're saving the world; they think we're co-operating with them."

The general laughed. "That's even better! How do you want them sent out?"

"The ones in the Bluelake area first. Better have some picked K.N.I. in native costume, with pistols, to go with them. They'll need protection, till they're able to get a hearing for themselves. After they're all out, the ones from Gonzales' area can be started." He thought for a moment. "I'll want four or five of them left here to help me when you start bringing more shoonoon in from other areas. How soon do you think you'll have another class for me?"

"Two or three days, if everything goes all right. We have the villages and plantations in the south under pretty tight control now; we can start gathering them up right away. As soon as we get things stabilized here, we can send reinforcements to the north. We'll have transport for you in three hours."

The general blanked out. He turned from the screen. Travis was laughing happily.

"Miles, did anybody ever tell you you were a genius?" he asked. "That last jolt you gave them was perfect. Why didn't you tell us about it in advance?"

"I didn't know about it in advance; I didn't think of it till I'd started talking to them. No cream or sugar for me."

"Cream," Edith said, lifelessly. "Why did you do it? Why didn't you just tell them the truth?"

Travis asked her to define the term. She started to say something bitter about Jesting Pilate. Miles interrupted.

"In spite of Lord Beacon, Pilate wasn't jesting," he said.

"And he didn't stay for an answer because he knew he'd die of old age waiting for one. What kind of truth should I have told them?"

"Why, what you started to tell them. That Beta moves in a fixed orbit and can't get any closer to Alpha—"

"There's been some work done on the question since Pilate's time," Travis said. "My semantics prof at Command College had the start of an answer. He defined truth as a statement having a practical correspondence with reality on the physical levels of structure and observation and the verbal order of abstraction under consideration."

"He defined truth as a statement. A statement exists only in the mind of the person making it, and the mind of the person to whom it is made. If the person to whom it is made can't understand or accept it, it isn't the truth."

"They understood when you showed them that the planet is round, and they understood that tri-dimensional model of the system. Why didn't you let it go at that?"

"They accepted it intellectually. But when I told them that there wasn't any chance of Kwannon getting any closer to Alpha, they rebelled emotionally. It doesn't matter how conclusively you prove anything, if the person to whom you prove it can't accept your proof emotionally, it's still false. Not-real."

"They had all their emotional capital invested in this Always-Cool Time," Travis told her. "They couldn't let Miles wipe that out for them. So he shifted it from this world to the next, and convinced them that they were getting a better deal that way. You saw how quickly they picked it up. And he didn't have the sin of telling children there is no Easter Bunny on his conscience, either."

"But why did you tell them that story about the Oomphel Mother?" she insisted. "Now they'll go out and tell all the other natives, and they'll believe it."

"Would they have believed it if I'd told them about Terran scientific technology? Your people have been doing that for close to half a century. You see what impression it's made."

"But you told them—You told them that Terrans have no souls!"

"Can you prove that was a lie?" Travis asked. "Let's see yours. Draw—soul! Inspection—soul"

Naturally, Foxx Travis would expect a soul to be carried in a holster.

"But they'll look down on us, now. They'll say we're just like animals," Edith almost wailed.

"Now it comes out," Travis said. "We won't be the lordly Terrans, any more, helping the poor benighted Kwanns out of the goodness of our hearts, scattering largess, bearing the Terran's Burden—new model, a give away instead of a gun. Now *they'll* pity *us*; they'll think *we're* inferior beings."

"I don't think the natives are inferior beings!" She was almost in tears.

"If you don't, why did you come all the way to Kwannon to try to make them more like Terrans?"

"Knock it off, Foxx; stop heckling her." Travis looked faintly surprised. Maybe he hadn't realized, before, that a boss newsman learns to talk like a commanding officer. "You remember what Ramón Gonzales was saying, out at Sanders', about the inferior's hatred for the superior as superior? It's no wonder these Kwanns resent us. They have a right to; we've done them all an unforgivable injury. We've let them see us doing things they can't do. Of course they resent us. But now I've given them something to feel superior about. When they die, they'll go to the Place of the Gone Ones, and have oomphel in the sky, and they will live forever in new bodies, but when we die, we just die, period. So they'll pity us and politely try to hide their condescension toward us.

"And because they feel superior to us, they'll want to help us. They'll work hard on the plantations, so that we can have plenty of biocrystals, and their shoonoon will work magic for us, to help us poor benighted Terrans to grow souls for ourselves, so that we can almost be like them. Of course, they'll have a chance to exploit us, and get oomphel from us, too, but the important thing will be to help the poor Terrans. Maybe they'll even organize a Spiritual and Magical Assistance Agency."

Introduction to "Graveyard of Dreams"

When I first heard of this particular story, Bill Tuning and several other people told me, don't bother it's just the short version of COSMIC COMPUTER. But I traced down a copy anyway; for one, as a collector I'm a completist, and for another, "Graveyard of Dreams" occupies a very interesting place in the Piper cannon. It and COSMIC COMPUTER are the last two tales of the Terran Federation. And what if it contained some vital piece of information not in the novel . . . afterall, there are some very fundamental differences between the novel version and serial version of ULLER UPRISING.

So I went down to Collector's Bookstore in Hollywood; if its an old pulp or movie poster you're looking for nine times out of ten they have it—if you can pay the price. The moment I got home I began to read . . . and eureka! Not only does Conn Maxwell, the young hero, end up with a different girl—Lynne Fawzi instead of Sylvie Jacquemont—but there is a gold mine of new information about the System States Alliance, the economic alliance that threatened the stability of the Federation.

Between "Graveyard of Dreams" and Space Viking, the next TerroHuman Future History story, there is a gap of some seven hundred to eight hundred years.

At the end of COSMIC COMPUTER we are left with the feeling that with the help of Merlin mankind might, if not change, avert this coming Age of Darkness. But in Space Viking, written either just before or just after Cosmic Computer, there is no mention of either Conn Maxwell's world Poitesme or Merlin; instead we have a galaxy of Space Vikings and Neo-barbarians . . . Someday we might discover a missing story that bridges these two novels, but until we do COSMIC COMPUTER and "Graveyard of Dreams" will stand as Piper's last statement on the grand Terran Federation.

172

Graveyard of Dreams

Standing at the armorglass front of the observation deck and watching the mountains rise and grow on the horizon, Conn Maxwell gripped the metal hand-rail with painful intensity, as though trying to hold back the airship by force. Thirty minutes—twenty-six and a fraction of the Terran minutes he had become accustomed to—until he'd have to face it.

Then, realizing that he never, in his own thoughts, addressed himself as "sir," he turned.

"I beg your pardon?"

It was the first officer, wearing a Terran Federation Space Navy uniform of forty years, or about ten regulation-changes, ago. That was the sort of thing he had taken for granted before he had gone away. Now he was noticing it everywhere.

"Thirty minutes out of Litchfield, sir," the ship's officer repeated. "You'll go off by the midship gangway on the starboard side."

"Yes, I know. Thank you."

The first mate held out the clipboard he was carrying. "Would you mind checking over this, Mr. Maxwell? Your baggage list."

"Certainly." He glanced at the slip of paper. Valises, eighteen and twenty-five kilos, two; trunks, seventy-five and seventy kilos, two; microbook case, one-fifty kilos, one. The last item fanned up a little flicker of anger in him, not at any person, even himself, but at the situation in which he found himself and the futility of the whole thing.

"Yes, that's everything. I have no hand-luggage, just this stuff."

He noticed that this was the only baggage list under the clip; the other papers were all freight and express manifests. "Not many passengers left aboard, are there?"

"You're the only one in firstclass, sir," the mate replied. "About forty farm-laborers on the lower deck. Everybody else got off at the other stops. Litchfield's the end of the run. You know anything about the place?"

"I was born there. I've been away at school for the last five years."

"On Baldur?"

"Terra. University of Montevideo." Once Conn would have said it almost boastfully.

The mate gave him a quick look of surprised respect, then grinned and nodded. "Of course; I should have known. You're Rodney Maxwell's son, aren't you? Your father's one of our regular freight shippers. Been sending out a lot of stuff lately." He looked as though he would have liked to continue the conversation, but said: "Sorry, I've got to go. Lot of things to attend to before landing." He touched the visor of his cap and turned away.

The mountains were closer when Conn looked forward again, and he glanced down. Five years and two space voyages ago, seen from the afterdeck of this ship or one of her sisters, the woods had been green with new foliage, and the wine-melon fields had been in pink blossom. He tried to picture the scene sliding away below instead of drawing in toward him, as though to force himself back to a moment of the irretrievable past.

But the moment was gone, and with it the eager excitement and the half-formed anticipations of the things he would learn and accomplish on Terra. The things he would learn—microbook case, one-fifty kilos, one. One of the steel trunks was full of things he had learned and accomplished, too. Maybe *they*, at least, had some value . . .

The woods were autumn-tinted now and the fields were bare and brown.

They had gotten the crop in early this year, for the fields had all been harvested. Those workers below must be going out for the wine-pressing. That extra hands were needed for that meant a big crop, and yet it seemed that less land was under cultivation than when he had gone away. He could see squares of low brush among the new forests that had grown up in the last forty years, and the few stands of original timber looked like hills above the second growth. Those trees had been standing when the planet had been colonized.

That had been two hundred years ago, at the middle of the Seventh Century, Atomic Era. The name of the planet—Poictesme—told that: the Surromanticist Movement, when the critics and professors were rediscovering James Branch Cabell. Funny how much was coming back to him now—things he had picked up from the minimal liberal-arts and general-humanities courses he had taken and then forgotten in his absorption with the science and tech studies.

The first extrasolar planets, as they had been discovered, had been named from Norse mythology—Odin and Baldur and Thor, Uller and Freya, Bifrost and Asgard and Niflheim. When the Norse names ran out, the discoverers had turned to other mythologies, Celtic and Egyptian and Hindu and Assyrian, and by the middle of the Seventh Century they were naming planets for almost anything.

Anything, that is, but actual persons; their names were reserved for stars. Like Alpha Gartner, the sun of Poictesme, and Beta Gartner, a buckshot-sized pink glow in the southeast, and Gamma Gartner, out of sight on the other side of the world, all named for old Genji Gartner, the scholarly and half-piratical adventurer whose ship had been the first to approach the three stars and discover that each of them had planets.

Forty-two planets in all, from a couple of methane-giants on Gamma to airless little things with one-sixth Terran gravity. Alpha II had been the only one in the Trisystem with an oxygen atmosphere and life. So Gartner had landed on it, and named it Poictesme, and the settlement that had grown up around the first landing site had been called Storisende. Thirty years later, Genji Gartner died there, after seeing the camp grow to a metropolis, and was buried under a massive monument.

Some of the other planets had been rich in metals, and mines had been opened, and atmosphere-domed factories and processing plants built. None of them could produce anything but hydroponic and tissue-culture foodstuffs, and natural foods from Poictesme had been less expensive, even on the planets of Gamma and Beta. So Poictesme had concentrated on agriculture and grown wealthy at it.

Then, within fifty years of Genji Gartner's death, the economics of interstellar trade overtook the Trisystem and the mines and factories closed down. It was no longer possible to ship the output to a profitable market, in the face of the growing self-sufficiency of the colonial planets and the irreducibly high cost of space-freighting.

Below, the brown fields and the red and yellow woods were merging into a ten-mile-square desert of crumbling concrete—empty and roofless sheds and warehouses and barracks, brush-choked parade grounds and landing fields, airship docks, and even a spaceport. They were more recent, dating from Poictesme's second brief and hectic prosperity, when the Terran Federation's Third Fleet-Army Force had occupied the Gartner Trisystem during the System States War.

Millions of troops had been stationed on or routed through Poictesme; tens of thousands of spacecraft had been based on the Trisystem; the mines and factories had reopened for war production. The Federation had spent trillions of sols on Poictesme, piled up mountains of stores and arms and equipment, left the face of the planet cluttered with installations.

Then, ten years before anybody had expected it, the rebellious System States Alliance had collapsed and the war had ended. The Federation armies had gone home, taking with them the clothes they stood in, their personal weapons and a few souvenirs. Everything else had been left behind; even the most expensive equipment was worth less than the cost of removal.

Ever since, Poictesme had been living on salvage. The uniform the first officer was wearing was forty years old—and it was barely a month out of the original packing. On Terra, Conn had told his friends that his father was a prospector and let them interpret that as meaning an explorer for, say, uranium deposits. Rodney Maxwell found plenty of uranium, but he got it by taking apart the warheads of missiles.

The old replacement depot or classification center or training area or whatever it had been had vanished under the ship now and it was all forest back to the mountains, with an occasional cluster of deserted buildings. From one or two, threads of blue smoke rose—bands of farm tramps, camping on their way from harvest to wine-pressing. Then the eastern foothills were out of sight and he was looking down on the granite spines of the Calder Range; the valley beyond was sloping away and widening out in the distance, and it was time he began thinking of what to say when he landed. He would have to tell them, of course.

He wondered who would be at the dock to meet him, besides his family. Lynne Fawzi, he hoped. Or did he? Her parents would be with her, and Kurt Fawzi would rake the news hardest of any of them, and be the first to blame him because it was bad. The hopes he had built for Lynne and himself would have to be held in abeyance till he saw how her father would regard him now.

But however any of them took it, he would have to tell them the truth.

The ship swept on, tearing through the thin puffs of cloud at ten miles a minute. Six minutes to landing. Five. Four. Then he saw the river bend, glinting redly through the haze in the sunlight; Litchfield was inside it, and he stared waiting for the first glimpse of the city. Three minutes, and the ship began to cut speed and lose altitude. The hot-jets had stopped firing and he could hear the whine of the cold-jet rotors.

Then he could see Litchfield, dominated by the Airport Building, so thick that it looked squat for all its height, like a candlestump in a puddle of its own grease, the other buildings under their carapace of terraces and landing stages seeming to have flowed away from it. And there was the yellow block of the distilleries, and High Garden Terrace, and the Mall . . .

At first, in the distance, it looked like a living city. Then, second by second, the stigmata of decay became more and more evident. Terraces empty or littered with rubbish; gardens untended and choked with wild growth; windows staring blindly; walls splotched with lichens and grimy where the rains could not wash them.

For a moment, he was afraid that some disaster, un-mentioned in the father's letters, had befallen. Then he realized that the change had not been in Litchfield but in himself. After five years, he was seeing it as it really was. He wondered how his family and his friends would look to him now. Or Lynne.

The ship was coming in over the Mall; he could see the cracked paving sprouting grass, the statutes askew on their pedestals, the waterless fountains. He thought for an in-stant that one of them was playing, and then he saw that what he had taken for spray was dust blowing from the empty basin. There was something about dusty fountains, something he had learned at the University. Oh, yes. One of the Second Century Martian Colonial poets, Eirrarsson, or somebody like that:

The fountains are dusty in the Graveyard of Dreams;
The hinges are rusty and swing with tiny screams.

There was more to it, but he couldn't remember; some-thing about empty gardens under an empty sky. There must have been colonies inside the Sol System, before the Interstellar Era, that hadn't turned out any better than Poictesme. Then he stopped trying to remember as the ship turned toward the Airport Building and a couple of tugs—Terran Federation contragravity tanks, with derrick-booms behind and push-poles where the guns had been—came up to bring her down.

He walked along the starboard promenade to the gang-way, which the first mate and a couple of airmen were getting open.

Most of the population of top-level Litchfield was in the crowd on the dock. He recognized old Colonel Zareff, with his white hair and plum-brown skin, and Tom Brangwyn, the town marshal, red-faced and bulking above the others. It took a few seconds for him to pick out his father and mother, and his sister Flora, and then to realize that the handsome young man beside Flora was his brother Charley. Charley had been thirteen when Conn had gone away. And there was Kurt Fawzi, the mayor of Litchfield, and there was Lynne, beside him, her red-lipped face tilted upward with a cloud of bright hair behind it.

He waved to her, and she waved back, jumping in excitement, and then everybody was waving, and they were pushing his family to the front and making way for them.

The ship touched down lightly and gave a lurch as she went off contragravity, and they got the gangway open and the steps swung out, and he started down toward the people who had gathered to greet him.

His father was wearing the same black best-suit he had worn when they had parted five years ago. It had been new then; now it was shabby and had acquired a permanent wrinkle across the right hip, over the pistol-butt. Charley was carrying a gun, too; the belt and holster looked as though he had made them himself. His mother's dress was new and so was Flora's—probably made for the occasion. He couldn't be sure just which of the Terran Federation services had provided the material, but Charley's shirt was Medical Service sterilon.

Ashamed that he was noticing and thinking of such things at a time like this, he clasped his father's hand and kissed his mother and Flora. Everybody was talking at once, saying things that he heard only as happy sounds. His brother's words were the first that penetrated as words.

"You didn't know me," Charley was accusing. "Don't deny it; I saw you standing there wondering if I was Flora's new boy friend or what."

"Well, how in Niflheim'd you expect me to? You've grown up since the last time I saw you. You're looking great, kid!" He caught the gleam of Lynne's golden hair beyond Charley's shoulder and pushed him gently aside. "Lynne!"

"Conn, you look just wonderful!" Her arms were around his neck and she was kissing him. "Am I still your girl, Conn?"

He crushed her against him and returned her kisses, assuring her that she was. He wasn't going to let it make a bit of difference how her father took the news—if she didn't.

She babbled on: "You didn't get mixed up with any of those girls on Terra, did you? If you did, don't tell me about it. All I care about is that you're back. Oh, Conn, you don't know how much I missed you . . . Mother, Dad, doesn't he look just splendid?"

Kurt Fawzi, a little thinner, his face more wrinkled, his hair grayer, shook his hand.

"I'm just as glad to see you as anybody, Conn," he said, "even if I'm not being as demonstrative about it as Lynne. Judge, what do you think of our returned wanderer? Franz, shake hands with him, but save the interview for the News for later. Professor, here's one student Litchfield Academy won't need to be ashamed of."

He shook hands with them—old Judge Ledue; Franz Veltrin, the newsman; Professor Kellton; a dozen others, some of whom he had not thought of in five years. They were all cordial and happy—how much, he wondered, because he was their neighbor, Conn Maxwell, Rodney Maxwell's son, home from Terra, and how much because of what they hoped he would tell them? Kurt Fawzi, edging him out of the crowd, was the first to voice that.

"Conn, what did you find out?" he asked breathlessly. "Do you know where it is?"

Conn hesitated, looking about desperately; this was no
time to start talking to Kurt Fawzi about it. His father was
turning toward him from one side, and from the other Tom
Brangwyn and Colonel Zareff were approaching more
slowly, the older man leaning on a silver-headed cane.

"Don't bother him about it now, Kurt," Rodney Maxwell scolded the mayor. "He's just gotten off the ship; he
hasn't had time to say hello to everybody yet."

"But, Rod, I've been waiting to hear what he's found
out ever since he went away," Fawzi protested in a hurt
tone.

Brangwyn and Colonel Zareff joined them. They were
close friends, probably because neither of them was a native of Poictesme.

The town marshal had always been reticent about his
origins, but Conn guessed it was Hathor. Brangwyn's
heavy-muscled body, and his ease and grace in handling
it, marked him as a man of a high-gravity planet. Besides,
Hathor had a permanent cloud-envelope, and Tom
Brangwyn's skin had turned boiled-lobster red under the
dim orange sunlight of Alpha Gartner.

Old Kelm Zareff never hesitated to tell anybody where
he came from—he was from Ashmodai, one of the System
States planets, and he had commanded a division that had
been blasted down to about regimental strength, in the
Alliance army.

"Hello, boy," he croaked, extending a trembling hand.
"Glad you're home. We all missed you."

"We sure did, Conn," the town marshal agreed, clasp-
ing Conn's hand as soon as the old man had released it.
"Find out anything definite?"

Kurt Fawzi looked at his watch. "Conn, we've planned
a little celebration for you. We only had since day before
yesterday, when the spaceship came into radio range, but

we're having a dinner party for you at Senta's this evening."

"You couldn't have done anything I'd have liked better,
Mr. Fawzi. I'd have to have a meal at Senta's before really
feeling that I'd come home."

"Well, here's what I have in mind. It'll be three hours till
dinner's ready. Suppose we all go up to my office in the
meantime. It'll give the ladies a chance to go home and fix
up for the party, and we can have a drink and a talk."

"You want to do that, Conn?" his father asked, a trifle
doubtfully. "If you'd rather go home first . . ."

Something in his father's voice and manner disturbed
him vaguely; however, he nodded agreement. After a
couple of drinks, he'd be better able to tell them.

"Yes, indeed, Mr. Fawzi," Conn said. "I know you're
all anxious, but it's a long story. This'll be a good chance
to tell you."

Fawzi turned to his wife and daughter, interrupting himself to shout instructions to a couple of dockhands who
were floating the baggage off the ship on a contragravity-
lifter. Conn's father had sent Charley off with a message to
his mother and Flora.

Conn turned to Colonel Zareff. "I noticed extra workers
coming out from the hiring agencies in Storisende, and the
crop was all in across the Calders. Big wine-pressing this
year?"

"Yes, we're up to our necks in melons," the old planter
grumbled. "Gehenna of a big crop. Price'll drop like a
brick of collapsium, and this time next year we'll be using
brandy to wash our feet in."

"I you can't get good prices, hang onto it and age it. I
wish you could see what the bars on Terra charge for a
drink of ten-year-old Poictesme."

"This isn't Terra and we aren't selling it by the drink.

Only place we can sell brandy is at Storisende spaceport, and we have to take what the trading-ship captains offer. You've been on a rich planet for the last five years, Conn. You've forgotten what it's like to live in a poorhouse. And that's what Poictesme is."

"Things'll be better from now on, Klem," the mayor said, putting one hand on the old man's shoulder and the other on Conn's. "Our boy's home. With what he can tell us, we'll be able to solve all our problems. Come on, let's go up and hear about it."

They entered the wide doorway of the warehouse on the dock-level floor of the Airport Building and crossed to the lift. About a dozen others had joined them, all the important men of Lichfield. Inside, Kurt Fawzi's laborers were floating out cargo for the ship—casks of brandy, of course, and a lot of boxes and crates painted light blue and marked with the wreathed globe of the Terran Federation and the gold triangle of the Third Fleet-Army Force and the eight-pointed red star of Ordnance Service. Long cases of rifles, square boxes of ammunition, machine guns, crated auto-cannon and rockets.

"Where'd that stuff come from?" Conn asked his father. "You dig it up?"

His father chuckled. "That happened since the last time I wrote you. Remember the big underground headquarters complex in the Calders? Everybody thought it had been all cleaned out years ago. You know, it's never a mistake to take a second look at anything that everybody believes. I found a lot of sealed-off sections over there that had never been entered. This stuff's from one of the headquarters defense armories. I have a gang getting the stuff out. Charley and I flew in after lunch, and I'm going back the first thing tomorrow."

"But there's enough combat equipment on hand to

outfit a private army for every man, woman and child on Poictesme!" Conn objected. "Where are we going to sell this?"

"Storisende spaceport. The tramp freighters are buying it for newly colonized planets that haven't been industrialized yet. They don't pay much, but it doesn't cost much to get it out, and I've been clearing about three hundred sols a ton on the spaceport docks. That's not bad, you know."

Three hundred sols a ton. A lifter went by stacked with cases of M-504 submachine guns. Unloaded, one of them weighed six pounds, and even a used one was worth a hundred sols. Conn started to say something about that, but then they came to the lift and were crowding onto it.

He had been in Kurt Fawzi's office a few times, always with his father, and he remembered it as a dim, quiet place of genteel conviviality and rambling conversations, with deep, comfortable chairs and many ashtrays. Fawzi's warehouse and brokerage business, and the airline agency, and the government, such as it was, of Litchfield, combined, made few demands on his time and did not prevent the office from being a favored loafing center for the town's elders. The lights were bright only over the big table that served, among other things, as a desk, and the walls were almost invisible in the shadows.

As they came down the hallway from the lift, everybody had begun speaking more softly. Voices were never loud or excited in Kurt Fawzi's office.

Tom Brangwyn went to the table, taking off his belt and holster and laying his pistol aside. The others, crowding into the room, added their weapons to his.

That was something else Conn was seeing with new eyes. It had been five years since he had carried a gun and he was wondering why any of them bothered. A gun was what a boy put on to show that he had reached manhood, and a man carried for the rest of his life out of habit.

Why, there wouldn't be a shooting a year in Litchfield, if you didn't count the farm tramps and drifters, who kept to the lower level or camped in the empty buildings at the edge of town. Or may be that was it; maybe Litchfield was peaceful because everybody was armed. It certainly wasn't because of anything the Planetary Government at Storisende did to maintain order.

After divesting himself of his gun, Tom Brangwyn took over the bartending, getting out glasses and filling a pitcher of brandy from a keg in the corner.

"Everybody supplied?" Fawzi was asking. "Well, let's drink to our returned emissary. We're all anxious to hear what you found out, Conn. Gentlemen, here's to our friend Conn Maxwell. Welcome home, Conn!"

"Well, it's wonderful to be back, Mr. Fawzi—"

"No, let's not have any of this mister foolishness! You're one of the gang now. And drink up, everybody. We have plenty of brandy, even if we don't have anything else."

"You telling us, Kurt?" somebody demanded. One of the distillery company; the name would come back to Conn in a moment. "When this crop gets pressed and fermented—"

"When I start pressing, I don't know where in Gehenna I'm going to vat the stuff till it ferments," Colonel Zareff said. "Or why. You won't be able to handle all of it."

"Now, Now!" Fawzi reproved. "Let's not start moaning about our troubles. Not the day Conn's come home. Not when he's going to tell us how to find the Third Fleet-Army Force Brain."

"You *did* find out where the Brain is, didn't you, Conn?" Brangwyn asked anxiously.

That set half a dozen of them off at once. They had all

sat down after the toast; now they were fidgeting in their chairs, leaning forward, looking at Conn fixedly.

"What did you find out, Conn?"

"It's still here on Poictesme, isn't it?"

"Did you find out where it is?"

He wanted to tell them in one quick sentence and get it over with. He couldn't, any more than he could force himself to squeeze the trigger of a pistol he knew would blow up in his hand.

"Wait a minute, gentlemen." He finished the brandy, and held out the glass to Tom Brangwyn, nodding toward the pitcher. Even the first drink had warmed him and he could feel the constriction easing in his throat and the lump at the pit of his stomach dissolving. "I hope none of you expect me to spread out a map and show you the cross on it, where the Brain is. I can't. I can't even give the approximate location of the thing."

Much of the happy eagerness drained out of the faces around him. Some of them were looking troubled; Colonel Zareff was gnawing the bottom of his mustache, and Judge Ledue's hand shook as he tried to relight his cigar. Conn stole a quick side-glance at his father; Rodney Maxwell was watching him curiously, as though wondering what he was going to say next.

"But it is still here on Poictesme?" Fawzi questioned. "They didn't take it away when they evacuated, did they?"

Conn finished his second drink. This time he picked up the pitcher and refilled for himself.

"I'm going to have to do a lot of talking," he said, "and it's going to be thirsty work. I'll have to tell you the whole thing from the beginning, and if you start asking questions at random, you'll get me mixed up and I'll miss the important points."

"By all means!" Judge Ledue told him. "Give it in your own words, in what you think is the proper order."

"Thank you, Judge."

Conn drank some more brandy, hoping he could get his courage up without getting drunk. After all, they had a right to a full report; all of them had contributed something toward sending him to Terra.

"The main purpose in my going to the University was to learn computer theory and practice. It wouldn't do any good for us to find the Brain if none of us are able to use it. Well, I learned enough to be able to operate, program and service any computer in existence, and train assistants. During my last year at the University, I had a part-time paid job programming the big positron-neutrino-photon computer in the astro-physics department. When I graduated, I was offered a position as instructor in positronic computer theory."

"You never mentioned that in your letters, son," his father said.

"It was too late for any letter except one that would come on the same ship I did. Beside, it wasn't very important."

"I think it was." There was a catch in old Professor Kellton's voice. "One of my boys, from the Academy, offered a place on the faculty of the University of Montevideo, on Terra!" He poured himself a second drink, something he almost never did.

"Conn means it wasn't important because it didn't have anything to do with the Brain," Fawzi explained and then looked at Conn expectantly.

All right; now he'd tell them. "I went over all the records of the Third Fleet-Army Force's occupation of Poictesme that are open to the public. On one pretext or another, I got permission to examine the non-classified files that aren't open to public examination. I even got a few peeps at some of the stuff that's still classified secret. I have maps and plans of all the installations that were built on this planet—literally thousands of them, many still undiscovered. Why, we haven't more than scratched the surface of what the Federation left behind here. For instance, all the important installations exist in duplicate, some even in triplicate, as a precaution against Alliance space attack."

"Space attack!" Colonel Zareff was indignant. "There never was a time when the Alliance could have taken the offensive against Poictesme, even if an offensive outside our own space-area had been part of our policy. We just didn't have the ships. It took over a year to move a million and a half troops from Ashmodai to Marduk, and the fleet that was based on Amaterasu was blasted out of existence in the spaceports and in orbit. Hell, at the time of the surrender, we didn't have—"

"They weren't taking chances on that, Colonel. But the point I want to make is that with everything I did find, I never found, in any official record, a single word about the giant computer we call the Third Fleet-Army Force Brain."

For a time, the only sound in the room was the tiny insectile humming of the electric clock on the wall. Then Professor Kellton set his glass on the table, and it sounded like a hammer-blow.

"Nothing, Conn?" Kurt Fawzi was incredulous and, for the first time, frightened. The others were exchanging uneasy glances. "But you must have! A thing like that—"

"Of course it would be one of the closest secrets during the war," somebody else said. "But in forty years, you'd expect *something* to leak out."

"Why, *during* the war, it was all through the Third Force. Even the Alliance knew about it; that's how Klem heard of it."

"Well, Conn couldn't just walk into the secret files and read whatever he wanted to. Just because he couldn't find anything—"

"Don't tell *me* about security!" Klem Zareff snorted. "Certainly they still have it classified; staff-brass'd rather lose an eye than declassify anything. If you'd seen the lengths our staff went to—hell, we lost battles because the staff wouldn't release information the troops in the field needed. I remember once—"

"But there *was* a Brain," Judge Ledue was saying, to reassure himself and draw agreement from the others. "It was capable of combining data, and scanning and evaluating all its positronic memories, and forming association patterns, and reasoning with absolute perfection. It was more than a positronic brain—it was a positronic super-mind."

"We'd have won the war, except for the Brain. We had ninety systems, a hundred and thirty inhabited planets, a hundred billion people—and we were on the defensive in our own space-area! Every move we made was known and anticipated by the Federation. How could they have done that without something like the Brain?"

"Conn, from what you learned of computers, how large a volume of space would you say the Brain would have to occupy?" Professor Kellton asked.

Professor Kellton was the most unworldly of the lot, yet he was asking the most practical question.

"Well, the astrophysics computer I worked with at the University occupies a total of about one million cubic feet," Conn began. This was his chance; they'd take anything he told them about computers as gospel. "It was only designed to handle problems in astrophysics. The Brain, being built for space war, would have to handle any such problem. And if half the stories about the Brain are anywhere near true, it handled any other problem—mathematical, scientific, political, economic, strategic, psychological, even philosphical and ethical. Well, I'd say that a hundred million cubic feet would be the smallest even conceivable."

They all nodded seriously. They were willing to accept that—or anything else, except one thing.

"Lot of places on this planet where a thing that size could be hidden," Tom Brangwyn said, undismayed. "A planet's a mighty big place."

"It could be under water, in one of the seas," Piet Dawes, the banker, suggested. "An underwater dome city wouldn't be any harder to build than a dome city on a poison-atmosphere planet like Tubal-Cain."

"It might even be on Tubal-Cain," a melon-planter said. "Or Hiawatha, or even one of the Beta or Gamma planets. The Third Force was occupying the whole Trisystem, you know." He thought for a moment. "If I'd been in charge, I'd have put it on one of the moons of Pantagruel."

"But that's clear out in the Alpha System," Judge Ledue objected. "We don't have a spaceship on the planet, certainly nothing with a hyperdrive engine. And it would take a lifetime to get out to the Gamma System and back on reaction drive."

Conn put his empty brandy glass on the table and sat erect. A new thought had occurred to him, chasing out of his mind all the worries and fears he had brought with him all the way from Terra.

"Then we'll have to build a ship," he said calmly. "I know, when the Federation evacuated Poictesme, they took every hyperdrive ship with them. But they had plenty of shipyards and spaceports on this planet, and I have maps showing the location of all of them, and barely a third of them have been discovered so far. I'm sure we can find enough hulks, and enough hyperfield generator parts, to assemble a ship or two, and I know we'll find the same or better on some of the other planets.

"And here's another thing," he added. "When we start looking into some of the dome-city plants on Tubal-Cain and Hiawatha and Moruna and Koshchei, we may find the plant or plants where the components for the Brain were fabricated, and if we do, we may find records of where they were shipped, and that'll be it."

"You're right!" Professor Kellton cried, quivering with excitement. "We've been hunting at random for the Brain, so it would only be an accident if we found it. We'll have to do this systematically, and with Conn to help us—Conn, why not build a computer? I don't mean another Brain; I mean a computer to help us find the Brain."

"We can, but we may not even need to build one. When we get out to the industrial planets, we may find one ready except for perhaps some minor alterations."

"But how are we going to finance all this?" Klem Zareff demanded querulously. "We're poorer than snakes, and even one hyperdrive ship's going to cost like Gehenna."

"I've been thinking about that, Klem," Fawzi said. "If we can find material at these shipyards Conn knows about, most of our expense will be labor. Well, haven't we ten workmen competing for every job? They don't really need money, only the things money can buy. We can raise food on the farms and provide whatever else they need out of Federation supplies."

"Sure. As soon as it gets around that we're really trying to do something about this, everybody'll want in on it," Tom Brangwyn predicted.

"And I have no doubt that the Planetary Government

at Storisende will give us assistance, once we show that this is a practical and productive enterprise," Judge Ledue put in. "I have some slight influence with the President and—"

"I'm not too sure we want the Government getting into this," Kurt Fawzi replied. "Give them half a chance and that gang at Storisende'll squeeze us right out."

"We can handle this ourselves," Brangwyn agreed. "And when we get some kind of a ship and get out to the other two systems, or even just to Tubal-Cain or Hiawatha, first thing you know, we'll *be* the Planetary Government."

"Well, now, Tom," Fawzi began piously, "the Brain is too big a thing for a few of us to try to monopolize; it'll be for all Poictesme. Of course, it's only proper that we, who are making the effort to locate it, should have the direction of that effort . . . "

While Fawzi was talking, Rodney Maxwell went to the table, rummaged his pistol out of the pile and buckled it on. The mayor stopped short.

"You leaving us, Rod?"

"Yes, it's getting late. Conn and I are going for a little walk; we'll be at Senta's in half an hour. The fresh air will do both of us good and we have a lot to talk about. After all, we haven't seen each other for over five years."

They were silent, however, until they were away from the Airport Building and walking along High Garden Terrace in the direction of the Mall. Conn was glad; his own thoughts were weighing too heavily within him: I didn't do it. I was going to do it; every minute, I was going to do it, every minute, I was going to do it, and I didn't, and now it's too late.

"That was quite a talk you gave them, son," his father

said. "They believed every word of it. A couple of times, I even caught myself starting to believe it."

Conn stopped short. His father stopped beside him and stood looking at him.

"Why didn't you tell them the truth?" Rodney Maxwell asked.

The question angered Conn. It was what he had been asking himself.

"Why didn't I just grab a couple of pistols off the table and shoot the lot of them?" he retorted. "It would have killed them quicker and wouldn't have hurt as much."

His father took the cigar from his mouth and inspected the tip of it. "The truth must be pretty bad then. There is no Brain. Is that it, son?"

"There never was one. I'm not saying that only because I know it would be impossible to build such a computer. I'm telling you what the one man in the Galaxy who ought to know told me—the man who commanded the Third Force during the War."

"Foxx Travis! I didn't know he was still alive. You actually talked to him?"

"Yes. He's on Luna, keeping himself alive at low gravity. It took me a couple of years, and I was afraid he'd die before I got to him, but I finally managed to see him."

"What did he tell you?"

"That no such thing as the Brain ever existed." They started walking again, more slowly, toward the far edge of the terrace, with the sky red and orange in front of them. "The story was all through the Third Force, but it was just one of those wild tales that get started, nobody knows how, among troops. The High Command never denied or even discouraged it. It helped morale, and letting it leak to the enemy was good psychological warfare."

"Klem Zareff says that everybody in the Alliance army

heard of the Brain," his father said. "That was why he came here in the first place." He puffed thoughtfully on his cigar. "You said a computer like the Brain would be an impossibility. Why? Wouldn't it be just another computer, only a lot bigger and a lot smarter?"

"Dad, computermen don't like to hear computers called smart," Conn said. "They aren't. The people who build them are smart; a computer only knows what's fed to it. They can hold more information in their banks than a man can in his memory, they can combine it faster, they don't get tired or absent-minded. But they can't imagine, they can't create, and they can't do anything a human brain can't."

"You know, I'd wondered about just that," said his father. "And none of the histories of the War even as much as mentioned the Brain. And I couldn't see why, after the War, they didn't build dozens of them to handle all these Galactic political and economic problems that nobody seems able to solve. A thing like the Brain wouldn't only be useful for war; the people here aren't trying to find it for war purposes."

"You didn't mention any of these doubts to the others, did you?"

"They were just doubts. You knew for sure, and you couldn't tell them."

"I'd come home intending to—tell them there was no Brain, tell them to stop wasting their time hunting for it and start trying to figure out the answers themselves. But I couldn't. They don't believe in the Brain as a tool, to use; it's a machine god that they can bring all their troubles to. You can't take a thing like that away from people without giving them something better."

"I noticed you suggested building a spaceship and agreed with the professor about building a computer.

What was your idea? To take their minds off hunting for the Brain and keep them busy?"

Conn shook his head. "I'm serious about the ship— ships. You and Colonel Zareff gave me that idea."

His father looked at him in surprise. "I never said a word in there, and Kelm didn't even once mention—"

"Not in Kurt's office; before we went up from the docks. There was Kelm, moaning about a good year for melons as though it were a plague, and you selling arms and ammunition by the ton. Why, on Terra or Baldur or Uller, a glass of our brandy brings more than these freighter-captains give us for a cask, and what do you think a colonist on Agramma, or Sekht, or Hachiman, who has to fight for his life against savages and wild animals, would pay for one of those rifles and a thousand rounds of ammunition?"

His father objected. "We can't base the whole economy of a planet on brandy. Only about ten per cent of the arable land on Poictesme will grow wine-melons. And if we start exporting Federation salvage the way you talk of, we'll be selling pieces instead of job lots. We'll net more, but—"

"That's just to get us started. The ships will be used, after that, to get to Tubal-Cain and Hiawatha and the planets of the Beta and Gamma Systems. What I want to see is the mines and factories reopened, people employed, wealth being produced."

"And where'll we sell what we produce? Remember, the mines closed down because there was no more market."

"No more interstellar market, that's true. But there are a hundred and fifty million people on Poictesme. That's a big enough market and a big enough labor force to exploit the wealth of the Gartner Trisystem. We can have prosperity for everybody on our own resources. Just what do we need that we have to get from outside now?"

His father stopped again and sat down on the edge of a fountain—the same one, possibly, from which Conn had seen dust blowing as the airship had been coming in.

"Conn, that's a dangerous idea. That was what brought on the System States War. The Alliance planets took themselves outside the Federation economic orbit and the Federation crushed them."

Conn swore impatiently. "You've been listening to old Klem Zareff ranting about the Lost Cause and the greedy Terran robber barons holding the Galaxy in economic serfdom while they piled up profits. The Federation didn't fight that war for profits; there weren't any profits to fight for. They fought it because if the System States had won, half of them would be at war among themselves now. Make no mistake about it, politically I'm all for the Federation. But economically, I want to see our people exploiting their own resources for themselves, instead of grieving about lost interstellar trade, and bewailing bumper crops, and searching for a mythical robot god."

"You think, if you can get something like that started, that they'll forget about the Brain?" his father asked skeptically.

"That crowd up in Kurt Fawzi's office? Niflheim, no! They'll go on hunting for the Brain as long as they live, and every day they'll be expecting to find it tomorrow. That'll keep them happy. But they're all old men. The ones I'm interested in are the boys of Charley's age. I'm going to give them too many real things to do—building ships, exploring the rest of the Trisystem, opening mines and factories, producing wealth—for them to get caught in that empty old dream."

He looked down at the dusty fountain on which his

father sat. "That ghost-dream haunts this graveyard. I want to give them living dreams that they can make come true."

Conn's father sat in silence for a while, his cigar smoke red in the sunset. "If you can do all that, Conn . . . You know, I believe you can. I'm with you, as far as I can help, and we'll have a talk with Charley. He's a good boy, Conn, and he has a lot of influence among the other youngsters." He looked at his watch. "We'd better be getting along. You don't want to be late for your own coming-home party."

Rodney Maxwell slid off the edge of the fountain to his feet, hitching at the gunbelt under his coat. Have to dig out his own gun and start wearing it, Conn thought. A man simply didn't go around in public without a gun in Litchfield. It wasn't decent. And he'd be spending a lot of time out in the brush, where he'd really need one.

First thing in the morning, he'd unpack that trunk and go over all those maps. There were half a dozen spaceports and maintenance shops and shipyards within a half-day by airboat, none of which had been looted. He'd look them all over; that would take a couple of weeks. Pick the best shipyard and concentrate on it. Kurt Fawzi'd be the man to recruit labor. Professor Kellton was a scholar, not a scientist. He didn't know beans about hyperdrive engines, but he knew how to do library research.

They came to the edge of High Garden Terrace at the escalator, long motionless, its moving parts rusted fast, that led down to the Mall, and at the bottom of it was Senta's, the tables under the open sky.

A crowd was already gathering. There was Tom Brangwyn, and there was Kurt Fawzi and his wife, and Lynne. And there was Senta herself, fat and dumpy, in one of her preposterous red-and-purple dresses, bustling about, bubbling happily one moment and screaming invective at some laggard waiter the next.

The dinner, Conn knew, would be the best he had eaten in five years, and afterward they would sit in the dim glow of Beta Gartner, sipping coffee and liqueurs, smoking and talking and visiting back and forth from one table to another, as they always did in the evenings at Senta's. Another bit from Eirrarsson's poem came back to him:

We sit in the twilight, the shadows among,
And we talk of the happy days when we were brave and
*   young.*

That was for the old ones, for Colonel Zareff and Judge Ledue and Dolf Kellton, maybe even for Tom Brangwyn and Franz Veltrin and for his father. But his brother Charley and the boys of his generation would have future to talk about. And so would he, and Lynne Fawzi.

Introduction to "When in the Course"

Of all the stories in this collection, "When in the Course" is the only one that has never before been published! But even more important than that; it occupies a strange half state between Piper's two major series, the TerroHuman Future History and his Paratime time travel series. But I'll get back to that in a moment.

I wasn't even aware of "When in the Course's" existence until one day about two years ago, when Jerry excitedly called me into his office. Earlier that morning we had received a package with the morning mail from Ace Books; nothing unusual there. "John, look at this!" I hurried in. "Here are two unpublished Piper manuscripts that Jim Baen found among Beam's papers. Would you take a look at them for me?"

Would I? Right then it would have taken a spaceship full of Slan to stop me. Midway through the third page I realized that I had "read this story before." Yes, it was in Analog: "Gunpowder God." But not quite; where was Lord Kalvan? The story, a chartered company come to claim a new world, was set in Beam's TerroHuman Future History: it took place on legendary Freya, a world mentioned throughout the early TFH stories—as far back as ULLER UPRISING—as a place where the women were even more beautiful than those of earth. Obviously, it had to be an old story, or one that Beam had carried in his head for years. But there is no denying it; except for the last half it is the story of Lord Kalvan of Otherwhen—except he's not in it and these Federation people are!

After a good deal of thought, it is my contention that Piper wrote "When in the Course," submitted it to John W. Campbell—who probably had fits over the central idea of parallel evolution, as any good biologist would (which means Beam probably had another ace up his sleeve as he did nothing by accident; but what?)—and therefore Campbell suggested some changes, as he was wont to do. "Beam, the story's good; why don't you set it in that Paratime series we used to run awhile back?" I have talked with both Perry Chapdelaine and George Hay, editors of the forthcoming John W. Campbell letters collection, and—when things get cleared up—they have promised me copies of the Piper/Campbell correspondence for a book on Piper I intend to do called The Piper Papers. But until then, if I can find the correspondence to explain what happened, this will have to remain H. Beam Piper's most unusual story.

WHEN IN THE COURSE—
H. Beam Piper

She closed her mind to the voices around her and stared at the map spread on the table between the two great candlesticks, trying to imagine herself high above everything, looking down like a bird. Here was Tarr-Hostigos, only a little mark of gold on the parchment, but she could see it all in imagination—the outer walls around the great enclosure with the sheds and stables against them; the citadel, and the inner bailey; the keep, and the watchtower, jutting up from the point of the ridge. And here, below, was the Darro, and she could see it glinting in the sunlight as it rushed south to join the Athan, and here was the town of Hostigos, and the bridge and the town-hall and the temple of Dralm, and, beyond, the farmlands and the squares of fields and the dark woods and the little villages. Oh, it must be wonderful to be a bird and fly above everything, and look down; ever since she had been a baby, she had dreamed. . .

A voice, harsher than the others, brought her back to the present she had been trying to flee.

"King Kaiphranos won't intervene? What's a king for, but to keep the peace? Great Dralm, is all Hos-Harphax afraid of Gormoth of Nostor?"

She looked from one to another of them, almost as though she were a stranger who had wandered unknowing into this windowless candlelit room. Phosg, the Speaker for the Peasants, at the foot of the table, uncomfortable in his feast-day clothes and ill at ease seated among his betters. The other Speakers, for the artisans and the townfolk and the merchants. The landholders, and the lesser family-members. Old Chartiphon, the captain-in-chief, with his heavy frowning face and his golden beard splotched with gray like the gray lead-splotches on his gilded breastplate. Xentos, even older, with the cowl of his blue robe pushed back from his snowy head and trouble in his gentle blue eyes. And her father, Prince Ptosphes of Hostigos, with his pointed mustache and his small pointed beard and his mouth thin and grim between. How long it seemed since she had seen that mouth smiling!

Xentos was passing his hand across his face in the negative gesture.

"The King said that a prince must guard his own princedom," he replied. "He told me that it was Prince Ptosphes' duty to keep raiders out of his lands. And then he laughed and turned from me, and that was all."

"Did you tell him it wasn't just raiders from the Strip?" the voice that had spoken earlier demanded. "We don't care for them; I've killed a dozen with this hand!" The speaker banged it, large and hairy, on the table. "It's war! Gormoth of Nostor means to take all Hostigos, the way his grandfather took the Strip, after the traitor we don't name sold him Tarr-Dombra."

That was the part of the map her eyes had avoided—the two little rivers to the north, flowing together from east and west to form the Darro. Once the land beyond, to the crest of the mountain, had all been Hostigos, until a brother of her great-grandfather had sold the castle that guarded Dombra Pass to the prince who had then ruled Nostor, on the other side. Now the Nostori called the country between the mountain and the rivers New Nostor, and the Hostigi called it the Strip.

"Gormoth's hiring mercenaries." That was a cousin on her mother's side. "He has near ten thousand of them, beside his own soldiers, and we have a scant two thousand, counting peasants with axes and scythes."

"We have five hundred mercenaries of our own," somebody mentioned.

Chartiphon snorted in contempt. "Bandits from Sastragath; all we can trust them to do is go over to Gormoth the first chance they get. No free-captain in his right wits would take service with us, the case we're in."

"I wouldn't, if I were a free-captain," her father said wryly. "Well, you know how things are. Now, what is in your minds that we should do?" He turned to the man at the foot of the table. "Phosg, you speak first."

That was the custom, for the least to speak first. The peasant representative cleared his throat.

"Prince, my cottage is as dear to me as this great castle is to you. I will fight for mine as you would for yours."

There was a quick mutter of approval—"Well said. An example to the rest of us!"—and the others spoke. The landholders and the lesser family-members agreed. Chartiphon said only: "Fight. What else?"

"Submission to evil men is the greatest of all sins," Xentos told them. "I am a priest of Dralm, and Dralm is a god of peace, but I say, fight with Dralm's blessing."

"Rylla?" her father said.

She started slightly when she heard her name in that cold, distant tone.

"Better die in armor than live in chains," she said. "When the time comes, I will wear armor, too."

Her father nodded. "Then we are all agreed. Gormoth of Nostor may take Hostigos, but we will not live to see it, and it will be long remembered what price we made him pay for our lives." He rose. "I thank you all. At an hour past sunset, we will dine together; the servants will attend you in the meantime. Now, if you please, leave me with my daughter. Xentos, do you and Chartiphon stay."

When they had gone, he drew his poignard and struck the gong with the flat, bidding a servant bring wine.

"Won't Sarrask of Sask help us?" she asked, when they had sat down again. "If I were Sarrask, I'd rather have you as a neighbor than Gormoth of Nostor."

"Sarrask of Sask's a fool," Chartiphon declared. "He's gathering forces to join Gormoth against us. Well, when we are dead and Hostigos is Gormoth's, Sarrask's turn will come next."

"No, Sarrask is acting with wisdom," Xentos differed. "He's not joining Gormoth; he hopes to gain enough ground north of the Athan to be able to fight Gormoth off his own land. And he dare not aid us. We are under the ban of Styphon's House. Even King Kaiphranos dare not help those whom the priests of Styphon would destroy."

Chartiphon fingered the hand-guard of his long sword, on the table in front of him. Then he raised his head.

"The priests of Styphon," he said, dragging the words out as though by main strength, "want the land in the Yellowstone Valley. They want to build a temple in Hostigos, and they want you to give them land and workers for a temple farm. I know, that would be bad, but. . ."

But not as bad as what Gormoth and his ten thousand mercenaries would bring when they came over Dombra Pass.

"Too late," Xentos said. "Styphon's House has already made a compact with Gormoth. They will help Gormoth conquer Hostigos; Gormoth will give them the Yellowstone Valley, and land for their farm, and the peasants he drives off their own farms will work for the priests. And all the world will see the fate of those who refuse Styphon's

House anything." A look of pain came into his eyes. "It was on my advice, Prince, that you refused when they asked it of you."

Her father put a hand on the old priest-counselor's shoulder. "Blame yourself for nothing, Xentos; I'd have refused even against your advice. I swore long ago that Styphon's House would never come into Hostigos. They build a temple. Then they demand land for a temple farm, and when they have it, they make thorn-hedges around it, and the workers on the farm never leave it and are never seen again. And they tax the ruler, and force him to tax the people until there is nothing left."

"Yes, you'd hardly believe it," Chartiphon said, "but they even make the peasants haul their manure to the temple farm, till they have none left for their own fields. There's nothing too petty for them to filch, once they get into you."

"I wonder why they want the Yellowstone," she said. "Is there something valuable there that we don't know about?"

"Something in the ground, that makes the water taste and smell badly," her father said. "They'd have mines there, and our own people would be the slaves that worked them. No, even if I'd known then that it would mean war with Gormoth, I'd have refused. Better be shot with a musket than stung to death by gnats."

Roger Barron watched the coffee-concentrate tablet dissolve, and wished somebody would start a fight. It might help morale, which needed it. Adriaan de Ruyter and Reginald Fitzurse and Lourenço Narvaes had returned and the two hundred foot hyperyacht was berthed again inside the thousand foot sphere of the *Stellex*. Now they were all together in the ship's lounge, ten men and

five women, and it was a worse gloom-session than six
months ago, and with less reason. Adriaan was trying to
point that out.

"Of course; if it had been uninhabited, we'd be able to
get clear title of ownership for the whole planet. But look
at the Thor Company, and the Loki Company, and the
Yggdrasil Company. They were all chartered for inhabited
planets, and they're all making money."

"But the people here are civilized!" That was Charley
Clifford, the doctor, who doubled as carniculturist. He'd
made that point a couple of times before. "Good Lord,
you all saw those cities."

"On only one continent," Karl Zahanov, the space-cap-
tain, said. He had a square-cut gray beard which gave him
a professorial appearance to match his didactic manner.
"There is no evidence of civilization on either of the other
two, and one of them's even bigger than the Eurasian
landmass on Terra."

"We didn't see any evidence of inhabitants on the other
two continents," Reginald Fitzurse, on the couch beside
him, said. He was a retired Terran Federation army officer;
when he made positive statements he was certain of their
correctness. "Any people whose works can't be seen at
five hundred miles with a three hundred power telescope
aren't civilized enough to mention. And I don't think much
of this civilization, as such, either. It's confined to one river
valley about the same area as the Mississippi-Missouri system in North Terra. There is nothing outside that except a
small and apparently unrelated patch at the northern corner of the continent. A really high civilization spreads itself
out more than that. Nancy, you saw all the photos; what
do you think?"

Nancy Patterson was sitting at the table, beside Karl Zahanov. She had dark hair and eyes, and a pleasant if

slightly remote face. She had been a secretary in the social science division of the University of Montevideo.

"Well, it's premechanical," she said. "Of course, that might be anything up to the level of say Sixteenth Century Europe. Fifth Century Pre-Atomic," she added, for which he was glad. They used Atomic Era dating exclusively on Venus, and he always had to count on his fingers to transpose to Christian Era, and he usually remembered too late that there was no C. E. Year Zero. "The cities are dark when they pass into the night-shadow, except for a few gleams of what might be firelight. They are all sharply defined, and look as though they might be walled."

"They are; at least some of them," Fitzurse interrupted.

"That would indicate warfare as a serious possibility, which would mean competing national sovereignties. All the cities are surrounded by belts of farmland; each one grows its own food. That would indicate lack of large-scale powered transportation. And, of course, we detected no evidence of nuclear or electric energy, no radio-waves of any sort, and no sign of aircraft."

"The other two continents may be completely uninhabited," Luther Smith, the chief engineer said. He had reddish hair and a thin, intense face. "Can't we land on one of them and claim it, and let this civilized continent go?"

That would be Luther; he was worried about the possibility of conflict. Luther, he recalled, had protested vehemently about the quantity of arms and ammunition that had been taken aboard when they had been fitting out, four years ago. Luther was a pacifist.

"No." Adriaan de Ruyter was positive. "With our resources, or lack thereof, we can't float a company on Terra without an exclusive-rights charter to operate on this planet, and we can't get that for one continent. What we will have to have is some kind of a treaty with some more or less sovereign power, guaranteeing us rights of entry and trade. Once we have that, we can get a charter. But on an inhabited planet, we must contact the inhabitants and establish friendly trade relations with at least some of them."

"Well, if that's what we have to do, let's get at it," he said. "We came out to find a Terra-type planet. We spent four years and visited six systems; now we've found one. We won't get another chance. Do I hear that statement disputed?"

He didn't. Luther Smith looked at Margaret Hale, the hyperdrive engineer; she'd told him just how many more jumps her Dillinghams were good for. Charley Clifford and Sylvia Davock were silent; both of them knew that the law of diminishing returns was rapidly overtaking both the carniculture vats and the hydroponic gardens, and Sylvia knew how much oxygen and water was escaping irrecoverably from the recycling systems. And they all knew how long the *Stellex* herself would last. The only reason they had been able to buy her had been because her former owners could no longer get her insured.

Julio Almagro set down his drink—hydroponic potato schnapps and soda.

"Well," he said, in a weary voice, "we can always throw it in and go back to Terra."

He had a plump face and a black mustache; he looked soft, but under the fleshy upholstery he was hard as collapsium. He had more money in the *Stellex* than any three of the others, except Adriaan de Ruyter—and if he went back, his creditors would eat him alive.

"Most of us—I'm not speaking for myself or Roger— could stay out of jail. Some of us could even get jobs. I doubt if any of us would actually starve to death. But every cent any of us has is in this ship. If we want it back, here's where we'll have to get it."

Sylvia Davock could get a job. So could Luther and
Lourenço. Maybe Karl Zahanov could get command of a
ship, again, though he was pretty old for that. Reginald
Fitzurse would have his army pension. Nancy could get
her old job back—but she had put every cent she had in-
herited from her mother into Stellar Explorations to escape
that job.

And if he went back, there was a warrant waiting for him
from the Federation Member Republic of Venus. That was
standard procedure. If you got voted out of office, they
indicted you for corrupt practices. There were no other
kind in Venusian politics.

"All right; for the record do I hear a motion that we land
on this planet?" he asked.

Almagro moved; Dave MacDonald, the scout, hunter
and naturalist, seconded. Luther Smith tried to shove in
an amendment forbidding hostilities against the people of
the planet. That brought Fitzurse to his feet, his mouth tight
under his gray mustache.

"No, You've all made me responsible for landing operations; I'm not taking down a landing party to have them
massacred because my hands are tied by instructions not
to use firearms. I've seen that happen before. Let's vote
on the motion as presented and seconded."

It passed. Zahanov wanted to know what Fitzurse
wanted done first.

"We know that this is, roughly, a Terra-type planet,"
Fitzurse said. "We do not know, however, that it will support Terran life. Yggdrasil is inhabited, and the Terran colonists there still have to eat hydroponic vegetables and
carniculture meat. For all we know, the animal life here
may be silicone instead of carbon-hydrogen. The water
may be deuterium-oxygen instead of hydrogen-oxygen.

Or there may be fatal allergens. And Charley can tell you about some of the micro-organism possibilities.

"The first thing will be to make small-party landings, on the apparently uninhabited continents—and keep the adverb firmly in mind; you can't see everything through a telescope, and the woods may be full of characters who throw spears first and yell halt afterward. Then, after we have satisfied ourselves about the chemistry, biology and so forth, we will make a landing in force to contact the inhabitants. This will *not* be anywhere near that big city at the forks of the river. We will land in some isolated district where news will not be likely to leak out too quickly, and we will try to ingratiate ourselves with the people there, learn the language, and find out all we can about the customs, religion, level of technology, social organization, and, above all, the power situation. I don't mean your kind, Lourenco," he told the nuclear engineer. "I mean who rules whom and how. You agree, Roger? The actual making of contact will be your job."

He nodded. "We certainly don't want to go blundering into some royal court and wading up to our necks into some high level faction-fight without knowing what it's all about. Not in the middle of a big city. We don't have enough machine gun ammunition for that."

"Here's a place I'd had in mind." Fitzurse put on one of the projection screens. "This is three hundred power telephoto at two hundred miles."

It was a wide cultivated valley, hemmed in by mountains on three sides; two small rivers flowed in at one end from opposite directions to form a larger stream. There was a town, and something like a castle on the point of a ridge overlooking it. The distance was still too great for details, but it looked feudal—lord's castle, market-town, peasant villages, farms; self-contained and apart from everything else. It reminded him of pictures he had seen of Switzerland and the Tyrol before the Atomic Wars.

"I think so, Fitz," he said. "It looks like just the place for us to stay for a while, till we're ready to move in on the big city. Which way is north, in the picture?"

"At the top. It's on the west of the big river valley."

He nodded. There was a road going north, beyond the juncture of the two smaller streams; it crossed the mountains at a pass guarded by another castle. He wondered if that were held by the lord of what he was beginning to think of as "our" valley. If not, mightn't it be held by an enemy? Better not mention that possibility in Luther Smith's hearing.

It was another road, rutted and dusty, that entered "our" valley from the east; five hundred yards up the slope, it emerged from the woods into a broad meadow. The grass beside it grew almost waist high, topped with silvery plumes that rippled ceaselessly in the wind. Real wind; not fan-stirred ship air recycled thousands of times. And there was a blue sky above, peopled with rolypoly white clouds, and a strange fragrance everywhere. It was all wonderful, after four years of the sealed steel world of the *Stellex,* and six airless, waterless, poisonous and otherwise abominable planets. But a day and a half here, and nothing. . .

He turned back to the camp—the seventy foot oval landing-craft, with the marquee-tent in front of it and the lorries and aircars on either side—and as he did, a couple of the others shouted his name. They had all left what they had been doing and were crowding in front of the screen tuned to the pickup on the airjeep in which Dave MacDonald and Arthur Muramoto were on watch.

"They have something," Reginald Fitzurse told him as

he hurried over. "Mounted party—Dave calls it cavalry—about twenty, coming up the road on the other side. He has the pickup at top magnification and centered on a stretch of clear road."

Karl Zahanoz was talking into the screen to the ship, telling Adriaan de Ruyter. Luther Smith was fussing with the photo reproducer on the jeep screen. Then Arthur Muramoto, who must have been using the binoculars, gave a yell from the screen-speaker.

"I can see their dust; be along in a couple of minutes. Get set for them."

Then, briefly, the cavalcade appeared and passed. The mounts were ungainly things, with bovine heads and short, stumpy legs; he was surprised at their speed until he remembered having seen dachshunds run. These things had the same sort of gait, their short legs blurring till they almost looked like wheels. One of the riders wore a scarlet cloak and a wide plumed hat. The others were in armor, either back-and-breast cuirasses or mail hauberks or plated brigandines, and they wore conical helmets and red-and-blue shoulder capes, and all carried long straight swords. A few had lances; the rest were armed with what looked like muskets.

Then they were out of sight, and the view shifted to another stretch of open road, and Arthur Muramoto's voice, from the screen-speaker, estimated ten minutes till they reached it. Luther Smith began getting photoprints out of the slot at the bottom of the screen and passing them to the others. Nancy Patterson took one.

"Why, they're *human!*"

If they weren't, they'd pass for it. Humanoid form, of course, was to be expected in any sapient race, with variations—the hairy, dog-faced Thorans, the faunlike Lokians, the grotesque but upright and biped natives of

Yggdrasil. In this case, the variation wasn't noticeable, but Charley Clifford was a stickler.

"Humanoid," he corrected. "Homoform, approaching tenth degree. But there'll be all kinds of internal differences, of course."

"You can call them cavalry if you want to, Dave; I'll go along with it," Fitzurse said. "They're better than anything I ever saw."

All the mounted warriors he had ever seen had been Eurasian barbarians of North Terra, the human debris of the Atomic Wars, against whom he had campaigned to protect the reclamation projects. He began wondering, audibly, what sort of guns they had, and if there weren't pistol-holsters on the saddles.

"All right, watch for them!" Muramoto called, and Luther Smith went back to the screen and took the button-cord for the photoprinter.

They had a better view, this time. Details were clearer, and the riders on the short-legged, broad-tailed animals looked even more human. They were light-skinned and fair; most of them had blond or reddish beards. Almagro became excited.

"The one in the red cloak; that's a woman!"

That could be imagination; Almagro's ran in that direction. The prints weren't positive evidence either way; the cloak and the wide-brimmed hat hid too much. Fitzurse was sure the guns were muzzleloaders, probably flintlocks.

"All right, we'll give them a fire-power demonstration," he said. "You all know the drill. Roger, you'd better take over from here."

Lourenço Narvaes and Nancy Patterson went to the other airjeep, Nancy at the controls and Lourenço at the twin 15-mm machine guns. Everybody who wasn't wearing a pistol put one on and everybody got a rifle except

Charley Clifford, who had a portable machine gun. They
formed a line in front of the camp, with the jeep on the
right and Charley on the left. He and Fitzurse took their
position slightly front and center. Katherine Gower, at the
screen, was giving instructions to the jeep at the top of the
mountain.

Then the riders came out into the meadow, bunching at
first and then forming a line of their own, with the red cloak
in the middle. Fitzurse raised the binoculars slung around
his neck.

"Gad, it is a woman," he said. "Beauty, too." He
started to lift the strap over his head, then let go of it and
unslung his rifle. "Here they come," he said.

The line stirred; the red-and-blue-pennoned lances
came down; the musketeers rested the forestocks of their
weapons on their bridle-arms. Then the woman in the red
cloak flung up her right hand, held it raised for a moment,
and then swung it down and forward. The line advanced,
first at a walk and then at a slow slope. Half way to the
camp, they were at full speed, and the woman was lifting
a long pistol from her saddle-bow. He brought his rifle to
his shoulder, aiming fifty feet over the heads of the charg-
ing cavalry.

"Ready!" He waited till they were a scant hundred
yards away. "Three rounds; fire!"

The rifle-butt punched his shoulder, and then punched
it twice again. Other rifles banged, and the light machine
gun chattered, stopped, and chattered again. Then the
woman in the cloak flung up her right hand, the gold
mountings of her pistol glinting, and pulled her mount
back onto its flat beaverlike tail. The whole line piled up
backward as the airjeep rose slightly, whizzed past in front
of them, and then turned. Its 15-mm's chugged and the
bullets cut a swath through the grass. Then, before the

woman and her troop could turn to flee, the other jeep, now directly behind them at a couple of hundred feet, fired a warning burst.

Angrily, the woman pushed her pistol back into its holster, said something to a man with a drawn sword beside her, and sat staring at them defiantly.

He handed his rifle to Fitzurse, who slung it, and went forward, his right hand raised in what was a peace-sign on Terra, Thor and Loki and ought to be one here. She *was* a beauty; hardly more than a girl, he guessed. He stopped twenty feet from her, lowered his hand, and bowed. She said something in a sharp, demanding voice. He smiled at her and asked her if she'd ever thought of going into tele-movies. She spoke again—different intonation, probably different language. He shook his head and replied from the *Iliad* in the original. She said something exasperated and quite possibly unladylike.

"Let's stop this foolishness," he said. Then he pointed to her and raised one finger. He pointed to the men on either side of her and raised three fingers. Then he dismounted from an imaginary—whatever they were—and pointed back to the striped canopy in front of the landing-craft, and pantomimed sitting down, pouring from a bottle, and drinking healths, wondering if that was one of their customs. Apparently it was; the girl smiled, jerked her chin toward her right shoulder in what looked like a nod, and spoke to the man beside her.

He and one or two others began raising objections. That convinced her that it was a good idea; kicking her feet out of the stirrups, she sprang to the ground, tossing her reins to one of the troopers, and started to unbuckle a belt on which she carried an unfemininely heavy and serviceable dagger.

"No! No!" He stopped herewith a gesture and signed

that she should keep the weapon, touching the butt of the
10-mm Colt-Argentine automatic on his own belt. She
smiled and nodded again. That made sense; an armed
host should not expect his guests to disarm.

The man to whom she had first spoken—big and
brawny, with a graying yellow beard and a gilded breastplate whose nicks and bullet-splashed showed that it
wasn't ornamental—dismounted and beckoned to two
musketeers, who slung their weapons and got to the
ground. There was a general dismounting along the line as
the girl and her three companions went over to the mar-
quee.

They sat down at a trestle-table which was provided
with screens and recorders and writing and sketching
equipment and a blackboard. Wine, or at least fermented
apple-juice, was poured. A five gallon jug of the hydroponic hard cider, to which a half-gallon of pure medical
alcohol had been added, was sent out to the troopers.
They'd settled the point that the biochemistry of this planet
was entirely Terra-type, and any people who had gotten
as far as castles, riding animals and firearms must surely
have discovered fermentation somewhere along the way.

It appeared that they had. They all drank with obvious
pleasure, surprised at the coolness of the drink. Evidently
they hadn't gotten as far as refrigeration. Then, after
everybody had drunk everybody else's health, they settled
down to language-learning.

He touched himself on the breast and said, "Me." He
tapped Fitzurse on the chest and said, "You," speaking to
him directly. Fitzurse repeated it to Charley Clifford, who
passed it on to Margaret Hale, who returned it to point of
origin. He turned to the girl, touched himself again, and
said:

"Me Roger Barron. You?"

"Me Rylla-dad-Hostigos,' she said. "Rylla-dad-Hostigos *tsan vovaro*. Roger Barron *doru vovaron*."

That was picking it up smartly enough. There were introductions. The man with the graying beard and the battlemarred cuirass was Chartiphon. He didn't bother trying to remember the names of the other two; the audiovisual camera had them. They went on from there. Some of it involved moving pictures; they startled the newcomers only at first. After all, if people had things that went up off the ground and guns that kept on shooting, why shouldn't they have pictures that moved and talked like live? More was done on the blackboard or on sketch-pads, or acted out. The girl thought it was fun. When she wasn't trying to keep an imperious expression on her face, she was lovely. She had a tilty little nose and a golden dusting of freckles across it.

Chartiphon and one of the musketeers tagged along faithfully. The third man dropped out, and he and Fitzurse began examining each other's weapons. Finally they strolled off to have a shooting-match between a 7-mm Sterberg and one of the big flintlocks.

"Place you come; where?" the girl was finally able to ask.

"Place name Terra; much far," he told her. "No word for say."

She gave one of her people's jerky nods. "Me place Hostigos." She pointed to the west and said something complicated.

"Place far?"

She grimaced and made a spread-fingered clawing gesture in front of her face. That was just what she had been trying to tell him. Then she caught up one of the seven-color pens she had learned to use and bent over a sketch-pad. First, a lance, with a red-and-blue pennon; she gave him the word for that. Then numbers. Their numeration was something like the Roman system—dashes for digits from one to four, a half-circle for five, and a circle for ten. Circle with stroke across it, fifty; circle with cross, a hundred. A lance was the unit of measurement, about ten feet, and a hundred lances were a great-lance; the prefix was *hos-*. It figured that she was about forty miles from home. One of the first blessings of Terran culture to be showered on these people would be Arabic numeration, he decided.

He took her to the other trestle-table, where the map Lourenço and Luther and Margaret Hale had been making from air photos was thumbtacked out, hoping that she knew what a map was. She did. As soon as she saw it, she clapped her hands delightedly and began babbling in excitement. After she became coherent, she began pointing things out, naming them.

The whole of "our" valley was Hostigos. So was the town beside the river; the castle on the ridge overlooking it was Tarr-Hostigos. It was her home. She went back to the other table and sat down with a pen, and this time she drew two little pictures, unmistakeably if indelicately masculine and feminine. Evidently prudery wasn't one of the local shortcomings. She connected them with a horizontal line, dropped a vertical line from the female symbol, and drew another symbol like it.

"Me, Rylla," she said. Then she pointed to the male symbol above. "Ptosphes." He was something-or-other—prince, duke, lord—of Hostigos. She drew a small stylized flame around the mother-symbol and made an equally stylized sound of lamentation. These people cremated their dead; her father, Prince Ptosphes of Hostigos, was a widower.

And they'd hoped to catch some wandering peddler or something of the sort for their first contact!

He touched the mark that represented the other castle, at the mountain-pass to the north.

"This Hostigos?"

"No! Nostor!" she replied. "Belong Prince Gormoth."

She used another word, and to explain it grimaced ferociously and drew her dagger in a threatening manner. The word would be enemy. He and Reginald Fitzurse exchanged glances.

"You go Tarr-Hostigos now?" he asked. "We go Tarr-Hostigos, make talk Prince Ptosphes. "You, me, me people, you people, all go Tarr-Hostigos." He pointed to the contragravity vehicles. "All go up, high; go Tarr-Hostigos fast."

Her eyes widened in wonder. "Me? Go up? High?" She pointed to the sky, and then bent, looking down. "See everything, like map?" Then she turned to her bearded henchman Chartiphon and began babbling excitedly again.

As soon as Chartiphon understood what she was saying, he began protesting. Even the two musketeers joined him, and they all shouted objections. The girl shouted back at them, banging a small and shapely but very firm fist on the table. She must have been taunting them with being afraid; the objections now became indignant denials. Finally she turned to him.

"We all go Tarr-Hostigos in sky-things," she told him.

Chartiphon and the two musketeers went to break the news to the rank-and-file. For a moment, it looked like a mutiny in the making. Then they came over, some to help get the camp things into the landing-craft and the rest leading the mounts—they were *oukry,* plural the same as singular—to be put aboard.

It had been just as wonderful as she had imagined—everything spread out below like a map, but real instead of pictures on parchment. It had been the most wonderful thing in her whole life, and she wished that it could have gone on for hours. There had been a little trouble, at first, when they came to the castle; everybody saw the sky-things and Chartiphon's son, Harmakros, had manned the walls and fired a warning shot with one of the cannon. She had been afraid that there would be more shooting and that the—the *Terrans*—would shoot back. But the Terrans had another wonder, a little thing she could hold in her hand, that made her voice so loud that she could call down from above and everybody in Tarr-Hostigos heard her. So they had come down safely into the great enclosure in front of the citadel, and there had been no shooting.

But much excitement. Her father and Xentos and Harmakros met them in front of the main citadel gateway, acting as though somebody came down from the sky to visit them every day, she was clearly proud of how calmly they behaved, but the castle-folk went almost crazy. Harmakros got forty or fifty infantrymen to push them back with pikestaves and musket-butts, and the score of cavalrymen of her escort got their oukry unloaded and helped. Finally things got a little quiet.

She had to help her father, using the few words of the Terrans' language she had learned and the words of her language that she knew they had learned, and her father made them welcome to Tarr-Hostigos, and sent Harmakros off to show them to rooms in the keep.

And now, at last, she and Chartiphon and her father and Xentos were alone in her father's little work-chamber.

Chartiphon sat down heavily, and then remembered to take off his helmet and his sword-belt.

"Wine, for the love of Dralm!" he said, and when Xentos poured him a cup, he emptied it at a gulp. "I have never been more afraid in all my life, not even when we fought the Dazouri at Sykrys! And this crazy daughter of yours thought it was all fun!"

"But it was! Father, it was—it was—" Even in her own language, she had no words for how wonderful it had been.

"Chartiphon, our Rylla is still up in the sky," her father said, and he was truly smiling, even if it was only a wan ghost of his old smile. "Till she gets back on the ground, you'd better tell me about it."

Chartiphon thought for a moment, and then began to tell how they had seen the strangers camped by the road, and thought that they might be Nostori, and how she had taken command and arrayed the little troop for a charge. And then he went on to tell what had happened.

"What could we do?" he asked. "They held our lives between thumb and finger; they could have wiped us out in less time than I speak of it. But they wanted to parley. It is my thought that they seek to be friends."

"But what do they want of us?" her father asked. "And where do they come from?"

"As to where they come from, they say it is a place called Terra, and that it is very far. It may be that they want to trade with us, or they may be exiles seeking a home. Or they may be scouts ahead of a great army."

"In that case, we had better make friends with them quickly," Xentos said. "And hope that Gormoth of Nestor doesn't."

The smile came back to her father's face. "Tell me about these guns of theirs, Chartiphon."

"They have small ones, half as heavy as our muskets, which load ten shots at a time and fire as fast as the trigger is pulled. They have pistols that load with twelve shots. They have guns a little heavier than muskets, and guns like small cannon, that shoot very fast, *ah-ah-ah-ah-ah!* as long as the trigger is held back."

He opened his belt-pouch and got out two brass tubes, as long as one of her fingers, necked like wine-bottles. One was empty; the other had a pointed metal cork. He handed them across to her father.

"I stole these," Chartiphon admitted. "I had to; I was afraid of making them suspicious if I asked for them, and I wanted you to see them. These are what they load the guns with. The pointed thing is the bullet; the fire-seed is inside, and there must be something like a bit of flint inside, too, to make the spark. Look at the empty one; you can see where something in the gun punched it. Every time the guns fire, one of the empty holders flies out of it, and a new one is put into the barrel. I think they use the kick of the gun to do that," he added, as though he had just thought of it.

Her father looked at the brass things and nodded. "That could be." He thought for a moment. "If they would use their weapons to help us, we could laugh at Gormoth, and Sarrask wouldn't even be worth that. The question is, would they?"

"If they were here as our guests when Gormoth invades, they'd have to help us to defend themselves," Chartiphon said.

"I think they will help us, anyhow," she said. "I don't know what they want here, but I think they want to be our friends." She felt herself smiling. "And the one who is called Roger likes me. He doesn't realize it yet, but he will."

"Princess!" Chartiphon was shocked.

"I think Rylla likes the Terran called Roger," her father said. "It is to be seen in her face when she speaks about him."

And now, as her face warmed, she knew that what was

to be seen on it was a blush.

"But we must learn their language," Xentos said. "We can't tell them about our troubles until we do."

"They'll learn ours first. They are very good at learning languages," Chartiphon said. "In just a short while, they were able to talk to us. Princess, tell them about the pictures that move and talk."

"Oh, yes!" And then she remembered the wonderful thing that Roger had given her, the silver thing that wrote like a pen, in black and red and blue and all the colors. "But let me show you this, first. . ."

The rooms to which they had been conducted were at the top of the keep, on the east side. The outer walls were twelve feet thick, pierced with loopholes big enough for a man to stand in and narrowing to apertures six inches by a foot. On the other side, wide arches gave onto a balcony, covered with flowering vines, above a garden in a central court. There was no window-glass, and the fireplaces had an unused look. Evidently it never got cold here.

The horde of servants who had helped install them had gaped in amazement at the contragravity skids on which they had floated their belongings up from the landing-craft, and then departed reluctantly. So, a few minutes later, had the young officer in the gilded armor—his name was Harmakros, and he was old Chartiphon's son—and now they were alone. They had a screen up and tuned to the ship; a crowd of them were in front of it, telling Adriaan de Ruyter and Lisette Krull and Sylvia Davock about the castle and their reception there.

He strolled out on the balcony and found Reginald Fitzurse and Nancy Patterson looking down into the garden.

"Well, this was much better than we expected," he said.

"Yes," Fitzurse agreed. "I thought we'd have to spend

a day or so convincing some backwoods farmer that we weren't really horrible monsters. I think you made rather an impression on the young lady."

"I wish I could be a little more sure of what we've gotten into," Nancy said.

"Ah. You were another who thought we were spending too much money on armament, when we were outfitting. Beginning to wish we'd have two or three times as much to spend, now?"

She looked at him sharply. "Are you getting that, too?" she asked.

"I got that the second little Rylla formed up her troop and charged us. Around here, stranger equals enemy; hit them before they hit you."

"And this castle; these walls, and all these cannon," Nancy said. "You know, I doubt if there are more than twenty thousand people in this whole valley, and the agriculture, or what I saw of it from the air, is the most primative sort. Yet there are at least two hundred soldiers, completely nonproductive, here at the castle. They wouldn't keep that many in idleness if they didn't have to."

"That's only a fraction of them," Fitzurse said. "I saw close to a thousand infantry drilling in the fields up the river, when we were coming in. And look how promptly they got the walls manned and got of that warning shot, when they sighted us."

And Prince Whoozis of Whatzit, who holds the castle at the mountain-pass; he thought of the professionally trained manner in which Rylla handled her big dagger to convey the idea of enmity. If she's really had him in front of her—

"I've been thinking about that. Let's don't mention it around Luther or Sylvia or Charley, it would only start another infernal argument, but all this red-carpet treatment may be on account of our potential value as allies."

"Oh, heavens, I hope not!" Nancy said. "We don't want to get mixed up in any wars."

"Not without knowing what they're all about," Fitzurse agreed.

He and the retired soldier exchanged glances past Nancy. People who want allies make treaties with them. Stellar explorations, Ltd., needed a treaty with somebody. Talk that over later in private. There was likely to be a serious division on policy.

They strolled into the big room where the screen was. Karl Zahanov was talking to de Ruyter, promising to get a relief ship-watch up as soon as possible. Charley Clifford, in the middle of a group sampling the wine the servants had left, was pontificating:

"No, we simply mustn't speak of them as 'human;' that is reserved for *Homo sapiens terra*. They're sapient beings, so we can call them people, but they are utterly alien to us, descended from a different though remarkably parallel line of evolution. We just can't call them human."

Phooie! He'd call them human, any day. Then another thought suddenly burgeoned within him. He'd go further than that. He'd be quite willing to call Prince Ptosphes father-in-law.

The feast had started at dusk and lasted until well past midnight. They knew, from the tests made by Sylvia Davock and Lisette Krull and Charley Clifford and Katherine Gower, that the food of the planet was edible by Terrans, without deficiencies of any essential vitimines or trace-elements. Properly cooked, it was also delicious. Now, with the sun beginning to peep levelly through the eastern loopholes, their quarters had been invaded by a posse of servant-girls with breakfast. It was an informal meal; they sat on cushions on the floor, with the bowls of steaming food and the baskets of fruit and pots of hot spicy tea in front of them. Nancy wondered if the ancestors of these people hadn't been nomads, accustomed to eating on the ground around campfires.

They were talking about a name for the planet. They'd need one to file discovery claim, and even among themselves they couldn't go on calling it Eta Stellex II, or "this planet."

"What do the people here call it?" somebody asked.

"They don't know it is a planet," Karl Zahanov said. "I was talking—well, sketching and making signs—with this old fellow Xentos. He took me to the castle library and showed me a map of what he called 'Everything.' The south-central part of this continent, a rough circle, with sea all around it. I tried to show him what a stellar system was. I don't think he understood. We hadn't enough idea-words in common."

That would correct itself. Nancy Patterson was worried.

"Well, you know, he's some sort of a priest," she said. "On this culture-level, cosmology's part of the religion. You might have been committing all kinds of sacrilege and heresy."

Julio Almagro was watching a couple of the servant-girls, shapely and lightly-clad.

"Pity Venus is a planet already," he said. "How about Aphrodite?"

Zahanov passed his hand in front of his face in the negative gesture he was teaching himself to use.

"The Astrographic Commission won't accept Helleno-Roman names for anything outside the Sol System. They prefer names from Norse mythology, as long as they last."

Somebody mentioned that Freya was the Norse Venus.

Zahanov jerked his chin at his right shoulder.

"Freya's good. The Chartered Freya Company," he said experimentally.

"We haven't been chartered, yet," Fitzurse mentioned. "We still have to get a treaty from somebody."

"I think we can get one from Ptosphes."

"Of course, there's the question of just how sovereign he is, here," Lourenco Narvaes said. "I know, he has an army, but he may be just a minor nobleman in something big."

Luther Smith wasn't thinking about that. "Look what we can give these people," he said. "Air transportation. Nuclear power. Telecast communication. Even take some of the minor things, like refrigeration, or paper and printing. . ."

Almagro took his eyes from the two girls—the two *Freyan* girls—and threw his bucket of cold water.

"If you think we're going to transform this planet with what we have here, think again, he advised. "We would need four or five shiploads of equipment, and fifty to a hundred technicians and engineers, just for a start. What we have is one ship that should have been junked ten years ago, Adriaan's yacht, and a couple of million sols in debts."

"If we get a charter, we can float a company, and then we'll have credit,"Zahanov said.

"You can't float a company just by waving a charter and yelling, 'Lookit, we gotta planet!' If Freya weren't inhabited, yes. Anybody will invest in a colonization company. But there are too many restrictions to colonizing an inhabited planet, and investors don't like that. What we'll have to do is find something on this planet that can be sold on Terra at a profit after space-freight costs, and space-freight costs are murder."

"Well, there's this tea," Dave MacDonald said, lifting the cup in his hand. "I had a helluva hangover, this morning, and one cup yanked me right out of it. Coffee isn't in it with this stuff."

"Sure," Almagro agreed. "In a couple of years, we'll be shipping it all over the Federation—if we're in business then. But you can't start an interstellar company on a new luxury-item. Too chancey; the big money won't risk it. We need something with an existing demand. Remember, the first thing we have to sell is stock."

They were still talking about that when one of the girls came over.

"You . . . want . . . more?" she asked bashfully, in precise Lingua Terra.

Nobody did. She and her companion began gathering up empty bowls and things. A little later Chartiphon's son, Harmakros, came in. He saw Nancy Patterson first of all, and they smiled at each other. Harmakros had been especially attentive to Nancy at the feast.

"You . . . all . . . sleep . . . good?" he asked.

"Yes, thank you," Roger told him, in his own language. "Sleep good. Good things for eat, this daylight; much good."

"Much happy." He spoke to one of the girls, and she want out. "Rylla, Xentos, come: We make talk."

They made talk, all that day and for days to come. Mostly it was with Rylla and Xentos and Hamakros; sometimes Chartiphon and, seeming to snatch the time from an endless press of other affairs, Ptosphes. Luther Smith and Lourenço Narvaes went back to the *Stellex* to relieve deRuyter and the girls, and thereafter joined the language classes by screen. Words for things or acts that could be shown; thing-and-act combination words; words for ideas, and for ideas about ideas. Sentence structure, and grammar. It was surprising how little grammar was needed to convey meaning, and how much trouble a little knowledge of grammar could make.

The language, they found, was called Sosti; it was spoken all over the river-valley system to which the Freyan civilization was confined. They learned the names of the river and its tributaries, and of the cities and their rulers. There were a surprising number of princely realms and sovereignties, and this bothered Nancy Patterson. It wasn't what the culture pattern indicated.

The civilization was an ancient one; the language was uniform, and the culture and the economy unified. These were a warlike people; the nobleman was first of all a warrior. Then why hadn't there been conquests and, long ago, a single empire? Apparently there never had been. Three great kingdoms existed in an area no larger than the Mississippi Valley on Terra, each a loose collection of minor princedoms. Prince Ptosphes, for instance, was a nominal subject of King Kaiphranos, at Harphax, the big city at the forks of the river—his kingdom was called Hos-Harphax—and so were the neighboring princes of Nostor to the north and Sask to the south. There was always trouble between Ptosphes and Gormoth of Nostor, and there was talk of impending open war, which disturbed Luther Smith and Sylvia Davock. What bothered Nancy was not being able to understand the situation. These kings should long ago have estabished their authority in their respective kingdoms, and then wars among them should have unified the whole civilization into one empire.

The language-learning gradually spread out from the big room at the top of the keep. Karl Zahanov and Adriaan de Ruyter spent a lot of time with Xentos in his study. Arthur Muramoto and Dave MacDonald and Margaret Hale were usually in the shop of the castle armorer, or the black-smith, or the carpenter. Julio Almagro, a horseman on Terra, haunted the stables. Charley Clifford found a professional brother in the castle healer, who had his dispensary and surgery across from the guardroom inside the main gate. And of course Reginald Fitzurse and Charti-phon became almost inseparable.

"You know, they never invented the socket bayonet here," Fitzurse said. "They have to mix pikemen and halberdiers with their infantry musketeres. So I just invented it for them; now every infantryman can have a musket. Trouble is, every one has to be individually fitted; it's only an accident when you find two musket-barrels with the same outside diameter at the muzzle. Take a year and a half to get them all fitted."

He was surprised, too, at the muskets. They were, he said, almost exactly like guns he'd seen in museums in Cape Town and Johannesburg, which had been used in the Great Trek.

"Well, that's like the physical resemblance of the people to Terran humans," Charley said. "You wouldn't claim, would you, that some Boers had their oxcarts fitted with Dillinghams, and trekked out here to Freya with their guns? No; if you have black powder and no percussion caps, there are only a few ways in which you can get fire to the charge in the barrel, and a flintlock's the simplest and best way to do it. Well, environmental conditions being the same here and on Terra, the same physical structure is the most efficient for a race of sapient beings."

Charley's insistence on the non-humanity of Freyans was getting a trifle tiresome, especially when one is thinking, at the moment, of a tilty little nose with a dusting of golden freckles across it.

"Charley, have you found one characteristic among

these people that differentiates them from us?'' he asked. ''Do they differ from any of us more than a full-blooded Mongoloid differs from a full-blooded Negroid or Caucasian?''

''Well, no,'' Clifford grudged. ''But they can't be human! They evolved here on Freya; there's no genetic connection at all between them and us.''

He was trying very hard to be convincing. Maybe it was Charles Clifford, M.D., whom he was really trying to convince.

They sat together in a double chair, just wide enough to be comfortably and agreeably close. Her golden head was bent over the notepad, and somehow his arm had managed to get up on her shoulder. When it had, she'd only snuggled a little closer.

''This is my name,'' she said. ''See; rrr-ih, lll-ah, Rylla.''

Two characters—they wrote from the bottom of the page up—each with a little dingbat like an accent-mark. Phonetic-syllabic; he'd been afraid of having to learn a thousand or so ideographs, or hire some scribe of questionable reliability.

''And here is yours.'' She switched from blue to red for that. ''See. Rrr-oh. Djjj. Eh-rrr.''

The accent-mark things were the vowels; you put them under the consonants when they preceded and over when they followed. This looked like an easy alphabet to learn.

''And here is yours, in our writing.' He did it in block capitals; time enough to go into upper and lower case when she had learned the letters. ''This is R-y-l-l-a.''

She looked at it in mock-horror, and then laughed.

''That—*me?*'' she demanded in Lingua Terra. ''But so many letters. And it goes on its side, and the wrong way.'' She made the funny clawing gesture in front of her face, which seemed to convey complete bafflement. "I will never learn this!"

"Oh, you've just had it, for now. let's take a break."

"Take?" She made a grasping gesture. "Break?" She snapped something imaginary with her fingers. "Break what?"

"Throw it in. Time out," he told her. "Stop this now and do something else."

"Yes!" She jumped up and caught one of his hands in both of hers. "Let us *take a break* in the flower-and-grass place. The garden."

"Good. Or would you rather take a ride in an aircar?"

He knew what the answer to that would be. As they went out, Nancy Patterson, trying to teach Harmakros the Arabic numeration and the importance of a figure for absolutely nothing at all, waved to them. Another Terro-Freyan romance sprouting; somebody else wouldn't listen to Charley Clifford.

The big policy debate started as soon as Karl Zahanov and Margaret Hale went up to relieve Luther and Lourenço on ship-watch. It wasn't that Luther wanted to make trouble; he'd just come to some conclusions the correctness of which he was positive. That was usual with idealists.

In the first place, he wanted them all to leave Tarr-Hostigos and go to Harphax. He'd heard, like everybody else, of the trouble between Ptosphes and Gormoth of Nostor, and he wanted to be out of Hostigos before a war started. Again, it would have been easy to do Luther an injustice. He wasn't a coward; he just thought all wars were wrong and he didn't want any part in one. Then, he wanted to start immediate trading operations. He and Lourenço and, by screen, Zahanov, had designed a hundred and fifty foot freighter with a wooden hull, which could be built by local labor and lifted with one of the heavy-duty contragravity generators. It looked more like a cantilever bridge than an airframe, but he estimated a five hundred ton payload and an airspeed of a hundred and fifty mph.

"We all admit we have to find something we can sell on Terra," he argued. "We won't find it sitting around here, and the best way we can learn about the products of this planet will be by trading-voyages."

Nobody denied that. What Barron couldn't see was the necessity of leaving Hostigos, especially when things were just getting good with him and Rylla. And he could see a great many objections to a move to Harphax.

"We still don't know what things are like there. We don't know what powerful established trading interests we'd come into conflict with, and neither do we know how soon this King Kaiphranos would get envious of us and try to grab our ship, not realizing that it wouldn't do him any good after he got it. We don't have that to worry about here."

"Well, can we trust Ptosphes?" Luther countered. "He's been very hospitable so far, but—"

"We can trust him," Fitzurse said. "We could wipe this whole castle garrison out at the first act of treachery, and he knows it. We couldn't defend outselves effectively in the middle of a couple of hundred thousand people in Harphax. Trade there, yes. But keep our base here."

"We still need a treaty. I think we can get one from Ptosphes; a better treaty than we could get from Kaiphranos, at least now."

'Well, Kaiphranos is Ptosphes' sovereign; a treaty with a subject prince wouldn't be as good as a treaty from the king. I doubt if Ptosphes has enough sovereignty to give us a treaty the Federation Colonial Office would accept,"

Luther argued.

"You know why we can get a treaty from Ptosphes? He
needs our help in case Gormoth of Nostor invades him. If
King Kaiphranos hasn't enough sovereignty to keep his
subject princes from making war on one another, he
doesn't have enough sovereignty outside the city of harphax to make a treaty with."

"That's another thing!" Luther began clamoring. "I've
heard about that, too. That's why I want us to get out of
here, before we get caught in the middle of a war."

There was, he had long ago learned, one infallible
weapon against the idealist, and that was moral indignation.

"You mean, you want us to tell Ptosphes it was nice
knowing him and thanks for everything, and then run out
on him when he needs help?" he demanded. "Abandon
him and his people to massacre and enslavement? Maybe
you could do that and still respect yourself; be damned if I
could."

"Yes: I thought I was the business-is-business guy, and
Luther was the idealist," Almagro put in. "If that's ideal-
ism, I'll take a plate of hash."

"And have you any idea,' Fitzurse asked. "what effect
a shameful desertion like that would have on our prestige?
Why, no Freyan would ever trust any Terran's friendship
again."

"Luther, it's our moral duty to help Ptosphes defend his
country." Surprisingly, the feminine voice came from the
screen-speaker. Generally Margaret Hale stayed completely out of these bickers, unless they involved the
Keene-Gonzales-Dillingham Theory of Non-Einsteinian
Relativity and the Dillingham hyperdrive. "You say you're
opposed to war; why, if we didn't help Ptosphes, we'd be
no better than passive accomplices of this Prince Gormoth

in an unprovoked war of conquest.''

Luther looked hurt and bewildered. Why, they were actually taking a lofty moral attitude toward *him,* instead of defending their own position. He said something, rather weakly, about what the Federation government would say.

"I'd hate to listen to what they'd say if we deserted Ptosphes, under the circumstances," Fitzurse told him.

There was a lot more of it, mostly repetitious, with Luther's position getting steadily weaker. In the end, Stellar Explorations, Ltd., voted to authorize Roger Barron and Reginald Fitzurse to offer Prince Ptosphes of Hostigos a bilateral offensive and defensive alliance.

"He was very happy to accept," Barron reported, the next afternoon. "There will be a meeting with the Council of Hostigos this evening to ratify the treaty. That is a pure formality; Ptosphes is really absolute ruler here. Now here's the situation. . ."

He showed them, on the map, the Hostigos-Nostor boundary, along the two small rivers that joined to form the Darro, and explained how the castle that guarded Dombra Pass had passed, almost a century before, to Nostor by betrayal.

"There's been raiding and barn-burning and cattle-rustling on both sides ever since; that's accepted. But lately, some outsider has made a deal wth Gormoth to furnish him with money and supplies and mercenaries and guarantee the permissive support or at least the non-interference of King Kaiphranos, in return for concessions after the conquest. This outsider, Styphon, is to get this section up here, called the Yellowstone Valley—"

"Did you say Styphon?" Nancy demanded. "Why, Styphon is one of the gods these people worship. Not here in

Hostigos, but other places. He's a fire-god, or sun-god, or something like that."

"Come to think of it, Roger", Fitzurse interrupted, "Xentos and Ptosphes never spoke of Styphon, at all. They talked about Styphon's House; they always used that expression."

"That's right; Styphon's House," Nancy said. "It's some kind of a theocracy; all the top priests are in Harphax, but they have temples all over. Tell me; what's fire-seed?"

"Fire-seed?" Fitzurse echoed. "Why, that's gunpowder."

"But they get it from the priests of Styphon. I thought it was some sacramental substance, maybe used in connection with their cremation rites. Are you sure?"

"It's all I've been hearing about. Sore subject, here; they're almost out of it, and can't get any more. I'm surprised Harmakros didn't mention it to you."

She and Harmakros would have had other things to talk about. Then he swore at his own obtuseness.

"Now it figures!" He swore again. "The whole thing figures. Say these priests accidentally discovered gunpowder, a few centuries ago. . ."

"Bet I know how," Charley Clifford interrupted. "Bet Styphon was originally a healer-god, like Aesculapius, and the priests were the doctors. Sulpher, saltpeter and Charcoal sounds just like the sort of mess early iron-age, try-anything empirics would mix up, and then I suppose they put it on the stove and got a big surprise. After that, Styphon went out of medical practice and into the munition business."

"Yes. Styphon's House is the only source of gunpowder; the priests make it, keep it a temple secret, and furnish it to the kings and princes. Firearms and artillery are just good enough that nobody without powder has a chance against anybody with it. That's why this place is cluttered up with this hodgepodge of petty sovereignties and tributary princes who don't pay tribute and kings who can't keep their subjects from fighting among themselves. Styphon's House wants a lot of rival rulers they can play off against each other. Anybody doesn't cough up with offerings to the temple, they shut the powder off on him and supply his rivals, and see what happens. I'll bet the offerings just roll in!"

"Yellowstone Valley," Arthur Muramoto said. "Can anybody show me where it is? I'll take a jeep and go look at it right away."

"Sulphur?"

"Sure; what else?"

"This is old-fashioned, country-style black powder?" Lisette Krull asked. "Well, if Arthur finds sulphur, you can tell Ptosphes that his ammunition worries are over. Little Lisette will make him all the fire-seed he wants, and she'll eat the first batch if it won't outshoot Styphon's Best."

"Where'll you get the niter?"

"The first thing I noticed, coming down, was that every farm has a manure-pile bigger than the farmhouse. The ground under every one of them is saturated with KNO_3. Anybody want to bet on how soon the priests of Styphon will be out on the sidewalk beating a drum for pennies?"

There was an electric light at the ceiling of Ptosphes' council-chamber, with its own nuclear-conversion unit, and three more stood on the table in place of the candlesticks. Some of the Council had never seen them before, and blinked in awe.

"Well, tell us all," Xentos was saying. "To what will we pledge ourselves?"

"We will pledge friendship and brotherhood with one another," Barron said. "We will pledge to aid one another in war. Prince Ptosphes will guarantee to the Company of Searchers Among the Stars the right to live in peace in his realm, and to buy and sell, and to buy land and erect buildings on it, and places to land our sky-things. The Company of Searchers Among the Stars will pledge themselves to respect the rights of the people of Hostigos, and to maintain the right of the house of Prince Ptosphes to rule in Hostigos, against enemies from without and treasons and rebellions within, and specifically against Prince Gormoth of Nostor and Prince Sarrask of Sask. And we will pledge ourselves to give weapons, as we can, to Prince Ptosphes and his people, and to make weapons and teach them how to make weapons. And we will make fire-seed, and teach the people of Hostigos to make it."

There was an instant's silence, and then the room blew up almost like a barrel of fire-seed. Everybody was shouting at once. Chartiphon was brandishing his sword and yelling, "Death to Gormoth! Destruction to Nostor!" Rylla ran around the table and flung her arms about his neck. Nancy Patterson and Harmakros were embracing. And Ptosphes had flung back his head and was laughing like a madman. It was the first time, now that he thought of it, that he had ever heard the Prince of Hostigos laugh. Things must have been pretty grim, up to now. Then there was a general cry of, "Wine! Wine!" Evidently there was only one way to make a treaty really official here.

"The making of fire-seed will take time," Ptosphes said, after things had quieted down a little. "The people must be taught, and the stuff to make it of must be gathered, and things to make it with prepared, and we know nothing of any of this. The priests of Styphon have kept it a secret since no man can remember."

Mark one up for Ptosphes; at least he had some faint glow of an idea of production problems.

"Well, I know what has to be done," Lisette said, "and I know what we don't have to do it with. I'll have to organize the niter production, first of all. How about you, Lourenço? How soon do you think you can get the mill ready?"

Narvaes estimated a week, doubled that, and then said: "That's for about fifty pounds a day. That can be increased gradually, after we get workers trained."

Arthur Muramoto was even less optimistic about sulphur production; he gave it a month, to be on the safe side.

"But we can't wait that long," Ptosphes objected. "Gormoth will learn of what we're doing, and he'll be across the mountains before we're ready for him."

"Don't let him find out," Fitzurse said. "Seal your frontiers. Haven't you done that already?"

Ptosphes wasn't exactly sure what he meant. Fitzurse told him.

"Cavalry patrols guarding every road and trail out of Hostigos; let anybody in, but let nobody out. How about this Sarrask of Sask, by the way?"

Ptosphes used some words that hadn't come up yet in the language-learning. Xentos said:

"He will attack as soon as he hears that Gormoth's army is across the rivers, but not before. At least, I don't think he will."

"Then we'll take care of him. But this Tarr-Dombra, the castle at the pass; that will have to come first. That's the key to the whole situation."

"Man, do you know about Tarr-Dombra?" Chartiphon cried. "Tarr-Dombra has never been taken. We would have it today, if it hadn't been sold to Gormoth's grandfather by Him Whom Phadrigos Slew."

"Father," Harmakros said reprovingly. "Tarr-Dombra has never been attacked with sky-things."

"That's right," Fitzurse said. "Give me a hundred men and a week to train them and the first cloudy night we'll take it, from the top down."

"Harmakros, pick your best hundred men," Chartiphon told his son. "Men able to learn from those wiser than they are, if you have that many. The Terran war-captain Reginald will teach them a new way to take castles."

"We ought to have a good fifth column, both in Nostor and Sask," he said, and then had to explain what that was. Ptosphes seemed to question the propriety of such a way of making war. Xentos had no such scruples.

"Styphon's House is established in both," he said, "and in both, the priests of Dralm are ill-pleased, because the people have no more offerings for them, after Gormoth and Sarrask make them give offerings to Styphon's House. They look to me for advice. I will send word to them."

"We'll airdrop agents outside both Nostor and Sask cities, with radios. You can give them contacts, people you trust. Then they can gather those who have been wronged or bear any grudge against the prince, and the can gather news for us, and spread tales, and get people to speak and act against Styphon's House."

For ten days, Karl Zahanov, on the ship, reported unvaryingly fair weather over the north-western part of the continent. Fitzure and Dave MacDonald took charge of the commando training, and at all hours men in black with long pistols and sawed-off muskets and short pikemen's swords were swarming out of air-lorries onto the battlements of Tarr-Hostigos. Arthur Muramoto had a gang of workmen up Yellowstone Valley; Luther Smith and Lourenco Narvaes and Charley Clifford took over a grist-mill and began converting it for mixing and grinding powder. Lisette Krull, with anybody she could press into service, began organizing niter production. There already existed a small charcoal-burning industry.

There was a shortage of everything, particularly skilled help. In the town of Hostigos, only three or four pot-tinkers knew anything at all about working sheet-metal, and one of these had to be dragged to a chopping-block and threatened with instant beheadment before he consented even to try to make evaporating pans for the sulphur refinery. There was also trouble with the peasants about the manure-piles.

Barron, Fitzurse and Almagro formed a general staff, along with Ptosphes, Chartiphon and Xentos. The latter was also busy fomenting treasons and plots among his co-religionists in Nostor and Sask by radio, and the three Terran members usually found themselves called away to show some Freyan mechanic how to use a monkey-wrench, or to land a spy outside one of the enemy capitals, or jockey a landing-craft to and from the ship. Barron had taught Rylla to fly an aircar, and Nancy had given Harmakros a few flying lessons; outside of them, all the air-transport had to be flown by Terrans, and when they were doing that, they couldn't be doing anything else. Nobody got much sleep. Everybody wished that he or she had been born quintuplets.

Along with everything else, he managed to find time to learn everything that Xentos or anybody else at Tarr-Hostigos knew about the operations of Styphon's House. One item of information intrigued him. Wherever there was a temple, there was always, nearby, a large farm, enclosed with high and impenetrable thorn hedges, to which a great deal of manure was hauled, and also bags of sulphur said to be used in religious ceremonies. He flew by night to take infrared photographs of the ones both at Nostor and at Sask.

Then, on the evening of the ninth day, everybody decided that the age of miracles had not yet ended. Charley Clifford, who had surprised nobody more than himself by developing a talent for the work, reported that the powder-mill was in production, to the extent of fifteen pounds. A charge of it drove one of the big two-ounce musket-balls an inch and a half deeper into a block of wood than an equal charge of Styphon's Best, and fouled the bore less.

It was decided to take time out for a feast the next evening. It had been a week since the last one, and feasts were important to Freyan morale. Chartiphon and Xentos wanted to open it by firing one of the bombards with the new powder, until they learned that the production being celebrated would be equal to about one-quarter charge for one of them. They finally settled on Rylla firing a musket down the banquet-table at a dummy robed in black and red like a priest of Styphon. That last was gratifying; Hostigos had come to recognize its real enemy.

The feast was still in progress when Margaret Hale called down from the ship.

"Get ready for it tomorrow night," she said. "Cold front moving in; heavy clouding with it."

The feasters broke into cheers when this was translated. He noticed that Nancy Patterson was clutching Harmakros' arm, and that her cheering was rather mechanical.

The firelight glowed brighter through the fog ahead; the guardians of Tarr-Dombra had built fires at the corners of the outside walls, and there were cressets over the gate. They were watchful, but they were watching the ground; with the wet fog swirling along the mountain-top, nothing could be seen from the watchtower, and only the lower ramparts were manned.

The aircar ahead, piloted by Nancy Patterson, hovered briefly over the tower, then moved away. After a moment, there was a faint glow, a cloth-covered flashlight. Katherine Gower, piloting the lorry in which he and twenty men were riding, brought it up over the tower. Checking the safety of his submachine gun and the sack of spare drums slung from his shoulder, he stepped down. It was a pity they had to double up on vehicles, but only a few Freyans had had any instruction on Terran firearms and none, not even Harmakros, who had only a 10-mm automatic, could be trusted with machine weapons.

In the faint glow of the covered flashlight, Harmakros showed him the head of the spiral stairway; they started down together, the man with the flashlight behind them and the rest softshoeing after. The light was uncovered after they were around the first turn. Outside, he knew, Lisette Krull and Dave MacDonald were bringing another lorry down to the top of the keep. Then they heard voices ahead.

There were a dozen Nostori soldiers in the vaulted room at the bottom of the steps, kneeling or stooping in a circle under a cresset, around a pair of dice and a handful of coins on the stone floor. They were completely unsuspecting; as one of them stooped for the dice and shook them between his hands, he slipped off the safety of the submachine gun and saw Harmakros lift the Colt-Argentine from his holster. Then, with shocking suddenness, a black-powder smoothbore bellowed somewhere outside, followed by the gibber of a submachine gun, and a dozen voices began yelling at once.

The man with the dice dropped them and snatched a long pistol from his sash, cocking it. Harmakros shot him dead at once. The rest flung their hands above their heads, clapping their palms together. One or two of them cried "Treason!" Considering the direction from whence they had been assailed, that wasn't an unreasonable assumption. Outside, the shooting stopped; the yelling continued, and the cry of treason was being raised there, too. Dave MacDonald came through the doorway from the battlements, fitting a fresh drum onto his submachine gun. From the lower and outer walls, more shooting began, mostly local black powder, with a few sharp pangs of Terran smokeless.

Half a dozen of the black-clad commandomen came in from outside, and the twenty who had landed with him on the tower came crowding out of the stairway. They found the stairs to the floor below. When they got there, they found more of their force, with Reginald Fitzurse and Arthur Muramoto; they had gotten in by the balcony from the central court. They had a crowd of prisoners—fifteen or twenty men and several women. Only one man wore armor; most were in night-dress, including a portly and dignified if badly shaken gentleman who was evidently the castellan himself.

That was the end of the Battle of Tarr-Dombra. By this time, landing craft were coming in with infantry, a few of them with Fitzurse's new bayonets on their muskets. Ptosphes was with the first one, and he was the first man off, with a big red-and-blue Hostigi flag, which he insisted on raising with his own hands before he did anything else.

"My friends," Ptosphes was saying, when the castle was secure and they were gathered in its council-room, "you have taken Tarr-Dombra from Gormoth, a thing nobody thought possible. Now, I will give it to you, the Company of Searchers Among the Stars. And when the Nostori are driven out of the Strip, you may have such lands there as you need, to make your buildings and places to land sky-things. This will be written into the agreement which we will sign."

"And we will make you one of the Company of Searchers Among the Stars," Barron replied, "with a thousand shares of common stock." Ptosphes wasn't quite sure what that was, but he felt that it must be a great honor. "What'll we do with these prisoners, now?"

"Well, the captain of the castle, Phebron, is a gentleman. He is cousin to Prince Gormoth. If you follow our customs, you will furnish oukry for himself and his family and servants and release him under pledge to pay you such ransom as you name. Any other gentlemen you will release in the same way. As to the soldiers, if they are mercenaries you may take them into your service, but you may not require them to fight against Gormoth as long as their captains are in his pay. If they are Gormoth's own soldiers, you may put them to work, as long as they are given soldiers' pay and soldierly treatment, but you may not require them to fight against anybody, and you must release them as soon as the war with Gormoth is over."

Count Phebron—at least, he had a title a few below prince—had expected an exhorbitant ransom. Instead, he was told that he would be freely released if he swore never again to bear arms against the Prince of Hostigos or the Company of Searchers Among the Stars, and to be their friend in everything saving his duty to the Prince of Nostor. He'd never heard of anything like that, and said so.

"We would rather have your friendship than any ransom of money, Count Phebron," Barron told him. "And it won't cost you anything."

The implication that neutralizing him was worth more than cash was flattering.

"But is it honorable for me to do this?" he asked.

"It is a common and an honorable practice among our people," Fitzurse assured him, without adding that it was chiefly used in pacifying the Northern Hemisphere barbarians on Terra.

"He should also swear," Ptosphes hastened to add, "that he will tell Gormoth nothing about the Terran weapons."

"Oh, nothing of the sort; we want Gormoth to hear all about them, and about the sky-things. And he can tell Gormoth that we are making our own fire-seed and don't have to depend on Styphon's House for it. We'll put the soldiers of Gormoth to work making it, and teach them how, and after the war they can return to Nostor and make fire-seed there."

Ptosphes was shocked. As soon as Phebron was out of earshot, he exclaimed angrily:

"What god has addled your wits, Roger? I never heard of such folly, to offer to teach an enemy!"

"Nobody who can make fire-seed is our enemy, Ptosphes, because Styphon's House will be his. If you don't realize that yet, it will take Gormoth time to learn it, but sooner or later he will.

Daylight filtered down through a fog that hung heavy on both sides of the mountain. Nothing happened on the Nostor side, except that a few carts and a pack-train, bound for the Strip, were turned back by Hostigi soldiers. There was a little shooting down in the Strip, the scattered reports floating up faintly. By mid-afternoon, the refugees began coming up, a few at first and then crowds of them. They had carts, and pack and riding animals, but no meat-cattle. Most were armed. Some of them stopped and shook their fists and shouted curses as they passed the castle, but that was all they did. There were too many guns staring blackly at them from the walls, and they could see the gunners' smoking matches.

Luther Smith watched them pass and go down the slope on the Nostor side. He was indignant; not because they had been driven from their homes, but because they had been allowed to keep their weapons. He said so to Barron. It wasn't the first time, Barron reflected, that he had observed the ruthlessness of an idealist committed to a war to end war.

"You'll notice, though, that they haven't anything to eat."

Luther hadn't; now that it was mentioned, he shrugged.

"I don't pity them. That land down there didn't belong to them; they stole it from the Hostigi in the first place."

Well, their grandfathers had. The distinction didn't seem important to Luther. Nostori had done it, these people were Nostori, therefore they'd done it. He changed the subject by asking Luther how soon. he could get work started on the contragravity ship.

A lot of angry people, with weapons and no food. They had all been advised, when evicted from the Strip, to go to the city of Nostor, and told that it was Prince Gormoth's duty to provide for them. He doubted if Gormoth would see it that way, and even so it was a two days' journey to the city, and they'd be hungry before they got there. Hungry, and armed, in a countryside full of food.

Have to alert the fifth column by radio. Mixed among those refugees were close to a hundred Hostigi infiltrators.

That night he and Rylla took a landing-craft into Sask to land three men and their oukry a few hours' ride from the city. One was an oukry-trader, suspected dealer in stolen livestock; one was a hunter, suspected smuggler; the third was a known and convicted thief whose head, by rights,

ought to be over the town gate at Hostigos. They had all
been promised free pardons and rewards if they followed
instructions and survived.

"The only thing I'm afraid of is that Sarrask won't believe it," he said as they lifted and turned back toward
Tarr-Hostigos.

"He'll believe it. It's such a big pack of lies that nobody
would stop to doubt it, and it's just what Sarrask has been
waiting for," she said. "But why do you want him to attack
us now? Why not just go on and finish Nostor at once?"

"And have Sarrask attack while all our soldiers are north
of the mountain? We have between two and three thousand, counting those hooligans from Sastragath. Gormoth
has over ten thousand, which would keep our army quite
busy. And Sarrask has five thousand of his own. There is
a temple of Styphon, and a powder mill, in Sask. We need
more powder than we have to conquer Nostor. Rylla, Reginald has a saying: 'The long way round is the shortest
road to victory.' He knows what he's talking about."

The next day started early and ended late. From before
daylight all the Terrans who could be spared were piloting
landing-craft and lorries, ferrying soldiers to the southern
border, and by noon only the five hundred Sastragath irregulars, patrolling and pilfering in the Strip, and a
hundred men under Julio Almagro at Tarr-Dombra, remained in the north. Fitzurse, Chartiphon and Prince
Ptosphes went south to take command in the field.

By noon, too, the skies had cleared, and Arthur Muramoto and Adriaan de Ruyter took airjeeps, each with a
hastily instructed Freyan machine-gunner, and flew reconnaissance over Nostor. They found long columns of
troops, with artillery, marching south toward Dombra
Pass, where an immediate invasion was evidently ex-

pected. When caught in inviting density, they were machine gunned from the air.

The spy radio reported consternation in the city of Nostor. Count Phebron, arriving in the morning after an all day and all night ride, had told his story. He had been accused at once of having sold Tarr-Dombra to Ptosphes and thrown into prison. There were also reports of clashes between the refugees and troops.

The invasion from Sask came at noon of the second day after the taking of Tarr-Dombra. He was in the banquet-hall of Tarr-Hostigos, now converted into staff headquarters, with Rylla, Xentos, Adriaan de Ruyter and a few others, when Reginald Fitzurse appeared in the screen.

"This is it," he said. "Their cavalry crossed just above the mouth of the Darro; our pickets gave them a few shots, bolted, and radioed in, according to plan. They're headed north along the main road to Hostigos, into the ambush we have set up for them. The main army's close behind; we can't observe them because we don't want to let them see our contragravity."

He gave a wave-length combination; Sylvia Davock punched it on another screen. The pickup was in a tree, and occasionally a spray of long triangular leaves would swing in front of it. It looked down into an empty village street, with thatched and whitewashed cottages on either side. Among and between them, hidden from down the road, infantrymen crouched. A few had pikes or halberds; most of them had muskets, a number with bayonets. More would be inside, waiting to fire out of doors and windows. An anvil rang intermittently in the smithy, and a cowbell—worn by something that looked not at all like a cow—went *clank! clank-clank*. Close to the pickup somebody, in a tone of subdued fervence, was imploring somebody else to watch the point of that unprintably qualified pike.

Then they could hear the slap-thudding of many oukry feet. The infantrymen tensed, and gunlocks clicked. There were a few shots. Then three cavalrymen in blue and red sashes and shoulder-capes came tearing, one firing a pistol behind him, and passed out of view. Their pursuers, about two hundred, in black and orange Saski sashes and the white shoulder-capes that meant mercenaries, followed.

They got to the middle of the straggling village, and then it blew up in their faces. The front of the column became a tangle of dead and wounded oukry and unseated riders. The rear kept on for a moment, pushing the middle off the road and among the houses, where they ran into pikes and the deadly novelty of bayonets. Then a howling tide of Hostigi cavalry, swinging long swords, swept in and chased the survivors down the road. There was a distant squall of musket-fire when they ran into another ambush.

"Main body's crossed the river, now," Fitzurse said, from his own screen. "They're in two divisions, about a thousand infantry in each, one two miles behind the other. We'll give you that from an airjeep." He gave another combination, and Sylvia, at the other screen, punched it out. "Ground troops are just going to demonstrate in front of them and stop them; we're going to let them form a battle-line and then bust it from the air."

The jeep from which this was being picked up was grounded, out of sight of the enemy. In the foreground, the Hostigi army was deploying; none of these infantrymen had bayonets, and there was a pike or halberd between every two muskets. Field-guns—the carriages were abominably clumsy—were being run into position, and troop-sized blocks of cavalry came up and skittered off to the flanks. Then one of the guns was fired, and another. The jeep rose slightly, to get a view over the heads of the infantry; the advance force of the Saski army, approaching along the road, was forming a line across the fields on either side of it. The Hostigi infantry began firing, the men in the front rank passing back empty muskets and taking loaded ones.

"All right; here we go," Dave MacDonald's voice said. "Ready, Gathlon? Don't fire till I tell you to, now, and don't fire unless there's something in front of your guns."

The vehicle rose rapidly, and the landscape below swung in the screen as it made a half-circle to get on the Saski left flank. Then it came rushing down on the enemy, and Dave yelled, "Let them have it, Gathlon' "

The blocks of cavalry on the flank simply exploded in all directions, leaving a residue of a few dead men and oukry. The infantry saw what was happening and bolted, all but a few with sluggish reflexes or the optimism to try to hit an airjeep with a smoothbore flintlock. A caisson beside one of the field-pieces blew up with a bang. The cavalry at the other end of the line simply weren't there.

By the time the jeep had turned and was approaching what had started out as a battle, two more jeeps and an aircar were at work, firing ahead of bunches of fugitives to stop them, and amplified voices were shouting offers of quarter. Whole companies were surrendering to aircraft, and Hostigi cavalry were arriving to disarm them.

"Well, that was the Battle of Whatzit," Fitzurse said. "Nancy and Harmakros and Lisette each have a jeep; they caught the other gang, a couple of miles south, and are herding them north under arms till somebody can take their surrender. Can you leave what you're doing and come down and give a hand?"

They began to hear firing, ahead, and Rylla, who was piloting the car, put on speed. It wasn't fighting, though. About a thousand Saski troops had been marched into fields beside the road and were discharging their muskets to empty them before stacking them in surrender. There were two landing-craft on the ground and a third lifting out, and a couple of hundred Hostigi, some of them infantry on captured oukry, were guarding the prisoners. Some trestle-tables had been set up, and as Rylla brought the car down he could see Ptosphes and Fitzurse and Chartiphon and a number of others, among them a dozen Saski in long black and orange cloaks and gilded armor, but without swords or daggers.

There were introductions. One of the Saski was a brother of Prince Sarrask, and the rest were dukes or counts or the equivalent. They were arguing about the pledge of peace and friendship, to which the Saski objected.

"But it is a well-known and honorable usage of war, on our world," Fitzurse was saying.

"You're not on your world, now,!" the brother of Sarrask retorted, with a belligerence the circumstances didn't quite justify.

"I wonder about that," one of his companions said. "A few more battles like this one and it'll be their world. Peace and friendship with these people might be worth having."

Ptosphes stepped aside a little. He looked as though the merry-go-round was going too fast for him.

"Roger, what are we going to do with these people?" he whispered.

"Can you trust this brother of Sarrask's?"

"Great Dralm, no! Not even chained in a dungeon! He's a bigger villain than Sarrask, and has twice as much wit. This war, and everything else, was his idea. All Sarrask cares for is wine and feasting and beautiful women."

"Then he's our boy. Long live Sarrask, Prince of Sask, vassal of King Ptosphes of Hos-Hostigos."

The conquest of Sask turned out to be a large-scale Tarr-Dombra operation in triplicate. Charley Clifford was in charge of the taking of the temple farm, three miles southeast of the city; most of the men he had with him had been workers at the Hostigos powder mill, and it was hoped they they would know what not to do to avoid blowing the place up. Reginald Fitzurse took command of the detachment to take the temple itself, making a cryptic remark to the effect that dealing with turbulent priests was a Fitzurse tradition. The main force, led by Barron, Chartiphon and Ptosphes, took the citadel-palace in the center of the city. At all three the surprise was complete, and only at the third was there any serious fighting.

An hour after it was over, they were gathered in Sarrask's throne-room. Ptosphes, who had by this time gotten used to the idea of being King of Hos-Hostigos, was sitting on Sarrask's throne, one booted foot resting lightly on the golden crown of Sask. Rylla stood at his right, clutching Roger Barron's hand but keeping a properly haughty Princess-Rylla-of-Hos-Hostigos expression on her face. The others were ranged on either side, and there were screens for Luther Smith and Adriaan de Ruyter at Tarr-Hostigos, Julio Almagro at Tarr-Dombra, and Zahanov and Margaret Hale on the *Stellex*. Prince Sarrask had been given time to dress—magnificently in cloth-of-gold—and was standing before his conqueror, his nobles about him. There was no fear in his face; only anger which had become utter fury when he saw what Ptosphes was using for a footstool.

"Is this an honorable thing, Ptosphes?" he was demanding. "To hire a gang of accursed sorcerers and witches, from Styphon only knows what place of abominations, and murder brave soldiers with many-shooting guns from sky-things? Is that a decent way to make war?"

"It's a way to win a war, when you've been attacked by treachery and without warning."

Sarrask actually became angrier, which hadn't seemed possible.

"And what a pack of dirty lies that was!" he fairly howled. "You sent those three rogues yourself; If I had them here now, I'd kill them with my bare hands if you shot me the next moment."

He was interrupted by a bustle at the door. Reginald Fitzurse, wearing his old Terran Federation Army tunic, with a blaze of decoration-ribbons on his breast, strode in. Behind him, soldiers frog-marched eight or ten prisoners, all in the black and red robes of Styphon's House, hustling them to the throne and throwing them to the floor at Ptosphes' feet. There was a gasp of horror from Sarrask and his nobles.

One of the priests picked himself up and glared at Ptosphes.

"There is still time," he cried, "for you to humble your-self and repent!" Then he pointed at Fitzurse. "But none for him! He threatened to kill me, an archpriest, at my very altar."

Now he knew why Reginald Fitzurse's name had always stirred something in his memory; now he understood the remark about turbulent priests. There had been a Reginald Fitzurse, centuries ago, who, with three comrades, had slain at his very altar a turbulent priest—Thomas á Becket.

"He would have saved me the trouble. Maybe it would have been better for you if he had," Ptosphes told the priest. Then he asked Fitzurse: "What did you find at the temple?"

"Oh, quite a treasure. Gold and silver bullion, specie, merchandise of all sorts, jewels. Five hundred fine new muskets, all alike. And ten tons of fire-seed, in twenty-pound kegs. Charley called me; he found fifty tons at the farm.''

Sarrask gave a strangled cry of rage. ''You lying old scoundrel!'' he shouted at the archpriest. ''You told me you only had a hundred small kegs. I wish he had killed you, and taken all day about it. And where did you steal those muskets? From my own armory, I'll wager.'' He turned to Fitzurse. ''You mean they have fire-seed at the farm, too? A hundred great casks of it?''

''Of course; that's where they make it. In a day or so, we'll be turning out about two hundred pounds a day there.''

''You mean *you* can make fire-seed? Just like they can?''

Nobody bothered to answer him. Ptosphes held the crown out on his toe.

''Sarrask, do you want this back?'' he asked.

''What good will it do me? It's the crown of Sask, and there is no Sask now; only Hostigos.''

They hadn't meant to proclaim the Kingdom of Hos-Hostigos until they had Nostor as well as Sask to support the pretension. It suddenly struck Barron that now, however, was the time to do it.

''Oh, no, Sarrask,'' he said. ''There will still be a Sask, and if you wish, you may be Prince of Sask. As a subject, of course, of his Majesty Ptosphes, King of Hos-Hostigos.''

Sarrask's jaw went slack for a moment, then tightened. That was evidently a Hos of another color.

''And I will be sovereign here in Sask?''

''You will be obliged to furnish me troops, at need, and there will be a matter of tributes for the support of the Kingdom, of course,'' Ptosphes told him. ''And you will never suffer Styphon's House to take root here again.''

Sarrask laughed. ''You think I'm crazy, to let these robbers come back, now that you've rid me of them?" he demanded. Then he looked at the crown, still dangling on Ptosphes' toe. "At least, you might have the decency to hand it to me on the point of your sword," he said.

"Oh, of course." Ptosphes wasn't wearing a sword; only a 10-mm automatic. "Chartiphon, lend me yours."

As soon as the conquerors came home to Tarr-Hostigos, Nancy Patterson and Xentos went to work on the proclamation. Nancy furnished the basis for it, from the microbook library, an old document from the Second Century Pre-Atomic. There were a few words in it to which Charley Clifford took exception, but, in Sosti translation, he agreed that they'd be appropriate. And there was the matter of a new flag for Hos-Hostigos. Ptosphes wanted to use the old red flag of Hostigos, with the blue halberd-head; it had to be carefully explained that that wouldn't do. What was finally adopted was a quarter-arc rainbow on a white field. No matter who got annexed later, he'd still be able to find his colors in the flag.

Sarrask and a score of his nobles, brought from Sask in a hastily luxurized landing-craft, gathered with the Hostigi nobility and gentry in the great hall and listened while Xentos read solemnly from the scroll:

"When, in the course of human events, it becomes necessary for one people to dissolve the political bands which have connected them with another . . . a decent respect for the opinions of mankind requires that they should declare the causes which impel them to the separation. . ."

A great many of the charges against King Kaiphranos of Hos-Harphax were grossly exaggerated; well, maybe the case against George III of England had been slightly overstated in Nancy's original. Nobody paid too much attention to that; they were in too complete agreement with the denunciations of the "rapacious priesthood of a false god," which made up the bulk of the proclamation. Finally, "we, the princes, nobles and people of Hos-Hostigos," after declaring themselves, as they of a right ought to be, free and independant, pledged allegiance to king Ptosphes I and undying friendship to the Company of Searchers Among the Stars.

One thing, Stellar Explorations, Ltd., now had a real treaty, with a real sovereign power. That was drawn up, in triplicate and bi-lingually, and signed by all parties.

The Saski were feasted; they tasted chilled wine, and ice cream. The net day they were taken by air to Tarr-Dombra. They looked at the *Stellex* through a telescope, and saw a screen-view of the planet from a thousand miles; they didn't quite believe that. But they did believe, because they saw and fired it, that the powder mill was actually making fire-seed, and when they returned home, loaded with presents, they found that Charley Clifford had production at the Sask mill up to a hundred and fifty pounds a day and increasing it daily.

Chartiphon was still at Sask, with five hundred Hostigi troops. One of the first things he did was empty the jails and recruit the inmates into a secret police, headed by the three disreputables from Hostigos. All Sarrask's mercenaries and half of his own Saski soldiers were shifted north to the Nostor border; the rest were put to work demolishing the temple of Styphon. It was incredibly rich; the gold that plated the minaret alone was worth enough to pay the mercenaries for a year. Sarrask got half the loot, which completely reconciled him to losing the war and his independence and insured that Styphon's House would hate him equally with Ptosphes and the Terrans.

The hangovers from the feasting had barely evaporated before all Hostigos was demanding the immediate invasion and conquest of Nostor. After Tarr-Dombra and Sask, nothing seemed impossible, and weren't they a mighty kingdom, now? Even Ptosphes was impatient to add Nostor to his realm, and Xentos flew up from Sask, where he had been re-organizing the government, to add his voice. He was worried about the possibility that King Kaiphranos would mobilize to recover his lost princedoms, and that Styphon's House, infuriated but not seriously damaged by the Sask expulsion and expropriation, would preach a general holy war.

That worried Nancy Patterson, too. "We're going to have this whole civilization against us," she prophesied. "Not just King Kaiphranos and Hos-Harphax; the other two kingdoms, down the river and along the coast, too. There are temples and priests of Styphon in all of them, and they'll all be preaching a crusade against us. Roger, this isn't just politics. This is religion. Religion isn't so important to us, but these people aren't rationalists; they're believers. The same mentality that existed in Europe at the time of the Crusades and the Reformation and counter-Reformation. We're the enemies of Styphon; the infidel."

Reginald Fitzurse wasn't underestimating the power of religious fanaticism, either. There was always some half-crazy messiah stirring up the Eurasian barbarians, and he knew how hard a holy war was to stop, once it started. But he also knew how dangerously low this ammunition, especially for the 15-mm machine guns, was. Thousands and thousands of rounds had been wasted during the Sask Blitz, by ill-trained Freyans who had had to handle the guns because Terrans were needed to pilot the vehicles. He was trying to explain that to Ptosphes and Xentos.

"We didn't have much to start with, and we can't get any more. We haven't the means of making it, and it would take our ship a year to go to our world and back for it." He didn't bother to add that in any case they had no money to buy any. "If we fight Nostor, it will have to be with your muskets."

Just the day before, Julio Almagro had been talking about seeing if he could get one of the huge 8-bore muskets rifled and fitted with sights, so that he could hit something with it.

Ptosphes looked hurt and puzzled; normal reaction to the discovery that the supposedly inexhaustible is close to being exhausted. Then he brightened.

"But there are the sky-things," he said. "Look at this fool of a Gormoth, massing his army in front of Dombra Pass, waiting for us to march over the mountain. Because the pass used to be the only road, he still thinks it is. He hasn't realized, yet, that the whole sky is a road now."

Mark another one up for Ptosphes. It had been quite a while after the fact, on Terra, before military, political and economic thinking had adjusted to that simple little fact.

"That's true, Ptosphes," he said. "But we haven't enough sky-things, or enough people to fly the ones we have. We'll have to train your people and teach them to fly. And we'll have to build big sky-things, that can lift a thousand soldiers at a time, and we'll first have to teach people to help us do the work. And we'll need more fireseed than we have. All that will take time."

"It will take work, also." Rylla had been sitting quietly beside him, saying nothing until now. "It will not be done by shouting 'On to Nostor!' or boasting about how we will feast in Gormoth's palace."

"No, it won't, her father agreed. "And too many of the people think the Terrans are magicians who can do everything for them." He turned to Xentos. "We will have a meeting of the Council tomorrow afternoon. Roger and Reginald and the others will explain what must be done.

Then, in the evening, we will have a great feast. Not only the namely men, but the leaders among the townsfolk and the common soldiers and workers and even the peasants; the ones to whom the others listen. Instead of tale-telling and drinking-songs, there will be speaking. Then they can go and inspire the others."

"We must strike quickly, that is certain," Xentos said. "There is much unrest in Nostor. We must act before it dies down."

He was right about that. The fifth column radio was calling for speedy invasion, too. With a fine disregard for chronology, they were spreading the story that Styphon's House had coerced Prince Gormoth into war with Hostigos because Prince Ptosphes had discovered how to make his own fire-seed and was no longer dependent on them. This was uncritically accepted by the people; there was a rising tide of anticlericalism, and everybody was blaming Styphon's House for everything. Nancy was almost chagrined at the lack of crusading spirit among the Nostori.

By this time, too, there were a large number of Strip refugees in the city of Nostor, clamoring for relief; the soup-kitchens Gormoth set up only insulted and infuriated them. Most of the land in the Strip had been tennant-farmed, and the absentee-landlord owners were, many of them, influential nobles. A few were gotten to and told that there was enough gold in the temple of Styphon to indemnify all of them.

Then there was Count Phebron. As soon as contragravity began appearing north of the mountains, it was realized that he had been telling the truth about how he had lost Tarr-Dombra. He was promptly released, and Gormoth sought his advise.

"Make peace," Phebron told his cousin bluntly. "One of these machines can wipe out a thousand men in the time it takes to drain a wine-cup. Ptosphes has made himself a king. If you submit, he will deal as fairly with you as he did with Sarrask. If you don't, he'll put your head up over your own gate."

"Suppose I put yours there?" Gormoth was reported to have said.

"Then, in time, Ptosphes will take it down to make place for yours. He has sworn friendship with me, and vengeance is the duty of a friend."

A good idea of Gormoth's state of mind could be gotten from the fact that Phebron was not even banished from the court. Gormoth may have thought that he might need somebody with whom the now King of Hos-Hostigos had sworn friendship.

And the mercenaries, even those directly in the pay of Styphon's House, were dissatisfied. Most of them were in the Dombra Line, awaiting the attack that didn't come. They had all hoped to enrich themselves by the plunder of Hostigos, and now that hope was vanished. Not a few of them had experienced, and all had heard about, machinegun fire from the air. They were business men, and they knew bad business when they found themselves on the short end of it.

Except for the difference in language and dress, and the absence of cigar-smoke, it could have been any political rally banquet he had ever seen since he had been a teenage illegal voter. It was a big success; the boys from the precincts came, were fed and liquored, received the Word, and went away full of party spirit. The next day, the work began.

Luther Smith now had a finely drawn set of plans for a contragravity ship. Nobody, himself least of all, expected it, when finished, to bear more than a coincidental resemblance to them. First, he had to design a jet engine that wouldn't set the ship's timbers on fire as soon as it was started. He solved that with a nuclear-electric engine and a big blower-fan from the *Stellex*. After that, he was faced with the problem of building a ship around it and the contragravity generator that would leave any room at all for payload. By this time, the estimated speed had inched down to eighty mph.

Lourenço Narvaes tried to take on the contragravity pilot training program, in the time he could spare from helping Luther on the ship and Charley Clifford at the two powder mills. He became disheartened by the total inability of any Freyan to grasp the theory of the contragravity field. Hell, they didn't even grasp the theory of gravity; things fell because down was the place for them. Rylla and Harmakros had become skilled pilots, and at a pinch they could handle a landing-craft alone. All they knew about it was that if you pushed this and pulled that, so-and-so would happen. With Nancy Patterson and, when he could find time, Dave MacDonald, to help them out of difficulties, they were able to handle it themselves, and almost all their alumni made good light-vehicle pilots. Many went on to lorries or helping on landing-craft, and a number were graduated to power equipment.

There was a lot of this. When the *Stellex* had been fitted out, it had been hoped that they would find an inhabitable but uninhabited planet; while Adriaan took a couple of them on the yacht and streaked back to Terra to file claim, the rest would dig in and make the colony self-sustaining. So they had lumbering machines and excavating and mining equipment and construction equipment and a lot of contragravity lifters of all sizes, and half a dozen big contragravity manipulators sprouting hooks and claws and grapples and pusher-arms in all directions. There was even a sawmill and a forging-hammer and a small nuclear smelting furnace. The lot of it was lightered down and put into use as soon as people could be taught to use it.

By the end of the second week, there were still very few visible and tangible accomplishments, but there were a lot of young Freyans around who could be trusted with manipulators and bulldozers and things like that and wouldn't do anything utterly disastrous with or to them.

Troop morale was good. Most of the soldiers on the Strip were professionals; they thought this was a wonderful war—plenty to eat and drink, lots of pretty girls, and nobody taking shots at them. They knew it wouldn't last, but they were going to enjoy it while it did. The five hundred so-called cavalry from Sastragath were different. There was no looting on this side of the mountain, and they all thought that every Nostori peasant was a rich miser with a crock of gold under the hearthstone. They were getting restless, and Fitzurse was worried. He had a talk with their captain, and explained that there would be no invasion until the big sky-thing was built.

"You'll never get it finished the way you're going at it," the Sastragathi told him. "I watched those peasants you have cutting timber over here in the Strip. Why, I have at least a hundred men who could each do more lumbering work than any five of those clodhoppers."

"It seems," Fitzurse said, reporting the conversation to Barron, "that after brigandage and cattle-herding, lumbering is the third largest industry in Sastragath. It occurs to me that we could put some of those fellows to work."

"It occurs to me," Barron said, "that we could buy cut timbers in Sastragath. Luther has his jet finished; he could build some kind of a temporary lumber-scow with it and the generator, and for a few kegs of powder we might get all the timbers we need."

After a visit to Sastragath, which was just west of north-ern Hostigos and southern Nostor, Fitzurse decided that the idea was feasible. He didn't think much of the manners and customs of the Sastragathi—the former he described as non-existent, and the latter beastly—but they did have timbers, logs up to a hundred feet long and four feet at the butt, and they could cut more as desired. They rafted it, when they had high water, into Nostor. That and the herds of *zhoumy,* big yak-like animals, were traded for anything they couldn't raise, make or pilfer for themselves. There was no temple of Styphon in Sastragath, and they were delighted to have fire-seed brought right to their log-stock-aded town. They couldn't understand, though, how the Hostigi were going to get the timbers out.

At first they couldn't, that is. The next day Dave Mac-Donald, who was in charge of lumbering, arrived with a landing-craft, Luther Smith, and three recently skilled Hostigi workmen. They unloaded the big generator, built a log frame around it and a log-raft around that, lifted it, and towed it out, detouring over southern Nostor to the alarm of the populace. There was a panic among the troops in the Dombra Line when they passed over them, too. The next raft was bigger. Its frame was built at the shipyard, it mounted the blower-jet, and it didn't have to be towed. This thing shuttled back and forth, usually car-rying a deck-load of boulders which could be dumped onto Prince Gormoth's army, for some time. Enough tim-ber to build three ships like the one under construction only cost a halfton of Styphon's Best from Sask.

Beside timbers, iron was needed. It was learned that there was a little princedom called Xanx, just south of Sask, where there were some bog-iron mines and a few crude furnaces and forges. Julio Almagro took one of the landing craft down and traded four kegs of powder for enough iron to load the vehicle. When he went back for another load, he was invited to dine with the prince, an elderly and rather shabby gentleman named Lykarses, who wanted to know how much he would have to give for a great-cask of fire-seed. That would be a half ton.

"Why, your Highness, I'm afraid I can't sell you that much," Almagro regretted. "King Ptosphes is at war with the Prince of Nostor, now, and he will only allow limited quantities to be shipped out of the kingdom. Now, if you were subject to King Ptosphes, of course, he would be obliged to give you all you needed for the defense of your princedom."

"But I'm a subject of King Kaiphranos."

"So was King Ptosphes, until very recently. I'll tell you what you do; come, with a few of your gentlemen, to Tarr-Hostigos and sign our Declaration of Independence and swear allegiance to King Ptosphes, and then Xanx will be part of the Great Kingdom of Hos-Hostigos, and. . ."

"Does King Ptosphes really and truly make his own fire-seed? I'd heard that said, but it's so hard to believe—"

He went to Tarr-Hostigos with five or six of his courtiers, all as elderly and shabby as himself, and when he saw the powder mill he cursed Styphon's House for almost ten minutes without repeating a single malediction. It seemed that, until now, he had believed that fire-seed was made by Styphon Himself, and that its manufacture was totally beyond any human power.

So Prince Lykarses swore allegiance and was given a pretty new rainbow flag, and a flashlight and a magnifying glass and a few other gadgets. He wanted to do his part in the war with Nostor by furnishing five hundred infantry. After he saw the shipyard, however, he agreed that fifty blacksmiths would be worth much more to the war-effort.

The contragravity ship was finished. She looked like old pictures of Noah's Ark, except that Noah's Ark hadn't had a sheet-metal jet-and-air-scoop assembly and an air-rudder on top or a big bulge amidships for a contragravity generator. After some hesitation, she was christened *King Ptosphes*. Ptosphes was delighted, even after seeing her, which only went to show that he'd never seen a real contragravity ship. On her trial voyage, CGS *King Ptosphes* reached sixtyfive mph, which at least made her a formidable competitor for oxcarts and river barges. She could carry five hundred cavalry and their mounts, or, badly crowded, two thousand infantry.

Naturally, everybody began shouting "On to Nostor!" again.

Luther Smith was one. This was a war to end war and make Freya safe for democracy and strike off the chains of theocratic despotism. Nancy was another; she wanted Nostor conquered before the crusaders began swarming in. And Reginald Fitzurse had drawn up an ambitious plan for beating the army of Nostor by detail through mobility. Only Roger Barron was against it.

"This isn't going to be any Sask Blitz," he told them. "You can't win a war on nothing but mobility; you have to have fire-power too, and we don't have that. It will take a lot of hard ground-fighting, with conventional Freyan weapons. That will mean damage to the country, and the people who'll be worst hurt by it are the ones who are most favorable to us now. Fitz, you've been quoting Clausewitz about the necessity to destroy the armed strength of the enemy; I wish you'd remember the Calusewitzian quotation everybody knows—War is a continuation of policy by other means. Policy is to add Nostor to Hos-Hostigos, without creating any more enmity than we did at Sask."

"Well, if we have to conquer Nostor with muzzle loaders, we'd better do it while we still have powder for them," Charley Clifford said. "Powder's seventy five percent niter, and I'm not getting enough of it."

"Well, don't look at me," Lisette Krull said. "I've been having to get it a shovelful from under this manure-pile and a shovelful from under that manure-pile, and we're just running out of manure-piles."

"Well, that's the way Styphon's House got it," somebody argued.

"They didn't attempt the sort of quantity production we're in, and they didn't scatter it around the way we're doing. A whole ton and a half to this Prince Lykarses of Xanx!" Charley fairly tore his hair. "We're using up the niter they accumulated over years, faster than it can be replaced. We can't keep that up."

"Can you keep it up three months?" Adriaan de Ruyter asked.

"I suppose so. What can we do by then?"

"Send the *Stellex* to Yggdrasil and back. It's only twenty light-years away. You know what Yggdrasil produces, don't you?"

"Guano." Terra was still importing huge quantities of it, for the soil-reclamation projects in the war-ruined Northern Hemisphere. "That's right; nitrates. What'll we use for money, though?"

"Foodstuffs," Almagro said promptly. "They still have to supply themselves by carniculture and hydroponics; Terran vegetation won't even grow in the soil. They have to process the guano before they ship it—Hey, with the processing plants they have, it'd be no trick at all to extract pure KNO_3. A shipload of pure niter would make an awful lot of fire-seed."

Everybody was happy. Charley saw his powder mills on full production. Lisette would at last get out of the barn-yards and oukry-stables. And when they called Karl Za-hanov, on ship watch again, he grinned in his gray beard.

In his book, planets were just places you took spaceships to and from.

Everybody was happy except the five hundred Sastragathi irregulars. The great sky-thing was built, and the promised invasion wasn't going to start at all. So they mutinied, fortunately when the *King Ptosphes* was available and could load a thousand mercenaries and Nostori regulars. The mutiny was put down, and the mutineers disarmed.

Their captain, forlorn without his weapons, was highly indignant.

"You promised us that we would be taken to Nostor; that there would be an invasion as soon as the big sky-thing was finished—"

"We promised nothing of the sort; we told you that there would not be an invasion till after it was built, and we said nothing about how long after. In any case, you have freed us from any promises to you by this mutiny. You are no longer soldiers of the King. You will be paid what is owing to you, and you will be taken back to your own country."

Barron talked to the captain privately:

"You know, I suppose, that the Sastragathi no longer need to trade with Nostor; we bring them fire-seed and everything else. Well, where you don't have to trade, you can raid." He paused, and the Sastragathi captain's eyes widened momentarily; that happy thought had not occurred to him before. "We will give your men their pay in fire-seed, we will give each one a good oukry, we will return their arms, and we will land them in Sastragath on the Nostor border. Will they that satisfy them?"

Satisfy them; it delighted them. When they were loaded, with their mounts, aboard the *King Ptosphes,* they were happily singing their folk-songs, all of which seemed to deal with the exploits of distinguished robbers.

There were six of the seventy foot landing craft; he and Rylla took one, Nancy and Harmakros took another, and the other four were handled by similar Terro-Freyan teams. The ship hauled iron from Xanx to Sastragath to trade for meat, Sastragathi hardwoods to Sask. Meat and grain and root-vegetables and fruit and casks of wine and bales of the dried blossoms from which the tea was made went up to the *Stellex*. Adriaan de Ruyter brought down his two hundred foot space-yacht *Voortrekker,* and she was berthed in an improvised and growing spaceport in the Strip. Three of the six landing-craft were also to be left behind; the berthing-space aboard the *Stellex* was thus added to cargo-capacity. Zahanov and Lourenço Narvaes and Margaret Hale and Sylvia Davock would take her on her voyage, with four young Freyans whom they had been training to do ordinary crewmen's work. They had learned considerable merely in the process of getting the cargo aboard and stowed. Finally, when the *Stellex* was crammed with every scrap of food that would go into her, there was a farewell feast and then she broke orbit and vanished into hyperspace.

Ten days later, a second and larger contragravity ship was finished. She was christened *Princess Rylla.*

While open to travel, the frontiers were closely guarded, and there were radios at most of the posts. One of these reported that a party of cavalry from Dazour, escorting two noblemen, had been halted by a patrol. The noblemen—Xentos recognized their names; they were members of the court of Prince Tabalkon of Dazour—said that they wanted to discuss pledges of friendship and trade between their sovereign and King Ptosphes. Maybe they meant that. Maybe Tabalkon wanted an embassy in Hostigos as a base for espionage and propaganda. Or maybe he was ready to launch an invasion. There had been some examples from Old Terran history of things like that.

The aircar ride to Tarr-Hostigos impressed the envoys. So did the spectacle, carefully arranged, of both the *King Ptosphes* and the *Princess Rylla* in the air, and the guard of honor of five hundred infantry, each with a long triangular bayonet on his musket. And, of course, the electric lights, and the chilled wine, and the screens and radios.

They began by talking about trade. They wanted iron and lumber and hides; they had textiles and wine and grain to sell. And they inquired, with elaborate nonchalance, if it were really true that the Hostigi made their own fire-seed, without the help of the priests of Styphon. They were shown that it was, but they were told that because of the war with Nostor, only very little could be released for export, and it was not too delicately hinted that if the Prince of Dazour brought his country into the Kingdom of Hos-Hostigos, he could have all he needed.

By this time, reports had gotten from the western border to Prince Gormoth's capital that the five hundred Sastragathi, joined by a thousand more of their countrymen, were pillaging and burning, committing all the usual atrocities and a few they seemed to have invented specially for the occasion. The spy radio reported that Gormoth had pulled a thousand troops out of the Dombra Line and ordered them west.

Their column was kept under air observation, and the two envoys from Dazour were taken for a look at them and the Dombra Line. The troops on the march were not molested, but the two Dazouri saw some bombing of the Dombra Line—empty oxygen cylinders packed with blasting explosive—and were horrified at the effect.

There was only one road across southern Nostor; about half way from Dombra Pass to the Sastragath border, it crossed a deep and narrow gorge on a wooden bridge. By the end of the second day, the Nostori column was within a few hours' march of it, and made camp. The next morning, when they took the road again, they were under observation of several aircars, including one in which Barron had the two Dazouri diplomats.

"We are going to show you something, now," he told them, when the head of the column was within two hundred yards of the bridge. "Watch this."

Then he dived and swept over the heads of the Nostori. Before any of them could do anything, he was zooming up at the bridge, and as he did, he let go his rocket-booster.

The aircar shot up to twenty thousand feet in a matter of seconds; when it was losing momentum, he turned in a wide circle and brought it down again. The bridge was blazing from one end to the other, and the road to the east of it was empty, except for a litter of discarded pikes and muskets and a few casualties who had been knocked down and trampled in the rush. Nostori soldiers, mounted and on foot, were streaming away in both directions, scattering as they went.

"That was an army, a moment ago," he told his passengers. "It may be an army again, but not for a couple of days."

"But why did you spare them?" one of the Dazouri asked. "You could have wiped them all out with the flame-weapon."

"Oh, that would have been too horrible! We would never do a thing like that," he assured them. "That is, not unless it were a case of national survival. If Hos-Hostigos were invaded by some overwhelming force—the only such enemy I can think of would be Hos-Harphax—we would find ourselves driven to use even worse weapons than that, of course. Beside, those are trained soldiers, though they don't look like it at the moment. When Prince Gormoth submits and brings Nostor into Hos-Hostigos, as he will inside a month, we will want them. Now, down there; there's the Dombra Line, again. Wait till I show you something. Here, use the binoculars. Those four big cannon, two on either side of the road. Bombards, throw three hundred pound stone balls. They're new ones, but they're probably the last of their kind that will be made. . ."

"We must go home to Dazour tomorrow," one of them said. "Prince Tabalkon must be told about this. Today, we have seen the whole world changed."

"I am glad," the other said, "that I am an old man. I will not have to live long in this changed world."

The next morning, the two Dazouri envoys got a closer view of Prince Gormoth's three hundred pounders. All four of them, with their mounts, were sitting in the outer enclosure of Tarr-Hostigos. The night before, Dave MacDonald and Harmakros, with two hundred of the commando force, had dropped onto the gun positions and held them until four Hostigi machine operators brought down contragravity manipulators and each snatched away one of the giant bombards. The whole operation cost three casualties and two hundred-odd rounds of rifle and pistol ammunition.

The two Dazouri heard the story, inspected the bombards, and then got into the landing-craft that was to take them back to Dazour.

Three days later, Prince Tabalkon of Dazour decided to repudiate his allegiance to Hos-Harphax and take his country into Hos-Hostigos. It took some argument to persuade him not to have the priests at the Dazour temple tied to kegs of fire-seed and blown up. Once he could get along without them, he had wanted to indulge what had long been his real feeling toward them.

On the way to Tarr-Hostigos from the discussions, Roger Barron detoured for another look at the Dombra Line. It was empty, marked only by the raw-earth scars of trenches and gun-emplacements. Swinging north along the road, he saw the army on the march toward Nostor. They were going to inform Prince Gormoth that the war was over.

A couple of days later, Count Phebron and several companions rode up the pass road to Tarr-Dombra and from there were airlifted to Tarr-Hostigos. Prince Gormoth, they said, wanted admission to Hos-Hostigos on the same terms as Prince Tabalkon. He also wanted assistance in suppressing the Sastragathi brigands who were ravaging the western part of his princedom.

Everybody was happy except Nancy Patterson, and she would have been except that she was convinced that the crusades were about to start. Kings and princes everywhere would be taking up the sword; huge armies would be marching to crush the infidel, joined at every crossroads by fresh throngs shouting "Styphon wills it!" Every day of postponemeny would make the final catastrophe that much more catastrophic. She said as much, one afternoon, when half a dozen of them were lounging in the room at Tarr-Dombra that had been fitted up as a bar and clubroom.

"Nancy, it isn't going to happen," he told her, a trifle impatiently. "Styphon's House is finished, even in Harphax."

"But you can't just wipe a religion out of existence overnight," she objected.

"Not a religion, no. But Styphon's House wasn't really

one. A religion needs more than priests and temples. It needs believers with deep emotional faith, believers who love their religion as the people who followed Peter the Hermit loved theirs, and that Styphon's House never had. Look at the way the people of Sask, and Dazour, and Nostor, turned on them. And the Prince of Balkron, south of Dazour."

He had been one of the more recent seceders from Hos-Harphax; to prove his sincerity, he had shipped the heads of eighteen priests of Styphon, each packed in a powder-keg full of salt, to Tarr-Hostigos. Nancy had been present when they had been opened; she grimaced at the memory.

"Where Styphon's House made their mistake was right at the beginning, by over-specialization. When they discovered the niter-sulphur-charcoal combination, they thought they had everything they needed, and they adopted this policy of supplying the rulers with powder in exchange for forced-levy offerings from their subjects. The people hated them, and they were stupid enough not to care. They thought they could control the people through the princes, and their only control over the princes was based on the secret of making powder and their ability to supply or withhold it. And now the secret isn't a secret any more, and their monopoly's busted."

"What I can't see," Almagro said, "is why King Kaiphranos hasn't gone to war with us on his own account. He's just sitting and watching his kingdom break up under him."

"That's all he can do. With the annexation of Balkron, we now have forty five thousand troops, not counting Sastragathi. King Kaiphranos has, in the original princedom and city of Harphax, a total of fifteen thousand. The rest of the military strength of Hos-Harphax is controlled by the—put it in quotes—subject princes. That was Styphon's House, too. They managed to keep the kingdom divided, every prince virtually independent of the Great King, and completely independent of one another. That's why we've been making these princes who join Hos-Hostigos turn the bulk of their troops over to us. What we want is a national army, because Hos-Hostigos is going to be a nation, not a snake-pit. We can do that, because we're something new and we're making it a condition of membership. If Kaiphranos tried to do it, he'd have a civil war on his hands. I'm about half expecting him to have one, no matter what he does."

"The mercenary captains aren't taking service with Kaiphranos, any more," Reginald Fitzurse remarked. "And we have to fight them off with a club."

Quite a few free-companies, he had been hearing, were going down the river to take service in Hos-Rathon, in the delta country, and in Hos-Bleth, to the east along the coast. The mercenary business itself wasn't too good, any more. Hos-Hostigos wanted no more of them. He thought of the many things, none of them good, that Machiavelli, out of long experience, had had to say about mercenaries—*They plunder you in peace and let your enemies plunder you in war. You cannot rely upon them, for they will always aspire to their own greatness. . . .* Maybe it would be a good plan to collect a lot of free-companies and use them in colonizing the other continents. He was turning that idea over in his mind when he became aware of what Nancy Patterson was saying:

"Well, gosh, I won't cry if there isn't any crusade. Then Harmakros won't be going off to war as soon as we're married."

"Huh?" Charley Clifford almost shouted. "You mean you and Harmakros are getting married?"

"Yes, we are, in about a week." She rose, picked up a bottle and carefully corked it. "You say one dam' word about him not being human and I'm going to smash this over your head!"

Then she set the bottle down and went out. Clifford looked at it silently until she was gone.

"I can understand her attitude, of course, but—" He shrugged. "I hope having a child by Harmakros isn't anything she's counting on too heavily. She won't, you know."

"Do you know that, or is that just your professional opinion?"

Having a child by him might be something important to Rylla. They hadn't discussed it, but he suspected that it would be. The curse of overpopulation hadn't put its mark on the Freyan mind as it had on the Terran.

"Well, look, Roger," Charley said. "Life here originated and evolved independently of life on Terra. We and the Freyans started from two different puddles of living slime, seven hundred light-years apart. You know the mechanism of reproduction. The sperm and the ovum are away up the structural ladder. Each contains twenty four chromosomes, with us; I don't know how many for the Freyans. Each of them contains thousands of genes. Here, for a simplified example, suppose a Terran locksmith made a lock, and a locksmith here on Freya made a key, neither knowing what the other was doing. What odds would you give against the key working in the lock? Well, that's almost an even-money bet beside the odds against a Terran spermatozoon fertilizing a Freyan ovum, or vice versa."

That sounded reasonable, until he began to think about it.

"Wait a minute, Charley. Every physical characteristic stems, originally, from the gene for it; that's correct, isn't it? And you, yourself, have admitted that Freyans do not possess any non-human characteristics, or lack any human ones."

"I see what you're getting at, Roger." Charley frowned. "Superficially, it sounds convincing. But, dammit, these people. . ." Then he changed the subject by shifting to the research work he intended doing once the powder mills could run themselves and he could get back to medical work.

The third ship was finished. She was almost twice as big as the *King Ptosphes,* and had a speed of a hundred mph. Luther Smith thought that now was the time to embark the armies of Hos-Hostigos and go to Harphax to tell King Kaiphranos that he was through. Julio Almagro was reminded of an old Spanish proverb about the converted Moor eating pork three times a day. And even if this beligerance hadn't been so incongruous for Luther, the idea was pure nonsense. Administrative problems were already piling up faster than they could be dealt with, without creating a host of new ones.

Beside, Kaiphranos would find out where he stood soon enough.

It didn't take him long. It was barely three weeks after Nancy's marriage to Harmakros before a big forty-oared barge came up the river to Balkron and an embassy from King Kaiphranos journeyed overland by oukry to Tarr-Hostigos. They brought friendly greetings from their king, who wanted to enter into alliance with the Great King of Hos-Hostigos and make agreements of peace, friendship and trade. Styphon's House, they announced, no longer existed in Hos-Harphax. The temples and farms had been seized by the Crown, and the priests expelled, but not before a number had been questioned under torture. As a result of this last, King Kaiphranos now knew how to make fire-seed for himself.

Why, in the five or six centuries that Styphon's House had been battening on the kings and princes and people of the Great River valley, this simple little idea hadn't occurred to anybody before would be one of the perpetual mysteries. Maybe everybody had been afraid Styphon really would do something about it.

Her father was alone at his writing-table, with piles of parchments and stacks of the soft white paper of the Terrans in front of him. For a moment, he did not hear them enter, and kept on writing. Then he raised his head and smiled at them, and picked up his poignard to strike the gong and call for wine. They sat down facing him.

"I'm not hearing any more complaints from western Nostor about Sastragathi raids," he said.

"Oh, no; that's stopped," Roger said. "I told their chief that if it didn't, there'd be no more ships with iron and powder, and we'd buy no more cattle and lumber from them. He accused us of being as bad as the priests of Styphon; I assured him that we were much worse. On that basis, we got along very pleasantly. Why, King Ptosphes, there is something we want to talk about."

"Why, of course, Roger." He closed his eyes and massaged them gently with his palms. "What is it; this visit of King Kaiphranos? We will have to entertain him very lavishly, and I'm afraid he'll find Tarr-Hostigos small and mean, by his standards. You know—"

"Father," she interrupted. "Roger wants to talk to you about us getting married. Why don't you listen to him?"

Her father didn't seem greatly surprised. He poured wine for the three of them and picked up his own cup.

Then he said something which horrified her.

"You understand, Roger, that Rylla is heiress to the throne of Hos-Hostigos?"

"Why, what a thing to mention!" she cried. "But for Roger and his friends, there would be no Hos-Hostigos. There wouldn't even be a Hostigos, by now, and our flesh would be rotting from our bones in the ruins of this castle."

Her father nodded slowly, straight forward, like a Terran. "I remember it hourly, Rylla, with thankful wonder," he said. "But Roger is a subject—a *citizen*— of the Terran Federation. Would he repudiate that?"

Roger passed his hand across his face slowly. "I will make no claim on the throne," he said. "Hos-Hostigos did not exist a quarter of a year ago; who knows what it will be when your daughter succeeds you? It may be all of this world by then. It may not even be a kingdom, but a Public Thing, such as we have in the Federation. There have been great changes, and none of us can guess what greater changes will come. Why talk now of things that may happen in a world the very shape of which we cannot guess?"

Her father nodded again. "Yes," he said, and tasted his wine—it would have been warm and tasteless, except for the cold maker, no, the *refrigerator,* of the Terrans. Who would drink warm wine, once they had tasted it chilled? "I suppose there is nothing impossible to those who go searching among the stars. But of course; you and my daughter must marry, if that is what you both wish."

Then he drank more wine, while they both told him how much they wanted it.

"And it will be a big, wonderful marriage," she said, "and everybody will be here, all the Princes of Hos-Hostigos, and all the people, and there'll be feasting and rejoicing and a happy time for everybody. . ."

When the *Stellex* had left, everybody had been busy—
the war with Nostor had still been on, and there had been
the annexation of Dazour and of Nostor and the other
princedoms afterward, and rebuilding the bridge they had
burned in front of Gormoth's soldiers, and airlifting a thousand Sastragathi to guard the northern border against the
plains nomads, and finishing the *Princess Rylla* and building the *Searcher,* and Nancy's wedding, and King Kaiphranos. . .

Then, gradually, it began to be realized that the *Stellex*
was almost a month longer gone than the estimated time
to and from Yggdrasil.

At first, nobody was much concerned; there might be
delays in getting the cargo sold, and refining the potassium
nitrate would take time. Then they began thinking of
everything that could go wrong aboard the poor wheezy
old *Stellex* between planets, and they began to worry.

Their main telecast station was at Tarr-Dombra, and
there were a dozen young Freyans of both sexes who had
learned to operate the screens; one or another of them
was always on watch at the activated but empty screen
tuned to the ship's wavelength. There was a button beside
it to press as soon as anything came in.

It was past two in the morning, on the hundred and
thirty fifth day after the *Stellex* had broken orbit off Freya,
when the girl on duty pressed it. Bells began jangling all
over the castle, and some soldiers on the ramparts, who
didn't know what was happening, let off a sixty pounder
and began ringing the alarm-bell.

When he and Fitzurse and de Ruyter got to it, they
found themselves looking through it into the astradome of
the spaceship, past Karl Zahanov. There was a card in
front of him, lettered, "5,000,000 Miles off Planet; 30 Second Lag."

"How did you make out?" de Ruyter wanted to know, at once; they waited for an endless half-minute and then Zahanov saw them and waved to them.

"Unbelievably well; we sold the cargo, and we have niter aboard for enough powder to blow Styphon's House into orbit. And a lot of machinery and power-equipment, and some contragravity vehicles. That stuff's all second-hand; the Yggdrasil Company sold it to us from their own equipment. They didn't lose any money on it, of course," he added. "And arms and ammunition. And there are twenty three Terrans aboard, fourteen men and nine women, all skilled technicians. They're willing to work for us either for salaries or for stock."

That would be stock. It takes money to pay salaries, and after Karl's buying spree. . .

"Well, that's wonderful, Karl." It was practically incredible. "How much do we owe the Yggdrasil Company?"

Thirty seconds later Zahanov heard him and started laughing.

"We still have a credit of a little under ten thousand sols on their books," he said. "I've commanded tramp freighters for a long time, and I never saw a cargo go quicker or bring better prices. I thought they were crazy till I tasted some of the stuff they've been eating, there. There's some kind of a micro-organism, something like a virus, that gets into the nutrients for both the hydroponics and the carniculture. Sylvia can tell you about it. Contact with Terran organic matter kills it, but it makes the food taste simply foul."

"Then we have prospects of regular trade with Yggdrasil?" de Ruyter asked.

"We have regular trade with Yggdrasil now," Zahanov told him. "As soon as I can get another cargo aboard, I'm going back. They'll buy all the food we can ship them. In a week or so, there's another ship coming in here, Pan-Federation freighter *Callisto*. She's bringing more niter, and blasting explosives—they've started manufacturing them on Yggdrasil—and general merchandise. A lot of that's paid for, too. And a Terran Federation Army captain and ten enlisted men, to represent the Government till something permanent can be set up. It was from the Federation Army that I got the arms and ammunition."

That was good. The Federation Army was authorized to furnish arms to colonies and exploitation companies; that meant that they had at least tentative recognition.

"You filed the discovery claim?"

"Yes, on the whole system, with the Army on Yggdrasil. And a photoprint of our treaty with Ptosphes, and I made first application for a charter. The Federation people there all take it as foregone that we'll be chartered, and are acting on that assumption. I have acknowledgements of the claim and the application, in case Adriaan starts for Terra at once and beats the ship from Yggdrasil there."

"That's possible," de Ruyter said. "The *Voortrekker's* faster than any of these Pan-Federation freighters and we're closer Terra than Yggdrasil. I'll have to wait till the *Callisto* gets in, of course. Tell me, somebody, why the devil we thought we'd have to export something to Terra when we have Yggdrasil right next door." Then he began muttering to himself about stock issues and the Banking Cartel and franchises.

They were in the bar and clubroom at Tarr-Dombra, the few of them who weren't busy showing the newcomers around or supervising work on the new spaceport. Adriaan de Ruyter was trying to make up a crew for the *Voortrekker*.

"I'll need two, beside myself," he was saying. "It oughtn't to be anybody who can't be spared here."

"I'm just getting this hospital system organized," Charley Clifford said. "And I have to run down to Harphax every now and then and help our noble ally chase some of the bugs out of his new powder mills. How about you, Fitz? Now that everybody has all the powder he needs, I doubt if there'll be any wars for a while."

"There are still Hos-Rathon and Hos-Bleth," Fitzurse said. "And Ptosphes has just made me commander-in-chief of the armed forces, and I have to keep an eye on our royal ally, too."

"I'll go," Margaret Hale said. "Luther and Lourenço can handle everything on the *Stellex*."

"That's good. I ought to have somebody who can help me talk to people on Terra. We have a company to organize, you know. How about you, Julio?"

"Hell, I'm Minister of Industry and Economics," Almagro said. "And I have to organize cargo procurement."

"Harmakros wants to see our world," Nancy said. "He'd be handy on the ship."

"And he'd be a lot handier on Terra," de Ruyter said. "Ptosphes could appoint him ambassador; he could have a lot of influence with the Government. And he'd be wonderful publicity."

"Wait a minute." Something seemed suddenly to have occurred to her. "How long's this voyage going to take? Six months, isn't it?"

"No, that's what it would take the *Stellex*. *Voortrekker* has a lot lower mass-to-power ratio, and better Dillinghams. About four months."

"Oh, that's all right. We can go. You know, the *Voortrekker's* a lovely yacht, Adriaan, but it wouldn't make a very good maternity hospital."

"You mean to tell us—?" Charley Clifford began.

"I am a married woman, Charley," she said. "And

when, in the course of human events, a couple of humans
of different sexes get married—"

Charley Clifford reached for the bottle and poured himself another drink.

"A couple of humans," he repeated. "Of two different
sexes, from two different planets. That's right," he agreed.

He really seemed relieved that it was settled.